Also by
Isabella League
in paperback and Kindle formats
on Amazon.com

The Scholar Gypsy

Darkest Magic

Murder Moon

Dragons' Pearls

Land of the Firebird

The Jongleur

Coronado's Gold

An Adult Fantasy Novel
by
ISABELLA LEAGUE

HELENENTHAL BOOKS

Coronado's Gold

The author may be contacted via E-mail:
isabella.league@gmail.com

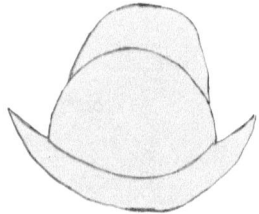

FIRST EDITION

10 9 8 7 6 5 4 3 2 1

ISBN-13: 978-1888071238 (Helenenthal Books)

ISBN-10: 1888071230

DEDICATION

For Copper –

Best of companions
on rides through woods and fields.
Still greatly missed after all these years.

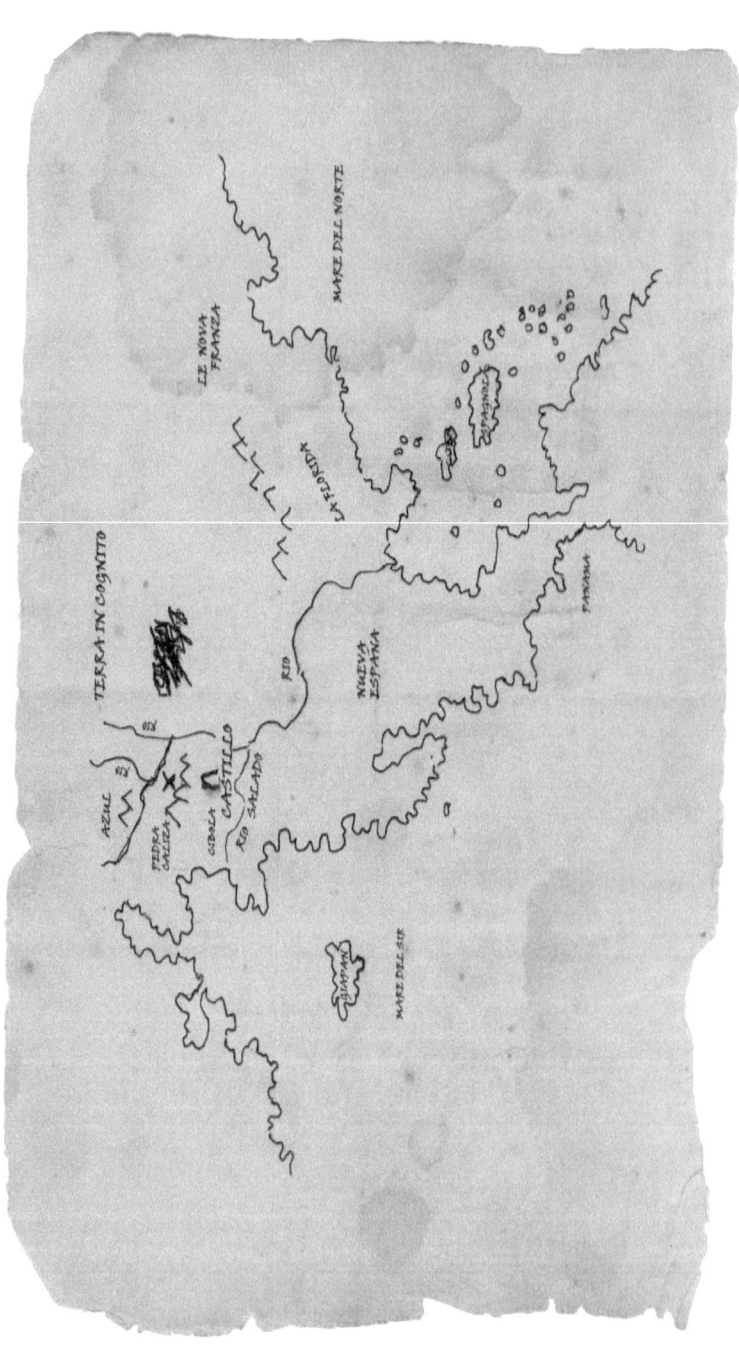

Prologue
The Map

New Spain, May of the year 1594, in the mission of San Cristóbal in the town of Mondrágon

Padre Eberardo Pérez y Montilla lay his quill pen down with a sigh, looking at the list he had spent the last hour compiling.

So many dead! So many gone of his parish, whom he had scarcely begun to know. The illness, whatever it was, had taken those from every strata of the small society here in Mondrágon, from the *hildago* family of *Don* Ignacio José de Arguello y Lucientes to the Indians and mixed bloods, the *mestizos*. No group had remained untouched.

The young priest had arrived in this inconsequential, poor mission scarcely six months earlier, from Spain. He had hoped for an appointment in a Bishop's household, as his family was related to the *Marqués* de Venegas.

But instead he had been sent somewhat to the north of Cúidad Mexico, to a little agricultural community that supplied much of the food to a nearby silver mine. Mondrágon was a small, sleepy town, with an equally small population. The Indians here were peaceful, and if they still indulged in heathenish practices the *padre* had been unable to catch them at it. They seemed devout enough, always attending the Church when it was expected of them.

Of course, Eberardo was not an Inquisitor. He was a Franciscan and not as concerned with heresy as were his Dominican brethren.

If people kept dying at this rate there would be no one left to attend the masses at San Cristóbal's. Every day, whenever he could, the priest had prayed that this terrible affliction be lifted from them. There was no doctor anywhere near and Eberardo had few nursing skills. Some of the Indian women had supposed remedies but none of them seemed to be doing any good. Every day one or two or even more died. The young priest had conducted more funerals than any other sacrament.

Tiredly, the *padre* rubbed at his eyes. He had had

very little sleep since this plague of sickness had begun. It seemed that every hour someone needed his services, either in prayer for the healing of the sick or easing a passing.

"*Perdóneme, padre,*" came a soft, hesitant voice from the doorway of the cell-like room.

The priest looked up to see a boy he knew quite well. Ciro Maldonado served as an altar boy and was a member of a large and devout family of this parish. They were poor *péons*, but good people, descendants of a man who had gone searching for the Seven Cities of Gold with Coronado, nearly fifty years earlier.

The priest knew why he had come. "Your *bisabuelo*?" He asked sympathetically. The boy's great grandfather was dying, not of the current illness, but of old age. Eberardo had expected this call.

The boy bobbed his dark head and twisted his straw hat in his hands. "*Sí, padre.* He has a great need to confess. He has been crying of how great a sinner he is and how even the good God can never forgive what he has done."

As he stood and picked up his satchel of essential items, for he had attended so many death beds lately that it seemed easier just to keep them in a handy satchel, the priest said in some puzzlement "But your *bisabuelo* made confession less than a week ago. He is a pious, Godly man! What could he have to confess that weighs so on his mind?"

Ciro, with a gesture, indicated that he did not know.

The boy's great grandfather, Aníbal Maldonado, was the patriarch of his family. Crippled in an accident many years earlier, he scraped a bare living making hats and baskets of straw and telling stories at the local *cantina*. His stories were always well-received, for they were of high adventure–tales of searching for gold, piracy on the high seas, stories of desperate men and evil-doers, told in a exciting, breathless narrative as if he had actually seen and done these deeds. Local people were more than happy to drop a *peso* in the bowl taken around by one of his numerous descendants, for his fabrications took them away to a different place for a little while, far away from the drudgery and boredom that was their daily lot. He would be much missed.

Eberardo followed the boy closely as they left the adobe church. The sun was going down and it lit the white buildings in the village with an orange glow. From many of the houses they passed they could hear the sounds of grief. The young priest rightly surmised that he would get little sleep again this night.

The Maldonado family lived in a too small house at the edge of the village. Several generations shared inadequate room with the family donkey, a pig and some chickens. As was nearly the entire village, the house was made of adobe, bleached white in the strong sun. Aníbal's sons, grandsons and great grandsons worked a small patch of land and sold squash, corn and melons to the mines and lived on the rest.

In spite of the close quarters and the presence of the animals, the house was kept scrupulously clean by Aníbal's wife, Candéla and her female in-laws and descendants, whom she ruled with an iron rod.

She waited anxiously in the doorway, peering down the street, a lighted candle in her hand as was proper to meet the priest who had come to give her husband the Last Rites.

As the priest and Ciro approached, her face lightened and she said *"Gracias, Padre!* I know that you must have many calls on your time now. But he has been so anxious to confess!" Her dark eyes filled with tears. "He cannot last the night, I think." She was very pleased to see the young priest. When he had first come to Mondrágon she had been afraid that he was too aristocratic to minister to such a community as this. He was tall, and rather handsome, an obvious *hildago* with dark good looks and she had been afraid that he would look down his nose at people such as herself and her family. Her mother had been one of the *putas* that came out with the *Conquistadors* a long time back and she had no idea which of the many soldiers had been her father.

But the *padre* had proved to be sympathetic and Godly and had more than proved his worth in the present crisis. Witness his now coming to the bedside of a poor old cripple when there were so many other calls on his time, not the least among them the family of *Don* Ignacio.

"Buenas noches, señora," the priest greeted her. "Where is your husband?"

Her round face look worried. "We have given him a room to himself, *padre*, so that you may hear his confession. I do not think that he will rest easily and go to God until he has

9

confessed. I do not know why he is so worried, for my Aníbal has always been a good man. Surely the angels will come for him!"

They passed into a room full of people, all wearing varying expressions of grief and anxiety. The head of their family was much beloved and they had already lost four family members to the mysterious illness.

The dying man had been allotted a small room in the back of the house. The *señora* conducted the priest there and left him alone with her husband.

It was a simple room of white-washed walls and a single window. The only light was a burning twist of rushes, floating in a shallow dish of oil. This burned fitfully, sending shadows leaping over the walls as the dusk outside deepened.

On a rough bed beneath a crudely carved crucifix lay the figure of an extremely elderly man.

Aníbal Maldonado was more than likely in his late eighth decade. He had come to *Nueva España*, as a much younger man, in the ranks of the *Conquistadors*. Once strong, active and big, he had been crippled in an accident involving a cart, nearly losing his leg. The pain he had suffered ever since was deeply marked on his face and body and he had been able to hobble about only on crutches for the rest of his life.

Now he turned sunken eyes to the priest. "*Padre!*" he croaked, his voice but a thread of what it had been. "Thank God you have come! I am dying and I must confess my many sins! I must or I will burn in the fires of Hell forever!"

"My son, I know you, and it is impossible..." said the *padre* soothingly.

"No, no, *padre!* My whole life here has been one of deceit," the sick man insisted.

Eberarado removed his stole from the satchel and kissed it, putting it around his neck, genuflecting to the crucifix as he did so. "Then confess to me if you will," he said quietly.

With difficulty, Maldonado crossed himself and said "Forgive me, Father, for I have sinned. I have sinned most grievously. I have murdered and raped and stolen, yes, and even stolen from the Church herself! I must make good for what I did. Under my pillow, *padre*, you will find a paper.

Please take it."

Puzzled, the priest did so.

The paper was an old piece of parchment, much creased and dirtied.

"Open it!" the old man insisted. "All of this I give to the Church in hopes of forgiveness." He coughed and clutched at his chest.

Eberarado unfolded the parchment. It seemed to be a map of sorts.

In the poor light it took him a moment or so to make it out.

It was a map to the Seven Cities of Gold, those that had been proven by Francesco de Coronado's expedition, back in 1542, to be illusory and nonexistent. The *padre* could read clearly the word "Cibola" upon it.

"Aníbal," said the priest almost chidingly. "What is this? There is no City of Gold, no treasure! You know this! You were there yourself with Coronado."

"There *is* treasure there!" the old man insisted. "Gold and silver, jewels, ropes of pearls, rubies, emeralds–riches beyond belief! And it is all for the Church, Father! To give it back will make up for how it was taken!" He began to cough again so hard that the priest lay the map aside and helped Maldonado sit up.

When the spasm was pass Maldonado lay back weakly against the pillows. His eyes were beginning to dim and he had difficulty speaking again. He seemed to be wandering in his wits for he murmured of piracy, of sacking treasure ships and cities; the very tales he had told to entertain the denizens of the local *cantina*. "Take it, take it all for the Church." he said again and again.

Eberarado forgave him, as the Church dictated. The poor old man seemed to be sinking into delirium, mixing facts with his fancies. If it comforted him to think he was giving the Church a great treasure, the priest could not see what harm it would to accept the map in the spirit it was given. Everyone knew that there had been nothing but poor Indian villages where Coronado had journeyed: no gold, no jewels, no Cibola, the city of Gold.

Maldonado was sinking fast. The priest would perform the Last Rites, with the family on their knees, all offering up prayer for the old man's entrance to heaven.

Eberardo slipped the map into his missal that he carried in the satchel. It had been a gift from his parents, when he had entered the priesthood, and was a fine one, made with beautiful art work and a bejeweled cover. But it had been dropped on the voyage from Spain and the back leaf that held the book to its cover had been loosened. Into this little pocket he slipped the map, thinking that one day he would take a closer look at it, one day when he had the time. At the least, it would serve as a remembrance of Aníbal. For the *padre*, too, would miss the storyteller and his tales. But there was no treasure of course. It was all the sick fantasy of a dying man.

But he never looked at it again. Three days later *Padre* Eberardo himself was dead of the fever that had killed so many.

And for nearly two hundred years the map remained hidden from sight.

Chapter One

The Lure

"There is no gold nor treasure, Mr. Lutterworth," said Ellery Delamar patiently to his visitor.

"I've the map to prove it!" insisted A.J. Lutterworth, slamming his hand down on Ellery's desk where a piece of ancient parchment lay between them. He was a rough-hewn, pugnacious looking man with an iron jaw and graying hair worn very close-clipped. He had hard, piercing eyes of granite and looked as if he would be a bad man to cross. All Ellery knew of him was that Lutterworth was an American businessman with a reputation for ruthlessness, a self-made millionaire, as men such as he who had made a fortune in land, railroads, and steel were beginning to be called.

Ellery looked at the map. It was purportedly of the Seven Cities of Gold in what was now, since the cessation of the war with New Spain, the American southwestern territories. He sighed quietly and removed his spectacles to rub his nose. "These maps are usually forgeries for the credulous –"

"I've had it authenticated!" Lutterworth interrupted. "By one of your own kind at Columbia University! This is a copy, but the original is old, and of the right era. The ink and paper have been Wizard proved. It was found by one of my surveyors, in a crumbling old church, smack in the way of my railroad. It was in the back of one of those little books the Catholics use."

"Mr. Lutterworth, since I first had your letter I had time to send for everything available on this so-called Coronado's gold and read it. There is no doubt in my mind that no treasure exists. There was no report of any sort of treasure. Coronado, Cortés, de Soto; they all searched in vain for gold in America. All of the riches of the New World seemed to be in Mexico and Peru," said Ellery, again, holding onto his patience. "All through history there have been examples of hoaxes such as this map. And it is incomplete as well." he observed. The upper left hand corner was missing.

"It is not a hoax!" Lutterworth shouted, his face turning red. "I thought you archaeologists were damned eager to dig up treasure! I came to you because you've got a reputation for being able to find the goods! And as for the missing piece, I tore that off myself. I don't want the whole world knowing where the treasure is! I'll show it only to someone who is committed to finding it and is working for me."

Ellery laid his spectacles down on the map and rubbed his forehead wearily. He and his visitor had been going round and round on this subject for nearly half an hour and it was getting tiresome.

Even at the young age of thirty-two Ellery was considered an expert in his field, which was that of ancient history and archaeology. No university as yet granted degrees in archaeology as it was considered a 'new' science. Therefore Ellery's advanced degree was in ancient history.

In appearance, he was quite tall, and in his youth had been extremely thin but the active outdoor life he now led and broadened and strengthened his long frame, tanned his skin and made his copper coloured hair gleam with light highlights, making his amethyst coloured eyes all the more striking.

Now he said again, "As I've told you before, my field is ancient Egypt. I am busy making plans for an expedition there in the autumn. Even should I believe in the veracity of this map I know nothing of the region. I daresay no one does, for until scarcely three years ago it was in the grip of the Inquisition. Why did you not offer this—ah—*opportunity* to some American archaeologists?"

Lutterworth flushed and looked slightly sheepish. "They weren't interested. They claimed they had other things going on," he said reluctantly.

More than likely they refused to even see him, Ellery thought. He wondered at himself, agreeing to talk to this man, and deciding that he was too well-bred, which sometimes was a marked disadvantage. "And so you came all the way to Ireland, to Trinity..."

"A fellow named Burton at Columbia gave me your name," said Lutterworth.

Hal Burton! thought Ellery in exasperation. *I shall kill him!* His American colleague was known for his quirky sense of humor and love of practical jokes.

"Really, Mr. Lutterworth, to mount an expedition would be a waste of time and money for any archaeologist," Ellery began again, wondering how he was to get rid of this man. He found it more than a little distasteful that a man so wealthy was grasping after yet more money. Ellery doubted that Lutterworth wanted to go after this illusory treasure for his love of history. If there was anything out there it would not be ending in a museum.

"But you're not just an archaeologist, Doctor, you are a Wizard archaeologist!" said Lutterworth, leaning forward in his chair. "Burton told me! He said old things *call* to you, right through the ground and walls! You can find things no one else can! Isn't that so?"

Damn Hal Burton! This talent was not one that Ellery liked to advertise.

It was a form of pyschometry, the ability to 'read' an object and all receive impressions of all that had happened to it during its existence. But Ellery tried not to use it. He preferred the normal techniques of excavation because of the heavy, often unsettling and even painful emotions that he could read on old objects. Violence, hatred and pain clung to objects tenaciously, particularly those used in war and conquest.

"I don't like or trust Wizards, on the whole," said Lutterworth. "I won't employ any as a rule. But they have their place. And time is of the essence in this case."

Ellery's right eyebrow rose, which gave him a skeptical look. "Why should this be so?"

"I have an option on the land where this treasure is found and my option from the government runs out in September unless my railroad through the area is completed. Congress wants the railroads pushed through as quickly as possible and if my company, the Taos, Albuquerque, and Phoenix, cannot complete work by September they will give the franchise to the Santa Fe. Damned fools in Congress have no idea what it takes to build a railroad!" growled Lutterworth. "And I will not lay rail over this treasure! So it has to come out of the ground *now*, not wait around for spadework! You can find it easily from what I have heard!" He leaned further forward until Ellery was tempted to draw back from his eager, greedy face.

"No, Mr. Lutterworth," Ellery said sharply. "I am most definitely not interested. You will have to find someone else to take on such a fool's errand! I doubt you will find any reputable archaeologist—"

"I've interested Dr. Marcus Beck!" Lutterworth interrupted. "He has agreed to join the expedition."

Marcus Beck! Ellery looked at him sharply. "Dr. Beck is a Classical scholar. His work has always been of the antiquities of Greece and Rome. What could you possibly offer him to tempt him?"

"Complete funding for his next expedition to Greece," said Lutterworth smugly. "And I am prepared to make a very large donation to this University if you will consent to sign on. I am a very wealthy man, Doctor, and universities are always hard up!"

If the Chancellor learned of this offer he would push Ellery to accept. Ellery himself was well-off, unlike many scholars, but the University always needed money. And to work with Marcus Beck....

Ellery had always admired Beck's work and hoped to one day work with him. Although they had never met, they had exchanged letters. Beck's works on Greece and the Levant, and more recently, Rome, when the Inquisition had collapsed and the Italian peninsula was open to scholars from the British Isles, were already considered classics. His books were meticulously researched, informative and most of all, readable, which many scholarly works were not.

"It would be difficult to assemble a staff at such short notice," Ellery said thoughtfully. "Most of those who intend to go with me to Egypt have made other plans for the summer." He himself had no definite plans for the Long Vacation other than assembling his notes from a recent expedition to Egypt into book form.

Lutterworth waved his hand as if this consideration counted for nothing. "I'm sure you can find someone interested in making a good money! If this treasure is found in a timely fashion there will be ample reward for everyone involved! Can I count on you, Doctor? Will you come?"

A sizable donation for the University and a chance at last to meet and work with Marcus Beck...it was tempting, too tempting to refuse, Ellery decided.

And the southwest was unknown archaeological territory. Very few people from The British Isles or even the United States had been there and reported on it. It could be fascinating. "Very well," he said at last. "I shall join you. But I warn you, Mr. Lutterworth, do not expect miracles. I still doubt the existence of this treasure."

The next day, late afternoon

Near the dragon pen, out behind the stables at Dragon's Rest, Nicholas Stillfield was oiling his dragon friend, Varian. Dragons needed frequent oiling as their scales, altered from the almost rock hardness of their feral ancestors, had a tendency to dry out and an oil bath made for a more comfortable dragon.

Varian was a most striking looking dragon and the only one of his kind in the British Isles. His father was Lakota, the dragon companion of Nicholas's grandfather, Sir Simon Stillfield. Lakota was a brilliant blue dragon from America, known as an American Opal, for the opal edges of his scales and horn striations. Varian's mother Cynara was an American dragon as well, a 'sport' known as a Luna, whose scales resembled the moon in all of its ever changing colours. She was the dragon of Nicholas's great uncle Sacha Kustodiev.

Their mating had combined to produce an egg of the palest green laced with silver. Varian, since his hatching had been described by admirers as being the colour of new spring leaves. He was a handsome creature with the silver eyes of his mother, most unusual in a dragon, and took after his father in length, bring now at the age of twelve, twenty-five feet long. He had been with Nicholas since he came from the egg when Nicholas was sixteen.

Nicholas was the holder of a doctorate in

Dracophilology, which now, since the mid-seventies, was a scholarly degree available here in the British Isles. Before, students who wanted to get an advanced degree in Dracophilology had to go to America, as had Nicholas's grandfather Sir Simon, and his great uncle Sacha.

Nicholas was a good-looking young man of eight and twenty, with dark hair and very blue eyes, with what was called 'black Irish' looks. Tall and slender and very fit, he made little work of scurrying over the dragon's back and rubbing the oil well into his friend's scales.

"Oh, that feels so good!" Varian sighed, a deeper sigh than that of pleasure, for they were all a little depressed this afternoon. A trip to Scotland had been planned for the Long Vacation, when Nicholas's teaching duties at Trinity were through, but they had received word this morning that their companions would not be able to go due to a death in the family. Now they were at loose ends for the summer, for the prospect of the trip did not seem so enticing without the company of their friends, which included a Wizard, another dragon and another familiar. "What are we going to do now, for the summer, Nick?" the dragon continued. This question to his human friend was followed by the asking of the same question of Nicholas's familiar. But only a soft snore greeted his query.

Varian lowered his head to the ground and nosed at the familiar, who had been sleeping curled up in a small ball near Varian's feet.

Cillian was a hedgehog and Varian was one of the few creatures that could actually poke at him without becoming stabbed by his quills. Even though his quills were not barbed they could cause pain. For him to ride on Nicholas's shoulder as familiars liked to do, his Wizard had to wear a quilted shoulder pad.

Hedgehogs slept quite a bit and when not actually needed for his duties as a familiar, Cillian could be found snoozing. Since hedgehogs had poor eyesight, like most familiars of his species, he wore strong spectacles that made the bright black eyes in his pointed face look enormous. He now yawned and stretched and said "I don't know! I was looking forward to the company of their familiars and perhaps meeting some Scots hedgehogs. What *are* we going to do now for the Long Vacation, Nicholas?" He uncurled himself and looked up expectantly at his Wizard, far above him on the dragons' back.

"What about a trip to America?" said a voice.

Nicholas looked up from Varian's scales to see his uncle Ellery below on the tiled floor of the dragon oiling platform. Ellery was only a few years his senior, for Nicholas's mother, Rosamunde Stillfield, was Ellery's much older sister.

"America?" he repeated. "Why America?" He had been to America a number of times, for they all had friends there and there had been any number of Dracophilology conferences there in the past.

"I am mounting an archaeological expedition to the southwest," Ellery said, shading his eyes with one hand against the bright sun that glinted off the oil on Varian's scales. "Oh, I know you're not an archaeologist," he said a trifle impatiently as Nicolas opened his mouth to speak. "But at this late date I cannot find anyone. It seems that everyone's made plans for the summer. Your mother told me that you were at sixes and sevens now that your scheme has fallen through. But you are a trained scholar, Nick, and that counts for something. And there may be new dragon species in the area, as not much is known about that part of the world. It is a new frontier. At any rate, this is a what will probably prove to be a futile search for treasure – "

"Treasure!" interrupted Varian, his eyes lighting. Dragons adored treasure. Their remote ancestors had collected and hoarded gold and jewels, going so far as to sleep on beds of it. Nowadays dragons banked and invested their money but the love of precious metals and jewels lingered. "Oh, Nick! We MUST go!!" he said excitedly.

Ellery laughed. "Erianne said the same thing." Erianne was his dragon companion, an Irish Emerald.

Cillian yawned. "And what does Bairre say?" Bairre was Ellery's familiar, a black-footed ferret.

"He is as eager as Erianne and Varian," said Ellery. "That area of the world is near to where his ancestors came from and he wants to see it."

Nicholas slid down from Varian's back, jumping first to the uplifted leg the dragon held for him and then to the ground. "It *would* be interesting to study some unknown

19

dragons," he said, beginning to brighten as he thought of combining a trip to a new and nearly unknown place with his passion for dragons. The depression he had felt since the Scottish trip had been canceled began to lift. "When did you plan to leave?"

"Almost immediately," said Ellery.

"Oh, wonderful!" enthused Varian. "I have always wanted to go treasure hunting! Erianne has told me about Egypt and I always though it would be so much fun to dig in the sand looking for treasure!"

"It's not treasure archaeologists look for, but knowledge," Ellery corrected. "Erianne is a trained excavator and she will teach you what to do. You must promise to obey her and do just as she tells you."

Varian said "Oh, I will!" His silver eyes were as bright as stars and his tail wiggled in delight.

"Whom else have you for staff?" Nicholas asked.

"Sabrina, of course," said Ellery, naming his younger sister. "I couldn't do without her. But I have yet to find anyone else and I am willing to consider almost anyone at this point. Four, and I include myself in that number, would be the absolute minimum I could do with. I would especially like to have someone who can take photographs. Sabrina is a fine artist, but I should like to have a photographic record as well."

Nicholas looked thoughtful. "Then why not ask Julian to go with us? He's a keen amateur photographer and it might be useful in a strange place filled with who knows what in the way of poisonous plants and animals and diseases to have a Wizard Healer with us. And at any rate, the poor chap's been at loose ends since it happened and it would do him good to get away from Dublin for a while."

Chapter Two
Setting Out

Sabrina Delamar paused in packing her portmanteau and checked off a mental list. She supposed that she would have to take much the same equipment as she always took to Egypt: cotton tropic clothing (she found it easiest to wear a divided skirt, such as ladies wore for dragon-back travel) wide-brimmed hats to protect her fair complexion from the sun, a pith helmet and several pair of stout boots that laced up the front, as well as the accoutrements of underthings, shirtwaists, and toilet articles. She would also need plenty of notebooks, pens and pencils and the full range of art supplies: paper for watercolour and sketching, pencils, brushes, watercolours, rubbers and tracing paper, as well as her Witchcraft supplies of bottles of various herbs, crystals and candles, and a selection of robes of various colours in case there were a call for any magical rituals.

And new this year was a typewriting machine. She was very proud of this. It was a brand new Remington Model 2, a shift-key machine. She was equally proud of her ability to use it without having had to resort to Witchcraft. She was a fast and accurate type-writer and completely self-taught. The machine would come in very handy to transcribe and maintain the multitude of records that were so essential to any archaeological enterprise.

She had been surprised yesterday when her brother Ellery had told her of the proposed expedition to America. She had not thought that they would be going anywhere until Egypt in the late autumn. But she was not inclined to refuse the chance to go excavating, for she liked to be active and busy and the thought of Dublin in the summer with little besides social functions to occupy her time was not a tempting one.

For the last seven years she had been accompanying her brother on all of his excavation expeditions. After the first year, when she had proved herself invaluable as artist, secretary and excavator, he never thought of *not* taking her along. She had set herself to learn all about Egyptology, including the reading of hieroglyphs and had succeeded so well that Ellery often declared he could not do without her. He treated her as a valuable colleague and never allowed any of the other men who might accompany them to treat her else wise.

She was very grateful to him, for when she had most needed it, he had offered her a new life. For seven years ago, at the age of twenty three, she had lost her husband of only six months, and the child she was carrying as well.

Hugh had been a doctor, not a Wizard Healer as were her father and her nephew Julian. His primary interest was research and in his laboratory he had picked up a minor infection that killed him, in spite of all that had been done to try and save him with both magic and non-magical treatments. The shock of his death had brought on a miscarriage.

When she was nearly well again she had been so low that her family feared she might never recover from the state of melancholia into which she had fallen. It was then that Ellery had offered to take her to Egypt. It was thought that the dry, warm air of that country would help her recovery better than a damp Irish winter.

At first she had been apathetic. But a series of exciting discoveries had piqued her interest and she had found in herself a passion for all things Egyptian and archaeology itself. Now, at the age of nearly thirty, if she hadn't a husband and children at the least she had a satisfying occupation. She supposed she would never marry again now, any more than she thought Ellery would. Her brother was married to his profession and had always expressed more interest in long dead, mummified women than in any living ones.

And now she hoped archeology would be a cure for another person who was hurting from a loss.

Of course, her nephew Julian Stillfield *had* a profession, that of Wizard Healer. And the woman he had loved had not died but cruelly left him standing at the altar in front of all of Dublin. She had used Julian's love for her to carry on a surreptitious affair with a married man and then run away with him on the day of her wedding to Julian. It was a terrible scandal and since it had happened less than a month ago Julian was still reeling under the shock of it. He had honestly thought that Sarah Gooding loved him and was eager to be his bride. But she had fooled everyone, including her parents and her *fiancé*.

Yesterday afternoon Sabrina had taken both Nicholas and Julian shopping in Dublin to buy what they would need for the trip. Nicholas was bubbling over with enthusiasm. He had a mandate from his grandfather Sir Simon Stillfield, the noted Dracophilologist, to be certain and search out any new dragon species and perhaps prepare a paper for the Royal Society on his return. There might even be a book in it.

Sabrina's familiar, Flann, a red tabby, was stretched out on the bed and now said as she watched her Witch pack, "I was after having a word with Siofra and it was glad she was that ye are taking her Wizard away wi' ye to America. Sure and hasn't he been glum and wi' a black dog ridin' in his shoulders since that senseless besom threw him over! 'Tis gettin' away from here an' all of the starin' and the gossip he needs to be doin'. And Torin is after agreein' wi' us."

Siofra was Julian's familiar, a very small gray cat, so small that most people still mistook her for a kitten. Her fur was very soft gray, like a sea mist, and her name, which meant 'sprite' in Irish, suited her well.

Torin was Julian's hippogriffe, the traditional transport for Wizard Healers. Both the 'griffe and the familiar were much concerned over their Wizard and had evidently talked over what was to be done for him. The animal familiars were probably as eager to leave Dublin and put this behind them as their Wizard was. According to Flann, the two animals looked forward to the trip and would not let Julian back out

It would be good to have a photographer on staff and Julian had a more than passable skill with his camera. Sabrina intended to learn all that she could from him whilst they were in America. Part of their shopping had been for photographic supplies and the only thing that had stirred Julian's interest at all had been the huge amount of plates and chemicals Ellery had instructed them to buy. Sabrina was well-used to Ellery's minute documentation of the smallest particles from his excavations. There were sketches from every angle and many write-ups and careful records. He would want the same amount of photographs taken as there were sketches drawn. She decided to take double the amount of art paper and typewriting paper that she had planned upon. When in Egypt she knew shops in both Cairo and Luxor where she might obtain these supplies, but the American southwest was an unknown quantity.

"Don't be forgettin' me brushes an' me drinkin' bowls!" said Flann.

In spite of the many advances in recent years, such as water infused with firestone, there was still not any way that a dragon might fly across the Atlantic without running out of dragon fire to ignite the internal gasses that kept him aloft.

Fortunately, in these modern times, to cross the Atlantic was a far more comfortable and faster proposition than earlier in the century. The new ocean-going liners, carrying steam and sail both, were the epitome of comfort for both humans and dragons. The dragon deck, which was towed by the steamship, was no longer an open platform, but had shelter and was bolstered so that a dragon could take off and stretch its wings and land again without subjecting the ship to the violent rocking of previous years.

The staterooms and saloons for both dining and leisure activities were equally luxurious on this elegant liner of the White Star line, the *Chivalric,* and the Delamar party was surprised to find that the modest staterooms they had booked had been changed to the most sumptuous on the entire ship. This was discovered to be the work of Mr. Lutterworth, who had already embarked for New York ahead of them, there to meet Dr. Marcus Beck.

Champagne cooling in ice awaited them, as well as enormous baskets of fruit and choice edibles. In Sabrina's cabin, which she did not have to share with a stranger as she had feared, was an enormous bouquet of yellow roses.

"Doing the pretty with a vengeance!" said Nicholas, surveying the largesse.

"There's bein' nothing for us!" said Flann indignantly.

The White Star line was well used to Wizards, Witches and their familiars and would accommodate them with a special table and separate menus, with chef prepared food to tempt familiar appetites.

Nicholas looked into a giant basket and said "Here, Flann, there's *paté* and caviar, all manner of things you will like. Can we expect this pampering on our entire trip, Ellery?"

His uncle shrugged. "Mr. Lutterworth seems to enjoy throwing his money about. He wanted us to go to the site on one of his railways in a private car. But we will fly."

"Of course, it will be so much faster," said Sabrina, laying aside her hat and its hat pin from her coppery curling hair with a sigh. She looked a great deal like her brother Ellery with the same hair, violet eyes and general body type refined to a delicate beauty.

She had felt that she should be a trifle fashionable for both the send-off by friends and family this morning in Dublin and the boarding of the ship. They had flown from their home to Liverpool and there boarded the steamer. But the deep blue straight-skirted gown with a double breasted jacket of slightly below the waist length she wore, in spite of the fact that she had not allowed the Dublin modiste to make the skirt as tight as fashion dictated, was by no means comfortable as her working clothes and was far too swathed with drapery for her taste. But fashionable clothing would be *de rigueur* until after New York. Indeed, they would all have to dress for dinner every evening. Sometimes she envied the familiars their one piece fur ensembles, suitable for all occasions and the men their comfortable belted Norfolk jackets and trousers.

Julian was very silent, merely looking about him as if he did not really care where they were. He gave the impression that they just as well might nave been in steerage as in the most luxurious accommodations on the steamer.

He was normally of a sunny disposition, and fair of complexion, with honey blonde hair that was nearly always a little long, that tumbled over his brow. His eyes were gray and usually held a smile but now they looked rather blank, as if his thoughts were elsewhere. He looked nothing like Nicholas, his brother, but this was not surprising as they were both adopted. Their parents, Alan and Rosamunde

Stillfield, unable to have children of their own, had adopted ten magical children, some unwanted by anyone else or even abused by the people who had had them in charge.

Now he said abruptly "I shall go and see if Torin and the dragons are comfortable."

Siofra exchanged a look with the three other familiars and scampered after her Wizard.

"I hope his spirits pick up on this trip," said Bairre, Ellery's familiar. He was a handsome black-footed ferret, with bright eyes in a black masked face.

"Just getting away from Dublin will be good for him," said Sabrina. "And as for the rest of us, we ought to treat him as if nothing had happened. Being dealt with as if one were made of glass becomes wearing. Everyone in Dublin was tip-toeing around him, afraid of further hurting his feelings. The more work you give him the better, Ellery."

"We shall all have to work very hard, I am afraid," Ellery answered, putting a case up upon a luggage rack at the foot of an opulent bed and pulling stacks of books and paper from it. "Four people is not an adequate staff for something that has to be accomplished in speed, but I am damned if we are going to be rushed through any findings of archaeological significance. Lutterworth seems to think it is just a matter of digging."

"I've the impression that you don't care too much for our patron," Nicholas remarked.

"I don't," said Ellery shortly. "If it were not for his contribution to the University and the chance to work with Marcus Beck...there's just something about the man that I cannot like. He has a reputation for being utterly ruthless in his business dealings." He shook his head, as if to clear his mind from the thoughts of A. J. Lutterworth. "I take it we all are fluent in Spanish and the languages of the Indians we shall come in contact with now?"

"Julian and I, our familiars, and Varian and Torin saw Oberon yesterday and he was most gracious. He said he gave us every language we would need," said Nicholas. The High King of Faerie, who had welcomed members of their families to his kingdom for nearly eighty years, freely 'gave' the gift of any foreign language needed. It made travel outside their homeland so much easier. Sabrina and Ellery and their

26

familiars and Erianne, Ellery's dragon companion, too, had been gifted.

"Sabrina has type-written some background information for each of you," Ellery continued, and handed a sheaf of papers to Nicholas. "Give one of those to Julian if you will."

Nicholas hefted it in his hand. It was not a small stack. "A little light reading for the trip?" he said with a grin.

At his feet, Cillian the hedgehog yawned. "There are some lovely chairs up on the deck where we can sit and read out in the sun," he suggested. "This voyage, I read, will take seven to nine days. Plenty of time for reading."

"An' for you to be sleepin'!" put in Flann the red tabby rather slyly. She enjoyed teasing the hedgehog about his frequent naps. He seemed to sleep even more than a cat.

"Do you think that there is any chance for there to be a real treasure, Ellery?" Nicholas asked his uncle. "Varian is already imagining coming home decked in gold."

"I doubt it," Ellery answered. "Since we can now get materials and books from Spain I requested everything I could find on the Conquistadors and their forays into the southwest. No one found any gold or jewels or fabulous golden cities. It seems to have been a ploy by the Indians to get rid of the Spanish. They kept telling Coronado and others like him that the gold lay further away. However, this is an opportunity to perhaps make some new archaeological discoveries in a region where excavation has been completely unknown, even if the search for gold proves to be fruitless, which no doubt it will. Coronado's gold, I am afraid, will prove to be as nonexistent as Faerie Gold."

"But if I can find some new species of dragons," said Nicholas cheerfully, "that will be as good as gold to me!"

Eight days later after a largely uneventful trip they steamed into New York harbor. The company on the trip had been pleasant if undistinguished; their party was the only magical one on board and there were not that many persons returning from abroad. Since the Inquisition had been disbanded three years earlier and the ocean 'greyhounds' had begun regular runs between the Continent and the British Isles, Americans had flocked to the countries across the sea. This time of year, in late May, people were heading towards the east, not returning to America.

Lutterworth did not meet them in New York as Ellery had thought he might. A young man from his railroad company, Melville Sinclair, met them at the dock, eager to get them on the train for the far West. He was a fair, clean cut young man, the type Sabrina thought of as very American.

He could not understand why they would prefer dragon-back and hippogriffe travel to that of a train, particularly a plush private car such as Mr. Lutterworth could provide. His employer had not told him that there would be dragons, and familiars. He seemed taken aback at the sight of the familiar animals and shocked when he was told there would be dragons and a hippogriffe in the party. They had flown ahead to a New York Dragon Park as their was no room on the dock for them.

"We're getting away from using dragons here," Sinclair said, frowning. "They're not very up-to-date, or cost-effective, are they? Mr. Lutterworth claims that within the next ten years we'll all be driving motor-cars and soon the horse will be as obsolete as the dragon! Even now some Congressmen are working to get the mail delivered by the railroads, not dragons. The railroads are much more up-to-date." Up-to-date seemed to be one of Mr. Sinclair's favorite phrases.

"And how long will it take us to reach New Mexico on a railway train, Mr. Sinclair?" asked Sabrina. Mr. Sinclair had been much struck by her good looks and had cast many admiring glances her way.

"A little over a week, Miss Delamar," he answered. "You'll have to change trains at – "

"But the dragons can fly right to New Mexico and probably in less than three days," Sabrina interrupted. "They can carry all our goods and, from the air, locate good stopping places for our nightly halts. And unlike a train, they can read a map! They are an excellent defense should we encounter any hostilities, which we understand are not uncommon as there are still pockets of Spanish resistance."

Mr. Sinclair looked taken aback and began to stammer that Mr. Lutterworth would not be pleased if his plans were upset. "He left with Dr. Beck and his party only yesterday. Why, you'll arrive there before he does! I shall have to telegraph and ask for instructions!"

"Do that," said Ellery. "In the meantime we shall *rendezvous* with the dragons at the Dragon Park in Flushing. The dragons are all packed with our necessities and we shall take to the air immediately." He felt rather sorry for Mr. Sinclair, who did not seem to know what to do without orders from his employer.

But Ellery knew that the rest of the members of his party agreed with him. Why journey on an uncomfortable railway train for above a week, with the necessity of changing from one train to another, when flight was so much faster and direct? Lutterworth, from Sinclair's expostulations, would not be pleased that his arrangements were to be upset. But Lutterworth had stressed the time factor, and with dragons to get them there quickly, they could begin the excavation at once. Ellery, with his excellent memory for such things, had done a rough sketch of the map that Lutterworth had shown him. Lutterworth had not given him a copy, nor allowed the original to leave his possession.

Already Ellery could see problems ahead. Lutterworth trusted no one and would no doubt be extremely difficult to work with. Ellery only hoped that they were not all going to regret this expedition. But the dragons would be invaluable not only as fast transportation and excavators. They would be a quick way out if all went badly.

Chapter Three
Atalanta

Atalanta Beck sat next to the window of the luxurious private car, watching the Kansas prairie. It was immense but not perfectly flat as she had imagined from her reading. It was more of an undulating landscape, with trees, and far too many scenes of devastation.

Kansas had suffered cruelly in the recent war between New Spain and the United States. It had been the scene, like so many border areas, of many bloody conflicts. The war had raged for nearly ten years and had only ended recently, in 1878. The main causes of it had been the increasing incursion of the Spanish into American lands and the terrible slavery of people and dragons practiced by the Spanish. No one was safe in the border areas, from the raids of the armies of the Inquisition, who needed more and more slaves for their mines, for the immense cattle and sheep ranches and vast agricultural enterprises. When diplomacy had failed, the United States had little choice but to declare war, rather than see an increasing amount of their citizens disappear into the maws of greedy New Spain, most never to be seen again.

And then in 1878, the new Pope, Leo XIII, had disbanded and forbidden any further activity of the Inquisition. Without Papal support and funding New Spain had collapsed and the war had come to an abrupt conclusion. All of its former territories now belonged to the United States, and, some optimists hoped, would eventually become states.

It was a part of the world that Atalanta had never thought to visit, much less work in. She had been shocked when her father had accepted Mr. Lutterworth's offer. With the opening of the Continent she had thought that for the foreseeable future their work would be concentrated in Italy, for Dr. Beck had long desired to study the Romans on their own soil, and see for himself the ruins of antiquity that had for so long been closed away from British and American scholars. The new Pope also desired normal diplomatic relations between the countries that had been closed by the Inquisition, and the countries of France, Italy and the others of the European Continent saw the advantages in trade and tourism at once and eagerly embraced the new society that was forming.

But Atalanta had little say in who her father accepted work from, or where they went. She was her father's secretary and had been, for years, the keeper of his papers and records.

She did not like Lutterworth in the least. From the first time she had met him, after her father had accepted the position with him, she had felt uneasy about him. He had taken one look at her and dismissed her as of no account, but she was quite used to that look from all the men she met. She knew she was too plain and too tall to interest any man and it was a look she deliberately cultivated for her own protection, dressing in severely tailored ladies' suits, her brown hair in a prim bun at the nape of her neck and steel-rimmed spectacles on her nose, shielding her hazel eyes.

Lutterworth was too brash, too confident and too certain that everyone else was wrong and he was right. She did not care for the way he treated his employees and most of all she did not like the greed in his eyes when he spoke of the 'treasure' of Coronado.

Her father seemed to see none of this. All he saw was the money Lutterworth had offered, money now already in the Beck bank account in New York, more than enough money to completely finance the next expedition. Seneca, the small college in upper state New York with which Dr. Beck was affiliated, was a fine but relatively poor institution and could spare but little for its antiquities department. The Becks had no private means and Atalanta's mother, at home in New York, was a semi-invalid who required frequent consultations with physicians.

This meant that almost all of their excavations in Greece and the Levant had been tightly budgeted, indeed, under funded. Most of their staff were poorly trained undergraduates, who had to be led by the hand and only started to become really useful just as the site work was ending for the season. The one advantage to the undergraduates was that they worked for free or for a minimal stipend.

But Lutterworth had offered enough money that the next expedition could hire professional staff and have decent accommodations at or near the site as well as all of the materials they would need for a successful dig. Dr. Beck was in alt, and not even the sheer foolishness of this treasure chasing expedition had depressed his spirits.

Like her father, Atalanta had read all of the material available about the *Conquistadors*, Francisco Váquez de Coronado y Luján in particular. There were journals and reports available, all in archaic Spanish, but Seneca was fortunate in possessing one of the new, less expensive portable translation tables. Atalanta had been acquainted with the college's librarian for some years and had no trouble gaining access to the translation table where the Spanish books could be inserted and magic made them appear to her as if they were in English.

What she had read made her think Lutterworth a greedy fool. Coronado had died a bankrupt, with no gold, no riches, ever found. There was nothing found in his explorations but an indigenous agricultural people whose wealth seemed to be in corn, not gold. The map was obviously a hoax of some kind.

She sighed and looked out the window at the setting sun falling over the vast reaches of prairie. The lamps had been lit in the private car by a soft-footed servant and they highlighted the plush interior of the parlour car.

Lutterworth had boasted to her father that this car had cost him above $38,000 and he paid nearly $6,000 a year in wages for a chef, two stewards, two waiters and a maid.

This parlour car was quite the most luxurious place Atalanta had ever been in. Carpet lined the floor, as if it were a home, not a railway car, and heavy crimson velvet drapes, be-tasseled with gold rope, hung at the windows. The chairs were of tufted gold velvet, again adorned with tassels on the arms and skirts, and what was more, they swiveled, so that the passenger could look out of the window or face into the room. From the high arched ceiling, decorated in gilded floral swags, swung four crystal chandeliers, lit by electricity.

Her father, she could see, was vastly enjoying being in the lap of luxury. He had been playing chess with Lutterworth, using a chess set from Medieval Europe, made of gold and studded in jewels. Balloon glasses of a very fine brandy stood on the table beside the chess board and in just a little while they would be served a meal that would rival anything from Delmonico's in New York. Not that Atalanta or her father had ever eaten at that famous restaurant, but that had been another boast of Lutterworth's.

She wished that she could shake the feeling that this entire venture was certain to turn out badly. What would happen when there was no treasure and came the inevitable disappointment, or, as she was afraid, Lutterworth's anger? Would Lutterworth turn on them? Would they be stranded out west somewhere? Would her father's reputation, as well, be ruined by this silliness?

She could see nothing but trouble ahead.

It had been excellent weather for flying. Even though the dragons had not been able to fly as fast as they could, for a hippogriffe was not as fast as a dragon, they had made very good time.

They had all been fascinated by the changing landscape below them and awed at the sheer size of America. Nicholas had been to America quite a few times, Julian only once, when he was small, to visit family friends, and Ellery and Sabrina had never been before. But not even Nicholas had been west of the Mississippi river, for all of his visits had been to Boston, New York, Charleston and Savannah which were all centers of draconic learning.

One night they spent out on a vast prairie, the horizon stretching into infinity with stars so large and clear overhead that they seemed as if they might be on another planet entirely, one with a far clearer atmosphere than the Earth.

The two dragons and the hippogriffe took it upon themselves to stand watch, and there were as well, nearly impregnable wards set around the tents, to warn of anyone's approaching.

Close to midnight, a vast rumbling rose in the air and woke everyone, drawing them from their tents. The noise drew closer and closer until at last a great sea of enormous brown creatures, running at speed, approached the camp site. The wards, of course, turned them away as if they were striking a fence.

"Oh, what are those animals?" cried Varian, his eyes shining. This was such an adventure!

They were immense, shaggy beasts, with a humped back and curved horns on a rather low hung head.

"Bison," said Ellery. "The Americans call them buffalo."

"We may get to taste them, Varian," said Nicholas. "According to what I've read, they are eaten by the Indians and their hides used for clothing and shelter. Many of the native dragons like them as well."

There were so many bison that nearly an hour passed before the last of the herd had galloped by. During that time the earth trembled beneath their feet and the noise of their passing was incredible.

When at last they had all gone by, Varian had a new ambition. He wanted to eat buffalo meat, like an American dragon. Perhaps his grandparents had eaten buffalo!

The final destination was one which was more than easy to find. Lutterworth's map had it clearly marked and Ellery had taken careful note of the landmark.

It was a huge bluff of sandstone some 200 feet in height, known since the time of the Conquistadors as *El Morro*, the bluff, or headland. It rose from the surrounding area of desert plants and junipers to tower over the landscape like a huge castle dropped in an arid environment. At the base of this bluff was a cache pool, full of good water, a natural stopping place for travelers for many centuries.

The dragons were at once excited by this bluff. Dragons loved few things more than sunning themselves and *El Morro* was a natural sunning shelf. Once unsaddled and relieved of the baggage they flew up to the top as their human friends set up camp near the shaded pool which was sheltered by ponderosa pines, while Torin took a dust bath and preened his feathers.

Varian discovered that the top of *El Morro* gave a view of the box canyon enclosed by the bluff. There were also archaeological remains of human habitation that Erianne determined to show to Ellery.

The sky above was intensely blue and to Varian's amazement, deep in some cracks on top of the bluff was what looked like snow! He touched it with his long forked tongue tentatively. It WAS snow!

When he pointed this seeming anomaly out to Erianne she said indeed it was snow. The snow that fell here, along with the rain, melted to fill the cache pool below. She had read of it, although it seemed strange to think of snow falling here in what amounted to a desert.

Below the bluff the tents were soon set up. The tents were magical, so there was enough room for comfort, sanitary and bathing facilities inside. Sabrina would share her tent with the expedition office, while the three young men shared the second and a third was designated as artifact storage with a fourth as a cook tent.

"Do you have any idea exactly where this treasure is supposed to be?" Nicholas asked as he and Ellery made a mage fire outside the largest tent with a pile of stones. Power drawn from the ley lines that ran beneath them would be drawn to keep this fire constantly burning and eliminating the necessity for wood in a place where there was not that much of it.

"Lutterworth was very careful not to let me see all of of the map," Ellery answered. "In fact, it had been torn off. I was fortunate to see the part that showed this landmark."

Nicholas pulled a face. "I hope we shall not have to do a great deal of shoveling!" Shovels, picks and trowels, along with brooms and brushes were part of the equipment that had come with them from Ireland.

"We'll let the dragons do a good amount of the preliminary digging. Erianne is a grand excavator and if she can train Varian we shall have a real advantage," Ellery said. "Tomorrow I shall lay out a practice grid and Varian can begin his training. In fact, you and Julian can learn a thing or two from Erianne. Speaking of Julian, where is he?"

"He said he was going to look around. The familiars

went with him. They're very curious about this place. Most of them have seen nothing like it. Only Bairre and Flann have any knowledge of this desert terrain."

"And this is not really much like Egypt," Ellery looked around. It was not such a bad place for there was shade and water and when they had done setting up the office, they would put up a shelter with folding chairs and a table where they could eat and relax. An etheric barrier to repel insects and curious creatures would be erected as well.

With a thump Erianne landed near the fire. "Some interesting features here!" she said cheerfully. "There are remains on top of this rock, Ellery, rather old, but not as old as we are used to in Egypt. I can see Mr. Lutterworth's railway about ten miles off, coming from the direction of Albuquerque. There's a very small settlement to the north, a scattering of buildings only. Other than that I saw little sign of any life in the area, human life, I mean. There may be dragons out at the railroad."

Varian suddenly joined them, landing a little clumsily. "Did you see it?" he asked excitedly.

"See what?" Nicholas asked.

"A big blue dragon went overhead! He was flying very high. I could barely make him out, but it was a dragon, I am certain of it and he was a handsome dark blue, darker than my father."

If Varian had been barely able to make him out the dragon had been very high indeed, for dragons had better long distance eyesight than hawks and eagles.

"Well, this looks promising for me!" said Nicholas, pleased. Searching out new dragons was more to his taste than digging in the dirt. And the blue Varian described was not a colour of any known American breed. Of course, it could be a sport, as Varian was himself. Tomorrow he and Varian would go up and see what they could spot from the air.

Walking about the base of the bluff of El Morro, Julian wondered, not for the first time, why, he had agreed to come on this trip

Everyone had been so keen on his going; his parents and siblings, and almost everyone else in the family. And both his 'griffe and his familiar had thought it a splendid idea.

He supposed it was better than staying in Dublin and seeing the glances of pity and the smirks he sometimes caught on people's faces. How, they seemed to say, could he have been so stupid as not to know that Sarah was playing him false?

That was what he wondered now. He had passed the first stage of wild disbelief and anguish and had begun to be angry, first at her and now at himself. How could he have been so stupid? To have missed the signs that were all now too clear? How she was hesitant to kiss him and let him hold her ... he had taken it for shyness and a becoming modesty. And all the while she had been sleeping with that man! Her excuses, so many of them, of shopping and wedding plans when all the while she was meeting *him* in various Dublin hotels. And he, poor stupid fool that he was, believed every lying word. It was worse than humiliating.

The familiars at his feet were chattering in excitement about the sights they were seeing, wondering what kind of animals could be in the area, what the weather would be like each day and what they might discover whilst here.

Nothing would be the answer to the last question. With little real interest Julian had read the material Ellery had provided and it had struck him at once what a futile quest this would be. He had not met Lutterworth but had already formed a low opinion of the man's intelligence.

"Oh, look, Julian!" came Siofra's voice. "There are after bein' pictures and writin' all over the rock here! Please to be liftin' me up so that I can see!"

She was a very small cat. Even standing on her hind legs did not give her much more of a view.

Julian ended with Siofra and Flann in his arms with Cillian and Bairre on his shoulders as all of the familiars wanted to see.

In spite of himself he became attentive for their excitement was infectious. There were primitive pictures of animals and stick figure humans. There were also signatures, many in Spanish with dates going back to 1605, in curving, almost florid calligraphy.

"Ye should be after getting a photograph of this!" said Flann.

A photograph! Suddenly it seemed an excellent idea, It would be a challenge, for he was far more used to taking pictures in the misty soft Irish air, while the desert air was sharp and brilliant, making everything stand out with extraordinary clarity.

"Let's go tell the others," said Bairre in his ear. "They'll want to be seeing this."

None of them noticed, high above in the brilliant blue cloudless sky, a darker blue dragon riding easily on a thermal. He and his rider had circled around and come back from their first pass overhead, filled with curiosity as to what was going on below.

"The railroad?" the dragon suggested, turning his head back towards his rider so that they might speak. He ordinarily would fly no place near the railroad, for, as even as big as he was, it made him fearful that he might again be enslaved. They might be in need of dragon strength to haul the timbers and rails.

The rider frowned. "I see no equipment such as the railroad people use," he said in Spanish. "There are no building materials for the tracks."

"I have never seen dragons like those," remarked the blue dragon. "They do not act like the ones who were in the mines, as I would be if it had not been for you."

His rider leaned forward and lay a loving hand on his neck. "We will have to keep watch over them. If they are a danger to us and our people they will have to be stopped."

Chapter Four

Buying Cattle

After supper that evening everyone retired early, for it had been a long day. But Varian lay awake, worrying over the blue dragon he had seen. To fly overhead without landing was not normal dragon behavior. Dragons were friendly creatures and it would be far more usual for a dragon, seeing other dragons that he did not know, to land and greet the newcomers, and introduce himself, perhaps even telling them about the area and the best spots for sunning and bathing.

Erianne had dismissed his sighting. Perhaps he saw a very large bird, up high, and he had mistaken it for a dragon, she thought. Why would a local dragon not come to call on them? In Egypt, they had many dragon callers, for there were a great many dragons in Africa and they found the archaeological excavations fascinating. He wanted to see other dragons, she said, for Nicholas's sake and it was a form of wishful thinking.

But Varian remembered a talk he had had with his father Lakota before they left Ireland about what he might find here in America. This area was the part of the world from which Varian's mother, Cynara, had originally come. She had been a slave in the mines of New Spain until rescued by Sacha Kustodiev and brought to Ireland.

She never spoke of the past, for it was far too painful. Lakota explained to his son that she had been terribly mistreated in the mines. Some of the dragons Varian might meet in the American southwest may have been in the same situation; they might even be shy of humans and even of other dragons. Although the war with New Spain had been over for nearly three years and supposedly all the slaves, human and dragon, had been freed by order of the United States government, this circumstance could not change their wariness overnight. It had taken Varian's mother quite a long time to adjust when first she came to Ireland. She had known only cruelty from humans, and had not known any other dragons.

Varian had trouble imagining such a thing as being afraid of humans. He loved Nicholas and the other members of Nicholas's extended family dearly. He was bonded to Nicholas in a special way. Nick had spent hours reading to him when he was in the egg, and talking to him, with the help of the draconic egg tenders at the Incubatory, who could talk to a dragonet still in the egg in mind speech. Varian had been even more eager to greet Nick when he had hatched than he had been to see his parents.

This strange dragon in the sky was a troubling situation. How was Nick to study the southwestern dragons if they were too wary of humans and even of others of their own species? Varian decide that the next time he saw another dragon he would fly up and greet it, and show it that they were friendly. He wanted to help Nick with his studies almost as much as he wanted to dig for treasure.

Just thinking about the possibility of treasure excited him. Erianne had explained that, like in Egypt, what they found did not belong to the archaeologists. Most of it would belong to the owner of the land or to the government, but they would probably be allowed to keep some items.

And tomorrow Erianne was going to teach them the principles and practices of scientific excavation, as she called it. Dreaming about what they might find and what his share of it might be, Varian finally fell asleep.

Ellery was the first to rise, shortly before sunrise. His familiar still slept. Rising early was a long time habit. In Egypt, it was the best thing to do, as by noon the heat, even in the winter, was intense and it was best to rest for the midday hours and resume work later in the afternoon.

After reading up on this area Ellery had concluded that it might not be as hot here. It was desert-like, rough terrain, but it was higher in elevation, over 7,000 feet, and in the winter it could see snow, as Varian had found yesterday. The sparse information gathered by the few government surveys here since the war had indicated that the summer temperature in July was an estimated average of 84 degrees Fahrenheit, sometimes falling as low as into the 50s at night.

It had certainly been cool last night.

The ley line fire had burned all night and it was an easy matter to bring a kettle to the boil for the morning's first cup of tea. As Ellery prepared it the sun began to rise.

Tea in hand, he began to walk about that area, enjoying the still cool air and the already brilliant blue sky. Birds sang in the somewhat scrubby trees but he did not see any other life, which was not surprising. Wildlife would stay away until they ascertained that the party was harmless. One of the dragons, the familiars or the 'griffe would probably talk to the local animals and assure them that these humans were not hunters.

The sun came up in a burst of golden rays and set fire to the rocky walls of El Morro. It gleamed like gold, and looking at it, Ellery could imagine why and how the legend of golden cities had arisen. The rock bore a distinct resemblance to a Faerie castle out of legend. One could imagine a gate, and turrets, even a Wizard's Tower in its crags.

He walked back to the fire and set a frying pan on the hot rocks. The smell of Irish bacon, kept fresh by a bespelled preservation box, would tempt the others awake and they could begin the day's work. There was a lot to do.

After a hearty breakfast of eggs, bacon, toast and potatoes, with boiled grains with milk and fruit for the dragons, they began to make plans for the day.

Ellery and Sabrina, it was decided, with Erianne's help would scout out a location for a suitable 'practice grid', for the non-archaeologically trained members of the party.

"What is a grid?" Nicholas asked as he broke the last bits of bacon into pieces for the cats and the ferret to share. Cillian, being a hedgehog, prefered chicken and fruit or even insects to the salty bacon.

"A grid is a new method of excavation," explained Ellery. "Archaeology used to consist of random digging, with no thought of where or how an antiquity was discovered. Much valuable evidence of the past was completely destroyed through overzealous digging and carelessness. Now we lay out a multi-squared grid pattern, divided into sections, of regular square trenches and we dig one square at a time, carefully noting everything in the one square, from the stratigraphy of the surrounding soil to the position any objects are in when they are found."

"That sounds so fussy!" commented Varian, lifting his snout from the last of his grain and cream.

"It is the way we work," said Erianne firmly. "If you cannot do it properly, you shan't be allowed to dig."

Varian looked a little taken aback but agreed that he would obey the rules; after all, he had promised to do so back in Ireland.

"We shall also have to find a source of fresh meat," said Sabrina. "We've a fair amount of preserved and potted meat, but with two hungry dragons and a hippogriffe, we need to find more."

"I saw what looked like a large farm from the air yesterday," said Nicholas. "Varian and I could go there this morning and find out if the farmer would like to sell us some beef. Want to come along, Julian?"

As he had been far too often lately, Julian had been quiet, looking as if his mind was elsewhere, while all of the others talked and made plans.

Now, as if coming out of a brown study he looked at Nicholas for a moment and said "Torin told me that there is a little town not too far away. I would like to see if I can find a doctor and question him about what the local medical problems might be. There was very little information available about what is endemic to this area and I might have to devise some new spells to keep us healthy."

"An excellent notion," Ellery approved. It might indeed be a very good idea for his nephew to find someone he could discuss medicine with. In Dublin he had arranged for a locum for his practice during what was supposed to be a lengthy honeymoon. The young man who was taking over Julian's practice would have been sorely disappointed and all his arrangements overset if this agreement had been abruptly canceled. At any rate, Julian's patients were as curious over their doctor's disappointment as had been the rest of Dublin and he had not been able to face their sheer nosiness.

But no one here knew or cared. Julian could enjoy discussing medicine with another physician without the other making comments about his personal life.

They went their separate ways shortly after drinking the last of the tea. Until they could hire a local person to cook, as Ellery and Sabrina always did in Egypt, they would take turns doing the cooking and the washing up. All of them had been raised on walking and camping trips where they had been taught to make simple meals and be self-sufficient. Even the familiars could scrape plates and help wash up.

Varian brought water for the tub so that Nicholas could do the washing-up. He thought it great fun to fly up with a bucket and dive down to the pool, scooping up water. However, he was impatient to be off. It was a wonderful day for flying, clear and sunny He would be able to glide in the many thermals that would be forming.

Cillian, of course, would be going as well. Even though he would probably nap in his basket on the back of Varian's six person saddle he would not want to miss out on any possible adventure.

Varian complained of the time cleaning up took as Nicholas finally began to saddle him. The dragon tack had been stored in the artifact tent overnight.

"If Cillian had helped you properly," the dragon grumbled, "we could have been in the air by now."

The hedgehog had climbed up onto a sun-warmed rock and said, on a yawn, "I could have dried the dishes, but the dish cloth becomes tangled in my quills. Nasty business, getting it out."

"Next time I'll use you to scrub the pots," said Nicholas, tightening the last girth. He picked up Cillian carefully and put the hedgehog in the basket, securing the lid.

Varian crouched low and put out his foreleg so that Nicholas could climb to the saddle from there. The dragon waited impatiently until Nicholas had done the safety check of harness and strapped himself in.

When all was secure, Varian thrust himself into the air with a combination of his powerful hind legs and a downward push of his half opened wings.

It was cooler up above the earth, but Nicholas had not worn a full flying suit, only a jacket that could be easily removed. They would not be going high or fast this morning as they would have to stay low to see if they could spot the farm Nicholas had noticed yesterday.

The country below them was rather arid, with scrub brush, not the rich green land they were used to back home. To the west not too far from this spot, lay the Continental Divide, which separated the watersheds of the eastern and western United States. There were other divides, but this was known as the Great Divide. Perhaps he and Varian would have a chance to explore it, Nicholas thought. Perhaps those mountains were home to dragons no one had yet seen.

"Look, Nick!" Varian's excited voice interrupted his thoughts. "Cows! Lots and lots of cows!"

Nicholas looked below and saw a vast herd of cows, odd looking animals with immense horns and of varied colours. They seemed to be beef cattle, as Nicholas could not imagine anyone keeping a dairy herd so far form any byre or barn where they could be milked. As the dragon's shadow passed over them they bellowed in fright and began to run.

They were being tended by several people on horseback, one of whom, to Nicholas's shock, raised a rifle and fired at Varian.

Acting on reflex Nicholas threw up a deflective shield to protect themselves. What did this idiot think he was doing, shooting at a dragon? And why were those cows so afraid?

"He shot at me!" said Varian indignantly.

"Get the sun in front of us and land," Nicholas said grimly. "I'll have a thing or two to say to him!"

Varian turned in the air, making a tight circle and eliminated the shadow that seemed to be terrifying the cows. The animals had all run away, pursued by most of the riders, by the time that they landed.

But one rider turned his horse and began to gallop towards them.

He was a superb horseman. Dropping the reins and guiding the horse with but weight and knees, he brought his rifle up to his shoulder and fired again at Varian and Nicholas.

The magical shield held and the bullet was deflected.

But the rider kept firing.

Nicholas swore and tore his wand from its pocket in

his jacket. He shouted *"Impedire!"* and leveled the wand at the fast oncoming rider.

The rifle stopped working immediately.

Nicholas was so angry that he unbuckled the safety straps and slid down Varian's side, generally neither a safe nor practical practice.

The rider did not stop coming. He shoved the non-working rifle into a sheath on his bulky saddle and took up a rope, which he began to swing around his head in a loop that grew larger and larger as he came closer.

"What is that fool doing?" Nicholas muttered to himself. He did not think that the rider even saw him there. All the rider's attention seemed to be on Varian.

Was he attempting to put a rope around Varian's neck? That was what it looked like. Exasperated by the sheer stupidity of any one who thought he could put a rope on a dragon Nicholas again pointed his wand at the rope and said *"Nodus!"*

The rope collapsed in mid-air, tangling itself around the horse and rider. The horse tripped and fell, sending the rider sideways onto the ground. Both animal and rider lay still.

Nicholas ran forward, closely followed by Varian.

The horse was wildly struggling to get to its feet but the spell had done its work well and the rope was tangled about its legs.

"Make certain it doesn't hurt itself," said Nicholas tersely to Varian. The dragon would speak to it in Animal and reassure it. Another spell would untangle the ropes.

Nicholas turned to face the rider, snarling "What the *hell* do you think you're doing?" and broke off in astonishment as the rider rather painfully sat up, wide-brimmed hat tumbling to the ground.

The rider, so skilled with rifle and rope, was a young woman.

"What am I doing?" she said in heavily accented English, a flush staining her olive cheeks and then switched to an angry torrent of Spanish. "I am protecting what is ours from attack! These cattle are our livelihood! They are not here for these great reptiles to feast upon at their will! And what business is it of yours? Where did you come from? Where is your horse?" She looked at him, her dark eyes narrowing. "*Madre de Dios!* You're a *Norteaméricano!*" She said it in the same tone a Wizard sworn to the Light would have said, "You're a necromancer!"

"No, I'm not. I'm an Irishman," Nicholas corrected absently. "I have no horse. I was riding the dragon. That's why I'm so mad that you shot at us." He extended a hand to her. "Here, let me help you up."

She glared at him and, ignoring his hand, got to her feet unaided.

She was small and slight, but very feminine. Looking at her now Nicholas was amazed that he had thought her a man. She had a mass of dark hair, rather curly, tied at her nape, that had been tucked up under her hat. She wore tight trousers, wide at the bottom, with silver medallions going up each leg, a white shirt, now considerably dirtied from its contact with the ground, and a leather vest over it.

She picked up her hat and used it to beat the dust from her clothes. "And what did you do to my horse?" she demanded. "Don't let your creature eat him!" she suddenly shrieked as Varian put his snout near the horse.

"I don't eat horses!" Varian exclaimed, sorely affronted. "And I don't steal people's cows! I like my food cooked, not raw!"

She looked shocked when Varian spoke. "*Madre de Dios!*" she repeated again and quickly crossed herself.

"Haven't you ever seen a dragon before ?" Nicholas asked curiously.

She gave him a glance that said he was one of the stupidest people alive. "Since the Inquisition was ordered from this place we have seen far too many of them! They raid our cattle and take what they please. And the new government will do nothing to help us!"

"Dragons don't steal!" said Varian hotly, miffed at this insult to dragon-kind. "Nick and I want to buy some of your cows but we would never take any without paying! And I would rather that they were dead before we got them," he added.

Her attitude completely changed. "You wish to buy some cattle, *Señor*? You have gold?" From being hostile she became brisk and business-like.

"I have gold or a bank draught or American dollars, whatever you would prefer," Nicholas answered, a little mystified by her sudden about face. A little absently he pointed his wand at the horse, who was now lying quietly, and pronounced *"Explicare,"* just as shouts and shots were heard rapidly approaching, accompanied the by the thunder of hooves and men calling out *"Señorita! Señorita!"* Anxiety filled every voice.

They all had guns out and with a sigh Nicholas leveled his wand and pronounced *"Obturare,"* halting all five riders in their tracks, the horses stopping so abruptly that four of the riders went off over their mounts' heads.

"Here we go again!" said Varian in disgust.

Chapter Five
The Hacienda del Sol

All about Nicholas were shocked and horrified faces. They looked at him as if he were the Devil incarnate. The men, picking themselves from off the ground, made the sign of the cross, several even making the sign against the evil eye.

"What was that you did with that *thing?*" the young woman demanded, pointing at his wand. She was pale, and had backed away from him. "What did you do to my *vaqueros?*"

"I stopped them from trying to kill my dragon," Nicholas said. "I'm a Wizard –"

In Spanish the word for Wizard was *brujo* and the moment that the men heard this they gasped and backed even further away from Nicholas. One older man, braver than the rest, ran forward and put himself between the young woman and Nicholas. "Let him kill me, *Doña* Marisela! I am old and have lived my life."

"I am not about to kill anyone!" said Nicholas, exasperated. What was wrong with these people?

"All we want to do is buy some cows!" put in Varian. "Wizards don't kill people! Nicholas is sworn to the Light!"

"I practice *magia blanca*–white magic," Nicholas said patiently. They seemed just as frightened of Varian's talking to them as they did of seeing him perform magic. "I don't know what I can do to reassure you that we mean no one any harm." He put away his wand as he spoke. "As Varian has said, we want to purchase some cows, that is all."

"Step aside, Curro," the young woman ordered. "He has gold, we have cattle. The *Hacienda* needs his gold too badly."

She gave Nicholas a hard look. "I will ask you, *Señor*, to restrain this beast of yours and to use no more of your *magia* upon me or my *vaqueros.*"

Varian was indignant at this. He certainly was *not* a beast, but at a look from Nicholas he subsided, although not without mutterings beneath his breath.

"I am *Doña* Maria Luisa Consuelo Felicidad Veléz y Serrano," she then announced. "And this is my family's

51

Hacienda, the *Hacienda del Sol*."

"Nicholas Stillfield," he said with a bow, wondering if he should inform her of his middle name as well. "And this is Varian," he said, nodding at the dragon.

"I shall take *Señor* Stillfield to see my father, so that a bargain may be made," she said to the *vaqueros*. "Curro, you may stay here and guard this beast and see that it does not eat any of our cattle."

"I am not a beast!" Varian began hotly.

"There is no need of that," Nicholas protested. "Varian does not need to be guarded as if he were dangerous!"

She did not believe him; he could see it in her face.

What was going on here? Were there actually dragons that were attacking and stealing and eating the cows? Nicholas had never heard of such a thing amongst civilized dragons. Only ferals, such as those in Scandinavia or the Ice dragons of Russia would behave so. And in Scandinavia the feral dragons left behind some of the gold from their hoards as compensation to the humans they took from, since their diet was usually wild deer and reindeer. Only the direst necessity would make them attack domesticated animals.

The dragons of the Americas had a long history of working with men, both with the Native Americans and with the colonists. Dragons from the Six Nations had come with the first settlers and mingled with the native breeds.

"Be patient," he said to Varian in Gaelic. "There is something strange going on here. I cannot easily believe that dragons are stealing the cows, but I want to know why these people are so hostile. And we do need the meat."

"I wish there was somewhere else to get it!" fumed Varian in the same language. "I don't like these people at all!"

"I shan't be long, I hope," said Nicholas. He went to the back of the saddle and opened Cillian's basket and took out the slumbering hedgehog. "I shall leave the shield up around you, Varian. With that up they could shoot a cannon at you and you would be perfectly safe."

He turned to find the young woman looking at him with hostility. "Is that *brujo* language that you speak?" she said suspiciously. "Do you think to put us under an enchantment?"

52

"I'm just reassuring my dragon that he will be perfectly safe while waiting for me to conclude my business." Such a prickly, mistrustful young woman he had never met!

"What is that animal?" she asked, pointing at Cillian.

"This is Cillian. He's a hedgehog." He used the word *erizo*, or urchin, as there was no literal translation of 'hedgehog' in Spanish, and even in the Six Nations, many people called hedgehogs 'urchins'. Hedgehogs were not native to the Americas or to Spain and he doubted she or any of the *vaqueros* had ever seen anything like Cillian. "He goes everywhere with me." Let her think Cillian a pet animal. Nicholas thought it injudicious at this point to try and explain the concept of a familiar. He knew, however, that if Cillian woke and found that his Wizard had gone off without him he would make a terrible fuss. Nicholas could just imagine how these *vaqueros* would regard a talking animal. More accusations of black magic, no doubt.

While they were talking, one of the *vaqueros* had brought up both her horse and Curro's. Both horses were snorting and rolling their eyes, but Varian said a quick phrase in Animal and they quieted.

They mounted and Nicholas settled Cillian in the crook of his arm, the leather of his flying jacket protecting him from the hedgehog's spines. Cillian, still sleeping, only sighed and snuggled in.

The saddle was the strangest Nicholas had ever ridden. It had a deep seat with a high pommel in front, crowned by what he later learned was called a horn. The cantle in the back was equally high and the stirrup leathers and the stirrup itself were deep and wide. It was comfortable, but he was used to a flatter saddle with less leather and more contact with the horse.

Tied to the saddle was both a coiled rope and a gun sheath, empty now, for Curro had kept his rifle. The reins, to Nicholas's surprise, were split and there was only one set of them.

The *Señorita* set a fast pace. She put her horse at once to the gallop, without looking back to see if Nicholas could keep up or was having any trouble. This was either a compliment or an insult; Nicholas could not decide which.

They rode steadily upwards through scrubby brush

and rather arid land until, suddenly, he could see a group of buildings ahead.

The buildings were surrounded by a high wall, of dazzling whiteness. A gate of intricate wrought iron stood slightly ajar and, as they approached, never slackening pace, a small figure ran out to open it. *"Buenos dias, Doña Marisela!"* the child screeched as they swept by.

She brought the horse to a sliding halt, with Nicholas's horse following suit. The child ran forward and took her reins. *"Gracias,* Chaco," she said to the boy. "Where is the *patrón?"*

"In his library, *Señorita,"* answered the child.

"Come with me," she said to Nicholas as another child came running from a low building with a red-tiled roof and took the reins of the horse Nicholas had been riding.

They were in a huge courtyard, with buildings on all four sides. Long covered walks, divided by graceful arches bordered the courtyard. Walking briskly, with spurs jingling, she led him through one of the arches.

This opened into another courtyard, quite different from the first. A large circular fountain,with a jet sending a cool mist into the air, stood in the center, while all around the edges were trees and plants in glazed terra cotta tubs. Between the plants were benches of stone, some piled high with brightly coloured cushions. The ground about the fountain was tiled as well. Due to the many trees it was cool, shady and very inviting after the dry and dusty countryside.

An older woman with graying dark hair sat on one of the benches, needlework in her lap. She wore a black gown of silk, and a graceful black lace *mantilla* fell from a high comb on her head. She looked up as she heard the sound of boots on the tiles and then came to her feet with an exclamation of horror.

"Marisela! You gave me your word that you would not ride about the countryside in those indecent garments again! If you must ride you should be wearing the habit from Spain and riding on your sidesaddle!"

"I cannot rope cattle from a sidesaddle, Mama," said Marisela impatiently. This obviously was an old argument.

"You should not be roping cattle!" her mother said. "However are you to make a good marriage if you insist on acting like a man! Little wonder that *Don* Rafael does not press his suit! And riding out without a *duenna!*"

"I have told you and *mi padre* both that I will never marry *Don* Rafael, even should it mean remaining unmarried all of my days!" Marisela said hotly. "He is an idiot! His family may be good but they bequeathed him but little brains! And as for dragging a *duenna* with me everywhere I go –"

Both of the women seemed to have forgotten or not noticed his presence and Nicholas thought it best to clear his throat loudly.

They both looked up at him, startled. "Why, who is this, Marisela?" her mother said, her face breaking into a smile at the sight of an attractive male. "*Perdóneme, Señor!* You must excuse my daughter's lack of manners! She should have introduced us immediately and not greeted you without her *duenna* and in proper dress." She bent a stern eye upon her daughter.

"*Señor*, may I present my mother, *Doña* Milagros Soledad Inmaculada Álvarez de Cordóba y Serrano," said Marisela, again with impatience in her voice. "*Mamacita*, this is *Señor* Stillfield. He is only a *Norteaméricano* who wishes to buy cattle from us."

Nicholas gave one of his best bows and murmured that he was charmed to make *Doña* Milagros's acquaintance. *Only* a *Norteaméricano?*

"Such delightful manners!" *Doña* Milagros, with an arch smile, picked up a black lace fan from where it lay beside her and unfurled it, flirtatiously.

"He is not come courting me!" said Marisela, angrily "I am taking him to Papa, to make a bargain. He has gold that we badly need."

She ignored her mother's gasp of outrage at this breach of etiquette and said brusquely, "Come, *Señor*, we shall see my father and strike a bargain."

She was very angry. Nicholas could see that easily. He could not blame her as he himself had experience of match-making Mamas in Dublin society. Even Nicholas, an adopted son, was considered an excellent 'catch' for both his connections and his fortune. He considered himself fortunate that his parents left matters of the heart in his own hands, unlike some who were always scheming to make a good 'match' for their children, either male or female. Obviously, the *Señorita's* mother was one of these.

"You must excuse my mother," Marisela said suddenly. "She persists in seeing every male under the age of eighty as having fallen victim to my fatal charms and panting to marry me. But she knows that Papa would never allow me to throw myself away on a *Norteaméricano.*"

"How fortunate that I am an Irishman!" Nicholas murmured. He heard a muffled chuckle and looking down to where Cillian still nestled in his arm saw the bright eyes of his familiar looking up at him.

If she heard this, she chose to ignore it, instead, increasing the speed of her walk.

The rooms they traversed were palatial: huge, with high ceilings and windows, carved pediments over the doors, bare floors of different coloured tiles, and elegant furniture which by its style, dated from the beginning of the century. Chandeliers of silver hung from heavily ornamented ceilings and rather dark paintings of what Nicholas assumed to be Spanish landscapes in heavily gilded frames graced the cream coloured walls.

Even hurrying through these rooms though, Nicholas had an impression of a place fallen on hard times. It was not as clean as a great house like this should have been, as if there were a lack of staff and some of the hangings, both tapestries and draperies were looking a little faded and shabby. The chandeliers were tarnished and the crystal prisms hanging from them were dusty.

Marisela paused before a heavily carved door and tapped lightly on it. "Come!" a voice called from inside and she opened it, gesturing to Nicholas to follow her inside.

Don Casimiro Antonio Caldéron Altamirano y Serrano was not a happy man. The recent war with the United States, resulting in what had been *Nueva España* now belonging to the *Norteaméricanos,* had almost ruined him. For the first time since his ancestors had, back in 1559, been granted an *encomienda* to the property of the *Hacienda del Sol* he did not have unlimited wealth flowing in. The Inquisition had demanded a levy of money and men from him to fight the heretics and it had not been paid back as promised. Instead the new Pope had disbanded the Inquisition and laid claim to their holdings. The outstanding loans, he had been assured, would one day be repaid, but he must understand that the affairs of the Inquisition offices were in disarray and he could be given no date as to when he could expect the repayment of his monies.

The *encomienda* he held from the original land grant meant that he had possessed the power of life and death over every soul living on his lands. He literally owned the Native Americans and he had possessed American slaves as well, both black and white, which had had obtained at little cost from the Inquisition.

Now the new government, which abhorred slavery, told him that he must free them all and further more, pay them wages! If he did not do so, there were immense fines to be paid. Representatives of the United States government regularly visited to see that the *Hacienda* was in compliance.

How was he to tend his fields of corn and agaves and care for the vast herd of Longhorns if he had to pay all the workers? And the silver mine lay unworked these three years since the war's end. He could not pay agricultural workers, *vaqueros* and miners all at the same time. But the thought of all of that money lying in the ground caused *Don* Casimiro to wake in the night, writhing in anguish. There was little money coming in and too much going out.

Don Casimiro was trying his best to get a contract from the United States army to supply beef to the new forts that were being erected everywhere in the southwest. But he had no skills in negotiating. Nor did he speak their barbaric tongue with any ease. In the old days, the Inquisition had come seeking him for provender; he did not have to dicker with *Norteaméricanos,* which was not appropriate for a *caballero,* one whose pure *hidalgo* blood went back to medieval Spain.

And then there was his daughter, his only child, now that his son Rodrigo had been killed in the war. Marisela seemed bent on taking her brother's place instead of marrying the well-bred and wealthy suitor he had chosen for her. She had refused to marry him, saying that she would not be happy with such an idiot. *Don* Casimiro could not believe his ears. What had happiness to do with marriage? He had dutifully married Milagros, a woman he had never even seen until she was brought from the convent in Spain where she had been reared. But her family was aristocratic, her dowry was ample and he had wed her.

In spite of exhortations from her parents, her *duenna* and the priest Marisela stubbornly refused to marry *Don* Rafael or to give up her hoydenish ways. She was getting old; she would be one and twenty next year, and soon no one would wish to marry her, especially as her dowry was now small and decreasing in value daily. She was the sole heiress to the *hacienda*, but soon it would be falling down around their ears and if the *Norteaméricanos*, as he had heard, levied a heavy burden of taxes, the *hacienda* would be ruined. What prospective son-in-law would wish to take on such a burden?

Now the door to his private sanctum, his library, with its furniture dating back to the sixteenth century and its many rare books and manuscripts, opened and his daughter, followed by a man he had never seen before, entered.

He was instantly aware of the man being a foreigner. No native of *Nueva España* had eyes of such a brilliant blue. And what was the strange little creature he cradled in one arm, covered in spines like a cactus?

"Papa," said Marisela "This is *el Señor* Stillfield. He has gold with which to buy our cattle."

Don Casimiro's eyes lit with pleasure.

"You are from the railroad, *Señor?*" the *Don* said eagerly. "You wish to supply the workers with good beef?"

"I'm afraid not," said Nicholas. "I do, however, represent an archaeological expedition that requires a fair amount of meat for our staff."

Don Casimiro frowned. He was a very tall, slender man, with silvered hair and an air of being able to drop into any court in Europe and fitting in there very well indeed.

"What is this *arquellogia?*" he inquired.

"My uncle, Dr. Ellery Delamar, is an historian and archeologist. I suppose the easiest way to explain it is that he goes digging   for evidence of the past. I am temporarily on staff for the summer and we have a dig near *El Morro*."

Nicholas was conscious of Marisela staring at him as he spoke with her father. She had gone to sit on the edge of his desk with her arms folded across her chest. From the pained glance that her father gave her he did not approve of this careless posture. The expression on her face was somewhat sardonic.

"The *Señor* does not tell you, Papa, that he is a *brujo* and he rides a dragon. Some   of our beef will end in dragon bellies!" she said mockingly.

"Marisela!" her father said in horror. "You bring such a person to our home?"

Cillian chose this moment to yawn and said clearly, "Show him the colour of our money, Nicholas. I daresay that will reconcile him to selling beef to Wizards and have it eaten by dragons!"

Don Casimiro recoiled in shock as Cillian spoke. Marisela started and looked hard at the hedgehog.

Stung by this blatant disapproval, Nicholas pulled a well-filled purse from his pocket and flung it on the desk in front of *Don* Casimiro. It spilled open, showing a good spread of the Spanish gold they had been advised to bring here.

"*Madre de Dios!*" said *Don* Casimiro at the sight, all his objections to Nicholas and his shock at the talking animal forgotten.

"Does that make me more acceptable?" Nicholas said sarcastically.

Chapter Six
The Missionaries

It took Torin scarcely ten minutes to fly to the little town that lay some ten miles to northwest of *El Morro*.

The small cluster of buildings scarcely deserved the designation as a town, Julian noted when his hippogriffe landed in a broad, dusty road. On one side of the street the few buildings were of adobe, while on the other they were all of wood, with porches shading the boardwalks that ran in front from the hot sun. These buildings had tall false fronts and ran to two or even three stories, while the adobe buildings were of only one story.

The whole little town seemed totally somnolent. Several horses, saddled and bridled, stood hip shot, tied to railings in front of the wooden buildings. They had scarcely stirred when Torin landed, as if it were too much effort to awaken and react to him.

In front of a building with a sign saying *"Sheriff"* a man in a chair tipped backwards slumbered, hat pulled down over his face. On the adobe side, several men squatted on the ground, sleeping, with extra large hats pulled down over their faces.

The wooden buildings all had rather pretentious signs: *"Big Dan's Saloon – Finest Booze this Side of the Rio Grande! Come in and See Our Beautiful Dancing Girls!"*; *"Charlie Simmons' Livery: Best Horses in the Territory!"*; *"Jim McGraw's Dry Goods Emporium - Unsurpassed Selection and Value!"*. Even the sheriff's office had a large sign with a star on it and stated: *"Famous Sheriff F. E. Post and Two Deputies. Check your guns!"*

But Julian did not see a doctor's office anywhere, nor any sign of other professionals such as a lawyer or a dentist. Nor was there a church or a school.

On the ship coming over, Nicholas had amused himself reading what were called in America 'dime novels', which seemed to be the American equivalent of the 'penny dreadfuls' found in most of the Six Nations. These were cheap pulp paper stories, inclined to be melodramatic tales of adventure. The American versions were largely detective

61

tales and stories of the frontier of the borders with New Spain. They featured tales of daring-do of 'cowboys', outlaws, and other frontier types. Julian had inadvertently been an audience to these stories as Nicholas read them aloud to an enthralled circle of familiars and the dragons and Torin.

Now Torin looked around, with a pleased expression on his beaked face. "It's just like the stories, isn't it?" he said. "Do you suppose we'll see any bandits?"

Julian dismounted and then opened the familiar's traveling basket on the back of the saddle. Since there was not that much space on a hippogriffe's saddle, as the saddle had to go behind the wings, space was very carefully thought out. Torin wore deep, magiced panniers for Julian's medical supplies and a breast harness as well in which he carried herb packets. Siofra's basket was lashed and magiced above the panniers.

"I'm not after wishin' to see any bad men at all!" Siofra said as Julian lifted her out of the basket she had traveled in. "Sure, an' who would want to be amongst all of the blazin' guns that Nick was after readin' to us about?"

"I don't think there is any chance of that," said Julian, as he put her on his shoulder where she habitually rode. "The entire town, what there is of it, seems to be asleep."

He was proved wrong, for a husky voice called out from up above him "Hey, handsome! Looking for a good time?"

All three of them looked up to see a woman hanging out of a second story window above the saloon. Her dark hair was a tousled mass of curls adorned by a drooping feather. She wore a deep red dress of some flimsy, shiny material, low cut, and held up only by thin straps of sequins. More sequins adorned the tight bodice. She wore heavy eye cosmetics and her lips were bright red. She was pretty in a hard way and now moved suggestively, putting her hands under her ample breasts and pushing them up.

"This would seem to be a brothel of some sorts," said Torin in a low voice.

Siofra spat and hissed and shrilled "Me Wizard has no need of such as ye, ye old besom! An' to be sure, doesn't he be knowin' better than to be after consortin' wi' diseased whores!"

The woman's eyes widened and she disappeared from

the window, slamming it shut.

"I was after tellin' *her!*" said Siofra in satisfaction. She considered herself not only the guardian of Julian's well-being but his morals as well, To her, the only permissible liaison outside marriage was one with an Elf, which was safe, as there was no danger of diseases from a connection with an Elf maid.

"I think she was frightened of you," said Julian thoughtfully. "I don't think she has ever seen a familiar before. Did you notice in all of those horrid novels Nick read to us that there was very little mention of Wizards or Witches?"

"But there are plenty of Witches and Wizards and dragons too in America," Torin protested. "Not as many hippogriffes, because my people were never inclined to leave the Six Nations. You would think that people here would be well-used to magical creatures."

"Don't forget, until just recently, this area was New Spain. And from what Laura Connelly told us, there were never that many Witches and Wizards on the frontier," said Julian. "Magical people and creatures were in danger from the Inquisition and its Cold Iron. The United States government advised magical people and creatures to stay away from the border areas." Laura Connelly, an American, was a non-magical family friend who had grown up in a mining town on the frontier of New Spain. "Perhaps, Siofra, you had best let me do the talking until we find out what these people know of magical persons and familiars." Julian suggested.

"I'll keep quiet as well," Torin promised. "They may be frightened or surprised at the sight of of me."

This would be no hardship for the hippogriffe as he was not especially talkative. But Siofra, for such a small cat, had decided, big opinions and no hesitating in voicing them. She took after her grandmother, Sinéad, Julian's mother's familiar, who was legendary in their family.

Siofra grumbled under her breath but she kept largely quiet as Julian stepped up onto the boardwalk. It creaked under his step and attracted the attention of the man dozing in the chair.

He came at once to attention, shoving the hat off his

eyes and putting a hand on the gun he wore at his side. From being lazy and sleepy he was instantly on the alert.

"Who are you?" he said, eyeing Julian suspiciously. "And what the hell is on your head?"

Julian had come out today in what Sabrina called their Egypt rig-out, linen clothing with knee-high laced-up boots, jodhpur type trousers, linen shirt open at the neck, with rolled-up sleeves and a pith helmet. A belt loop held his wand.

"It's a pith helmet, protection against the sun," Julian answered. "And this is a cat," he added, unsure as to whether the man was referring to his helmet or to Siofra.

A grin, showing some bad teeth, split the man's unshaven face. "Well, I'll be hornswoggled!" he said, chuckling. "If that don't beat all! Wait 'til the boys at the saloon get a load of that! You're a tenderfoot for sure!" With this he suddenly gathered up a gob of something in his mouth and spit into a brass receptacle to the right of his chair.

Chewing tobacco, Julian thought in some disgust, a particularly nasty habit and unhealthy as well.

The man lowered his chair to the boardwalk. "I'll have to check your gun, stranger. Sheriff don't allow no gun-totin' here in Diablo, 'specially if you was plannin' to frequent the saloon."

"I haven't a gun," Julian pointed out. "And I am not about to go into the saloon." What an odd name for a public house. "I am looking for a doctor. Is there one hereabouts?"

"You sick or somethin'? If so, you're out of luck. Closest doc's in Albuquerque or over to Phoenix. Better get on your horse and hustle!" He laughed "An' hope you don't die before you get there!" He gave a great guffaw, obviously enamored of his own wit. But he continued "Closest thing we got to a medical man is them missionaries out past town. They take in sick folks, mostly kids. Wouldn't want to go near 'em myself as you got to take a whole mouthful of that holy stuff they preach with your treatment. Rather die of gunshot or snakebite, than be plagued to death by a bunch of Bible-thumpers. But it's your funeral, stranger." He stood and pointed to the direction of the missionaries. He then stared beyond Julian into the street and his face turned white underneath his tan. "What the *hell* is *that?*" he almost yelped.

64

Julian turned around to look where the man's goggling eyes stared and only saw Torin in the street.

A hippogriffe *would* be an odd sight to someone who had never seen one. As big or bigger than most horses, he had the head of an eagle, the body of a lion and the hindquarters of a flying horse, with a lion's tail. His front feet were taloned, like an eagle's, and he had a pair of immense wings. He was covered in smooth bronze feathers.

"He's a hippogriffe," said Julian. "He's my transportation. No, you don't!" he added sharply, as the deputy's hand went to his gun. Without taking out his wand he said "*Impedimente!*" and the gun would not come out of the holster. It was as if it was glued there.

The deputy pulled at it and cursed a blue streak when it would not budge. "What the hell is wrong with this damn thing?" he grunted. "I'll get me a rifle!" he said and turned towards the door of the building.

"No you won't!" said Julian. "I told you, he is my transportation and will harm no one. I cannot understand this predilection for wanting to shoot everything!"

The deputy stared at him. "You sure talk and look funny," he said. Then he slapped his thigh and gave out a hoot. "I know what it is! You can't put one over on P. K. Purvis! You're with a circus, ain't you?"

"Holy Bastet!" said Siofra in Julian's ear. "Is it the village idiot we've stumbled across?"

Julian went to Torin and sung up into the saddle, Purvis following him with eager questions about the arrival of the circus. Torin turned his head and looked at the man in amazement until Julian was settled in the saddle and had tucked Siofra in the front of his shirt. "Fly!" Julian said brusquely to the 'griffe, who took off with a quick running start, almost knocking the deputy over with his unfurling wings.

"Hot damn!" yelled the deputy after them, cupping his hands around his mouth. "I just can't wait to see me the show!"

Prudence Cromwell felt like crying as she scrubbed the floor of the little Covenanter's mission. It was suffocatingly hot in the small building as Reverend Brewer would not allowed the doors or windows to be opened. Her dress was the proscribed black wool of the Covenanter women with white collar and cuffs, high to the throat and long-sleeved, covered in a very plain white apron. It was a garment ill adapted to the climate. A close white cap as well covered her hair, but little deep brown curling tendrils insisted on escaping about the edge. Sister Rebecca would rebuke her for that later as curls were 'worldly' and a vain adornment. Sister Rebecca would give her a heavy penance, no doubt, even though Prudence could not see how she could prevent her hair from curling.

But it was none of these things that made Prudence so near tears. No, it was the children who made her want to cry.

Most of the occupants of the mission were sick children. They were of mixed blood, Spanish, American and Indian offspring of the former female slaves of the mines in the area. Brother Ezekiel Bradley, his wife Sister Rebecca, and the Covenanter minister of this mission, Reverend Joshua Brewer, had been horrified to learn that these children were the fruit of rape in most cases. "Born of sin," as the Reverend, a most pious young man, said. He was younger than Brother Ezekiel by over twenty years, but he was a full minister, while Brother Ezekiel was but a Deacon and therefore Reverend Brewer was in charge of this mission.

They were here to convert the heathen. The Church of the Covenant, back in Ohio, had greeted with joy the opening of the territories with so many heathens to bring into the fold.

The Reverend or his helpers knew but little of medicine. As the Church of the Covenant believed in most cases that prayer healed, the only treatment the children received was being prayed over, some soup, and exhortations to convert. The ones who were dying, the Reverend declared, were the ones who would not repent, and clung to the false beliefs of paganism, in which the Reverend included the beliefs of the Catholic Church, which he often declared, was corrupt and evil, a front for Satan. Death, and Hell were their punishments for refusing to see the Light.

Prudence had trouble believing that God would punish innocent children, furthermore children who had already been punished by being made to work in the mines. Most had been forcibly separated from their mothers and starved and beaten as well. Now many of them suffered from a coughing sickness.

When Prudence prayed by herself, in the solitude of the woods near her home, she was filled with Light, with a sweet, loving warmth that told her that the Creator was good. She felt his love and His embrace. He would not hurt children. But since coming here and living under the thumbs of the Reverend and his two helpers she had not felt that love and connection. It was as if God had gone away. She felt deserted.

She could not please Sister Rebecca, whether it was her hair curling or the way she did her appointed tasks. She was here as a Handmaiden, to serve, as was required of all girls between the age of 17 and 22. And her parents expected her to come home betrothed to Reverend Brewer. But there was small chance of that, for as Sister Rebecca had pointed out, a young Handmaiden who put herself forward, who argued with her elders, would scarcely be looked upon with favor as the prospective wife of an ordained minister.

Only this morning Prudence had begged Sister Rebecca to please try and find a doctor for the sickest children. Even at home, the sickest persons, when all else failed (especially those who were particularly pious and Godly) would be treated by a doctor from a nearby Outlander town, as the Covenanters called everyone else who was not one of the Fold. The minister would announce that God had revealed to him in a dream him to call a physician, an Outlander who would be brought to the New Jerusalem settlement, there to save the life of Brother This or Sister That.

The children were suffering terribly and ought to have a real doctor! They cried very little, for their short lives had been so bad that many of them were used to enduring horrors with dumb resignation. But their eyes! Their eyes haunted Prudence waking and sleeping. She could barely speak to them, only try and comfort them with gestures, as none of the mission had considered it essential to learn a word of Spanish or any Indian tongue. Prudence, guiltily, had wondered what good the endless Bible readings did children who could not understand what they were hearing. But it was thoughts such as these and expressing them that had gotten her into trouble, all her life, both with her parents and the church.

In spite of the heat Brother Ezekiel sat at a small desk with the Reverend Brewer, both in clerical blacks, going over the mission's accounts. They received generous donations to run the place from back home, as every Covenanter believed fervently in missions, whether foreign or domestic, and all tithed towards their support.

Sister Rebecca sat in a chair, her back rigid, endlessly knitting, mostly stockings of heavy worsted wool. These were destined to be stockings. Wool was the only approved fabric. A Covenanter woman was never allowed to knit garments for herself as she might be tempted to embellish them with vain adornments, such as a bright colour, or even fanciful stitches. Such was the work of the Devil.

A knock came at the door and Sister Rebecca rose, as was proper, to answer it, in spite of the fact that both the Reverend and her husband were closer to it. But a woman's lot was to serve.

A stranger stood there. They had had but little to do with the local people, so his appearance was a surprise. The Reverend at once hoped that here at last was a convert.

"Good morning," said the stranger pleasantly. He presented an odd appearance to Prudence, because she had never seen a full grown man without a heavy beard nor he was not black clad. Even at less than thirty years of age the Reverend sported a full beard that might have been envied by a patriarch. "I was told in the town that there might be someone here with a knowledge of medicine?" the stranger inquired.

Prudence let her stiff brush drop into the pale. He had an odd, clipped way of speaking.

"Are you in need of physic?" inquired the Reverend, coming to his feet. "We can pray for you...."

One of the children began to cough, a deep, rasping sound and the stranger looked around sharply and went at once to the child's beside. He looked around the room again and frowned deeply. "Good God, are you trying to suffocate them in here? Lung disease needs fresh air!" he exclaimed angrily. He gave a wave of his hand and all of the windows flew open with a crash.

"What deviltry is this?" the Reverend yelled, nearly overturning the table.

"I'm a doctor," the stranger announced. "And by the look of things, you need me desperately." He then said to the child, a boy of about ten, in what Prudence assumed to be Spanish: "*Hola!, hijo. Soy médico. ¿Cómo se llama Ud?*" He laid a gentle hand on the boy's forehead as he spoke.

The boy calmed as he felt the Healer's magic in Julian's hand. This touch was to reassure a patient, to make him or her relax so that Wizard Healer could establish a trusting relationship almost immediately.

"*Me llamo Tomaso,*" the boy whispered.

"How do you feel, Tomaso?" asked Julian quietly. He took his hand from the boy's forehead and, pulling out his pocket watch, took the boy's pulse.

"It hurts here, *Señor el Médico,*" said the boy, touching his chest.

Prudence was watching breathlessly. Her prayers had been answered! He was a doctor, a real doctor! The air coming in the windows felt wonderful. She did not know how he had done it but already the children looked happier and even seemed to be breathing easier.

Both the Reverend and Brother Ezekiel were making angry noises in the background, but they were ignored. "You cannot come in here and–" the Reverend blustered.

"This is criminal negligence!" the Doctor switched back to English and glared at the Reverend "You could be up on charges! I would be violating my oath if I did not do my best to help these children. And before you ask, yes, I am properly licensed to practice here. As a mater of fact, I made certain that I was licensed for any part of America before I left Ireland. The American Ambassador eased my way."

Then, switching back to Spanish, he said to Tomaso, "This will not hurt at all. You'll just feel warm." He held his hands over the boy's chest and green light began to flow off them. The boy closed his eyes and smiled.

Sister Rebecca fainted dead away.

"Devil!" shrieked the Reverend. Brother Ezekiel backed up against a wall, eyes wide in horror.

But Prudence saw only the good Light.

Chapter Seven
First Flight

Don Casimiro looked up at the tone of Nicolas's voice. "Please, *Señor*, I am sorry if we have offended you. But we know nothing good of *brujos* and these flying fiends of Satan that you call *dragóns*. The Church has taught us –"

"If by the Church you mean the Inquisition, the Church is wrong. The new Pope has admitted as much by the dissolution of the Inquisition and the opening up of the Continent. Before I left Ireland the Pope welcomed our ambassador to Vatican City. The Irish Ambassador is both a Wizard and a Druid," Nicholas interrupted. "All magic is *not* evil. Black magic is forbidden in my country and all of us are sworn to the Light. And dragons are not flying fiends of Satan! I have studied them all of my life. In point of fact, studying and teaching about dragons is my profession. I am a professor of Dracophilology at Trinity University in Ireland." There was no Spanish translation for the word "Dracophilology".

Don Casimiro smiled apologetically. "The habits of a lifetime, *Señor,*" he said.

Nicholas noted how the man's eyes slid towards the gold spilled on the desk top. He had a feeling that if it were not for the gold coins, *Don* Casimiro would not be apologetic or even pleasant. He would probably order his servants to begin gathering wood for an *auto de fé* to burn the brujo.

"Shall we then make a bargain, *Señor*? Tell me how many of my cattle you need and how often you will need them and we shall sign a contract," said the *Don*.

"Might I have my spectacles, Nick?" piped up a small voice from where Cillian still rested in Nicholas' arm. "I shall read the contract through for you, if you like, *before* you sign it."

Again, both the *Don* and his daughter started and looked at Cillian, shocked. "It speaks!" *Don* Casimiro croaked, his voice seeming to have almost deserted him.

"No, it is more of his *magia*," said Marisela, glaring at Nicholas. "He makes it speak, Papa, animals do not speak! It is against the laws of God and nature."

71

"My dear young lady," said Cillian equably. "I am Nicholas's familiar. All familiars speak. Of what use would we be to our Wizards and Witches if we could not talk to them and read and write as well?" As he spoke, Nicholas put him down on the desktop. Cillian sat up, peering nearsightedly at their hosts until Nicholas took the familiar's spectacles from an inside pocket and fitted these over the hedgehog's nose.

"Ah, that is better!" Cillian said and took a good look at *Don* Casimiro and Marisela. "My, what a pretty young lady you are! Now, where is that contract? I trust you have a standard form?"

Marisela, escorting Nicholas back out to where the horses still waited, could not resist stealing a look at him out of the corner of her eye. She had never imagined anyone like him, someone who could perform magic, who rode a dragon as if it were a horse and had a talking animal. It had been a day of wonders; not in the least of which was the gold, gold that was badly needed by the *Hacienda*, to pay wages, to do repairs, needed in so many places.

She had watched in amazement as the animal had dickered with her father over the terms of the contract, almost as if it was an *abogado*. "Cillian's as good as any solicitor," Nicholas told her when he saw her staring at his familiar. "He reads law as a hobby. If urchins could be called to the bar he'd have taken silk by now. He read up on American law before we came here."

The spiny little *abogado* now rested again in the curve of his Wizard's arm, fast asleep. Cillian had corrected *Don* Casimiro when he referred to Nicholas as the hedgehog's "master". "Nicholas is my Wizard, and my friend," the hedgehog said with immense dignity. "There is no master or servant in our relationship. I chose him above all others, to be friends, helpers and companions for all our life together."

Marisela kept her silence as they mounted the horses for the ride back to where the dragon waited. The *Norteaméricano* rode well, she noted, although not in the *la jineta* military style she was used to. He had kept up well coming here.

During the return she kept to a controlled canter, riding a little ahead of him. Her mind was full of questions. The presence of a *brujo* and a talking animal had made her father fearful. She had realized that only the lure of the gold made him able to contain that fear.

She was not afraid. She feared very little. But she was curious. How and why did one become a *brujo?* Why did he ride a dragon? And what was he doing here? The explanation he had given her father made little sense to her. Why were they digging in the dirt?

She had also been surprised that the little animal insisted that the cattle be delivered butchered and ready to cook. She had expected that the animals would be sent to the dragons to be torn apart and devoured. She hated to think of this; she had had to learn not to become sentimental over the cattle.

Nicholas was quiet as well. He was still more than a little angry. How he hated the stupid prejudices of non-magicals! Even at home some non-magicals had the most idiotic ideas of what Wizards and Witches could and couldn't do. This in spite of the fact that people like his father went out of their way to teach them otherwise and even devised many spells to help both magicals and non-magicals.

This Inquisition based prejudice was even worse. At least few persons in the Six Nations (with the possible exception of radical Evangelical Christians) believed Wizards and dragons to be *evil*. Evil! That rankled!

As they reached the place where Varian waited, Nicholas could see at once that his dragon friend was not happy. He lay with his head resting on his forelegs and his tail wrapped around him. His expression was both angry and impatient.

As far away as they could get without letting him out of their sight, the *vaqueros* sat around a fire, drinking coffee. Their rifles lay across their laps, ready to be used if Varian made any move towards the cattle, which actually were nowhere close.

"Oh, Nick!" Varian saw his friend coming before the *vaqueros* did and brightened visibly. "I am so glad you are back! These men are so rude! I tried to engage them in conversation but they would not talk to me! They have been drinking coffee and didn't offer me any. Any time I even stretched they threatened to shoot me! I hope you are ready to go back to camp. I've had enough of these people. I don't like them at all!" His tone was indignant. He spoke in Spanish; he hoped the men heard him.

Nicholas pulled up his horse next to the campfire where old Curro came to his feet and walked over to take the horse. Nicholas thanked him for the use of the animal and then bowed to Marisela. "Thank you, *Señorita*," he said and began to walk towards Varian. "May I expect three cows delivered to *El Morro* tomorrow as we agreed?"

"Wait!" Marisela called impulsively, dismounting from her horse.

Nicholas turned to look at her, a quizzical look on his face.

"What is it like to fly upon a dragon?" she asked, feeling somewhat breathless.

"Do you really want to know? Aren't you afraid of the touch of the Devil or that you might disappear into his fiery maw and burn in Hell for all eternity?" Nicholas said a little bitterly.

"Flying is very nice," said Cillian, on a yawn. 'It's the quickest way to get from here to there. I always fall asleep when we're aloft."

"I do wish to know," she said. Her curiosity was stronger than any fear she might have felt. "Describe it to me. Tell me why you ride such a creature."

"Stop calling me a creature!" said Varian, extremely irritated. Small puffs of steam came from his nostrils and his tail lashed.

"As Varian says, he is *not* a creature," said Nicholas. "Come here with me and meet him properly."

The thought of getting closer to something so large and with such big teeth did give her pause. The *vaqueros*, in the background, became agitated and protested until she snapped "*¡Cállate!*" and they subsided to mutters.

She was too proud to let anyone see her fear. She followed Nicholas right up to the dragon, to where it could have snapped her up if it wanted.

"Varian, this lady is *Doña* Maria Luisa Consuelo Felicidad Veléz y Serrano. *Doña* Marisela, my dragon friend, Varian," said Nicholas.

"What a long name," remarked Varian. He was a little hostile, not quite as friendly as he would be in normal circumstances.

"Do you magic it to talk as well?" Marisela asked.

Exasperated, Nicholas said, "Neither Varian or Cillian is magiced! They are sentient, thinking, intelligent beings with their own opinions. They don't need to be magiced; they are born that way."

"Does she think we're stupid, too?" Varian was affronted and drew up his neck to stare down his snout at Marisela, a posture indicative of draconic disapproval. "And I am not an it! I am a male dragon, which you would know if you knew anything at all about dragons, which you obviously don't!"

"It's up to us to teach her, Varian," said Nicholas soothingly. "That's why I think it would be a good idea to take her up."

"Up?" Marisela looked at him, startled. "Do you mean to fly, up in the sky? Me? But is it not dangerous?"

"There is a safety harness on the saddle," Nicholas pointed out, "and there is a retractable handle as well. You're much less likely to fall from a dragon than a horse as no dragon would ever dream of taking up an unsecured rider. And dragons are so fast that if you did fall, they can catch you."

Varian did not look very pleased at the idea of having her as a passenger but when Nicholas said, "please" he gave his consent. "Where shall we go?" he asked as Nicholas placed a now snoring Cillian into the basket and secured the lid.

Marisela's heart was beating very fast. Part of her was afraid but the largest part wanted to do this. To fly, to soar in the air...she had often dreamed of it when her nurse had told her fanciful stories when she was a child. It felt as if she was going to live a dream.

"We'll fly back to camp and we'll show her where to deliver the cows. She's curious about the dig as well," Nicholas said.

"We'd better get back," Varian agreed. "I don't want to

miss my excavation lesson. You'll have to show her what to do, Nick."

Marisela was looking up at the saddle on Varian's back. "It is so high –" she said, turning a slightly pale face to Nicholas.

He remembered his very first dragon flight so long ago. He had been only ten and very nervous, but elated. But he had grown up in a place where dragons carried the mail and hauled transport goods; he had been used to seeing them in the sky. He had never thought of dragons as evil.

"Don't worry," he said. "We'll help you mount. Varian?"

The dragon crouched low to the ground and extended a foreleg. "I'll give you a leg up," said Nicholas " and then let Varian lift you. When you are opposite the first seat on the saddle, step over and sit down. I'll be right behind you and I'll help you get secured."

The *vaqueros* were begging her to get away from the beast, some almost moaning in anguish "What am I to tell the *patrón*," old Curro called out, "if you are eaten? Do not do this, I beg of you!"

"She'll be fine," Nicholas called as he helped Marisela onto Varian's leg. "We'll be back in about an hour."

Nervously and trembling a little Marisela found herself on Varian's leg, almost losing her balance as the dragon lifted her.

When he realized that she was frightened, Varian moved very slowly and said soothingly "I won't let you fall and neither will Nick. Just lean towards the saddle. There you go! Now put your leg over and settle in. Wasn't that easy? Nothing to be nervous about!"

It was very high up. The saddle was deep and comfortable and a few moments later she felt Nicholas swing up behind her. He leaned forward and showed her the safety harness. One strap as secured around her waist, the other went over one shoulder. "There's a handle on the pommel that can be pulled out and stirrups that can be pulled down as well," he said.

"There is no bridle?" she queried, hoping that he did not hear the tremor she felt in her voice. She wanted the security of both handle and stirrups.

"Varian doesn't need one. He knows where he is going better than I do. Dragons have a marvelous sense of direction. We're all set, Varian. All secure."

"Cillian too?" the dragon asked.

"He's already asleep," said Nicholas.

"I'll fly low and slow, Nick, since this is her first flight," Varian promised. "And she hasn't a flying suit. She could get cold."

Marisela felt the bunching of very powerful muscles underneath and the wings snapped open. With a sudden thrust he was in the air and gave a downward push with his wings.

Her hands, white knuckled, gripped the handle in front of her and she tightened her legs against the saddle as he began to spiral up. She wanted to close her eyes but could not seem to do so. At once horrified and fascinated, she watched the ground recede further beneath her.

Below, the *vaqueros* had mounted up and were sending their horses galloping along beneath them. Varian snorted as he saw them. Even the fastest horse could not keep up with him!

The wind whipped her hair about, tearing some of it loose from its tie. But the wind felt good. It was cooler up here.

And suddenly it was exciting too. They were high enough that things seemed smaller, much smaller, beneath them. It gave her a view that she had never even imagined.

The speed was exhilarating! She had always liked to be on a galloping horse, feeling free and wild. This was so much faster! Marisela lifted her face into the wind as Varian banked to the left and climbed with one thrust of wings. He had caught a thermal, rising from the desert-like earth and now opened his wings to the fullest extent and glided.

A voice said, very close to her ear," Do you see now why I like to fly?"

"Oh, *Sí!*" she said. She laughed exultantly, wanting to fling up her arms and shout. This was the most wonderful thing that had ever happened to her! The only basis she had for comparison was when Rodri, her brother, had taught her to swim and they had floated inside the water tank, in secret, hiding from her mother's disapproval. There had been the same delicious thrill of the forbidden, of detachment from the earth, of coolness and only the blue sky above.

Too soon the dragon began to descend. Marisela saw a cluster of tiny tents below and the massive rock of *El Morro*. They were here already? They had been up in the air such a short time.

She was conscious of a deep feeling of disappointment that it was over so soon.

"Begone, ye foul fiend of Satan!" Reverend Brewer pulled a wooden cross from out under his clerical vest and thrust it towards Julian.

Julian looked up from his examination of the boy Tomaso. "If any one here is a fiend, it is not me!" he said firmly. "How dare you sir, keep children as ill as these in such conditions? They need fresh air, good food and cosseting, as well as immediate treatment. They do not need Bible tracts and piety!"

"Can you help them?" Prudence had crept ever closer, ignoring Sister Rebecca's huddled, still unconscious form on the floor and Brother Ezekiel, still propping up the wall. "What was that green Light? It was good; I felt it!"

"Prudence! Mistress Cromwell!" gasped the Reverend in shock. "You are consorting with a fiend of Darkness! Has Satan indeed infected you?"

Julian and Prudence both ignored him. "I am a Wizard Healer," Julian explained. "The green light is my Healing magic."

"And it is good–I know it!" said Prudence her eyes shining. "God sent you here to help these children! You can even talk to them!"

"Mistress Cromwell, do you do not realize that you are being seduced by the wiles of Satan? This is the very guise he uses, that of a handsome, smooth-talking fiend who leads the virtuous astray!" Reverend Brewer wanted to go and pull her away from the fiend. She was too close. But he was afraid of the magic. What if the fiend changed him into something unholy? He was a powerful fiend indeed for he should not have been able to enter this building, blessed as it had been. But he was making himself at home. And where had Brother Ezekiel gone?

"Who are these people?" Julian asked Prudence. She seemed the only sensible person in the room, although over impressed by his magical skills.

She recited their names and positions in the mission and told him that they were Covenanters.

He had never heard of the sect. There seemed to be far too many of these religious groups about nowadays and all of them seemed bent on viewing magic, and even Healing, as evil. How any sane person could swallow such claptrap was beyond Julian's comprehension. How could Healing someone be evil?

The others seemed to be afraid of him, Julian thought, which might be all to the good. They might be too scared to interfere. There were eleven children in the room who needed an examination and then a course of treatment, which probably would have to be later, if, and it was a large if, any of the children were able to be Healed at this late date. What he had seen in Tomaso's lungs had appalled him. If they were all that badly off all he might be able to do perhaps was ease their passing and let them go into the Light in the company of Raphael, the Healer's Archangel.

The Reverend Brewer was frozen with horror. He had sometimes dreamed of wrestling with the Devil, of proving his worth to man and God, but now that the fiend had come he could do nothing but watch helplessly, overcome with terror.

Reverend Brewer was a small man, with receding brown hair and a frail figure. This was thought to be a measure of his piety by the female members of his congregation, for it showed that he was not long for this world, and therefore too good for the world as well. He had never before regretted his physical limitations but now, surveying the tall, well-grown fiend he wished that he were more like Samson of Biblical fame. His limbs felt leaden and his hands shook. He was not filling with the strength of God's grace as he had always imagined.

Glancing about, he saw Brother Ezekiel, who was taller and stronger with a dark, truly patriarchal beard heavily flecked with gray. He was a great deal bigger than the Reverend but he stood rigid against the wall, looking as if he moved one step he would fall over. His brown eyes were staring at the fiend in supreme shock.

Sister Rebecca, a stern woman of high moral character and strength of mind, was a broken reed, still on the floor, insensible. The Reverend did not blame her, for what good Christian woman could retain her senses in the presence of magic?

Which made Mistress Cromwell's behavior all the worse. She was actually talking to the fiend, showing him the children! Acting as if he was not a minion of the Great Deceiver! The Reverend moaned. How could things get any worse?

But they did. "Sure an' what is after takin' ye so long?" came a voice from one of the newly opened windows. The Reverend swung around sharply. Perhaps this was a Godly person who might break the spell cast by the fiend!

But there was no one in the window save a small gray cat. Cats were often in the company of Witches and other evil-doers and black cats were the imps of Satan. If it were not for their vermin catching abilities cats would not be allowed in New Jerusalem. But without cats they were overrun by mice and rats. So they were tolerated–barely. There was no such thing as a pet cat in the whole settlement.

The cat yawned and stretched and spoke as the Reverend reeled in shock. "We'd best be after gettin' back, Julian, for 'tis time and after we were to be having our lesson in diggin'," the cat announced.

There was a heavy thump from behind Reverend Brewer. Brother Ezekiel had fainted as well.

Chapter Eight
The Discovery

Atalanta Beck felt extremely sorry for Mr. Melville Sinclair.

When Mr. Lutterworth had received, in Topeka, the telegram from Sinclair telling him that Dr. Delamar and his staff had gone on ahead, on their own initiative, there had been an explosion of rage. He had at once telegraphed back to New York, demanding that Sinclair join him, to account for this upset of all Lutterworth's carefully laid plans.

Somehow Sinclair had done it. He had moved heaven and earth and had actually been waiting for them in Wichita, looking exhausted and apprehensive.

Lutterworth wasted no time in beginning to berate the unfortunate young man, not even waiting until they had gained the seclusion of the private car, but shouting at him on the platform of the railroad station. The stationmaster, much distressed at this display and the attention it was attracting, managed to herd them into the private car, where the diatribe continued unabated, about Sinclair's incompetence, stupidity and failure to follow his orders.

Dr. Beck, his daughter knew, hated loud, angry voices. He was capable of as much verbal cruelty as A. J. Lutterworth, but it was a more refined, withering sarcasm uttered in his dry, pedantic voice, not a red-faced, choleric, profanity laced screaming fest. And to dress down the young man in front of his guests was outside of enough.

"That is quite enough, Mr. Lutterworth!" Atalanta said crisply, her voice carrying quite easily. "We have been subjected to an ample supply of your spleen. To blame Mr. Sinclair for failing to have some foreknowledge of Dr. Delamar's having dragons in his party is foolishness. Had you read any of Dr. Delamar's published works you would have been aware that he always uses dragons at his excavations. Indeed, he gives the credit for several important discoveries to a dragon." She stared through her spectacles at Lutterworth. She was not afraid of him in the least.

Lutterworth looked at her in both anger and surprise. He did not like her at all. The damned woman was like a

81

schoolmarm with that precise manner of hers. Nothing seemed to upset or impress her and he actually found himself feeling like a naughty schoolboy around her. It was a feeling he hated. She could put him in his place with one look. She did not seem to appreciate who she was dealing with.

"And what does it matter, Mr.Lutterworth, whether Dr. Delamar arrives before us or after us?" put in Dr, Beck. He was a rather slight man of sixty-five, with a white goatee, silvered hair and *pince-nez* spectacles attached to a cord that hung about his neck. He give the impression of being made out of parchment, pale of complexion and always dressed in cream coloured linen of a very fastidious neatness. "There is a great deal to accomplish when one is setting up an efficient archaeological dig," he continued. "Even though Egyptology is not my field I have not only read Dr. Delamar's works, but have corresponded with him as well and my impression is most favorable. His colleagues speak highly of his scholarship and methodology. His arrival beforehand will no doubt mean that we might begin excavating right away."

"How did he know where to go?" Lutterworth demanded belligerently, turning his attention to Dr. Beck and away from a grateful Sinclair. Atalanta poured Sinclair a glass of sherry from a silver and crystal drinks tray. He looked as if he needed it.

Dr. Beck smiled faintly. "You showed him the map as you did me, did you not? A trained scholar, Mr.Lutterworth, notices important things; notices and remembers. To not have trained one's mind to do so would be injudicious to say the least. Many times an important discovery may hinge on minute observation and the remembrance of that observation. Why, I daresay I, or even my daughter, could sketch a good representation of the map we saw, except, of course, of the part that you so obviously removed."

Lutterworth ground his teeth. He stalked to the drinks table, pushing past Sinclair, and poured himself a stiff whisky, which he downed in one gulp.

He did not like dealing with these damned intellectuals. His own education was rudimentary. He was a self-made man who liked to boast that the had dragged himself up by his bootstraps. He was far more comfortable in the company of men such as himself, men to whom money was the all in all. But it had been forcibly represented to him by Senator Marden, his contact in Washington D.C., that he had better legitimize this search for treasure with some respected scientists. The government was getting prickly about the amount of thieves and adventurers who were flocking to the new Territories to take every advantage of furthering their own fortunes. The new President, James Garfield, was anxious to welcome what he hoped would become new states into the Union without any bad blood developing between the current inhabitants and the people now rushing into the territories for settlement and, unfortunately, exploitation. Therefore, a scientific archaeological exploration sounded much better than a treasure hunt.

And even with the map, Lutterworth was not really certain how to go about finding this treasure. He needed people who were trained to deal with old maps and treasure. From what he had been told there was more to the matter than just digging. After Senator Marden's warnings he did not want some government agency interfering. No, he and he and he alone would be in charge. That meant he hired the scientists and they worked for him. What they found would be his.

However, he did not like what he saw as Ellery Delamar's defiance. It had been Delamar he really wanted to upbraid, not Sinclair, but Sinclair was here and Delamar was not. But Lutterworth would have something to say to Delamar when they arrived in New Mexico.

"Where *is* everyone?" said Erianne rather crossly. The grid had been all laid out since mid-morning and now it was getting on towards noon. She was anxious to begin training her 'pupils' in the techniques of proper archeological excavation. At this rate they would not get started until early afternoon. Everyone would come back hungry and would insist on eating a mid-day meal before working.

Sabrina and Flann looked at her in sympathy. They

too, hated waiting when everything was all prepared. his was not a full grid, but only a quarter of one. A test pit had determined that this was probably a rubbish dump of some sort, for *El Morro* had long been a stopping place for water and rest for travelers heading west onto to Arizona and points beyond or those heading east from California.

Sabrina had thought a rubbish pit the ideal practice place. It would give the new 'archaeologists' the pleasure of discovering something on their very first dig, even something as mundane as broken crockery.

Sabrina was also concerned about Ellery. He was pacing up and down, frowning and kept rubbing at his forehead, which was not a good sign. It often indicated, she had noticed in the past seven years, that something, some artifact, was 'calling' him.

She well understood how he felt about this unwanted 'gift' of pyschometry. She had seen how badly he could be affected by an artifact that still held the echoes of violence about it. Things such as spear points, arrows and other weapons could make him physically ill, for he could 'read' the past on artifacts such as these and it was as if the object had been used just for death just yesterday, not thousands of years earlier.

Fortunately, their work in Egypt generally involved tombs, not battle fields. Many of their fellow archeologists envied Ellery this dubious talent only seeing how easy it was for him to sometimes locate artifacts. But Sabrina did not envy him in the least, for she had seen the painful results of it too many times. And now his behavior was making her uneasy. But Bairre was with his Wizard. Sabrina could trust the ferret to come and tell her if anything more than a vague feeling developed for Ellery. Sometimes that was all it was: a feeling. Sometimes it was an overwhelming compulsion.

"Oh, thank goodness!" Erianne's voice interrupted her thoughts. "Here's Varian and Nick at last! But they have a passenger!"

A passenger? Sabrina stood up from the canvas folding chair she had been sitting in. It stood beneath a canvas awning by the site of the grid. Together with Erianne and Flann she watched as Varian landed near the spot that had been designated a sand wallow for the two dragons and

Torin. When Varian had folded his wings and crouched down for his riders to dismount she headed their way, followed by a curious Flann and Erianne.

"There is another dragon?" Marisela asked as Nicholas helped her off the dragon saddle. Her legs were a trifle wobbly but her eyes were shining. She found the thought that she had to fly again to get home exhilarating.

"Yes, that is Erianne. She's bonded to my uncle. My brother has a Hippogriffe, and of course we all have our familiars," Nicholas answered. Judging by her face, she was a convert to the joys of dragon-flight.

"It's about time you got back!" Erianne scolded as she came up to them. "We've been ready for you for ages! And now you've brought a guest!" More delays, her tone seemed to say.

Nicholas smiled at her as he took Cillian out of his basket. As usual, the hedgehog was deeply asleep. "Everyone, I'd like you to meet *Doña* Marisela –" he began in Spanish.

"Her whole name is very long," interrupted Varian.

"Most *Norteaméricanos* say only Serrano. They find it easier," said Marisela to the young woman in the divided skirt, knee-high boots and comfortable looking blouse. Marisela warmed to Sabrina at once. Here was a woman who, like herself, believed in comfort, not convention.

"The *Señorita's* family is going to sell us as many cows as we need. They'll be delivered, all butchered, beginning tomorrow," Nicholas continued after he had introduced everyone. Ellery, too, had noticed Varian settling down and walked over, Bairre on his shoulder. To Sabrina's relief her brother did not look as if whatever called him had moved on to the compulsion stage. Of course, sometimes it was difficult to tell. Ellery could be very good at hiding what he was feeling.

"A good morning's work, Nick. Digging increases the appetite, especially that of young dragons," said Ellery.

"And I want to dig *now*!" Varian said impatiently.

"Come with me," said Erianne. "I'm glad to have at least one pupil!" The two dragons headed towards the practice grid.

"What do you do here?" inquired Marisela, looking about at the tents with interest.

"I'll show you around if you like," Sabrina offered, and

took Marisela off with her and Flann, leaving Nicholas and Ellery staring after them.

Nicholas made a face. "She's getting on better with Sabrina than she did with me!" Then abruptly, he said. "Ellery, there's something very strange going on here. According to *Doña* Marisela, dragons have been attacking and carrying off their cattle." He briefly told his uncle the circumstances of his first meeting with Marisela.

"It hardly seems possible," Ellery agreed. Although he was not a Dracophilologist he had grown up around dragons and had never heard of a dragon behaving in such a manner. "It certainly is something that should be investigated. The United States will no doubt be establishing a Dragon Post throughout this area and I am quite certain that the couriers will not want people shooting at them and their dragons, thinking that they were protecting their property."

"Ought we to alert the authorities?" Nicholas asked.

"I am not certain who..." Ellery said slowly and then was struck by a thought. "Why don't we send a telegram to Nate Connelly? With his connections in Washington he would know who might help."

Family friends Nathan and Laura Connelly lived on the east Coast, in Connecticut, where they had a horse stud. Several years ago at the urging of his neighbors and the governor of their state, Nate had run for a Senate seat and won. Now he was involved with the integration of these new territories, having grown up on the frontier himself. He was the ideal person to contact.

"I'll look about for a telegraph office," Nicholas promised.

"Remember, Julian went into the town this morning. I trust he will have noticed if there were a telegraph office. He should be returning soon as well." Ellery rubbed again at his forehead.

"Headache?" inquired Nicholas sympathetically. The sun was very bright here, especially when compared to Ireland. Nicholas was glad of the broad-brimmed hat he wore.

Just then they heard an excited dragon trumpet. "Ellery, we've found something!" Erianne called. "And it's not just broken crockery!"

Everyone began to run towards the site.

"Thank you, Miss Beck," said Melville Sinclair gratefully. He was now comfortably ensconced in one of the velvet chairs, She had first given him a glass of sherry and now he had a thick ham sandwich on a plate, with a nice cold dill pickle and a mug of beer. He was starving. He had done little than travel at top speed for the last few days, only to arrive here and be screamed at by his employer. His job paid very well but sometimes he wondered if it was worth it, having to put up with Lutterworth's terrible temper.

"Is he always this way?" Atalanta asked. "Unreasonable, demanding and wrong?"

Sinclair flushed. He still felt some loyalty to his employer, for, after all, A.J. Lutterworth signed his paychecks. Rather than answer her he took a bite out of his sandwich.

"Never mind," she said. "It's really not fair of me to ask you that, is it?"

"I never imagined that there would be dragons," he admitted after swallowing the delicious mouthful. "I did order one of Dr. Delamar's books. It was called *Temples and Tombs*, I think. But the bookstore I get most of my books at didn't get it in on time for me to actually read it. And Mr. Lutterworth is not a reader. He only reads the financial sections in the newspapers. I don't know a lot about dragons either. They're not an up-to-date form of transport."

In the background Atalanta could hear her father talking to Lutterworth. Papa seemed to have succeeded in convincing the railroad magnate that Dr. Delamar's arriving ahead of them might be a good thing. However, Atalanta did not like the way Lutterworth was downing the whiskey. By her estimation he had drunk at least three good-sized glasses. When he rose unsteadily (cutting her father off in mid-sentence) and made his tipsy way to the room that he used as an office she was glad.

Mr. Sinclair rose as if he would follow Lutterworth but Atalanta put out a hand and pushed the hapless young man back in his chair. "Finish eating," she ordered. "He's had so much to drink that he will probably just fall into his chair and sleep it off."

But she underestimated Lutterworth's capacity for hard liquor. In a few minutes he was back.

"I just sent a telegraph to Dodge City," he said.

"How can you do such a thing?" protested Dr, Beck. "We are traveling at a great rate of speed and as I understand it, telegraph messages travel over wires."

"That's one thing these damned Wizards are good for," said Lutterworth, pouring himself another glass of whisky. "I've got a magical connection to any telegraph wire in existence from this car." He smiled grimly. "Those fucking Wizards have their uses, damn them."

"Really, sir," said Dr. Beck angrily. "I must demand that you moderate your language in front of my daughter! I will have you remember that she is a lady!"

"It's all right, Papa, he's drunk. And I've heard far worse from the men on some of our digs," Atalanta said calmly.

Lutterworth flushed, reading censure in her voice. "You all will be glad to know," he said loudly and sarcastically, "that our next stop is Dodge City, and that from there we will be able to get to New Mexico pretty damn quick! Some idiot has opened a dragon transport firm there and I booked us a flight. We'll be at the site by late afternoon!" He grinned in triumph and downed his glass in one gulp.

Before he saw what Varian had unearthed Ellery could feel it: a mass of churning chaos, of a violent, dark terror of emotion.

"Good heavens," he heard someone –Sabrina? – say. "It's some sort of jewelry!" He could not seem to focus his vision to see what they were looking at. There was a roaring in his ears.

"It's very small," said Varian. "This is so exciting! Look at that green thing in the middle! Is that an *emerald*?" He sounded as if he were very far away, his voice, like that of the others, distorted.

"Don't touch it!" said Erianne sharply. "It hasn't been documented yet. Sabrina, we need your sketch pad. Oh, why isn't Julian here with that camera?"

"Ellery? Ellery? Is something the matter?" came Bairre's anxious voice in his ear.

But Bairre and everyone else around him faded away and suddenly he was somewhere else where there was a terrible noise of shouting and screaming. There was the sound of gunfire and clashing steel. The deck pitched under his feet,

The *deck*? He was on a ship! All about him men were fighting and dying. From someone else's eyes he saw the scene, as vividly as it were taking place right now. The rational part of his mind that he still retained a small hold upon knew this was pyschometry but the terror that he felt was so real that his heart beat fast, his breath quickened and he trembled. These men meant him harm.

Suddenly an unshaven, nearly toothless face blocked his view of the deck. "Nice," this ugly apparition said. "Me an' the boys ain't had us a woman since we was last in Tortuga. An' what's these little baubles then?" He reached out a hand, filthy with dirt and caked with drying blood and gave a tug. Ellery could feel the pain around his neck as the chain broke.

He was seeing all this through the eyes of a woman, afraid for her life...no, he *was* the woman and felt the pain as the necklace was ripped from her throat and the earrings jerked from their holes.

"Ellery! Ellery!" he heard from far off and on some level he was conscious of hands touching him, holding him up.

But the scene on the deck was far more real and more urgent. Now the ugly man was advancing on him/her, closer and closer until he/she could smell the rank breath and see the evil intent in his eyes.

And that was the last he knew before everything went black.

Chapter Nine
Gray Wolf

When he awoke a blurred, unfamiliar face hung above him. "Oh, good, you're awake!" said a crisp voice.

Ellery reached out and groped for his spectacles, which he always made certain were on the bedside table.

They were put into his hand and he hurried to hook them over his ears. Whoever was at his bedside was not Sabrina. Her copper curls, even to someone hyperopic, were unmistakable.

A strange face came into view as he settled the spectacles onto his nose. Bairre, who had obviously been sleeping cuddled close against his Wizard's side, sat up and said "Ellery, this lady is Atalanta Beck. She and her father, Mr. Lutterworth and Mr. Sinclair arrived here yesterday afternoon."

"Yesterday afternoon!" echoed Ellery in dismay. "How long have I been out?" He still wore his clothing, now considerably rumpled, but someone had removed his boots.

"It is now nearly mid-day of Sunday, the 22nd of May," said Atalanta. consulting a ladies' watch that pinned to the breast of her tailored gray jacket.

"The twenty-second!" Ellery repeated, feeling foolish. "I have lost nearly an entire day?"

Bairre nodded. "We were all very worried, Ellery! Miss Beck offered to sit with you as Sabrina was up nearly all night. Julian has been in several times and said that the best thing we could do is to treat you as if you had been laid low by a Great Working."

"In fact," said Atalanta, "your sister left a mug of beef tea for you as soon as you awoke. Oddly enough, it is still warm."

"Oh, it's magiced!" said Bairre, his black masked face looking a bit surprised that she did not know this.

Since her arrival at the dig, Atalanta had been required to make a great many adjustments. She was not used to magic, Wizards and Witches, dragons and familiars. She knew such things existed, of course, and even Seneca College was lit with mage lights and had a magiced translation table, but there was no Department of Magic as there was at nearby Cornell University or Ithaca College and no Wizards were on the staff. No one in the area kept a dragon although one saw them in the sky, not infrequently. And their foreign expeditions had never had sufficient funding to use Wizards or dragons.

But Atalanta was a pragmatist, and she thought that her life's motto ought to be "What cannot be cured must be endured". One must adjust instead of fighting against things and moaning about how it was not what one was used to. She had observed the easy intercourse between the talking animals and the Delamar party and decided that she would talk to them in the same manner, as if they were rational beings.

But her father and Lutterworth were going to have a difficult time of it, she could see already. Dr. Beck was not an animal lover. She had never been allowed to have a pet. And Lutterworth somehow did not strike her as an animal lover or a lover of anything else save money and having his own way. He was incensed enough on arriving at the dig to find Dr. Delamar unconscious and that Miss Delamar would not let him examine their find.

Ellery sat up and Atalanta kindly put a cushion behind his back. He still looked pale and worn, she thought and handed him the mug of beef broth when he was situated.

She was going to have to make another adjustment there, as well. It had been another surprise to find that Dr. Delamar was a personable young man. She had expected a scholar of her father's age. She realized that this was illogical, for all scholars started out young. They were not born elderly, but everyone at Seneca, save the students was superannuated. And most of the time she often felt at least one hundred years older than the students.

Being around young men made her uncomfortable. She felt as if they were judging her and finding her lacking. She coped with this by being as brisk and efficient as possible.

"Thank you," Ellery said as she handed him the beef tea

"Drink every bit of that down!" scolded Bairre. "You need to get your strength back after an episode such as that!"

"What exactly happned to you?" Atalanta asked

92

curiously. Her tone that which she would have used with one of her father's ancient colleagues. "Miss Delamar tried to explain to us but I could see that Mr. Lutterworth thought it a pack of nonsense."

Ellery's mouth twisted wryly. "I suffer from the curse of pyschometry, Miss Beck. It's a psychic ability that allows the unfortunate person who has it to 'read' on an artifact emotions, long dead emotions and sometimes present and future as well. My curse, thank God, is limited to the past. Normally one has to touch or even hold the object to one's forehead, but it is thought that because I am magical, I don't even have to be particularly near it. Sometimes it as if the object is screaming at me. It's particularly strong when the object has been involved in violence. In this case the item, a necklace, was pulled from the neck of a young woman by some sort of brigand."

"I can imagine that such an ability would be uncomfortable, to say the least." said Atalanta sympathetically.

Ellery lowered the mug of beef tea he had been about to drink from and stared at her. "You are the first in our field that understands!" he exclaimed, amazed. "Most other archaeologists envy me for possessing such a 'gift'. It is a gift I could very well live without."

Atalanta warmed to him at once. He had included her in 'our field' and amongst 'other archaeologists', without hesitation. Nor had he made any clever remarks about her Christian name as did most classical scholars, asking her if she had slain any boars or had participated in any foot races lately. Even her father thought it amusing to remark to other scholars that she was still unmarried because no modern young men were possessed of any golden apples.

The Atalanta of classical mythology had been a huntress as good as any man and had killed the enormous and dangerous boar of Calydon. She had declared that she would not marry until the suitor for her hand could beat her in a foot race, and since she was extremely fleet of foot, no one *could* beat her. A suitor named Hippomenes obtained three golden apples from the goddess of love and beauty, Aphrodite. Every time Atalanta came near him in their foot race he tossed one of the apples behind him. This proved so irresistible that she simply had to stop and pick it up. Three times she did this, and her stops allowed him to get ahead and beat her to the finish line.

"Miss Delamar determined that the work is colonial Spanish, probably made from Aztec gold. My father confirmed this. It seems as if my father and Miss Delamar studied the same books," Atalanta continued. "She also said to tell you that she contained it and it was draining."

"Good!" said Ellery, pleased. "That means" he explained "that she put it in a magical field that prevents it from leaking out any of the emotions and that they are being pulled out from the object. My sister's husband, Alan Stillfield, devised a spell that will strip the object clean."

"Mr. Lutterworth takes this as proof that there is indeed a treasure buried near here," said Atalanta.

Ellery sighed in exasperation. "I am certain that you too, must have studied the literature, Miss Beck, and realized how extremely unlikely that is. The necklace probably came here via a passing traveler. Many times artifacts turn up in the most unlikely places, far away from their origin."

Again she was inordinately pleased with being talked to as if she were a colleague. "Mr. Lutterworth will be a difficult employer," she ventured.

"If it were not for a sizable contribution to Trinity I would not even be here," Ellery admitted. "And I look forward to the opportunity to work with your father," he added.

Atalanta hoped he still felt that way after getting to know her father. Many of their archaeological colleagues now felt otherwise.

She was also grateful that Dr. Delamar had not asked her *why* she had been named Atalanta. It had been a blow to her when she had discovered the reason.

The Atalanta of myth had been the daughter of King Iasus of Arcadia and as a girl child, was a disappointment to her father. The baby was abandoned on a hillside, exposed to the elements. But a she bear took her in and suckled her, and later she was brought up by hunters.

It was clear to Atalanta Beck, though, why she had been named so. For like the Greek Atalanta she was unwanted. She was supposed to have been a boy, a boy to follow in her father's footsteps, to bring further archaeological glory to the name of Beck.

But after her birth the doctors told her father that there would be no more children. Indeed, complications of her birth had made Atalanta's mother almost an invalid.

It mattered little how much Atalanta learned and studied or how great help she was in the field to her father. She would never be anything but a secretary to him, for although there were now female universities, none as yet granted degrees to women. She was not a male and who would pay the least bit of attention to a female? Many men in their field, and in other fields as well, thought a learned female an object of derision, a freakish anomaly.

She would always be unwanted, always a disappointment.

He stood on the top of a mountain, looking towards another. He was some nine thousand feet up, the mountain towards which he stared was over eleven thousand feet. It was called by the Navaho people, the *Dineh*, *Tsodtzil*, the Turquoise Mountain, and in the light of day it did indeed appear to be a giant slab of turquoise, capped with white snow. The *Dineh* believed that it was one of the four sacred mountains of the cardinal directions, defining the boundaries of the traditional homeland, the *Dinetah*.

But that was all he knew of it. He had heard talk by the Spaniards that it was an extinct volcano, surrounded by a group of inactive volcanoes. As a child he had imagined the volcanoes coming to life again, spewing forth fire that would kill the Spaniards and return this land to the People, to the Navaho, the Hopi, the Zuni and his mother's people, the Chiricahua Apache.

Now of course, as a man he realized how foolish this was. A volcano was indiscriminate. It would kill the People as well as their cruel overlords.

He was called Ramón by the Spanish, who promptly renamed all of the Natives that they captured and kept in slavery. The Inquisition wanted them to have no link with their pasts at all. They were Christianized and punished for speaking their own languages. Their own tongues had to be kept secret and they learned but bits and pieces of these.

His mother had tried to teach him as much of his heritage as she could, in the stolen moments they had together. He had been born in the mines, a child of rape, and his mother had never been certain which of the men that took her by force was his father.

His mother, Sonsee-array, Morning Star, had been stolen from her home on one of the many raids conducted by the soldiers of the Inquisition. Their mines, their lands and vast herds of sheep and cattle needed constant working and stolen slaves were the easiest form of cheap labor.

His mother, unfortunately for her, was a very beautiful young girl when she was stolen away. The first night that she had been taken to the silver mine where she would spend the rest of her life she was passed from man to man and this continued to be her fate. Days were spent digging for silver ore and nights in various beds.

A year later Ramón was born. He was fortunate; many of the women in the mines had rejected their children, for they were the get of the Spanish, of the soldiers of the Inquisition, and of the corrupt *Norteaméricanos* who satisfied a bent for cruelty by working for the Inquisition and keeping the slaves in line with whippings and starvation.

But from the beginning Sonsee-array had loved her small son and did her best to teach him what it meant to be one of the People. It was traditional that the first lessons came from the mother: she would teach the boy the legends of their People, and taught him of the sun and the sky, and of the stars and the clouds. She taught him to pray to Usen, the Life-Giver. But she lamented that he had no father to teach him the way of the warrior, and no one to teach him the way of the *diyin*, the medicine man. For His grandfather had been one and had known the ways of plants and the songs for healing. More than likely that would have been his way of life as well.

But there was so little time to learn. All day, from the time he could barely toddle, they had worked in the mine. Most evenings, the masters of the mines came and took her. She was with one of the overlords, sometimes until dawn. The slaves were allowed to rest only one day a week, and that was when she told him of his heritage, in whispers.

Now he did not know where he belonged, any more than the band of ex-slaves who looked to him for guidance did. They were a mixed bag of peoples: Zuni, Hopi, Apache, Navaho, and black and white Americans who had been stolen from their homes. Most of them were women and many were children and most of these of mixed blood.

Ramón did not know precisely how he had fallen into the role of their leader. The few men in the mines (woman and children were easier to intimidate) were like him, born there, and many were fearful as the result of bad treatment. He could not explain why he had not been cowed by the relentless cruelties and hard labor. Perhaps it was pride; perhaps it was, as his mother had often claimed, the fact that he was a *diyin* born. How she knew this he did not know.

But this little band had clung together when the silver mine had closed, shut down by the new government. They did not know where to go or what to do. The United States had told them to 'go home' but where was home for these people? Many of them had no idea what tribe they came from or what family they might have had. They did not know any language fluently save Spanish, and most were illiterate, nor did they have any skills, other than mining. The mines would reopen with American owners, they were told, but no women or children under fourteen would be employed.

When released from the mine it had been Ramón's idea that they go to the mountains, now being called the Zuni mountains by the *Norteaméricanos*. It was forested there, with wildlife and there were mines that perhaps the few men of their 'tribe' might get work.

At first it had been safe. By trial and error they learned to hunt with primitive slings, spears and traps. They learned in the same manner what plants were safe to eat.

But then came the railroads. Logging had begun in the mountains and the little tribe had been chased from place to place. And now there were these strange people at *El Morro*.

Even more disturbing, he had felt something in the earth, a stirring of power that had both elated and frightened him.

He wished he knew more! If he was a *diyin* he needed to know more of the healing plants, more of the songs of healing, more understanding of the forces of nature. It was like being blindfolded, groping in the dark after knowledge. There was so much that he needed to know! There were so many in the tribe that were sick. Some of the children had been so sick that he had unwillingly taken them to the missionary people. He could do nothing for them and perhaps the missionaries could.

"Nantan Lupan," said a voice behind him, "why do you look so sad and serious?"

He turned and looked a the great blue dragon behind him.

The dragon had been called Bluey or Azul in Spanish at the mine where he had dragged an ore cart. But Ramón's mother had given him the Apache name of Nah-kah-yen, or keen-sighted, for even in the dark of the mine his eyesight was remarkable.

"I am worried about our people," Ramón admitted. "Every day it seems there is much more to worry about."

"Those new people we saw, for one," the dragon said. He was completely deep blue, with no metallic edges on his scales or around his horns. and unlike most dragons, his wings were not fragile but tough and leathery. His eyes were golden, with pupils of dark blue and he had four talons on each foot. "I have never seen dragons like those two. The smaller one was a very odd colour but I am almost certain that the larger green one was a dragoness!" he added "She was very pretty. I wonder if she was mated to the other?"

Nah-kah-yen was one of the few dragons left in the area. The others had all run off when released from the mine. They had run, literally, for most of them had been wing-bound, unable to fly.

But Nah-kah-yen had been bonded to Ramón since they were both ten years old. The boy had come across the young dragon, crying, in one of the many shafts. The blue dragon had been stolen from his parents and the Native Americans whom they worked and lived with, the Cheyenne, when he was but a hatchling. He still had memories of them and of another life, including a young Cheyenne with whom he had bonded. He desperately needed someone to be a friend and a bond-mate and Ramón, who also needed someone, was exactly what was right. They had been together for fifteen years now and would never part.

Ramón had hesitated to tell even this trusted friend about what he had felt. But now he thought he had to discuss it with him and find out what he had to say. Animals were wise; they had knowledge even the most learned of *diyins* did not.

Nah-kah-yen listened intently and said at last "I felt something too. A stirring in the powers of the earth. It was not unlike when the evil sorceries of the Inquisition made their black magics, but this was different. I thought it good."

"Good magic?" repeated Ramon bitterly. His experience with magic had all been bad.

"There are two sides to everything," said the dragon thoughtfully. "Day and night, black and white, good and bad. It stands to reason that there should be good magic. Just because we have never seen any does not mean it does not exist."

He looked at his friend, who was still frowning. "It is a heavy burden you bear, Nantan Lupan," the dragon said in sympathy. "The people look to you for guidance; you are the Chief and the Medicine Man in one. Perhaps they think because of your silvered hair you are wiser than you are!"

Ramón smiled wryly. His hair, which at his age should still be dark, had been, since he was twelve, coated with silver. This had prompted his mother to give him the name of Nantan Lupan, or Gray Wolf.

He would have to be as cunning as his namesake to deal with all of the problems facing him as the erstwhile leader of his little tribe of mixed bloods. There was the encroachment of the logging companies, the coming of the railroad, and now these strange and a little frightening people at *El Morro*. What would tomorrow bring? Whatever it was it was certain that it would probably not be good.

Chapter Ten
The Vision

Ellery felt more himself after he had cleaned up and put on fresh clothing. It was amazing the difference a bath, a shave and clean garments could make.

He had anticipated, from what Miss Beck had said, that Lutterworth would be all impatience to see him. When he finally joined the others, with Bairre on his shoulder, it was to find everyone save Lutterworth sitting in the shade beneath the canvas canopy while Lutterworth paced up and down in the hot afternoon sunlight, muttering to himself.

"It's about time!" Lutterworth snarled as he caught sight of Ellery. "I'm not paying you, Delamar, to loll about and take it easy! Time is money!"

"And good afternoon to you as well, Mr.Lutterworth," said Ellery pleasantly. He was determined not to let the railroad baron put him in a bad mood. "But where is Julian?" he inquired, looking about and finding a member of their party missing.

"There are some very sick children in the little village not too far from here. Diablo, I think it is called," answered Sabrina. "He is treating them as there seems to be no doctor at all within two hundred miles in either direction." She was petting Flann, who lay in her lap, looking slightly sleepy. Cillian, in Nicholas's lap, was sound asleep.

The two dragons lay a little behind the awning. Varian said eagerly, "Tell us what you saw, Ellery! We've been trying to guess while you were recovering."

"This is a most – er – *interesting* conjecture, Dr. Delamar," said Dr. Beck rather dryly, as if he did not really believe that Ellery had 'seen' anything.

Lutterworth made an exasperated noise. "I told you, Beck, that he can feel these things! That's what the man at Columbia told me anyway. He didn't mention that it would put you out of commission for almost two days!" He turned and glared at Ellery. "If you keep collapsing every time we find something we'll never make the deadline! I want to know what is going on and I want to know now!"

"Why don't you both sit down and have some of this

101

nice cool drink Miss Delamar has prepared and talk rationally, Mr. Lutterworth? You look as if you are about to explode. It can't be good for you, marching about in the sun," said Atalanta.

As usual, her calm, no-nonsense voice had the effect of deflating Lutterworth, and he collapsed into a chair, muttering under his breath.

Ellery was glad to sit down and sip at a blend of fruit juices. "Where is the artifact now?"

"Here," Sabrina pulled out the small drawer of a little table and gave it magical push. It moved through the air to come and hang suspended in front of Ellery.

It was a golden cross on a heavy chain. It was quite large, about five inches long, and heavy appearing, with a good sized emerald in the center. Smaller stones, appearing to be crystal, went across the arms and down the center of the cross above and below the emerald in varying sizes, from large near the center emerald to very small at the ends. Other than beveled edges and the fact that the ends were curved in a rather Moorish style, the rest of it was quite plain. But it was a handsome piece. The chain, of gold as well, was broken in one place.

"It seems more like something that would be found on a priest than a young woman," Ellery said.

"You saw a young woman?" asked Nicholas intently. He had known that his uncle had the talent of pyschometry but he had never seen it in use.

"I not only *saw* her, I *was* her for a brief moment," Ellery answered. "From the very beginning I saw through her eyes and then I felt her emotions, her complete terror, as well, for her emotions became mine."

"It was on the deck of a ship," he continued. "All about were men fighting with swords and pistols. The deck was red with spilt blood. A most villainous looking fellow approached and he grabbed the cross from about her neck and pulled. It broke–I felt the pain of it as if it had happened to me." He paused and then said, "I have been thinking about this since I awoke and trying to remember the whole experience more clearly. More details have come back. From the dress on some of the people I saw it was the sixteenth century. There was another ship, close to, from which more men were coming.

From its rigging hung the pirate flag of skull and crossbones, the Jolly Roger."

Lutterworth made a noise indicative of disbelief. "Are you crazy?" he said contemptuously. "Are you trying to tell us that this necklace came from a pirate ship? Do you see any ocean anywhere near here? This is *Conquistador* jewelry!"

"It does, indeed, defy reason," Dr. Beck agreed. "What could be the possible explanation for pirate loot to end in the desert here? We are many miles from where pirates plied their trade."

"Weren't pirates around much later in time, like Blackbeard, in the eighteenth century?" put in Melville Sinclair rather timidly, as if he were afraid his employer would quash him.

But Lutterworth took this for support. "There!" he said triumphantly. "Even Sinclair knows what's what!"

"There were pirates in the Caribbean as early as the mid 16th century!" said Varian indignantly. "Didn't you ever read about the Spanish Main and Sir Francis Drake and the English Sea Rovers? There were all sorts of pirates and privateers, French and English and lawless men of every country, going after the Spanish galleons—the treasure ships, filled with doubloons and pieces of eight and fabulous jewels. I've read all about it!"

Lutterworth looked as if he wanted to dismiss anything Varian had to say but he thought twice about arguing with someone who had such large teeth.

"Is this some sort of reincarnation, Dr. Delamar?" asked Dr. Beck. He had steepled his fingers and was looking over the top of his *pince-nez* at Ellery. "I am afraid that I give little credence to the claims of people who insist that they were Egyptian pharaohs, Caesar or Napoleon in another lifetime."

"It's not reincarnation," said Ellery, suddenly feeling very tired. "It's a psychic vibration of past events. It's a vision, a small window into the past. But it has very few details. I don't know who this young woman was, or even exactly when this happened to her, or what became of her, although I suspect she was raped and murdered. It's the moment of violence that clings to this necklace. And unfortunately, the violence resonates to me far more than anything else." He was tired of trying to explain something he barely understood himself.

"Pyschometry is defined is an ability to read the past history of an object by usually touching it," Sabrina explained. "Ellery usually doesn't even need to touch it."

"And do all you so-called magical persons have this ability?" inquired Dr. Beck.

"No, it's rather rare," Sabina answered. Her opinion of Dr. Beck so far had not been favorable. She much disliked the way he ordered his daughter about and he had been equally dismissive of anything she herself had said. He had argued with her about dating the cross, until he came to the same conclusions himself, and even then would not admit that she knew what she had been talking about. Obviously he was one of those idiot men who thought that no woman could contribute anything of value to any scholastic endeavor. Unfortunately there were all too many of those around. She was more thankful than ever for her brother's open-mindedness and ability to accept anyone, male or female, whose scholarship was sound.

Lutterworth was as bad. He had actually told her not to worry her pretty little head over the artifact. Sabrina did not know what she hated more—a man who thought she could not be intelligent because she was attractive or one who thought her learning meaningless because she was female.

"So-called magical persons?" Nicholas inquired. "Surely, Dr. Beck, coming from the part of the world that you do, you know that magic is real!"

"My father and I have had little to do with Wizards, Dr. Stillfield," Atalanta put in quickly. She was far too used to acting as peacemaker for her father. He seemed to enjoy setting up people's backs. Even now he looked singularly pleased with himself. "Seneca College has no Department of Magic, nor even one of Dracophilology," she said, with a smile at him. "I believe that both our sister institutions, Cornell and Ithaca, do, however."

"I taught a summer course at Ithaca once," said Nicholas, returning her smile. He liked her; he was not sure about her father.

Lutterworth had been sitting silently for a few moments, pulling at his lower lip. "I don't care where this damned necklace came from originally!" he suddenly burst out, slamming his fist down on the fragile arm of the canvas chair. It nearly buckled beneath this assault. "What this necklace says to me is that the *Conquistadors* were here! It was probably lost from one of the treasure chests! I say that we start digging right now!"

"You'll have to show us the rest of the map, Mr. Lutterworth. We can't work in the dark," said Ellery. He found himself exchanging an amused and exasperated glance with Atalanta Beck.

Lutterworth laughed. "That's precisely where you *will* be working!"

"Oh, look!" said Varian excitedly. "There's that blue dragon again! I'm going up to talk to him!" He moved away from the awning area and launched himself into the air, over Erianne's protests.

It had been a long morning for Julian and Siofra.

He had achieved an uneasy alliance with the Reverend Brewer and his helpers. As he had thought, they were really too afraid of him and what his magic could do, or what they thought it could do, to interfere too much.

The Reverend kept up a running litany and actually wrung his hands as Julian began to work with the children. Julian had never imagined that anyone outside of an old fashioned Gothic novel actually did such a thing.

Brother Ezekiel and his wife sat at the table and watched, obviously filled with trepidation.

But Miss Cromwell followed him about, her eyes shining, so thrilled to see the children being helped.

They were not as badly off as Julian had dreaded as first. Most of them could be helped. Only one was beyond any aid.

There were eleven children all together, ranging in age from five to fifteen. Six were boys, five were girls and all were of what the Reverend persisted in referring to as "mixed blood" as if they were somehow inferior. It appalled Julian that children of this age had been set to work in a mine. The dust that they had inhaled had damaged their lungs, which was much more serious for still growing children. Some were asthmatic, very badly so, some had emphysema, and others chronic bronchitis. All had some sort of bronchopulmonary disease. This had been worsened, he found as he questioned them, by the fact that they lived, worked and even ate and slept in the mines. They never had fresh air, or been outdoors in the sunlight. Had it not been for the war they would still be slaves in the dark and unhealthy air of the mines, to pass their entire lives there and even die when they were too old or too ill to be of any use. As far as Julian could ascertain, the Inquisition had never employed doctors of any type. The sick were allowed to die as it was too easy to obtain more slaves from constant raids on the Native peoples and on the border towns. Slaves were even imported, illegally, from Africa and brought from the prisons of the Inquisition on the continent of Europe.

As had non-magical medicine, Healing magic had made many exciting advances since the beginning of the present century. A Great Ritual was no longer needed for many Healings as it had been in former times. Healers could do more on their own as techniques had been simplified. Preparations were now at a minimum and often times a Wizard Healer needed little besides his wand, an incantation, a potion, few props and his in-born Healing talent. The one exception was what had come to be called a "passing" Ritual, where a gravely, incurably ill person who desired it, was released into the care of the angels, and quietly and without pain, passed on.

But magic still had a price. It was exhausting and draining as the Healer took the illness or injury into himself and then passed it into the earth's energies where it would be safely dissipated.

Julian knew that he could hope to Heal no more than three of the children at a time, and then he would need to recuperate. Siofra would keep strict watch over him. She could tell even before he could at times when he was overextending himself. This was for the patient's sake as well as his. A Healer needed all of his strength to assure the best treatment. To try and Heal when exhausted was doing the patient little good.

Siofra helped in other ways as well. Children especially responded to her and relaxed when they listened to her purr and petted her soft fur. This as well as the Healer's bond, made them much more receptive to the Healing.

For the first session he chose two of the boys and a girl. She was worse off than they were, suffering from severe emphysema. At thirteen she had been exposed to the mine longer than they had. Her name was Angelita, given her by the mine overseers; she had no other name. She remembered no life save that of the mine. She had no memories of a mother or any family and had no idea where she came from.

Julian was very grateful that he had gone to Oberon and been given the gift of Spanish and Native tongues. Some of these children spoke a blend of Spanish and Hopi or Zuni or an Apache language, depending on what they had learned from mothers, brothers and sisters and other slaves.

Prudence Cromwell stood by as he made the simple preparations. He lit candles of green at the foot and the head of Angelita's narrow bed. With his wand he drew a Circle around her and himself, cautioning Prudence to not step inside it. Large-eyed, she nodded. The candles hung in the air and the wand left a visible trail of green fire around the cot.

Angelita, who would be strikingly pretty if she had her health, watched him with eyes as big as Prudence's. She had dark hair, black eyes and golden skin, which now had a grayish tinge. Every breath was a struggle and she coughed incessantly. She liked the *Señor el médico* but she did not really believe that he could make her well. She was somewhat resigned to dying as she still did not believe that the Inquisition was gone and she would not be dragged back to the mine. To her mind, being dead was preferable to that. She was only grateful that she had been spared the lustful attentions of the overseers.

Siofra lay under Angelita's hand, purring. She could feel the girl relaxing and turned up the volume of her purr as Julian placed his hand on the girl's forehead and opened himself to the ley lines. The Healing had begun.

It was as if the earth shook.

It was just after noontime when Ramón felt a tremor run through every part of his body. All his senses quivered.

Fortunately he was seated on a rock or he might have fallen. They had just finished their inadequate noon meal of corn tortillas and squash. No one had many cooking skills and there was not much to work with. The tortillas were lumpy and charred and the squash overcooked. But it was food, and not much worse than what they had eaten in the mines.

Tadeo, one of the few other men in the group of about twenty persons, said quickly "What is it, Ramón? You look strange!"

"There is a disturbance in the earth," Ramón answered slowly. "It stirs."

"An earthquake?" Tadeo asked anxiously. Here in the mountains was not a place to be if there was to be an earthquake. He was a man of near Ramon's age, the offspring of a mother who had been an African slave, a Watusi from the interior of the African continent, she had claimed, and a Spanish overseer. Like Ramon, he had been born in the mine. He was tall and regal of bearing with skin the colour of black coffee and abundant tightly curled black hair.

"I am not certain what it is," Ramón admitted. "If only I understood these things, Tadeo! Of what use is it being born a *diyin* if I have had no training and do not understand what things mean?" His voice was anguished.

Tadeo looked at his friend in sympathy. He well understood how he felt – all of the people here had frustrations, perhaps not as bad as did Ramón, but every one of them felt as if they belonged nowhere and knew nothing. They had few skills other than mining; even the most basic of survival skills such as hunting, growing food and cooking their food, were beyond them. And it hurt that many of them had no knowledge of who their people were, their traditions and a family history. They were truly lost.

"Someone is using magic," said a voice from near their feet.

Ramón looked down into the eyes of a gray fox that lay there. This animal had suddenly appeared when he had left the mine a few years earlier. Ramón had been shocked when the animal spoke to him in human language and announced that he was the helper of a *diyin*, who would intercede for him with the spirits and guide him in his medicine work. His name was Gian-nah-tah, which meant "always ready". But it seemed to Ramón that the fox had made a mistake in coming to him, for he was no Medicine Man and the life they now shared was a poor one.

"Like the black sorcerers?" Ramón queried. Like many of the others, he was never sure if the horrors of the Inquisition's occupation of the land would return.

"No," said Gian-nah-tah. "Feel it; open yourself to it. This is good magic! You should go and seek it out, Nantan Lupan." Like the dragon, the fox always used his Apache name. It still sounded strange to Ramón, who always thought of himself with the name the Spaniards had given him. He knew little of his mother's language as she had never been able to learn but a bit of it. There had been no time and she had died when he was only fifteen.

Half an hour later, persuaded by the fox, he was flying towards the source of the magical disturbance. The blue dragon wore a patched-up, discarded Inquisition cavalry saddle with a girth of woven grasses. He had been uneasy about taking his rider up without one and in truth it was more comfortable for Ramón as well.

The closer they came to *El Morro* the more Ramón could feel the surges in the earth's energies. Nah-kah-yen circled the area, going lower with each pass as Ramón tried to pinpoint where the feeling came from.

Neither of them was paying much attention to their surroundings. It was a clear day–no chance of lightning–and dragons had no natural enemies so that there was little need to be on guard.

Therefore they were both startled when a voice said, suddenly, "Hello! I knew that there had to be other dragons here!"

Chapter Eleven
Don Rafael

Marisela was angry and disappointed. She had wanted to deliver the cattle to the archaeological dig out at *El Morro*. She found the archaeologists fascinating, and, she admitted, hoped for another ride dragon-back.

Her mother had protested her intention to do this, which was bad enough. The scolding was nearly unendurable. Her mother seemed to have no idea when a subject was exhausted.

But then, unexpectedly, her father had put his foot down. She would stay here, and not go riding off in the company of only *vaqueros*. Curro could deliver the butchered beef to the *Norteaméricanos*. She would dress properly, and receive their guests in the company of her *duenna*.

"Guests?" Marisela had demanded, with a sinking feeling. This neighborhood was a limited one now. Guests could mean only one thing— the idiotic *Don* Rafael and his obnoxious mother, *Doña* Paloma, of the neighboring *Hacienda del Desértico*.

"You will behave as a proper young girl of noble blood should!" *Don* Casimiro had ordered. "I have invited them to come for the Mass as well, now that we again have a priest."

When the Inquisition had departed this circumstance had left them without a priest and the mission church of San Gabriel had stood empty for a long time. But *Don* Casimiro, a devout man, had spoken to *Don* Rafael, who had written to an acquaintance in Mexico City, one who knew the Bishop there. Two weeks ago *Fray* Felipe had arrived and had at once set about putting the mission to rights and once again the mission bell was heard ringing the canonical hours. It was still a small congregation, since many of the Spanish in the area had fled to Mexico and South America, particularly those who had officiated at the mines, as they were afraid of prosecution by the Americans.

Therefore, Marisela found herself at noontime on Sunday, sitting near the fountain in the company of her mother and her *duenna*, *Doña* Trinidad de Narváez, a spinster of nearly sixty, who, Marisela was certain, had never known what it was like to be young. The woman had been born old. When she was younger Marisela had fancied that *Doña* Trinidad was a prune in a gown. The *duenna* had never been known to wear any other colour than black and was sober, pious, humorless and a dead bore.

Marisela was clad in an uncomfortably tight white dress designed to show off her feminine charms, although supposedly in a modest, demure fashion. It was made tight to just below the hips, then fell to the ground in a cascade of four ruffled flounces. These flounces were repeated in the "butterfly" sleeves of innumerable flounces that showed her bare arms as they came only to a midpoint on her upper arms. Her dark hair and been pinned high and a tortoise shell *pieneta*, shaped like a convex comb with large prongs, added the illusion of height. Over this was draped a lacy white mantilla. She also had white roses in her hair. To complete this ensemble she wore gold hoop earrings and a tiny gold cross in the V of the bodice. She felt miserable and longed for the freedom of her trousers. She thought of the woman she had just met, Sabrina Delamar, who wore sensible split skirts and a comfortable short-sleeved blouse.

And all of this (for her parents and *duenna* wore their best too) to impress a man she thought of as a moron, that she would *never* marry, no matter what her parents wanted.

They had seen him in church that morning. The five of them the only *hidalgos*, seated in the front near the altar, while the back of the church was crowded with Indians and *mestizos*.

Don Rafael and his mother had gone home after church, for the ladies could not be expected to appear in the same clothing at the midday meal that they had worn to church. Church garb was more modest, less decorative.

All during the Mass Marisela had been conscious that *Don* Rafael's eyes were upon her, not upon *Fray* Felipe. In spite of the fact that she considered him mentally negligible Marisela did not like his gaze upon her, or his sweating palms when he took her hand in his. He made her skin crawl.

Pedro, their major-domo, only kept on now because he was superannuated and almost beyond any work, tottered into the room, peered at his employers and announced "*Don* Rafael Amancio Orfeo Mateo de Veláquez y Montillo! And his lady mother, *Doña* Paloma Maria del Pilar Miramontes y Montillo!"

With his usual smirk of self-satisfaction *Don* Rafael entered the room, his mother on his arm.

He was a man of medium height, with thinning hair, slicked back with hair oil, the beginnings of a paunch and a thick mustache of dark hair flecked with gray. His eyes were dark and restless, and in Marisela's opinion set too close together. His lower lip was flabby and always wet. *Don* Rafael was also a fop; he wore a suit of light blue, heavily embroidered on the breast of the jacket, the arms and the sides of each leg, with black work and spangles. His waist sash was bright red and his shirt ruffled to such a degree that it made him look like a pouter pigeon. Marisela wondered that he did not fall over from the weight of the embroidery and the ruffles. In spite of the fact that they had come in a carriage he wore immense, jingling silver spurs on the heels of his shiny boots. One hardly ever saw *Don* Rafael on horseback as he was a poor horseman and much preferred the comfort of his well-sprung carriage.

His mother, even though her Christian name meant "dove", more strongly resembled a vulture. She had an immense beak of a nose, of which she was inordinately proud, as it resembled that which could be seen in some of Goya's portraits of the Spanish royal family to which she was distantly connected. She too, had beady eyes too close together under a very high forehead and a long thin, rather emaciated neck set in hunched shoulders. She always wore black silk, all crowned with a black mantilla. She was very thin and actually taller than her son by an inch or so.

Don Rafael had been talking out in the hall, He continued to talk as they advanced into the room, about one of the carriage horses and its lameness.

He talked a great deal but actually said very little. He repeated himself endlessly and none of it was interesting. He remembered the most obscure details and padded out a story with them so that a simple anecdote that should have taken but a few moments took forever to relate. Marisela was not certain whether he was talking to Pedro or to his mother, or even to some invisible entity at the moment. Any of these was preferable to his talking to her.

"*Buenas tardes, Don* Rafael, *Doña* Paloma!" her father interrupted the stream of talk. "Welcome to our home! We are all very glad that you could honor us with your presence."

Doña Paloma snapped open a black lace fan and waved it languidly in front of her face. "We are pleased to be here as well," she said. She had a curiously deep voice. She sounded more male than did her son. "Are we not, Rafael?"

"*Sí*, Mamacita," he agreed, looking at Marisela and licking his already wet lips. "How beautiful the *Señorita* looks today! I thought her exquisite at church but now she takes my breath away." He advanced on her with mincing steps and took her hand in his, lifting it to his lips.

Marisela had all she could do to stop from pulling her hand free and wiping it on her skirt. She could not believe that her parents were smiling at this idiot, this buffoon. *Doña* Paloma looked pleased as well, smugly so. She thought her son a matrimonial prize, a paragon of all the virtues.

Suddenly Marisela had a vision of the *Norteaméricano* she had just met, the *brujo* Stillfield. *Don* Rafael seemed even worse than normal in comparison.

Marisela badly resented her time being taken up with this *idiota*. She could have been talking instead with her new acquaintances; she could have been riding a dragon! What would it take for her parents to realize that nothing would ever make her consent to a match with the stupidest man in *Nueva España*?

She turned away from *Don* Rafael as if she were a modest, retiring girl and sat back down beside her *duenna*. Her eyes were lowered; she did not want her father to see the contempt that she felt or she would be taken to task for it later.

She did not see the calculating look given her by the *idiota* as he began a long, pointless story about a carriage that he had ordered from Madrid ten years earlier and what had happened to it. That look might otherwise might have given her pause.

Startled, Nah-kah-yen back-winged as a strange pale green dragon seemed to drop out of the sky in front of them.

Ramón slid in the saddle and grabbed at one of the dragon's back ridges to steady himself. If he fell, he would be killed, no doubt about that.

"Who are you?" Nah-kah-yen ground out when he had steadied himself and sensed that his rider was again secure. His tone was hostile. "And what are you doing here, you and all of those strangers?"

"We're an archeological expedition," said Varian. He could not understand why this dragon spoke in such a way and looked at him so suspiciously. He was trying his best to be friendly.

Neither Ramón or Nah-kah-yen knew what he meant. They had never heard the word 'archeological' before.

"What are you doing?" Varian continued. "You seemed to be searching for something. Perhaps I can help you find it?" He spoke eagerly, hoping that an offer of help would make this dragon more sociable.

"It's none of your business–" said Nah-kah-yen, but Ramón interrupted him, remembering what the fox had said just before the dragon took flight. "Help will come in finding the source of the magic. Seize it and use it."

"We seek a user of magic," he answered.

"All of the humans in my party use magic," said the strange dragon cheerfully. "But if you are taking about using magic right at this moment it's probably Julian. He was planning to Heal those sick children this afternoon."

"There is a Medicine Man here?" Ramón queried sharply. "A Medicine Man who can heal?"

"I don't know if you could call him a Medicine Man," said Varian. "But he's a doctor, a Wizard Healer."

"Take me to him!" Ramón demanded. He was suddenly excited. Perhaps this was why the fox had come to him! To lead him to another Medicine Man! Perhaps he could learn from this man!

"We're not too far away," said Varian. "Just follow me!"

The two dragons had been gliding; now Varian began to go down in a lazy spiral.

Nah-kah-yen's first impulse was to fly as fast as he

could in the other direction. He was suddenly afraid of a trap. Having escaped the mines once he did not want to go back, or see Ramón have to return to forced labor.

But through their bond he could feel his rider's rising excitement. He knew, for they had talked of it many times, that Ramón would do almost anything to become a true *diyin*, to be able to heal and help the sick. This was the first true Medicine Man they had ever met. Even Nah-kah-yen could feel the magic calling to Ramón for it was powerful and gave rise to emotions in his rider that the blue dragon could easily read.

Against his own inclinations he began to follow the oddly coloured dragon down to the earth.

"That is after bein' enough!" said Siofra firmly to her Wizard. "'Tis near dead on your feet ye are an' ye'll be after doin' these wee ones no good passed out on the floor. Torin an' I will be takin' ye back to the camp and see that Sabrina is tuckin' ye up in yer bed! There's always bein' tomorrow."

Julian had to admit that his familiar was right. He was exhausted right down to his bones. He still had to show the missionaries how to brew the cough tea and make up a thyme bath for the children. Fortunately he had asked Sabrina to type out the instructions the night before.

A little shakily he stood up from the end of the cot where he had been sitting and looked down at the boy Benito, who was eight. Like Angelita and Guillermo before him he now had healthy colour in his face and the look of strain was disappearing. "It does not hurt!" he said in wonder, looking up at Julian, his black eyes beginning to sparkle. "The pain, it is gone." He rubbed at his chest, where the deep cough of chronic bronchitis had caused so much misery. He usually coughed up some nasty sputum and wheezed, his breath short, when he exerted himself.

But now for the first time in ages he could take a deep breath. "Is it gone, *Señor el médico?* Is it truly gone? It will not come back?"

"Yes. Just stay out of the mines." said Julian, smiling at the boy in spite of his utter fatigue.

"Oh, *sí, Señor*, I promise!" said the boy fervently. He took a deep breath as if he could not get enough air. A blissful smile spread over his face as this breath did not bring on the all too familiar cough.

Prudence, standing beyond the green Circle drawn around the bed was full of wonder. She had never seen anything like this. The children were completely cured, not just given something that would help their cough.

Angelita, Guillermo and Benito were all looking healthier, and the first two were now sleeping easily.

As Julian took down the Healing Circle and snuffed the candles with a wave of his hand, she asked eagerly. "Are you going to help the others now?"

"An' can ye not be seein' that he is after bein' drained from three Healin's?" demanded Siofra belligerently.

"I would like to, Miss Cromwell, but it is beyond me at the moment. Tomorrow, after I rest, I will be able to help more of them. By the end of the week I think that they all will be feeling much better." *Except Tomaso*, Julian thought to himself with a pang of intense grief. Even all the Healing skills in the world would not help that boy. It was amazing he was still alive. His lungs were virtually in tatters. Tomorrow he would aid the boy's passing into the Light.

"I have some instructions here for a herbal tea and thyme baths for the children," Julian continued, reaching into his shirt pocket and pulling out a folded paper.

"Let me have that," Unseen by either of them, Sister Rebecca had left her seat at the table and held out her hand. "I am a herb mistress."

"She is considered very knowledgeable back home in Ohio," Prudence said, at Julian's inquiring look.

"I think you will find everything on that list familiar, except for the last item," Julian said, watching as she read the list.

"These are all good, Healing herbs!" she said almost accusingly, looking up at him with a frown.

"I keep telling you, ma'am, that I am a servant of the Light. What do you expect, hembane and nightshade?" Julian asked.

She continued frowning but read aloud "Plantain, coltsfoot, elm bark, knotgrass, mallow flowers, licorice root, star anise–I have all of these in my stores, except this last."

"Eucalyptus," he supplied. "I can give you that."

"We were administering a tea of plantain, coltsfoot and mallow," she said, "but it seemed to be doing little good."

He forebore mentioning that it was the Healing magic that would help the most. He would bespell the eucalyptus so that she could blend it with the other herbs and the magic would spread throughout the tea.

"There's dragons comin'!" Siofra interrupted.

"Nick and Ellery?" Julian inquired, but before she could answer the door opened and a man Julian had never seen before entered.

He was a ragged man, clad in rough trousers and shirt that had seen very hard use. A bandana tied around his forehead held his shoulder length, gray streaked dark hair our of his eyes, His skin was copper coloured, his eyes a deep warm brown and his cheek bones high. He scanned the room rapidly, at last his gaze fastening on Julian.

"Ramón!" Benito cried out joyfully. "Ramón, come and see! The *Señor el médico* has made me well! I cough no more!"

Ramón took a deep breath to steady himself. He almost trembled with excitement. "Is this true?" he demanded of Julian. "You have made them well? With magic?"

"An' haven't ye be havin' the eyes in your head?" demanded Siofra. "Sure and is he not a Wizard Healer an' bearing the traces of th' Healin'? Sit down before ye fall down!" she said sharply as behind her Julian slightly staggered as his fatigue began to catch up with him with a vengeance.

Ramón started. Outside he had seen the strangest creature he had ever seen, a sort of feathered horse to which the pale green dragon talked and now here was another animal that spoke as a man, although its speech was strange indeed. This was indeed magic! "Teach me, teach me what you do!" Ramón said hoarsely to the Medicine Man.

Chapter Twelve
The Map

"It is about time," said Dr. Beck in his dry voice, "that we see this treasure map of yours. Mr. Lutterworth. And what is this about working in the dark?"

Lutterworth chuckled and reached inside his jacket pocket. "You'll see," he said in a mysterious and exasperating fashion. "Sinclair, clear off that table top and make certain that it is clean." He pointed at a collapsible table that still bore the remains of a late luncheon.

Sinclair leaped to obey him. Sabrina and Nicholas assisted, earning a look of gratitude from the hapless young man.

When it was clean Lutterworth took out a sealed oilskin packet. "What you saw, gentlemen, was a copy. This is the original map." They all crowded about the table to look at it, the familiars looking down from their magical partners' shoulders.

It was smaller than the copy, on ragged and stained parchment. It was drawn in the fashion of the 16th century, with little regard to proportion and limited by what was then known of the world. Mexico was fairly well recognizable but Baja California was a mere bump on the continent as was Florida. It showed the tip of South America and the Isthmus of Panama. Japan, identified as Gaipan, was far closer to the North American Continent than it was in reality as was the land mass of Asia

"They told me at Columbia's Geography and Cartography Department that this is based on one drawn in 1566 by a man named Bolognino Zaltieri," said Lutterworth, stumbling a little over the Italian name.

"Yes, that would be the map commemorating the discovery of New France," murmured Atalanta. "It was one of the first maps to identify the strait between Asia and North America, the Strait of Anian." She had noticed that Lutterworth left the "ladies" out of his discussion, although she had been present when he had shown the copy to her father and she had studied it as well.

Lutterworth shot her a glance of extreme dislike but

went on without comment.

"They helped me figure out where this actually was because a lot of the names have changed or just weren't there. But the little drawings helped." He pointed to a small sketch of El Morro and those of mountains. "The rivers are fairly accurate. See, here's the Rio Grande–" his finger traced the route of the river as it lead down from *'Terra in cognito'* to Mexico, where it emptied into the sea.

"This river," again he pointed to the map and traced a route that seemed to be a tributary of the Rio Grande "would seem to be the Rio San José. It goes through the mountains here. It passes between the San Mateo Mountains the north and the Zuni Mountains to the south. Look at this–there are two mountains shown here, one above the other. I'm willing to bet those are Mount Sedgwick and Mount Taylor. Here is where we are at *El Morro*."

"Most of the rivers are not even named," said Nicholas. "In fact, the entire map is short on names and places. It seems to be marked in a mixture of Latin and Spanish."

"But this river," Lutterworth said jabbing at it on the map *"is* named! The Rio Salado! It's below where the San Jose and the Rio Puerco join to flow into the Rio Grande. The San Mateo mountains are to the right of the San José and the Zunis are to the left, below it. And here, this little drawing says 'castillo' That's castle and this *El Morro* looks like a castle, doesn't it? And this mountain on the other side of the river is marked '*azul*'. That means blue! Don't the Indians call Mount Taylor the Turquoise mountain? And here," he pointed to a cross on the map "is the treasure! Between the two mountains and to the north of the river! And look at this – it says '*cueva*',which is Spanish for cave! And these other words are *tesoro oculto*–treasure trove!"

"Traditionally, treasure maps have more than a vague set of directions, Mr. Lutterworth," said Sabrina. "Even the person who supposedly hidden this treasure might have trouble finding it again with such an indeterminate route marked out."

Ellery found himself exchanging a look with Miss Beck. She felt just as he did; he could read it in her eyes plainly. Lutterworth was clutching at straws.

"I have something no one else has," said Lutterworth with a smirk of satisfaction. "I have Dr. Delamar. He can sniff out the treasure for me. If you could find such a small thing as that necklace you can find an entire treasure!" he said to Ellery.

"I did not find the necklace," said Ellery in protest. "Erianne and Varian dug it up—"

Lutterworth pooh-poohed his objections. "I had you thoroughly investigated after they told me at Columbia what you could do," he said. "You've found things other people have missed in places where it was said there was nothing to be found!"

Nicholas had taken a small pocket magnifier from his vest and was bent over the map. "There's another word or so here, near the cross marking the location of the cave. Even with a magnifying glass it's hard to make out." He took his wand from the belt loop and commanded "*Amplicare!*" touching the map with the wand's tip.

It was suddenly twice as large and though smudged, was easier to read. "*Piedra caliza,*" Nicholas read aloud. When he had made this out he said "*Reducto,*" and the words returned to their normal size.

Erianne had been standing behind the awning listening with interest. "But that means limestone!" she said surprised. "That means, Ellery, that even if you can't find it, I can!"

"What do you mean?" Atalanta asked.

"Limestone is our firestone that we chew to make our dragon gasses so we can fly," Erianne explained. "All dragons can always locate firestone no matter where we are. It's an absolute necessity for us. Varian and I were planning to try and find some tomorrow as we are running low on what we brought with us. *El Morro* is sandstone and useless for firestone. Besides that we would not wish to deface this place. But a cave would be perfect!" She gave a delighted wiggle.

Dr. Beck had been bent over the map as well and now he straightened up and took off his *pince-nez,* rather absentmindedly beginning to polish them with an immaculate handkerchief. "How can you be certain, Mr. Lutterworth, that the rivers are the ones you think there are, or be positive as to the identity of the mountains? Not only is this area rife with

121

mountainous terrain but from what I have read the Rio Grande has many tributaries, at least a dozen as I remember. Perhaps this map refers to the Pecos river, another long–"

"That's the trouble with all of you people!" Lutterworth interrupted angrily. "You spend too damned much of your time reading and not enough looking at the real world! Even a blind man could see that there could be no other way to read this map! At any rate," he continued, folding up the map and replacing it first in the oilskin pouch and then into his breast pocket, "I'm footing the bills for this expedition and I say that tomorrow we'll begin looking for this treasure cave just where this map indicates it will be!" He glared at all of them, his square jaw set and giving his face a decidedly pugnacious look. "Sinclair, go into town and arrange for some horses."

"I doubt such a small place will have sidesaddles available," protested Sinclair, with an apologetic look at Sabrina and Atalanta.

"The women won't be coming along," said Lutterworth carelessly.

"The women certainly are coming!" said Sabrina heatedly. She was more than a little tired of Lutterworth's attitude towards the female members of the party. "And how is Mr. Sinclair supposed to get into town, pray? Walk all that way in this heat?"

"Don't you have some cooking or laundry or something female to do here?" Lutterworth demanded of Sabrina. "Isn't that what you're here for?"

"Mr. Lutterworth," Ellery spoke before Sabrina could retort. "It is time you realized that my sister and Miss Beck are trained scholars and as such are just as valuable as any man here." His voice was cold and his eyes as he looked at Lutterworth were contemptuous.

"They are more valuable than I am," said Nicholas cheerfully. "I'm no archaeologist! Neither is Julian."

"And why should you hire horses when we have two dragons available? They can carry all of the equipment as well as all of us. We both have six person saddles," Nicholas continued.

" Varian and I can get you there much faster than any horse!" said Erianne, surprised that he would even think of using horses.

Lutterworth scowled. He much disliked having the arrangements taken out of his hands. But the thought of getting there earlier in the day was appealing. "All right," he said at last, rather grudgingly "but remember one thing! I'm in charge here!"

"I don't think that there is any possibility of any one forgetting that, Mr. Lutterworth," said Atalanta sweetly, which earned her another glance of aversion from him.

But she didn't care. Dr. Delamar had stood up for her! He considered her valuable! She felt as if she was walking on air, although she did wonder how he knew that she had viable scholarly skills. She determined to ask him at the earliest opportunity.

Marisela thought that the afternoon with the unwanted guests would never end. *Don* Rafael seemed more boring than normal and his mother more obnoxious with her scarcely veiled hints about a wedding and (dare she be indelicate? *Doña* Paloma had tittered in an arch fashion) grandchildren.

Don Casimiro and *Doña* Milagros had smiled on this display of stupidity benignly. How they could tolerate that insufferable bag of hot air she could not understand, much less think that she would ever marry him!

At long last they left, promising a return invitation to their home. Marisela stood with her parents and *duenna* at the gate of the *hacienda*, watching the carriage drive off.

"He still wants you, daughter," said *Doña* Milagros happily. "Crook your little finger and he will come running. He could not take his eyes off you during the meal!"

"Which is why I was so nauseated!" Marisela muttered.

"It will be a great match," said *Don* Casimiro happily. "He is willing to accept both your inferior dowry and your scandalous behavior." He had taken *Don* Rafael into the library for a cigar after dinner, where the two men had discussed details.

"You forget one thing!" Marisela said sharply. "I have not consented to marry him and I never shall! I cannot abide him!"

"It is not your place to decide these things," *Doña* Trinidad rebuked her charge. "A young girl leaves these decisions to her parents, who know what is best for her."

Marisela lost her temper. "My parents do not have to share a bed with him and endure his embraces! I would rather be raped by *banditos!*" she declared passionately.

Doña Trinidad gasped in shock. That a young unmarried girl would even mention such matters!

Doña Milagros said in shocked horror "Maria Luisa!" She turned on *Don* Casimiro. "Now you see," she said shrilly, "what your indulgence has lead to, letting her go about with Rodrigo instead of sending her to a convent school in Cuidad Mexico as I wanted! You said it would do her no harm to have a little freedom! I can only shudder when I think what other foul matters she learned from so much male company! Letting her ride with the *vaqueros* as well! I wonder that a good, respectable man such as *Don* Rafael even wishes to look at her, much less take her to wife!"

Doña Trinidad added her voice to this argument, whining tearfully that she had done her best to install good principles, modesty and female skills into her charge but that Marisela was willful and obstinate and refused to listen or practice her embroidery or the harp. *Don* Casimiro had to defend himself against the two women and was rapidly losing the argument.

Marisela took the opportunity to slip away, running towards her room. She jerked the *mantilla* from her head as she ran, crushing the lace in her hand, and pulled the roses from her hair, letting them fall to the ground.

She found her maid, Conchita, waiting for her, big-eyed with news.

"*Señorita,*" she said in her breathless fashion, for everything was exciting to her, "I have done as you asked and my mother's cousin, Lupe Garcia, the one who has twelve children, is willing to go as a cook to the *Norteaméricanos!*"

"*Bueno!*" said Marisela. "Help me from this dress, Conchita. I shall want my trousers. When does this Lupe feel she can go to the *Norteaméricanos?*"

"She is packed and ready to go now," said Conchita. "My mother says that she needs a holiday from the children and her husband. He is one lazy *hombre*! He will learn how much Lupe does for him if she leaves him for a while. And they need the money. Lupe never imagined she could earn so much!"

When Marisela had been out at the camp near *El Morro* Sabrina had asked her if she knew of someone who would like to earn a good wage cooking for the expedition. The sum she had mentioned paying a cook had made Marisela blink, but she promised to ask if anyone on the *hacienda* might want the job. Conchita knew everyone's business in the small world of the *Hacienda Del Sol* as she was an enthusiastic gossip.

"I shall take her out there myself, right now. I will finish dressing myself. Go to the stables and tell Pedro to saddle Vittoria and have a wagon ready to convey Lupe. I will need him to drive the wagon as well." A good gallop would chase away the disgusting memories of *Don* Rafael. And perhaps there might be an opportunity to ride the dragon again!

"*Sí, Doña* Marisela!" Conchita bobbed a curtsey and scurried off to do her mistress's biding as Marisela began to pull on trousers, shirt and vest, reveling in the freedom that these clothes gave.

Marisela would not have recognized either *Don* Rafael or his mother as they leaned back at their ease in the carriage on the return trip to their *hacienda*.

For once, both were silent.

"She does not wish to marry you, my son," said *Doña* Paloma at last.

Don Rafael shrugged. "She will do as her father tells her. He is greedy for gold. When I mentioned how much I was willing to pay for her he nearly fainted."

"Do you really wish an unwilling bride?" she asked. All traces of affectation had disappeared from her voice.

He shrugged. "It matters little. She is most suitable

for our purposes, *Madre*. *Don* Casimiro assures me that she is still virgin."

She nodded. "When will the wedding take place?"

"As soon as possible. Now that we have a priest–"

She began to laugh. It was not the titter she had used at the table at the *Hacienda del Sol,* but a full, rich laugh.

Don Rafael joined her in hilarity that nearly became hysterical. They understood one another very well.

Chapter Thirteen
Dynamite

"You don't seem to have many lanterns," Atalanta said to Sabrina as the latter began assembling their equipment. They were outside the supply tent, inspecting the contents of several mesh bags, while Erianne watched. Ellery and Dr. Beck were still in an increasingly acrimonious conversation with Lutterworth, with a harassed looking Sinclair standing by. Nicholas, was engaged in scanning the sky, no doubt wondering where Varian had disappeared and what was keeping him so long.

Atalanta was used to supplies in heavy wooden crates and hauled everywhere by mules, donkeys or wagon and these bags seemed very flimsy to her.

"We'll use mage lights," Sabrina said. "We can throw up as many as we need in the cave and use our wands. These lanterns will be lit by mage lights as well." She did not add that in their experience, many non-magical people felt strange about having a light floating in the air without a lantern or a candle and even balked at the idea of a light tipped wand.

Atalanta nodded. What an advantage! They had always been hampered by the limits of oil lamps and candles. "These bags are not very sturdy," she ventured.

"But they are easier to pack into a dragon's breast harness and panniers," Sabrina said, "Which reminds me...have you a split skirt like mine? The dragon saddle hasn't a sidesaddle on it and you will need either trousers or a split skirt to ride."

"Trousers?" Atalanta said wryly. "My dear Miss Delamar —"

"Call me Sabrina," the other woman interrupted. "Christian names are more comfortable."

"Very well, Sabrina," Atalanta agreed. "I am afraid that my father would never recover from the shock should I appear in trousers!"

"I have a skirt I can lend you," Sabrina offered. "I think we are much of a size."

Her new friend was one of the few other women she

had met that was as tall as she was, Atalanta reflected. And Dr. Delamar was even taller. She was too used to most men being shorter. She was taller than both her father and Sinclair and could look Lutterworth in the eye. He did not like that as she was well aware. He made himself stand higher when she was near, putting his chin up and balancing on his toes.

Thinking of Dr. Delamar made her think again of how he had seemed to know that she was not a mere dilettante. "Your brother spoke of me as a valuable colleague," she said. "How did he know that I did just not accompany my father as a secretary or was someone who has little real archaeological knowledge?"

Sabrina smiled at her. "When we went out to Egypt last year we had a young archeologist called Michael Whitney on our staff."

"He worked with us two years ago," said Atalanta.

"And he was quite impressed with your knowledge and told us all about you," said Sabrina.

Atalanta actually felt herself blushing. She had no idea that young Whitney had even remembered her. The surprise that she felt showed in her face.

Sabrina felt a spurt of anger. How terrible that this learned and competent young woman was not appreciated by her father! He ought to be treating her as a partner, not as a lackey. Whitney had sung her praises, including how much help she had been to him personally, as that dig had been his very first field work.

"Where can Varian be?" Erianne said suddenly. "If he doesn't come back soon I shall have to go and look for him! Nicholas is anxious as well." She glanced to where Nicholas stood a short ways away, Cillian snoozing in the crook of his arm, scanning the sky. The younger dragon had been gone quite a long time now.

The red tabby Flann, who had been dozing in the sun, sat up and stretched as Bairre scampered over to them and joined the cat on the flat rock she occupied. "That Lutterworth is a jackass!" said the ferret scathingly. "He's arguing with Ellery and Dr. Beck over excavation techniques! He wants to use dynamite to blast our way into the caves if necessary!"

"Dynamite!" echoed Sabrina, horrified.

Atalanta looked equally appalled. "Blast an archaeological site! Is the man mad?"

"If there are heavy rocks to be moved that magic cannot shift, Varian and I can do it," said Erianne indignantly. First that man wanted to hire horses and now this!

"Did Lutterworth bring dynamite with him?" Sabrina inquired. "Did you hear about that, Bairre?" She did not like the fact that the crates Lutterworth had unloaded from the transport dragon might have explosives in them.

"He did not. Ellery wanted to know that right away but Lutterworth said he could get the dynamite from the railroad site as they very often need it for blasting when laying the track. "

"And it can stay at the railroad site!" said Sabrina decidedly.

"That's what both Ellery and Dr. Beck told him. In fact, Ellery said he refused to go any further with this ridiculous farce if Lutterworth ever brought up the subject of dynamite again." Bairre sat up on his haunches beside Flann, at the alert, as upset as his Wizard had been.

"Lutterworth was none too pleased at that, I am willing to bet," said Atalanta dryly.

"He's far too used to having his own way!" said Sabrina angrily. "The man is a menace! I shudder to think how he is going to act when we fail to find a treasure!"

"Are ye bein' certain that there is nothing to find?" Flann asked. "No painted tombs like those after bein' in Egypt?"

"We probably will find some things of archeological interest," said Sabrina. "But Lutterworth doesn't care about pottery shards or evidence of Pre-Columbian peoples. He's a greedy bastard who only wants more and more money. I doubt if there *were* a treasure that any of it would end in a museum where it belongs. Lutterworth would sell anything for what it would fetch on the antiquities market."

"There's a horse and a wagon coming," said Erianne, turning her long neck sharply towards the sounds only she and the other animals could hear.

"Who could this be at this time of night?" said Sabrina. "It will be dark soon."

"Let us hope," said Atalanta "that it is not a wagon load of dynamite for Lutterworth."

From his seat on the cot Julian stared at the man who had entered the mission. Benito called him Ramón, and his Indian blood was as obvious as the children's.

"That is the man who brought the children here," said Brother Ezekiel, almost accusingly.

Ramón's face was alight with eagerness. He scarcely even noticed that this Medicine Man was not the venerable Native that he had expected, but instead a *gringo* of his own age or even younger. All he was aware of was the fact that his man could Heal. A glance at some of the children told him that they looked, in spite of their thinness as healthy children should. He knew Angelita, Benito and Guillermo very well and they bore little resemblance to the sick little ones he had left at this mission over a week ago.

"It's not something that can be taught, precisely," Julian began. "You have to have an inborn–Good God!" he exclaimed as he used his Othersight and looked at Ramón's aura.

It was a brilliant, pure green: the aura of a Healer. It pulsated with latent power.

"You've had no training at all in Healing?" Julian asked incredulously. It seemed impossible that someone had not recognized his natural bent and given him the training he needed to awake to his full potential. Some of the young men at Julian's *alma mater*, Edinburgh, the largest school for Wizard Healers in all of the Six Nations, did not have an aura this strong.

"There was no one to teach me," said Ramón simply. "My mother told me that my grandfather was a *diyin*, a Medicine Man, and that I would have been given to his care when I was but a boy, to be taught the ways of the Healers of my people. She said that I was born a *diyin*."

"It seems that she was right," said Julian on a sigh. He was suddenly exceedingly tired and wanted nothing more than some food and a bed. "I shall want to have a long conversation with you tomorrow," he said "The boy said your name is Ramón? I am Julian Stillfield."

"Yes, I have no other name as do the Spaniards and the *gringos*," he answered.

"More properly, he is Nantan Lupan," said a voice from the doorway.

The gray fox, Gian-nah-tah, stood there. Ramón wondered how the animal had found him.

"Gray Wolf?" Julian translated.

Ramón was further delighted. "You speak the tongue of the People!"

Siofra went up to the fox, a little stiff-legged with a straight tail and ruffled fur. "And who would you be ?"

"I am Nantan Lupan's guide," answered the fox.

"His familiar, would ye be meanin'? I was never seein' a fox that was bein' a familiar!" the cat said frankly. "'Tis only good for the chase, fox are bein', back home in Ireland."

"And I have never seen a creature like you," the fox said frankly. They studied one another.

Reverend Brewer, the Bradleys and Prudence had all watched this little drama in silence, eyes going from one to the other as each spoke, as intent as play-goers on what was happening, even though they could not understand what was being said, for Julian and Ramón spoke in rapid Spanish.

But they could scarcely comprehend at all what had happened here lately. Prudence had been thrilled at the wonder of the children's being made well while Sister Rebecca, herb list clutched in her hand, was beginning to think that maybe this young man was not the devil, while Brother Ezekiel could not make up his mind as yet.

Reverend Brewer, however, was still certain that the devil was somehow involved in all of this. To him the Healing Magic seemed unnatural. God had afflicted the children for their sins. It was not man's place to remove the punishment. That reeked of blasphemy.

And now this new man arriving with yet another talking animal made him very uneasy, if not frightened. He did not like it that this new man was an Indian. All the Covenanters firmly believed in the inferiority of the dark skinned races, even though one had a duty to bring them to

131

God, the Covenanter God, and lift them from the burden of paganism.

Julian was conscious of the Reverend's eyes upon him, almost as if Brewer thought he could understand what he and Ramón were saying, if he just concentrated hard enough. He did not like the look on the Reverend's face.

But he was too fatigued to cope with the Reverend now. He made plans to meet Ramón here the next day, explaining to him that Healing such as he had done today required that the Healer rest before he Healed again. For now it would be up to Sister Rebecca to make up the Healing herbal potions and dose the children with them.

Ramón brightened again when he heard about the potions. This Medicine Man also had knowledge of the healing plants that his mother had told him about! Perhaps he even knew the songs and dances. He glanced at Gian-nah-tah. The fox had been right. He had known that Usen, the Life Giver would send a teacher.

After concluding the argument with Lutterworth Ellery walked over to the supply tent. Dr. Beck headed towards one of the two tents that He and Lutterworth had brought, saying that he was going to lie down before dinner.

Lutterworth, completely out of temper by the archaeologists' refusal to agree to blast through the rock if necessary, brusquely commanded Sinclair to go and pour him a whiskey and stalked off to his own tent, muttering beneath his breath, his brow thunderous.

"Well, what a happy expedition this is turning out to be!" said Ellery sarcastically as he came up to Atalanta and Sabrina. He looked both tired and harassed. "That man is impossible! He argues over everything!"

"Bairre told us of the dynamite," said Sabrina sympathetically.

"And Sinclair just let drop another thing that completely appalled me, Miss Beck!" Ellery said, turning to Atalanta and looking indignant. "Lutterworth expects Sinclair to share your father's tent with him. He has made no provision for that hapless young man at all. He says Sinclair snores too loudly and refuses to share the tent another night with him. And where are you to sleep? I can scarcely credit that no thought was given at all to your comfort!"

"Usually I share the tent with my father. We hang a blanket up across the middle so that we can each have our privacy. But if Mr. Sinclair is to be with us, that will not do," said Atalanta.

"You may share with me," said Sabrina warmly. "There is plenty of space and I have a private bathing room."

Atalanta's heart warmed to them both. She had never before met with such consideration and she thanked them warmly.

"Here comes the horse and rider!" Flann announced.

"And Varian—at last! And Torin with Julian," stated Erianne. "I shall have a thing or two to say to that young dragon!"

Nicholas was pleased to see Marisela again. He had been conscious of a feeling of disappointment earlier in the day when she had not come with the promised beef. Somehow, he had expected her to come. She had seemed fascinated by the camp, and the dragons and had said that she wanted to have another dragon-back ride as soon as possible.

"I have brought you a cook," she said, riding her horse, a handsome Andalusian black gelding, right up to Nicholas. "The wagon bearing her follows. She is a very good cook and has twelve children eager for work should you need more servants. *Hóla*, little urchin," she added a little hesitantly as Cillian blinked and looked up at her. She felt so strange, talking to an animal in a human fashion.

Cillian returned her greeting and said "The beef was very good, tender and juicy. We all enjoyed it."

"Welcome back," said Nicholas as she slid off the horse. "I was hoping that you would return earlier."

Marisela made a face. "My parents insisted that I remain at home after church and entertain some most disagreeable guests." Once again she was struck by how badly

Don Rafael compared to this *Norteaméricano*. Nicholas, in his now rumpled casual linens, looked far better than *Don* Rafael in his absurd finery. And the *Señor* Stillfield actually had a chin and a nice strong jaw, and his bright blue eyes were not too close together. This foreigner was more of her notion of what a man should be than any other, from the limited amount of her acquaintance.

"I was going to come and see you," Nicholas continued. She tied her horse to a nearby ponderosa pine, and fell in beside him as they began to walk towards the group that contained Sabrina, Atalanta and Ellery. "It's very possible that we may be moving the camp soon, to the other side of the mountains. If we do, one of the dragons will come and fetch the meat, as it is a great deal further away."

"Moving further away?" she echoed in dismay. She had hoped that they would be here for a long while. She looked forward to more visits with them. She had liked them all and found their lives so different from hers and fascinating. She was also interested in the possibility of the treasure that Sabrina had told her about, although she knew for a fact that Coronado had found no gold. She also hoped for more dragon rides. To her surprise, Nicholas looked as disappointed as she felt.

"Here is Lupe," she said when she heard the creaking of the old wagon coming. "I will introduce her and you will show her where she is to cook, *sí*?"

"Yes," he said. "I will. Oh, here comes Varian!" he said in relief, looking up to where both a pale green dragon and a hippogriffe were making their descents. "If he is not too tired, *Señorita*, I could take you up again," he said impulsively. "Why do you not join us for dinner and then I will take you flying. Sunset is a wonderful time for it and the sunsets here, I've noticed, are particularly beautiful. Please stay. We're having curried prawns which are especially delicious. Lupe shan't have to cook her first night here."

It was the thought of another dragon-back ride that decided her. It was a long ride back to the *hacienda* in the dark, and could be dangerous as well, but she had no desire to return to her home too quickly as there would only be more arguments and recriminations. Far better to sail above the earth in the light of the dying day.

Chapter Fourteen
Legal Complications

Nicholas lay awake a long time that night thinking about Marisela and how much he enjoyed her company. They had flown together until it was quite dark and the stars had started to come out, not speaking, just contented to be where they were at that moment.

The rest of his family seemed to like her as well. Even Varian was beginning to forgive her for shooting at him. The dragon had no objections to taking her up after dinner and had obligingly flown rather far afield, almost to the site where they would begin their search on the next day and then in a wide circle southerly to the volcanic country that Marisela said was called *Mal Pais*, the Badlands, where walking or riding an animal was very difficult. Nicholas remembered reading about the difficulties that Coronado's men had encountered in traversing this desolate area in the material that Sabrina had typed up for them.

Instead of her riding home at once when they landed, Marisela and Nicholas talked and talked. She told him about her family, how much she missed her brother, Rodrigo and how terrible a blow it had been when he was killed. He told her of his own large family, with five brothers and four sisters, of which he was the eldest, with the youngest, Dinah, only two, just adopted last year, with Hilary, eight, and Oliver ten, studying Wizardry at The Tara Druidry, fourteen year old Phebe still at school, Cary at Oxford and about to take Holy Orders, Alasdair studying like his older brother, Dracophilology at Trinity, while Nicholas's oldest sister Felicity was a teacher at a girls' school and Nicola was a historian, specializing in Roman Britain. She taught at a woman's college.

Marisela marveled that none of the older ones were married and that, according to Nicholas, his mother was not concerned in the least that they were not. "She only wants us to be happy," he said.

Ireland seemed like a dream to Marisela, so different from what she knew, with dragons in the sky and the streets lit by mage lights that she could not hear enough about it.

In the end, Nicholas ended in flying her back to the hacienda as it was growing very late. Arrangements would be made to fetch her horse on the next day. Before she left, however, she made him promise that should they indeed discover a cave he would take her to see it.

Breakfast was quite early the next morning. Lutterworth was more than a little eager to start and was impatient with the routine of eating, getting ready and packing up the dragon saddles with provisions and equipment.

Ellery flatly refused to move the camp until they had seen the conditions in the new area and see if they were suitable. With dragons available it would take no time at all to get there and back each day.

He was finding that the best way to deal with Lutterworth was to take a firm line as the least bit of giving in would allow the man to ride roughshod over everyone. The danger in this, however, was that Lutterworth would explode one day when he was too often thwarted. As it was, poor Sinclair bore the brunt of Lutterworth's temper.

Another uproar was forthcoming when Julian asked Nicholas to help him with the passing ceremony for Tomaso, as two Wizards were required for this. Lutterworth could not see why Julian was concerning himself with the bastard children of slaves when he should be doing what he was brought along for, namely, taking photographs.

This was so outrageous that Julian did not even argue with Lutterworth. He left on Torin, asking Nicholas to join him later after they had all been transported to the site of the proposed dig.

"Do you realize what a passing ceremony is, Mr. Lutterworth?" Ellery asked coldly when Julian had flown off, leaving Lutterworth sputtering. "My nephew is going to help an incurably ill child die peacefully. It's not a task one undertakes lightly and it does need two Wizards, fortunately not two Wizard Healers. I have no argument with Julian using his medical skills to help these people. Indeed I would think the less of him did he not use his skills in such a cause. I quite fail to see why it should be any concern of yours. After all, he is on *my* staff."

Atalanta sent up a silent cheer.

When they finally boarded the laden dragons Lutterworth was still muttering to himself. He was riding Erianne with Ellery, Atalanta and Sinclair, while Varian took Nicholas, Sabrina and Dr. Beck. Dr. Beck, somewhat nervous of dragon-flight had said he would feel more comfortable with a smaller dragon.

"It's too bad Erianne can't make certain that Lutterworth falls off," Nicholas muttered to Varian as he checked that the carry-all on the dragon's chest was adjusted properly and its weight evenly distributed.

"Nick!" said Varian, shocked. "No dragon would ever let a human fall to his death! How can you even suggest such a terrible thing!"

"Sorry, Varian. It's just that I cannot abide that man. He is rude and arrogant and a know-it-all," Nicholas said with a sigh. They were speaking in low, confidential tones. "Imagine cutting up stiff because Julian wants to help sick children! I can imagine what my mother would have to say to that!"

Varian chuckled, "She'd send Lutterworth to the right-about, wouldn't she?" he agreed.

"Let's get this show on the road!" Lutterworth shouted from Erianne's back. "Stillfield, you've checked that freight enough! Let's go!"

Varian and Nicholas exchanged a look of perfect accord.

It was an area of cottonwoods, *piñon* pines and juniper, the forest mixed with canyons and arid areas, but a far cry from the green of Ireland. From above they had seen the Rio San José, flowing between the two mountains, or rather flowing between two mountain chains, the Zuni and the San Mateo, towards the Rio Grande and eventually the sea, far down in Mexico.

Mount Taylor, an inactive volcano, was indeed blue looking. It was heavily forested and sometimes snow could be seen on its peak. It had been called *Cebolleta* by the Spanish but recently renamed by the United States in honor of former President Zachary Taylor.

"There is definitely limestone here," said Erianne, sniffing the air after they landed. She could feel it. Dragons had a sixth sense about the presence of fire stone.

"Sandstone and shale and other things as well," agreed Varian as the various members of the party began to dismount. "There'll be more than one cave."

"More than one!" echoed Lutterworth. "How the hell can we tell which is the right one?" He glared at Ellery and said "Do whatever it is you do, Delamar, and find me my treasure!"

"I can't just make it work," said Ellery. "It's not something I can control."

Lutterworth looked taken aback. "What do you mean?" he demanded belligerently.

This question was to remain unanswered for with a sharp whine, a bullet passed by their heads, very close.

"Down!" Ellery yelled and pulled out his wand. Nicholas and Sabrina did so as well as they hit the ground and rolled, throwing up a shield of violet light.

The two dragons trumpeted and leaped into the air. They were still carrying the familiars in their baskets and the gear. But the weight of this did not prevent them from getting speedily into the air and spying out the situation.

Ellery, who had pulled Atalanta down with him, saw Erianne wheel and dive as quickly as a raptor. When she rose again she was holding a man, screaming and struggling, in her talons. As she gained height a rifle dropped from his hands and the man began yelling in terror as she went higher in the sky and he saw what a long way his gun fell before striking the earth.

Everyone rose to their feet as Erianne, followed closely by Varian, swooped in low and, at Ellery's nod, dropped the man to the ground. Ellery broke his fall with a command of "*Tarde*" and the man came gently to the earth, looking shocked as he landed lightly on his feet. Behind the members of the expedition two dragons landed quietly.

"What the hell do you think you're doing shooting at us?" Lutterworth went right up to the man and pushed him with a rough hand.

"Ow! That hurt!" the man said and backed away from Lutterworth, looking at him with a pained expression. He was a scruffy-looking, unshaven individual in clothes which had seen better days: worn denim pants, a faded shirt and a scratched leather vest. He also wore run-down boots. "Damn!" he said. clapping his hands to head. "Where's my hat? I was just trying to do my job and you send a big old lizard after me! Now I lost my hat and my rifle!"

"Your job?" said Atalanta. "Shooting at people is your employment?"

The man snatched at his head as if to remove a hat and then remembered again that it wasn't there. "Howdy, ma'am," he said. "I been hired by the railroad to make sure that there's no trespassers on this here piece of property. This here's going to be a spur line down alongside the river."

"What!" Lutterworth sputtered and took a step closer to the man again. staring at him threateningly. "Listen to me, you jackass! Do you know who I am?"

"Can't say as I do," the man drawled. He seemed to have recovered from being snatched up by a dragon relatively quickly.

"I'm A. J. Lutterworth and I OWN the railroad! No one at the Taos, Albuquerque and Phoenix is sanctioned to hire someone like you without my say-so! What is your name and who hired you?" Lutterworth demanded. His face was red and his voice loud.

The scruffy man looked at him with a lop-sided grin. "The thing is, Mister," he said "that I ain't been hired by the whatever you said it was. This here is the property of the Texas and Pacific railroad."

Lutterworth nearly had an apoplexy.

Sabrina, ever practical, made a ley line fire and

unpacked a kettle, cups and the makings of tea. Everyone else sat down around the fire while Lutterworth raged and stalked up and down, muttering imprecations against someone called Rankin.

The man introduced himself as Yancy Yates and accepted a cup of tea, sniffing at it dubiously. "Sure you ain't got any coffee?" he asked wistfully.

"You see, Mr. Yates, most of us are British and we are a nation of tea-drinkers," said Sabrina.

"Even the big lizards?" he asked, watching as Nicholas poured out dragon-sized mugs for Erianne and Varian.

Varian rolled his eyes and Sabrina said. "They are not lizards, they are dragons. Haven't you seen dragons before, Mr. Yates?"

"Can't say as I have, ma'am. I hear tell that there was some of them critters in the mines here abouts but I ain't never worked in no mine. I'm a cowboy and working cattle's been my whole life. I worked mostly up to Colorado and Wyoming, but I got me an itchy foot and I'm always roving. A pal of mine claimed there was a lot of big cattle ranches over this way and I thought I'd get me a job here. But no one was hirin' so I ended up workin' for the railroad since I was down to my last dime." he explained.

Dr. Beck had drunk his tea while watching Lutterworth pace back and forth. He now said "Mr. Lutterworth, I was under the impression that this land we are going to excavate belonged to you or your company! Is there some doubt as to the ownership of it? If so, I refuse to become involved in this matter any further! I was in a nasty situation in Greece once where we thought we had permission from the landowner to excavate. It proved that he was not the owner and a lawsuit nearly resulted. I do not want to find myself in such a situation again!"

Ellery felt much the same. In Egypt, he had to obtain a firman from the Department of Antiquities to dig in any given area and trouble could arise from indiscriminate digging. Permission from the proper authorities was always a necessity.

"I have an option on all the land between Taos and Phoenix!" snarled Lutterworth. "And that option doesn't run out until September! That damn Rankin is here illegally! Sinclair! Why didn't you know about this?" he turned on his assistant.

Sinclair was utterly taken aback. "Sir, I've only been out here as long as you have! New York is my base of operations!" he protested. "I have no idea of what Mr. Rankin may be doing, legally or illegally."

"Who is this Rankin?" asked Nicholas.

In relief Sinclair turned to him. "Mr. R. T. Rankin owns the New York, Boston and Washington railway. He has been expanding into the Midwest with the Chicago and Omaha line and now wants to expand into the southwest with his latest venture, the Texas and Pacific."

"Expand!" growled Lutterworth. "Take over, you mean! Only some pretty fancy footwork prevented him from taking over the Union Pacific! Texas and Pacific! That means he has ambitions so of running his damn line all the way to California. The bastard undercuts me at every turn!"

"Mr. Rankin owns his own steel mill and makes his own rails, therefore he can underbid everyone for railway contracts. Mr. Lutterworth is in negotiation at the moment to buy a steel mill as well," Sinclair explained. He left unsaid the obvious–Rankin was Lutterworth's chief rival.

Lutterworth paced up and down a few more minutes and then said "I've got to get to Albuquerque and send a wire to Washington. I've got to put a spoke in Rankin's wheel and stop the bastard in his tracks! Can you fly me there?" He turned to Ellery urgently. "I'll pay anything you like!"

"There's no question of that," said Ellery. "Erianne?"

She considered it. "It's early in the day yet and Albuquerque is only about one hundred and fifty miles away. We could be there in about two hours."

"Two hours!" Lutterworth said, looking happier than he had since the bullet had passed by their heads. "You, what did you say your name was?"

Yancy Yates looked startled and repeated his name.

"You're working for me now, Yates," stated Lutterworth. "I'll pay you twice what Rankin was for guarding this land from those bastards at the T and P!"

"The Texas and Pacific was payin' me a dollar a day," said Yates. "You mean you're gonna give me two whole dollars

141

a day?" His eyes lit up at the thought.

Lutterworth winced and choked out "Yes." This was a high wage to pay but he had said 'twice' and he would have to hold to that in front of all these witnesses.

The arrangements were made and it was decided that the rest of the party would return to the camp at El Morro until the legal matters were resolved. Ellery and Bairre would go with Lutterworth to Albuquerque where they would send his telegrams and wait for a reply. Ellery would also take the opportunity to telegraph Nate Connelly about the dragon problem.

Ellery and Nick transferred the rest of the gear to Varian so that Erianne could fly lighter and make better time.

"I wish we had been able to look for treasure," said Varian wistfully as they watched Erianne and her passengers fly off in the direction of Albuquerque. He was standing in a little depression a little ways away from the ley line fire.

"Let's finish up this tea and head back," said Sabrina. "Nick, perhaps we could find Mr. Yates' hat and rifle for him."

"Why, I'd take that right kindly, ma'am," said Yates gratefully. "Can't do my job with no rifle and I purely feel naked as a jay bird without my hat."

"I'll do it," said Nicholas and stood up. He made a sweep with his wand at the area from which Yates had been brought and said "*Invenire.*"

A few moments later a shabby, broad-brimmed hat and a rifle came speeding towards them.

"How useful!" said Atalanta.

"If that don't beat all!" Yates marveled.

Nicholas deftly caught the rifle out of the air and a little magical push settled the hat on Yates' head.

It was at this moment that Flann, who like Cillian had been dozing comfortably by the fire, sat up with a shriek, waking even the hedgehog.

"What the hell?" yelped Yates.

Before anyone else could react there was a sudden loud and violent cracking noise and where Varian had been standing was an enormous hole. There was no sign of the pale green dragon in the cloud of dust that billowed upwards and set everyone to coughing.

"Varian!" cried Nicholas in anguish.

Chapter Fifteen
Sinkhole

"Stay away from the edge, Nick!" Sabrina said sharply as Nicholas started to run forward. "We don't want you going down too. The edge may be unstable." She put a hand on his chest to restrain him.

"Good heavens!" exclaimed Dr. Beck. "That hole must be thirty feet across! Is it safe for us to remain here?"

"We have to rescue the dragon, Papa," said Atalanta patiently. She was embarrassed that her father had thought of his safety first, without expressing any concern for the dragon that had been swallowed up.

"But what can we do?" said Sinclair. "If the edge is unstable..." As he spoke another piece fell off and raised more dust.

"Let's clear the air first," said Sabrina. "No, don't shout, Nick," she said as her nephew looked as if he were about to yell down to Varian. "Mr. Sinclair is right. The whole thing is precarious and we have to stabilize it before we can proceed. Even shouting could dislodge more stone and injure Varian." She raised her wand and pointed it at he dust cloud. "*Lucidus*," she said.

The dust cloud gathered in on itself, rather like a small cyclone and lifted into the air where it spun off into the distance, leaving the whole area clear and more visible, the air once again easier to breath.

Unfortunately this revealed the frightful extent of the hole into which Varian had fallen.

As Dr. Beck had observed it was at least thirty feet across and again that wide. Varian was twenty-five feet long and it had swallowed him as easily as quick-sand. It was so deep that they could not see a sign of him. not even the tips of his horns.

"Now we'll use those rock stabilization spells your father devised, Nick," said Sabrina. "Ellery and I use these in Egyptian tombs," she explained to the four others. "They work marvelously well."

She had to prompt Nicholas, who wore such a stricken anxious look on his face that Atalanta's heart went out to him.

Working together, the Witch and the Wizard commanded "*Firmare!*"

Dr. Beck, Atalanta, Yates and Sinclair felt a movement beneath their feet, almost like a small earthquake. The broken edges of the pit shimmered and took on a more solid, substantial appearance.

Flann had had to restrain the hedgehog from rushing forward as well. Cillian and Varian were great friends and all traces of his habitual sleepiness had disappeared as he stared towards the hole where his dragon friend had vanished.

Nicholas ran to the edge and cast himself down on his stomach, peering into the pit. "Varian!" he shouted. "Can you hear me? Are you all right?"

There was no sound for a moment as everyone waited breathlessly for any sign of life.

Then, at last, they heard a deep cough and then Varian's voice, hoarsely, "Nick, it's a sinkhole! I fell into a big cave!"

"Are you hurt? Can you move?" Nicholas called down.

"I think I'm all right," the dragon answered, his voice a little doubtful. "I can't move my wings much–there isn't enough room to spread them..." his voice trailed off. "I *think* they're all right but you'll have to check when I get out. How am I going to get out? I can't fly!" He began to cough again and said "I'm so thirsty! My throat is full of dust! But one good thing, this cave is all limestone!"

"We can send you a drink, Varian," said Sabrina.

"Oh, thank you!" the dragon called up and coughed again.

She filled one of the dragon-sized teacups with water from one of their water vessels made of magiced canvas. It was fresh, sweet and cool. It was the work of a moment to lower it magically so that Varian could drink. He drank it eagerly, draining the cup.

Nicholas rolled over on his side and turned to Sabrina. "How are we going to get him out of there?" he asked worriedly. "If Erianne was here she could pull him out with a little boost from us. Can we magically lift several tons of dragon? How much can you lift? I doubt that I can do more than a ton!"

146

"In concert Ellery and I have lifted nine tons," she said absently.

Nicholas looked impressed. "What spell do you use?"

"*Effere*," she said, frowning as she tried to think of an easy way to get Varian out of the hole.

"Not *tolere*?" he asked, which was the standard lifting spell.

"No, with *tolere* you are limited to about a ton. Your father helped Ellery develop a spell that could easily lift huge blocks of stone and mortuary slabs. *Effere* is a spell of lifting *up*, not lifting alone. It's probably the best solution in this case. And if Varian could use his legs to push, as if he were getting into the air, that would help us."

Nicholas's father, Alan Stillfield, was the head of a spell development laboratory and had devised many useful spells.

"They seem to be using an illegitimate form of Latin for these spells," Dr. Beck remarked in an under voice to his daughter.

Nicholas called down to Varian again, asking if he could crouch down and thrust as they tried to lift him with magic.

Varian thought that he had enough room to do so and agreed to wait for their signal.

"You'll need to get on one side while I stand on the other," Sabrina said to her nephew. "The power will meet in the middle and wrap around him"

Nicholas got to his feet and went to the other side of the immense pit. Like they all were, he was covered in dust but even more so for having been on the ground.

"You'll have to direct your wand to send the widest possible stream of power out to go beneath Varian," Sabrina cautioned. "it's rather like making a rope, only we want it to be as large and as broad as possible.

She then asked the others to move away, for their own safety in case they dropped the dragon.

All of the others were interested in what was happening as they had not much experience with magic. Yates had never seen any magic at all before today and his eyes were wide with excitement as he watched and listened.

At Sabrina's suggestion Varian at first stood up so

that they could easily direct the light of power underneath him to make a type of sling to lift him up. This had the adverse effect of causing the rubble he was laying on to shift, sending up more dust. Another spell of *Lucidus* was needed before they could proceed.

Tapping the strength of the power in the ley lines that ran beneath them Nicholas and Sabrina pointed their wands down at the trapped dragon and commanded *"Effere!"*

Fountains of violet light spouted out the end of each wand through the focus stones on the wand's tips (Nicholas used a fire opal while Sabrina's was a pink topaz). The two streams began to spread at once, widening as they bent down into the hole and met under Varian.

"That tickles!" the dragon said.

"Crouch down now and get ready!" Sabrina called as the violet light came back up again to both wands. In effect, she and Nicholas were now each holding a huge sling from the tips of their wands.

As Varian shifted his weight Nicholas could feel it pulling at his wand. Could they really lift this much weight? Sabrina seemed quite confident that they could manage this. He wished that Ellery were here. If he and Sabrina had done this before....

But there was no time to waste on wishful thinking. "Push!" Sabrina yelled down to Varian and lifted her wand to shoulder height.

"It's working!" shouted Varian. "I'm coming up!"

To those watching it was as if he slowly rose from the earth on a platform of violet light. First they saw his horns appear over the edge of the hole and then his head. He was dust covered, but did not seem to have sustained any injury. He looked oddly enough, eager and excited.

"Unfurl your wings, Varian, as soon as we withdraw the light," Sabrina directed when he had cleared the hole and was hanging above it. Her arms and Nicholas's were now over their heads. "You've got to be fast! Can you get into the air?"

"Certainly!" Varian said and snapped his wings open. With a downward flap that raised more dust, he launched himself into the air and then landed again, away from the hole as Nicholas and Sabrina lowered their wands, the violet light dissipating.

Nicholas felt the strain all through his shoulders and back and abruptly sat down as the force of the ley lines left him and sank back into the earth. Varian hurried towards him as Cillian toddled up to his Wizard looking anxious.

"Oh, thank you, thank both of you!" said the dragon. "I did not know I was to ever get out of there! Are you all right, Nick?" He nuzzled Nicholas and then sneezed suddenly from all of the dust.

Sabrina was far more used to the strain of this particular spell and remained on her feet. "You'll feel better in a minute," she said sympathetically to her nephew. "It's hard the first time. It's a great deal of power."

"We have to go back down there, Nick!" said Varian abruptly. His silver eyes gleamed with excitement. "There are chambers all around the hole. It's a big cave system! And I am almost certain that I saw something in one of the caves off to the side!"

"Treasure?" asked Sinclair eagerly. If the treasure was to be found so easily Mr. Lutterworth would be very pleased indeed and they could go back to New York.

Varian shook his head. "Dragon eggs!" he said in thrilling tones.

Ramón had been almost unable to sleep the night before. He had sat up late, talking to Tadeo about what had happened to him that day, about the Healer and his promise to help.

"But a *gringo*, Ramón!" Tadeo had protested. "They're as bad as the Spanish! You can't trust them! Remember how the *gringos* in the town treat us! They'll take what little money we have or hire us for next to no money but they spit on us otherwise. They don't want us living near them," he said bitterly. He found occasional work at the livery stable and the other men there treated him as if he was inferior, as he was one of the bastard children of the mines.

Gian-nah-tah lay at their feet. He looked up and said. "This *gringo* can be trusted. He is a servant of all that is good."

149

"Does he serve Usen, Fox?" asked Tadeo sarcastically. "The *gringos* at the mission house say that there is no Usen, that only their God is real and that we are wrong to pray to Usen." Tadeo had taken Ramón's faith as his own, since he had no knowledge of the beliefs of his mother's people and the Spaniard's religion seemed perverted, embracing as it did slavery, rape and torture.

"The Light of Good has many names," said the fox wisely. "Goodness shows itself in many forms so that different men may understand it in their own way. It matters little what the Light is called."

Ramón was reassured by what the fox said. Tadeo's protests had begun to raise doubts in his mind after his first euphoria. But Gian-nah-tah was, he considered, his spirit guide, sent directly from Usen. He was not even certain that the fox was real and not a complete spirit. He looked and felt real, but Ramón had never seen him eat or drink and he had a disconcerting habit of showing up in places where he was completely unexpected, as he had earlier today. Ramón had left the fox behind high in the mountains here before he took flight on the blue dragon, only to have the fox turn up at the mission later, in far less time that it would have taken a man on a very fast horse to get there. It was very mysterious. One, of course, did not question spirit guides. But they *could* be completely trusted. And so if Gian-nah-tah said that they could trust the *gringo,* he could do so with a whole heart.

All the same, Ramón lay awake until nearly dawn, wondering what the next day would bring. He could hardly contain his excitement. At last he would begin to learn the secrets of something that he could feel but could barely touch.

Ramón arrived quite early at the mission to wait for the Healer to arrive. He had flown there on Nah-kah-yen. The dragon did not remain; he flew off to the east, to the vast grasslands above the mountains, where the buffalo roamed, there to hunt. One buffalo would provide a great deal of meat for the tribe, something they needed badly, as the diet of mostly corn *tortillas* and a few vegetables was inadequate.

Gian-nah-tah had accompanied Ramón as well. The fox made the ride tucked in the front of Ramón's shirt. He wanted to converse again with the strange creature belonging to the Healer.

Ramón did not intend to bother the missionaries at all. He neither liked nor trusted them. They had no right, he felt, to tell others that their Gods were false. Tadeo understood English (he had learned it from one of the mine supervisors who was an American) and he had explained to the others what the missionaries had been preaching. It was only with great reluctance that Ramón had delivered the sick children to them. But something had told him to do so and now he knew why that was. It was all part of Usen's plan for him.

But Prudence heard the dragon land and, thinking it was Julian, went outside eagerly, her face alight with welcome. She hoped that he could at least Heal three more of the children today.

Her face fell when she saw Ramón. "Hello," she said hesitantly. "Are you waiting for the doctor?"

Ramón shook his head. He did not understand her. *"Lo siento, pero no habla ingés,"* he said apologetically.

It was still very early; in fact most of the children and even Reverend Brewer and his two helpers were still asleep. But a Handmaiden was expected to rise early and see to the breakfast, fetching in water and do any other necessary chores.

Prudence sighed. Why had they not at least learned some basic Spanish before they left Ohio when they knew that the mission was to be here? She felt continually frustrated at her inability to talk to the children in a language they could understand.

She thought that the Indian looked tired; perhaps he was hungry as well? "Are you hungry?" she asked him, making the motions of putting food into her mouth and chewing.

"She wants to know if you are hungry," said Gian-nah-tah.

Ramón was suddenly conscious of being very hungry indeed as savory smells began drifting out of the mission. He nodded yes at her, feeling a little wary of her. She seemed to be kind and looked after the children but one never knew with *gringos*.

She hurried back into the mission and emerged a few moments later with a laden plate.

Covenanters were great believers in eating well. "One cannot serve God on an empty stomach," was a favorite saying and church members were required to save and store as much food as possible against want. Ever since Prudence could remember she had joined the other girls and women every harvest in canning, pickling, salting and preserving. Every Covenanter home had an immense storage pantry and all were required as well, to turn a tenth of their canned and preserved goods over to the church, where it was stockpiled and doled out to those in need.

The plate she gave to Ramón was filled with sage sausage, eggs, potatoes with onions fried in the sausage fat, and some golden pumpkin preserves, as well as an apple from the barrel that had come with them from New Jerusalem, a chunk of yesterday's bread and a piece of cheese.

Ramon had never seen so much food at one time and he took the plate eagerly, with murmurs of "*Gracias, Señorita, gracias!*"

"Eat slowly," the fox cautioned. "You are not used to that much food and you might be sick if you wolf it down! Do not eat like your namesake, Nantan Lupan!"

Ramón did not need his caution as he had seen how sick people became when they overate after long deprivation. Besides, he wanted to savor every bite of the wonderful food. His opinion of the missionaries went up. It was good of her to feed him.

"Oh, here comes the doctor!" Prudence announced a bit later in relief. It felt rather awkward, standing here watching him eat. The poor man was trying to hold back, but he ate as if he was very hungry indeed. She had thought that all of the children were thin because they were sick. Had they actually been hungry?

Ramón, wiping the now empty plate with the remainder of the bread looked up to see the feathered horse descending from the sky. He wiped his mouth with the back of his hand and straightened up. Here he was to start his new life, a life as a Medicine Man.

Chapter Sixteen

Black Magic

As she flew at high speed towards Albuquerque Erianne had time to reflect on what Varian had told her about the blue dragon he had meet yesterday. Of the humans, only Nicholas had been as interested as was Varian, for the others were occupied with getting ready for the dig.

This new dragon seemed very strange. He was not at all forthcoming and had refused to answer Varian's friendly questions as to how old he was, where he came from and what breed of dragon he might be.

This was not normal draconic behavior. Dragons were congenial souls and liked to talk, to other dragons, humans and familiar animals.

What made Erianne uneasy was the blue dragon had asked about her—was she indeed a dragoness and was she mated to Varian?

Varian had found this very funny indeed. At only twelve years of age he was far too young to think of mating.

But Erianne was twenty and had been thinking about mating for some time now.

She had been with Ellery since she was hatched and he was twelve.
Ellery's best friend growing up had been a boy named Gareth Sunderland, from a neighboring estate. Gareth had bonded to his dragon at much the same time Ellery had. In fact Erianne and Gareth's dragon companion, Cormac, had been hatching mates at the Dublin Dragon Egg Incubatory. Like Erianne he had been an Irish Emerald, although from another family.

From the beginning they had been close and they had always assumed that they would be a mated pair when they grew up.

But Cormac had not lived that long. When he was Varian's age he and Gareth had been killed in an accident in the Scottish Highlands. A sudden, unexpected downdraft had caught Cormac and slammed him into a mountain. Both he and Gareth had been killed in the resulting explosion.

Erianne and Ellery were inconsolable. Their grief drew them closer together. And when Sabrina had lost her husband so young no one had understood her loss better than Erianne.

But for the past year or so Erianne had been thinking about a mate, and most especially, about an egg.

All the same it made her feel uncomfortable to have an unfamiliar dragon express an interest in her. She knew of course, that she was not obligated to return his interest but his surly behavior made him sound as if he was ill-bred and next to feral. Who knew what he might do? There seemed to be few or no other dragons in the area and males could become very anxious and needful of a mating flight. There was no such thing as rape or forcing a female against her will amongst dragons but a male could be very persistent and Erianne did not wish to become involved with a foreign dragon. Her home was in Ireland, with Ellery, and she had no desire to leave him and her very satisfying life of excavating and all her friends both in Ireland and Egypt, even for an overwhelming passion. And at any rate, she doubted she could ever feel again what she had felt for Cormac, who had been the pulse of her heart, the other half of herself. But she did think about that egg far too much.

If and when she chose a mate he would be an Irish dragon, not some unknown, ill-mannered alien.

That was that, she decided, and began to spiral down as below her she saw what must be Albuquerque. They had made good time with little exertion on her part.

In another cave, not too far from Varian's discovery, but higher in the San Mateo mountains, a strange ceremony was taking place.

The cave itself was quite different from the limestone cave Varian had inadvertently discovered. It was a lava tube from one of the extinct volcanoes in the mountains, made of dark, porous stone which was the result of the cooling of the hot lava after it had poured out of the volcano during one of its ancient eruptions. These lava tubes were made by volcanic gasses expanding inside the lava during an eruption and served as conduits for further lava flows.

It had been a long, long time since any of these volcanoes had erupted and many of the lava tubes had collapsed.

This particular cave was unusual in another way as well. It had a floor made of ice.

The temperature in the cave never rose above 31 degrees Fahrenheit, for the lava provided heavy insulation. The perpetual ice was some twenty feet thick and thousands of years old, created by rainwater and snowfall seeping into the cold cave. Petrogylphs made by Pueblo Indians in prehistoric times decorated the rock walls and the sunlight that came through a tiny hole showed the ice to be blue-green, coloured by an Arctic algae.

It was a great deal like another Ice Cave, in *El Mal Pais*, which was better known. But this cave was a secret and had been deliberately kept that way by the men who had used it for their own purposes for almost three hundred years.

To prevent collapse the cave had been shored up top and sides with massive timbers. The slaves who had done the work had afterwards been killed. A small square room had been hollowed out and the floor of ice was kept leveled.

The only entrance was down a rope ladder through the small hole. The entrance was carefully hidden by a boulder and piled brush that was rolled back whenever the occupants were finished.

The other furnishings were a brazier of bronze, a small round table and four chairs, a storage cupboard, a number of black candles on tall stands and a broad altar set under a crucifix on the wall. Torches hung in cressets on the dark walls.

The crucifix was hung upside down and depicted a pain-wracked figure drenched in blood.

On this particular day the brazier burned, doing little to take the chill from the air. Two black-robed, hooded figures were busy lighting the black candles and laying out various accoutrements on the table.

On the altar, flat on her back, lay a naked female. "It's kinda cold in here," she complained in accented Spanish as one of the black robed figure came close to her.

"Too cold for you to be in a state of nature?" said the

157

robed figure. The hood completely obscured his face for it was deep, and cast a long shadow over his features. Only his hands were visible and on one hand he wore a blood red ruby. On the breast of the robe was embroidered a goat's head.

"I guess not," she drawled. "For what you're paying me I'd put up with a lot worse than being cold. Am I going to take on both of you or what?"

"Oh, yes, my dear," he said in a soft, silky voice. "We will both be enjoying your many charms. It's part of the little ceremony I told you about." He looked at her voluptuous nudity and licked his lips. How he would enjoy this one!

The other black robed figure came to stand beside him. "Wherever did you find her?" he whispered. "Her body is luscious! This will be much more enjoyable than normal! I don't like using little girls as they barely look female. Look at those tits!"

"Lana is one of the whores from the bordello in Diablo," the first man replied. He raised his voice slightly. "She expressed her desire to do anything we required of her, didn't you, my dear?"

The whore giggled. "Anything you gents want. I ain't fussy. I've done it all: back, front, and in between, two, three at a time–it's all the same to me as long as you pay."

"Oh, we will enjoy this!" said the second man. He had an upside down cross embroidered on the front of his robe. Like the taller man only his hands were visible and he too wore a ruby ring. "We'll take our time, won't we, and satisfy our every desire? It's been so long..." he added, sounding wistful.

"By the time we leave here you will be sated, Brother Daemon," the taller one promised. "Do whatever you like. You heard Lana: she is willing to gratify your every wish, no matter how perverted in the eyes of the Church."

"Damn the Church!" said Brother Daemon forcefully.

The taller one laughed. "Come, brother, let us begin. The sooner we finish the sooner we can take our pleasure on Lana's body."

The taller figure–he was known as Brother Satyr–helped the other set about their task.

If Lana had been a Catholic she would have recognized what followed as a perversion of the Catholic

Mass. They stepped on the cross, used urine for Holy Water and used a black piece of leather for the Host. The traditional Mass was performed backwards, in Latin. Brother Daemon led the mass, with the help of the other brother.

Brother Satyr drained some blood from his own veins and painted strange symbols on her body. She did not protest a this; men had paid her to do stranger things and it was all the same to her.

After a long exhortation in Latin and hands waving complicated passes over her, Brother Daemon climbed on her and did what she had been paid for. He was followed by Brother Satyr.

Still on top of her, Brother Satyr whispered in her ear "This is just the beginning, my dear. We will keep you very busy indeed for a long time yet. And we have a friend coming as well, someone you will find interesting and very inventive as to sexual pleasures."

She hoped so. She had been rather bored so far. She did not understand the language they had been intoning.

Suddenly the atmosphere in the room changed. It had been so cold that Lana had gooseflesh. She had been warmed only when they had started banging her. Now suddenly she was hot.

A sulfurous stench arose and a lurid red light began to gather in the cave. Lana watched in amazement as a man sized cloud began to form.

From it stepped the strangest figure she had ever seen, half man and half goat, with horns on his head and shaggy hair covering his animal like legs. He had a long, forked tail. He also had the largest genitalia that she had ever seen.

"Hail, Beelzebub!" the two men dropped to their knees on the icy floor and folded their hands in an attitude of worship.

The creature grinned. His name was not Beelzebub but these mortals fancied that he was actually the Prince of Darkness himself. As if this pathetic conjuring could call up his satanic Majesty!

No, he was only a lower level demon, but even a lower level demon had his powers and it amused the Prince to send him here and then listen with mirth to the poor efforts of

159

those on earth.

And the demon loved consorting with human females. His red eyes lit up as his saw Lana on the altar.

"For me?" he said. "Is she virgin?"

"No my lord, but she is experienced," answered Brother Satyr.

"Then we may all partake of her," said the demon. "Come gentlemen, join me."

Eagerly, the two black clad figures scrambled to their feet.

Lana was suddenly afraid and tried to scream only to find that her throat could make no more noise that a whimper. Nor could she seem to move at all. She was helpless as the three advance on her, the goat man's eyes gleaming red.

Three hours later, when they had done every possible thing that could be done to her, Brother Satyr cut her throat, laughing as he did so.

After a long rest, Julian had sat up late the night before, trying to think of how he might teach Healing to the man calling himself Ramón. He wondered if he had made too rash a promise, as, for one thing, Ramón was more than likely illiterate.

Healing itself was an in-born talent. According to the history of Healing that Julian had read whilst at Medical school, early Healers had worked without training in the parts of the body, or learning the many ills and plagues that afflicted mankind. Julian himself had learned his Healing magic from his grandfather, Wizard Healer Stuart Delamar, when very young. Medical School had refined his talent, taught him a minute knowledge of the human body and given him the names, causes and symptoms of disease, much as a non-magical student would learn it. He had also learned how to perform surgery when magic was not necessary or proper, as well as learning his herbs, potions and spells in classes for the magically gifted.

This had taken five years, from the time he was

sixteen until he was twenty-one. He had then walked the wards in a large London hospital for two years, before going into practice in Dublin.

Obviously, this programme would not be viable for Ramón. But someone with that much inherent Healing talent needed and deserved *some* training.

He would have to begin with the basics–grounding and shielding and perhaps making a mage light....

Nicholas and Ellery went to bed and as not to disturb them Julian moved outside in front of the ley line fire. With no insects due to the etheric barrier against them the night was cool but pleasant with a myriad of brilliant stars sparkling over head.

Julian scribbled as many things as he could think of that he might teach a person who had no access to books on a notepad with a stub of a pencil. He threw up a small mage light to aid his vision and was quite comfortable on one of the flat rocks they were using for seats.

Everyone else was asleep, even the dragons and Torin. The other familiars had gone to bed with their Wizards and Witch. Only Siofra was up with him, in spite of his urging her to go in and rest. She yawned loudly several times but stubbornly stayed up as the hour grew late and Julian kept writing.

"Julian, there's somethin' I had best be after discussin' with ye," the little gray cat said at last.

"What's that, Siofra?" he asked absently, scribbling away and not even raising his head to look at her.

"It's somethin' I have been noticin' the last few days and I am not likin' it at all," said the cat.

"You don't approve of me teaching Ramón to Heal?" Julian put down the pencil and stared at his familiar.

"'Tis not that," said Siofra. "I was after seein' his aura too an' he's a natural born Healer and ye should be doin' somethin' to help. No,'tis that Mistress Cromwell. She's in a fair way to be fallin' in love we' ye."

"Don't be absurd!" Julian said shortly.

"She's thinkin' that ye are God, St Luke, Aesculapius an' Hippocrates all rolled in to one."

"Siofra–!" said Julian angrily "I'm certain that Miss Cromwell has too much sense to be so foolish."

"I've been after watchin' her eyes when she is lookin' at you," his familiar insisted.

"Nonsense!" snapped Julian.

"Are ye after thinkin' that since that Sarah creature is throwin' you over that no female can be lovin' ye?" said the cat softly.

Julian stood up abruptly and slammed his notebook shut. "I'm going to bed," he announced and went into the tent.

Siofra looked after him sadly. She was very much afraid that the fear she had just voiced *was* what was wrong with her beloved Wizard. And she did not want to see him cut off from love forever. A flirtation, even a mild love affair with this Cromwell girl would do him a world of good. It would restore his confidence and ease the pain of Sarah's rejection.

Humans! They were hard to handle and harder to understand. If Julian was a Tom cat there would be no problem. He's just go out and find himself a female in heat with out thinking two things about it. But humans had to complicate everything, even love relationships, which should have been as natural as the sun coming up in the morning.

Chapter Seventeen
The Eggs

Before they returned to the camp at *El Morro* Nicholas thoroughly examined Varian for any injury.

Dragon-hide was tough but wings were fragile and a rip or a tear could ground a dragon for months. Nicholas was not certain if Julian could Heal dragons as that was usually the job of a veterinarian who specialized in draconic Healing.

Varian was impatient with the length of the examination. He wanted to fly the others back to the camp so that he and Nick could return and find what he was sure were dragon eggs.

"But we haven't seen that many dragons here, Varian, and the one you have met was a single male," Nicholas said reasonably. "Why would there be a cache of eggs here?"

"I don't know—maybe they had to leave and forgot them."

"No mother would leave an egg behind!" protested Sabrina. She was looking under his wings with a mage light while Nicholas looked down from the dragon's back.

"Maybe these eggs were stolen!" said Varian. "Like my father's egg! Remember, those agents of the Inquisition stole them from their proper guardians, the Lakota Sioux, until they were found and rescued!"

"We'll come back and look, Varian, but I think that you'll find that what you saw are only some egg-shaped rocks," said Nicholas. "I don't see any sign of serious injury," He added in relief. "Sabrina?"

"None here either." She came from beneath the dragon's widespread right wing. "I think there is no wing damage because his wings were folded when he fell into the sinkhole. There are a few minor scrapes on his hide but we've salve for that."

"Can we go now, please?" said Varian, almost dancing in anxiety.

"Just let me check the saddle and girths," Nicholas said. "I have to do that anyway," he said as the dragon snorted with impatience.

Varian knew that Nick needed to pick up some

supplies. He had 'egg kits' that were back at the camp. These consisted of egg holders, a stethoscope, calcium tablets, a small medical hammer to tap the eggs, magiced cloths to keep eggs warm, and a thermometer among other things. They had not come out this morning thinking to find eggs, but dig for treasure.

He was restless as they all mounted, save Yates, who was going back to his job of protecting the land from incursions, now from those of the Texas and Pacific.

"Don't shoot at us when we come back!" Varian said to Yates as he waited for Dr. Beck to climb aboard, followed by Atalanta and Sinclair.

"Nosiree," said Yates. "I ain't gonna be snatched up in the sky again! From now on shootin' at dragons is gonna be off my list, I reckon."

Nicholas made certain that his passengers were safely strapped in and then climbed into the first saddle and fastened his own harness.

Varian flew back to camp in record time, blowing a great deal of the dust from his passengers. He was restive as Nicholas fetched the mesh bag of egg kits and inserted them in his breast harness. He did not want to wait for the panniers of tools and the rest of the equipment to be unloaded, but Nicholas insisted, keeping only a shovel and a chisel, which were sometimes necessary and of more use than even a spell.

Varian took off again as soon as Nicholas was secured in the saddle, in a great hurry to return to the site. Cillian was still slumbering in his basket.

"Do you think that there will actually be real eggs?" Atalanta asked Sabrina as they stood together watching Varian disappear back towards the mountains.

"There is always the possibility," said Sabrina. "The Spanish not only stole humans to work as slaves, but they stole dragons as well. And it was far easier to steal eggs and force them to hatch, than to enslave an adult dragon who could defend himself with fire and talons, and could fly away from danger. A newly hatched dragonet is not much bigger than a large dog, has no flame and cannot fly.
They could easily be enslaved."

"How horrible!" said Atalanta feelingly. "How could

they justify—"

"Miss Delamar!" interrupted Dr. Beck's rather querulous tones. "I fail to see such a thing as a large kettle for heating bath water. Pray how is my daughter to heat my bath? I feel in urgent need of a bath! I am considerably disheveled and choking in dust! Really, Atalanta, you should have made that your first consideration!"

The words "Get your own damn bath!" trembled on Sabrina's tongue but one look at Atalanta's face stifled this impulse. "You don't need to heat the bath water on the fire," she said. "I'll magic it. Go into the bathing room and open the lid on the portable tub. It will be full of water. By the time you get there it will be exactly right in temperature. Mr. Sinclair," she called to the young man who, near the men's tent, was rather ineffectively trying to dust himself off with a handkerchief. "If you'd like a bath after Dr. Beck is finished I'll make certain the water cleans itself and is nice and hot for you as well."

He looked pathetically grateful. "Thank you," he said appreciatively. Dr. Beck had gone off without a word of thanks.

"Why don't we go into the canyon? "Sabrina suggested to Atalanta. "There's another cache basin there big enough to swim in and we can combine a bath and a swim. I could use the relaxation."

"I haven't a bathing dress," said Atalanta in some regret.

Sabrina looked at here a little surprised. "Neither have I," she said. "But why would we need them?"

"Oh!" Atalanta discerned her meaning at once and felt a little shocked and then mentally shrugged. When in Rome...and the thought of submerging herself in water was considerably appealing. She was dust covered and itchy. Usually she had to content herself with a sponge bath while at a dig. Her father was the only one to have the luxury of a bath.

"I'll just speak to Lupe about the noon meal and then we'll go," Sabrina said. "Dr. Beck and Mr. Sinclair seemed to find their breakfast a little spicy." Lupe had cooked an egg dish that had some piquant topping, all sitting on a corn tortilla. But everyone had liked her sugar glazed breakfast buns and the coffee with a touch of chocolate.

"My father is rather particular about his food," Atalanta said carefully.

"Fussy and demanding, Sabrina thought, *would better describe it.* "You seemed to like it," she said aloud.

"Oh, I like trying unfamiliar things," her new friend said. "I've really come to like Greek food. But my father always prefers American dishes."

And I'll daresay it is you who ends in cooking it for him, thought Sabrina. The man was impossible! Ellery had told her last night that Dr. Beck was not what he had expected. Her brother had sounded disappointed.

Another tent had been erected for Lupe to use as a cook tent. Atalanta had been surprised at how much the Delamar party had brought with them as to cooking accoutrements: a grill, frying pans and different sized pots as well as preserved foods and seasonings. Lupe was quite happy with her circumstances and the goods and provisions she had been given. She was a little nervous of the dragons, but seeing *Doña* Marisela actually ride one of the creatures had made her feel better about being near them.

While waiting, Atalanta went into the comfortable tent she was sharing with Sabrina and fetched fluffy towels and soap, which smelled of lavender. These she had seen when Sabrina had shown her around the surprisingly large tent. There was even a liquid soap for washing the hair, boxes of talcum powder and bottles of toilet water.

I shall become quite spoiled by all of this! Atalanta thought to herself as she loaded all this bounty into a basket.

Nicholas would not let Varian go back down into the sinkhole until he had created a dragon-sized, sturdy ramp out of dirt and debris with his wand. "I don't want to have to lift you out of there again. I could not do it by myself," he cautioned the dragon.

Varian was exceedingly impatient but he was forced to wait until Nicholas had finished. When it was indicated that it was safe, he hurried down the ramp and forged ahead through the fallen limestone, sending up another huge cloud of dust in the wake of his passing.

Nicholas was forced to clear the air once more as he followed the dragon, more cautiously.

He could hear Varian up ahead, pushing his way through the rubble of the cave-in. He hoped Varian was not too disappointed if the eggs turned out to be just rocks.

The noises made by Varian's passage ceased and he heard the dragon gasp. Then he shouted "Nick! Nick! Come quickly! It IS eggs! And I think some of them might be ready to hatch!"

Regardless of the treacherous footing Nicholas ran the rest of the way.

They found fifteen eggs of varying breeds, some of which Nicholas did not recognize. Usually the breed of a dragon was readily apparent from the colour and sometimes the size of an egg. The egg indicated the colour of the dragonet inside.

The eggs were in a pile, all close together. All of the eggs were hard. Nicholas examined then with his stethoscope, his face growing grim as he did so. This took some little time, as he was very careful and examined each leg minutely.

"What is it, Nick?" Varian asked anxiously.

"Some of these eggs have petrified, Varian, and others are cold," Nicholas answered.

Varian gave a low moan of anguish.

"Petrified?" queried Cillian. He had woken up and was peering over the edge of his traveling basket, standing on his hind legs.

"That's what happens when a dragon egg is ready to hatch and for some reason the dragonet hasn't enough strength to break out. The dragonet dies and his corpse becomes rock-like. It's also a result of forced hatching such as the Inquisition practiced," Nicholas answered.

"That doesn't happen at home," said Cillian.

"No, that's why we have incubatories with trained

attendants, both human and adult dragons, who are there to help the hatchlings if they can't get from the shell on their own. The idiots who mishandled these eggs probably used a hatching spell and then just walked away and left the eggs, never thinking that the dragonets could use help," Nicholas explained to his familiar, his voice full of disgust. "And some of these eggs became cold and the embryo never had a chance."

Varian's head was down and he was nosing at the eggs, his eyes bright with tears. "This is so terrible!' he moaned. "Are they all dead?"

Four eggs in the middle of the pile were huddled close together. Nicholas had worked his way inwards, examining each egg with stethoscope and hammer.

Now he pressed the bell of the stethoscope against one and listened intently. He laid a hand against the egg and felt it, quickly moving to the other three that leaned against it.

"These may be viable!" he said excitedly. "Varian, can you mind-speak them?"

Dragons were able to speak to one another via mind-speech and could talk to the unhatched dragonets. This ability was thought to date from the days over one thousand years ago, when they were still feral and traveled in huge flights at top speed, and stayed in communication through this form of telepathy. It was still a very useful skill, particularly with eggs, who could tell an adult dragon in mind speech exactly when they were about to hatch or if there were any problems.

Varian looked happier and bent back down to the eggs, with the slightly blank look in his eyes that Nicholas knew meant he was speaking mentally.

"Nick!" he said, looking up, his whole look changed to one of intense pleasure and elation. "They're talking to me! They say that no one has talked to them in a long, long time and they are ready to come out of the shell now!"

"Good grief! Now? All four of them?" said Nicholas in dismay. Four hatchlings at once? That was more than even occurred on the average at an Incubatory in one day.

"We'll need meat, Varian and some help. Four of them at once is too much for us to handle by ourselves," he said.

Varian nodded. "I was thinking that. There's plenty of

beef from our meal last night left. I'll fly back and get Sabrina and all of the meat. I'll hurry!"

"Nicholas, I'll stay here if I might," said Cillian and indicated that he wanted to be lifted down from the basket. His small dark eyes were bright with interest and he requested his spectacles so that he might see clearly what was happening.

Varian had not been gone for five minutes when one of the eggs cracked, with a sudden sharp noise. Then one by one, the others followed suit, showing a fissure at the top, where all dragon eggs began to hatch first.

"Hurry, Varian!" Nicholas said to himself. These dragonets were suddenly very eager to join the world. And they would need food as soon as they were out of the shell. Sometimes it could take days for a hatching but the average time was twelve to twenty-four hours. But somehow Nicholas did not think that these dragonets would take that long.

Sabrina and Atalanta were much refreshed by their swim. It had taken all of Atalanta's resolve to shed her clothing and go into the water unclothed. She had felt shy, vulnerable and exposed, even though there was no one about save herself, Sabrina and Flann.

But it was surprisingly liberating to leave her corset and tight restrictive clothing on the bank of the pool, along with her hair pins, and float in the water that appeared as blue as the sky above. She had learned to swim when she had started traveling with her father as a precaution, as much of their traveling was done on shipboard. Just in case there was ever a disaster she did not want to be unprepared.

Sabrina was surprised at how much younger Atalanta looked with her stiff formal clothing gone, her hair let loose from its confining bun and her spectacles laid aside. In the sunlight her hair had golden lights and a natural wave. Her figure was far more womanly than could be seen beneath the mannishly cut suits. Sabrina had thought Atalanta at least forty; now she revised that estimate downwards considerably.

And after her first hesitation she seemed to enjoy the freedom of no clothing and the sleek feeling of the water caressing bare skin.

They stayed in the water some little time, leaving it reluctantly to dry off, resume their clothes and go back to camp. By the angle of the sun Sabrina could see that it was almost time that Lupe would soon be serving the noon meal. Sabrina hoped that both Nicholas and Ellery were back. She did not expect to see Julian until much later and, like yesterday, he would most likely go straight to bed after a little food. She ought to remind Nicholas that he had promised to go and help his brother with that passing ceremony.

When Sabrina and Atalanta got back to the camp it was to find Marisela waiting for them and being entertained by Mr. Sinclair while Dr. Beck had decided upon a nap.

Marisela had been unable to stay at home without quarreling with her mother and *duenna*. *Don* Casimiro, tired of female voices raised in anger, had retreated to his library and closed the door and gave orders that he was not to be disturbed.

The argument, of course, was about *Don* Rafael and the marriage that her mother so ardently desired. In vain did *Doña* Milagros tell Marisela of the beautiful bride clothes she would receive, of how *Don* Rafael would take her on a bridal trip to Madrid, the jewels that would be hers as the wife of such a wealthy, important man, of the sumptuous *Hacienda* she would be mistress of.... Marisela cared for none of those things. None of them were worth putting up with *Don* Rafael as a husband, a prospect that made her want to be sick. All the clothes and jewels in the world could not reconcile her to marriage to such an *idiota*, a man she could not like, much less respect.

The argument ended, as they usually did, with Marisela flinging out of the house to mount her horse Vittoria and ride away as far and as fast as she could.

Generally she had no destination, only riding fast and hard until she had regained control over her anger. But now she found herself heading for *El Morro* and her new friends.

She was very disappointed to find that Nicholas and

Varian were gone. A flight would have calmed her and she would have liked to talk to Nicholas again.

It could not be said that Mr. Sinclair was successfully entertaining her. His Spanish was rudimentary; her English was slightly better but not fluent. Marisela was very glad, after some fifteen minutes of labored conversation, to see Sabrina and Atalanta approaching. *Señorita* Beck spoke little Spanish as well, but she was fluent in French, which Marisela had learned as a young girl. And *Señorita* Delamar was as fluent in Spanish as Nicholas.

They had scarcely greeted one another when Varian suddenly dropped out of the sky, obviously highly agitated. "Sabrina!" he said, sounding almost breathless. "Sabrina! They *were* eggs! And there are four hatching right now! We need help and all the meat we have! Can you come right away?"

"What!" said Sabina in surprise. "A hatching? Four eggs at once?"

Varian nodded.

"Baby dragons?" Marisela said, her eyes brightening when this had been translated for her. "But I would love to see this!"

"I should not mind seeing such a thing as well," said Atalanta. "It would be highly educational."

"Good," said Sabrina. "you can both come. Four hatchlings are a handful and we could use all of the help we can get, even inexperienced help. Now we've got to pack up all the meat available as they will be ravenous after coming from the shell. Luckily I've still meat in tins as well as the fresh beef we cooked last night. We'll take it all."

171

Chapter Eighteen
Dragonets

When they reached the sinkhole and had gone down the ramp, they found that Nicholas had pulled the viable eggs out of the pile and had put each one in an egg cradle so the dragonet would have more room to hatch and spread out when at last each one emerged from the shell. He had also thrown up a number of mage lights so that the dark cave was now well lit.

The limestone cavern the eggs were in was enormous. There was plenty of head room and width for dragons. Stalactites hung from the ceiling and stalagmites were in blunt mounds on the floor of the cave. Atalanta knew that much, although she had never been in a cave before. She saw many other formations of rock that appeared to have been caused by dripping water and minerals and at once wished she had a book about caves.

Marisela went at once to where Nicholas was kneeling by an egg, earpieces of the stethoscope in his ears and the bell of it against a big pale gold egg that had bands of darker gold running through it.

He looked up at her briefly, with a smile, and then bent to his task again, not taking his attention more than momentarily from what he was doing. As Marisela watched, more cracks appeared in the top of the egg.

Varian had gone straight back to the dead eggs and was nosing at them, tears gleaming in his eyes. Somehow the fact that Nick had had to push them aside so that they lay, not on their big ends as was proper but on their sides, brought the sadness at their unnecessary deaths back to him. Sabrina joined him and laid a sympathetic hand on his neck.

"Oh, Sabrina, this is dreadful! All of these dragonets who never had a chance at life!" he said in a low, choked voice. "It just isn't right!"

"The Inquisition has a lot to answer for. Both their treatment of people and of dragons was an atrocity." She thought of the ill ex-slave children of which Julian had told her.

"All of the eggs are different colours," Atalanta

remarked, coming up beside them.

"It's according to the breed," Sabrina explained. "I'll tell you about it as we unpack the meat. We need to start a fire to warm it for them." She gave Varian another stroke on his neck and drew Atalanta away, knowing that the dragon would rather be alone in his grief.

Nicholas took off his stethoscope. "They're rapidly progressing," he announced. "I wouldn't expect to see this amount of cracking for nine to twelve hours yet." He then ran his hands through his hair and let out a long, angry sigh. "That damned Inquisition! They ranged far and wide in their thievery! This one," he patted the egg he had been listening to, "is a New York Gold!"

"Are you sure?" Sabrina said. "And then she said " I'm sorry, Nick, of course you're sure–it's your profession!"

This conversation had been in English and Marisela had not followed it very well. Nicholas obligingly translated for her and she said in confusion. "New York? But is that not in the United States? How did it get here?"

"They more than likely stole it. This means they had agents working right in the States. New York is all the way out on the east coast." He pointed to the other eggs "That one," he indicated a copper coloured egg that gleamed with richer striations of very bright copper, "is a California Copper. The third egg is a Maple Dragon egg." This was a curiously coloured egg of red, green and yellow, with the colours all blending together. The colours had veins like leaves. It was smaller than the others. "Those dragons are found only in New England, in the northeastern United States."

"What is that purple one?" Marisela inquired, looking at the fourth egg. "It looks like twilight with bands of stars strung about it, no?"

"I have never seen an egg like that," Nicholas said. The egg was the colour of the deep purple that was sometimes found at dusk and Marisela's description of the striations was a good one. They were neither gold nor silver, but a crystalline colour that had the qualities of star-shine.

Flann translated this conversation for Atalanta as Miss Beck and Sabrina busied themselves getting the meat ready. There were enough Dracophilologists in her family and Sabrina had attended so many hatchings that she knew what was needed. Four pots were filled with meat and broth and she asked Atalanta to help her gather rocks for a ley line fire. Unlike many Witches, Sabrina had been trained to use the ley lines.

But when she touched the ley lines to bring up power for the fire she had a shock. There were remnants of black magic in it. She let out an exclamation. "Nick! Did you feel this?"

"Yes," he answered, "I'm sorry, Sabrina, I should have warned you. I daresay it was one of the Inquisition's black magicians using the ley lines to warm these eggs. Whatever spell they used it wasn't really powerful as the warmth had almost disappeared. There's not much residue left but what there is, is rather nasty."

"We'll have to clean that," she said distastefully. "I'll warm their food manually. I really don't want to touch it."

"I don't blame you," he agreed. It had been a very disagreeable experience to feel that presence of evil.

Sabrina warmed the four pots with a short spell. Nicholas walked over and stared down at he meat, frowning. Atalanta and Marisela had both been drawn to the cracking eggs, which were quite audible now.

"What's wrong?" Sabrina inquired.

"These are American dragons," he said, sounding troubled.

"So?" She raised an eyebrow.

"American dragons search for their bond-mate immediately upon hatching. From what I have read the necromancers of the Inquisition bespelled them before they were scarcely out of the shell. But they feel the absence of that bond-mate all of their lives. Look at Cynara—when Sacha took the spell from her that kept her enslaved she immediately declared that she was his. Grandfather studied extensively the bonding ceremonies that brought together riders and dragons amongst the Native Americans. There would have been an entire group of young boys tending the eggs, talking to them and waiting for the hatchings, at which the dragonet would then make its choice. But there's no one here for them to choose."

Sabrina looked at him with a sardonic expression. "Really, Nick? What are Atalanta, *Doña* Marisela and I?

Invisible?"

"But you're female!" he said, surprised. "Dragons don't bond with women! It's against tradition! It's never been–"

"Just because it's not been *traditional*," she said rather scornfully, "doesn't mean it can't be done. Think about it, Nick! Why would these four eggs all start hatching at once? I've heard enough dragon talk to realize that it is the presence of the bond-mate that starts the egg hatching, even if it means like in Lakota's case his egg had to be brought all the way to Ireland from Colorado for Uncle Simon. Give me one good reason why a woman can't bond with a dragon!"

"You sound like a suffragette!" he said.

"I *am* a suffragette and proud of it!" she returned. "Woman have been oppressed for too long. I'm surprised at you, Nick, especially considering the example of your mother and the other women in our family who run businesses, have careers and are independent."

"I'm sorry," he said, admitting his mistake. "It's just that I never heard of such a thing happening." He paused and sighed. "But there are only three of you and there are four eggs hatching. I'm already bonded. Dragons seem to know that and won't infringe on another's territory. Even Julian would not be chosen, as he has Torin and their closeness is almost a bond. A dragonet would respect that."

"Perhaps Mr. Sinclair, Lutterworth or Dr. Beck is meant to have a dragon companion," Sabrina suggested.

Nicholas pulled a face. "I would doubt that any dragonet would chose Dr. Beck or especially Lutterworth!" he declared." Dragons have better taste than that!"

"Oh!" they heard an exclamation from Atalanta as a particularly loud crack sounded, the noise magnified by the cave. "There's a hole forming on the gold egg!" she called.

"The tongue will be coming out it a minute!" Nicholas exclaimed. "I have never seen eggs hatch this fast! Here, we'd better get this meat close to hand."

Varian hurried over to the eggs as well. He bent his head to the golden egg. "He's hungry!" he announced. "And he says he feels his bond-mate near and hopes she has food for him!"

"She?" queried Nicholas sharply. "He definitely said *she?*"

Varian nodded. "That's what he said."

"Just think of the monograph you'll be able to write about this, Nick!" said Sabrina, laughing a little at the expression on her nephew's face.

"Bond-mate?" Atalanta inquired, looking from Sabrina to Nicholas. "What does that mean?"

Sabrina explained briefly that a rider and a dragon, particularly American dragons, made a mental bond with each other on the dragonet's hatching. "It's a bond of love and trust and deep friendship, rather like that we Witches and Wizards have with our familiars. One and one's dragon are a part of each other. This dragonet will more than likely choose one of the three of us as a bond-mate when it is hatched."

Flann, sitting with Cillian near the hatching eggs, obligingly translated this for Marisela.

The *Señorita* looked both shocked and elated. "Does this mean that I will have my own dragon?" Her eyes began shining and her breath quickened. "But which one?" She gave no thoughts to any practical considerations as to how, for instance, she was going to explain the acquisition of a dragon to her parents.

"The dragonet will choose when he hatches completely," said Nicholas absently. He pulled a notebook from his pocket and began scribbling notes rapidly with a pencil. He was very glad that he had set himself to learning shorthand, especially now that this record-breaking hatching was taking place. A hatching like this and female bond-mates—what a paper this would be! And an opportunity to study a brand-new, unknown breed, for the purple egg was something unique in Nicholas's experience. As the first to see this breed, it was his privilege to name it.

"Only the copper is female," announced Varian, who had been listening to the eggs again. "All of the others are males."

The gold egg made another immense crack and a forked tongue emerged from the hole. The dragonet was testing the air and taking its first gulps of the air outside.

"It normally takes about 14 hours to get to this stage!" Nicholas said. "This is really the most amazing hatching!"

"They really want to come out," said Varian. "They have been in the shell too long, they say. And their bond-mates are here."

"New York Golds usually spend a year in the shell," said Nicholas thoughtfully. "And they hatch much more quickly than some of our British breeds, but not usually this fast!"

As they watched more cracks spread out from the hole in the top half of the shell and a head appeared. The dragonet was panting slightly. Emerging from a rock hard egg was quite an exertion and at this stage his talons were soft and his teeth small. A single long tooth protruded from his mouth right in the middle of his upper jaw. This was the egg tooth, its only purpose to help tear away the shell. It would fall off in a day or so.

"Oh!" said Atalanta on a note of wonder and delight. She fell to her knees beside the egg.

He was a beautiful little dragonet of pale gold with huge amber eyes with dark slitted pupils. At this age his horns were mere stubs and his snout short. His scales were still covered with the remnants of the albumen that he had existed on during his time in the egg.

"Hello!" said the dragonet, looking right into her eyes. "I'll be out soon! Will you have something for me to eat? I'm so hungry!"

He spoke in English. They were to find later that he also spoke Spanish.

"I have a big pot of meat for you, " Atalanta said.

"Oh, thank you!" said the dragonet. "What is your name, please?"

"He's only concerned with your Christian name," said Sabrina in an under voice.

"Atalanta," she answered the dragonet.

"Oh, that's pretty! Will you give me a name, Atalanta?" the dragonet asked, looking up at her trustingly.

"Seneca," she said. The first thing that came into her head was the name of the college. It also seemed appropriate for a New York dragon.

"Seneca! I like it!" He gave a wiggle of delight and another piece of eggshell fell off–this a large one that allowed his two front, taloned legs to emerge. "Will you help me from this shell?" he said to his new bond-mate.

Atalanta looked at Nicholas, the dragon expert. He

nodded. Sometimes dragonets, particularly the impatient ones, wanted help and it was perfectly permissible. Some breeds scorned any help and wanted to do it all by themselves.

Atalanta eagerly tore away the rest of the shell , as eager to see her dragon as he was to finish hatching.

No sooner than he was free from every bit of shell than he said again "I'm hungry!"

Atalanta gave him the pot of meat, holding it carefully with two cloths, for it was quite warm, although not hot, but a perfect eating temperature.

Sabrina gave Atalanta a pile of cloths as the dragonet plunged his snout into the pot after a quick word of thanks.

"Dry off his scales," said Nicholas. "In the wild a mother dragon would lick him dry. It will help promote the bond."

"He's so beautiful!" Atalanta marveled as she knelt beside him and applied the cloth. Seneca wiggled with pleasure as he heard the compliment.

Cleaned of albumen his scales were revealed as pale gold with darker, bright gold edges. His back ridges were mere bumps and his tail was stubby and short. He was about the size of a large dog such as a Labrador retriever. His wings were quite small and at Nicholas's direction, Atalanta carefully pulled each wing out and dried it. The wings were translucent gold. Seneca appeared to enjoy her attentions.

"When he has his full growth at about ten years of age he'll be thirty-five feet long with a very wide and well-developed wing span," Nicholas told Atalanta. "New York Golds are fast flyers and very able in the air. It will be about a year before he can fly any distance and he won't be able to bear a rider until around nine months. He won't flame for nearly a year as well. In the next two weeks he'll nearly double in size and it will seem like he eats constantly. When he is finished with that meat, try to get him to eat the egg shell. It has calcium he needs for his bones."

"I don't know anything about dragons," Atalanta said a little apologetically as she knelt by her dragon, stroking him with a cloth. Already she loved him and could not even think of being parted from him. The thought of one day flying with him filled her with joy.

"Until the dig is through you'll have all of us to help you and then Nick can recommend some books. His grandfather, Sir Simon Stillfield, has written at least ten books on dragons," offered Varian.

"And with the help of a draconic veterinarian, two on dragon health and care," added Nicholas.

"The other egg, this purple one, cracks!" called Marisela excitedly. From the first she had been attracted to the purple egg.

This egg was only a little smaller than the gold had been but it was cracking just as fast. By the time the others, except Atalanta joined her, the tongue was sticking out, waving in the air.

Contrary to any other hatching that Nicholas had ever seen the shell suddenly burst open, falling away in shards from a deep purple dragonet with very well developed horns, which again, was highly unusual.

"*Hola!*" he said in Spanish to Marisela. He was very advanced in growth for his age, with a longer tail that had been curled around him in the shell. "I'm very hungry! Please, may I have some food? Tell me your name while I eat."

Marisela gave him the pot of meat and he said again and again "*Gracias! Gracias!*" before putting his snout into the fragrant pot. He sighed in pleasure as Marisela began to dry him off.

His scales and horns were all tipped with what Marisela thought as starlight. His wings, when spread out and dried, were iridescent and caught the light of the mage lamps in the cave with a beautiful rainbow sparkle.

"I shall call you Francisco, after San Francisco, the saint who so loved animals," said Marisela. "But you will be Pacho for short."

"I'm afraid I can tell you nothing about his breed," Nicholas told Marisela, "for I have never seen one like. We'll ask him if he knows, when he is finished eating."

"It is fortunate he speaks Spanish, no?" said Marisela, Like Atalanta had been she was totally charmed by her dragon. "My English, it is not good."

"I suspect his breed is native to this area," said Nicholas. "Dragons generally speak the first language that they hear, although they do pick up language far easier than humans, even learning to speak it when they hear it while they are still in the shell."

"I could speak both English and Gaelic when I was hatched," said Varian a little smugly.

But the newly christened Pacho did not know what breed he was. He had been very small–perhaps only just have developed from an embryo–when his egg had been roughly handled and moved. To Nicholas this sounded as if his egg had been stolen just after he developed enough to be a viable dragonet. He did not remember his parents at all and could only remember one other adult dragon 'speaking' to him in all of the time he must have been in the cave.

Nicholas named him a New Mexico Twilight. The little dragonet liked this name so much that he kept repeating it softly to himself. After dutifully eating his shell he lay down with his head in Marisela's lap and went to sleep, as Seneca had done with Atalanta. Sated with meat, they would sleep for a while and then wake, demanding more food.

The copper egg and the Maple began both began splitting at the same moment.

Sabrina felt a strong pull to the California Copper egg and went to kneel beside it as the little dragonet emerged.

"I'll see to the Maple," Varian offered. "If his bond-mate is not present it will help him to have an adult dragon near by."

The Copper struggled from the shell first and immediately bonded with Sabrina. She was the only female of the four eggs. Sabrina named her Eda, which was a Celtic word meaning "fiery woman"; most appropriate for a female California Copper as they had the largest and longest flame of any dragon.

The California Copper superficially resembled the Cornish Copper of the British Isles, being a dull, tarnished copper with brighter copper scale edges. But the California, when fully adult, had longer horns banded with an onyx-like black, and four talons on each foot instead of three. The tail ended in a spike as well, with sharply defined back ridges and dark eyes. The wings were black.

Nicholas warned Varian that Maple dragons were very shy. They were like chameleons, with the colour of their hides changing to match the maple groves they lived amongst.

They bonded only to the Native Americans who tended the sugar maples in the New England states, who, like their dragons, were solitary people, wary of strangers. They were very small dragons, seldom becoming much more than fifteen feet in length, with unusual brown eyes with green retinas. They had a smaller than normal wingspan and did not fly very fast or far and never willingly carried more than one rider at a time.

When the Maple dragonet's head emerged from the egg he took one looked at Varian and said wistfully "You're not my mother."

When Varian said very gently that no, he was not, the little dragonet looked around the cave as if searching for someone that he failed to find. He then said. "I'm sorry, but I'm so hungry. Can I come out of the shell, please, if it isn't too much trouble?"

Nicholas brought over the pot of meat as Varian helped remove the rest of the shell with talons and teeth. The little Maple thanked Nicholas and said "You have a dragon already." Like the New York Gold, he spoke English.

"Yes, that's me," said Varian. He felt very sorry for the dragonet, imagining what it would have been like Nick had not been there when he had hatched.

"He's not here. I can't feel him at all," said the Maple sadly. "You'd better give me a name, please, while I am waiting," he said to Varian.

"Don't worry, I'll be your friend until he comes," Varian assured the dragonet. "I'll call you Amyas. It's a name I heard in a song once." The Maple nodded shyly in affirmation.

Varian, with Nicholas helping with a soft cloth, licked Amyas clean as the Maple dragonet ate his first meal. He was more hesitant that the others had been.

In appearance he was a great deal like his egg: red and yellow and green blended into one another. But even as they cleaned him his colour began to change to all green. When Varian wanted to know why, Nicholas explained that he was becoming the colour of the maple trees in New England at this season. The fact that his egg had been the autumnal hues of the trees indicated that fall had been the season when his egg was laid. His underbody was the colour of red maple leaves, a dusky colour, and his wings veined with red as well. His scales were becoming solid green and his incipient horns striated with red as well. In the winter he would be a grayish colour that matched the bark of the leafless maple trees. He had three toes and a short tail, with no bumps indicating back ridges.

"I will have to read your grandfather's books, Nick!" said Varian, looking up from his washing of the little dragon— he was quite the smallest of the four. "I don't know enough about my own species!"

It was at this moment, when all of the dragonets had finished eating that they heard first Ellery's voice and then Erianne's, calling out.

"Down here!" yelled Nicholas. Varian had asked Sabrina to leave a note for Ellery explaining where they had gone and why.

The other dragonets did not even stir from their sleep but the little Maple, Amyas, was instantly on the alert, peering to where the voices came from.

When Erianne came in sight Amyas shrieked "Mama! Mama!" and breaking free from Varian and Nicholas, ran towards her as fast as his little legs could carry him.

Chapter Nineteen
The Art of Healing

"There's your pupil, Julian," said Torin as he slowly made the descent to the ground. Hippogriffes did not fly as high as dragons did, not were they as fast. "He certainly is eager."

"I hope that he learns at a rate to match his eagerness," said Julian. "Since he is illiterate, as far as I might ascertain, he will have to memorize everything; no helpful books such as I had."

"I read up on the Native peoples here before we left Ireland," said Torin. "They are held to have excellent memories and capable of assimilating large blocks of information, as theirs is an oral tradition. They are also noted for being at one with the earth. If that holds true with Ramón it should ease his training in grounding and shielding considerably."

Both Ramón and his vulpine companion came forward as Torin landed with a few running steps. At the door of the mission house Julian could see Prudence Cromwell waiting for them as well, her eyes shining eagerly.

Julian regarded her uneasily. What Siofra had talked of had kept him awake for a little while the night before. He liked to believe that she awaited his coming so fervently because of what he could do for the children. He did not wish to be an object of her affections. If she did entertain tender feelings for him, he was quite certain that they were the same feelings that many people had for their physicians, those of gratitude and trust. But having patients "in love" with one was an occupational hazard. The emotion usually wore off with time.

All the same, he thought it best to perhaps maintain some degree of formality with her as not to encourage any warmth she harbored towards him. The very last thing he desired at this point was any emotional entanglements.

To Ramón's surprise the very first thing that he was told to do was to take a hot bath and become extremely clean. His new mentor took him to a stream near the mission hose where the Covenanters bathed, and heated the water with his wand. Ramón was instructed to wash every inch of himself, including his hair, with a soap that smelled like herbs. Particular attention was given to his hands where the dirt from the mines was deeply ingrained. Julian ended in using a scrubbing spell most often used for very grubby children on Ramón's hands before the dirt would all disappear.

While Ramón was bathing Julian sat beside the pool and stressed the importance of absolute cleanliness in the treatment of patients. The Medicine Man and everything he used in treating a sick person must be immaculate.

To Julian's relief, Ramón understood this concept at once. He had seen in the mines how a dirty wound would fester and grow worse. Practical observation made more sense to him than if Julian had attempted to explain the new discoveries by such men as Louis Pasteur and Robert Semmelweiss, of the science of microbes and bacteria.

When Ramón was squeaky clean Julian gave him some clothes from his own wardrobe.

Ramón could see at once why people liked to be clean. It felt wonderful and the clothes were the finest he had ever worn. He hoped that he would be taught how to make the water hot for the bath. He would then make certain that all of his tribe could indulge in a hot bath and share this feeling. It was almost like being reborn.

While Ramón had been bathing Torin and Siofra had been busy with some of the supplies that Julian had brought from camp. Gian-nah-tah sat close to where they worked, watching intently with his bright eyes.

In a clear area a little removed from the mission house they had spread a soft blanket of green wool, the colour of leaves. A thick green candle sat on a flat stone, with a rounded chunk of black obsidian in front of the candle. To one side was a bundle of blue candles that would be needed later. Ramón's first lesson was to be in grounding himself. Without proper grounding he would not be able to channel the energies from the earth that made Healing possible.

Once Ramón was properly grounded and shielded

Julian intended that he be given some practical training: to let him watch as Julian Healed three more of the children. The grounding and a minor spell would enable him to 'see' what Julian was doing in the body of the sick child. This was how Julian himself had begun, as a boy, watching his grandfather, asking questions and closely observing, until he and his grandfather Stuart had been confident that he understood, and then beginning to Heal minor ills.

How successful this training would be without a background in Wizardry Julian could not tell. However, Ramón's Healing aura was amongst the brightest he had ever seen in an untrained person, and from what the Native had said, he already felt the power of the ley lines. With any luck Ramón was what was called a 'natural Healer', which was so rare as to be almost non-existent nowadays. But there were documented cases of such a Gift. Many of these rare people could Heal even without training.

Prudence had somewhat embarrassed herself by following the two young men almost to the bathing pool. She was very interested in what was going on. It was only when Ramón began pulling off his shirt that she blushed and fled back to the mission house, her cheeks flaming scarlet.

After they walked back from the pool Julian began explaining the concept of grounding to Ramon. Once again he was grateful for Oberon's gift of Spanish.

"The earth," he said to Ramón, "is the root of our being."

Ramón nodded. "The earth is our mother," he said.

"Exactly," his mentor went on. "The earth means steadiness, a foundation on which the other elements of water, air and fire move. The earth is where we Medicine Men get our power to Heal," Julian had decided that to use the term 'Medicine Man' would make more sense to Ramón than any other.

"Today I will show you how to properly ground to the earth so that you can pull the Healing power from it," he continued. "Without grounding you would be swept away by the power and perhaps badly harmed here." Julian put a finger to his forehead. "You've felt the pull of the earth before, Ramón, have you not?"

"Yes," he answered, "but I did not understand what it was trying to tell me. I felt it when you made the children well."

"After today I hope that you will understand," said Julian.

Ramón felt almost light-headed with joy. To know–at last! He would pay strict attention to everything that was said and do exactly as he was told.

They came to the clearing where the three animals awaited them. Torin had folded his long legs and was laying down with Siofra perched on his hip, a favorite resting place. Close by, Gian-nah-tah watched.

Julian had Ramón sit cross-legged on the green blanket, in front of the candle, which he lit with his wand. The flame burned straight and true. This was always a good sign. Julian checked again for any signs of psychic dirt. The area was remarkably free from malignant influences, which surprised him at first until he realized that the Covenanters must have blessed this place before they built the mission house.

Since grounding was not a Great Ritual there was no need of anointing oils, ribbon-bedecked candles, a Chalice and altar of tokens representing the four elements. It was a simple ceremony, among the first taught to any beginning Wizard or Witch.

Julian gave Ramón a grounding, or as it was sometimes called, an 'earthing' stone. This was obsidian, a black glass stone of volcanic origin. This type of stone had been used as weapons, spear points and such for centuries. It was easy to break and was so sharp that modern surgical scalpels were made from it. Because it came from the very core of the earth it was one of the best grounding stones to be had.

"It is warm," said Ramón in surprise as Julian gave him the stone and told him to hold it lightly in his hands.

In the background Siofra began purring. This was a good sign. Gian-nah-tah nodded in agreement.

"Close your eyes," Julian instructed, "Breath slowly and deeply. Think about a tree, a large tree that has roots deep in the earth. Think about it till you can see it. Sit quietly, empty your mind and think only of the tree. Think of how it grows down into the earth, how the roots make it strong against the wind and the water, how the earth supports it. Think of the roots going down deep, down to the earth's core. Think of yourself, like the tree, connecting to the earth. With each breath you take feel your energy flowing down into the soil. You may be able to see this as a stream of light passing through you and going through your feet. You can see this without opening your eyes," he suggested as Ramón's eyelids fluttered.

Ramón frowned but then a light broke over his face, "I see the light!" he said excitedly. "It comes out from my feet."

"Quiet, keep your mind quiet," Julian cautioned. "Feel how the constant strength of the earth lies beneath you, supporting you like a mother. Breath in and out, deeply and quietly. With each breath in feel how the earth's strength flows back into you. A green energy flows up from the roots of the tree you see in your mind. It goes into the tree trunk and the branches that is your body."

Visualization was all. Some Wizards took many tries before they could imagine the tree and see the light. Julian, with the aid of Othersight, could almost see Ramón's visualization of a strong piñon pine.

"Think of the power flowing into you until you feel calm and centered, feeling at one with the earth and calm and peaceful," Julian directed.

He kept Ramón practicing until his pupil could draw the energy in with each breath and have it flow back into the earth with each outward breath.

Julian was elated. Ramón had managed it easily. He could imagine what a sensation a pupil such as this would have caused in Edinburgh. To be so receptive at such an age was unique as well. Training in Wizardry and Healing was started early, at about eight years of age, for the younger the pupil the greater the connection he or she still had to the natural world without all of the sometimes stifling trappings of civilization in the way.

Then he taught Ramón to Shield himself from psychic

damage. This would guard him against both being overwhelmed by the power from the ley lines and from attack by malign forces.

This involved a small ritual: a circle of blue candles, with each cardinal point, beginning in the east, acknowledged with Ramón seated, facing the west, and the pupil visualizing a white light that he would completely wrap about himself.

At the end of just over an hour, Julian was satisfied that Ramon could ground and shield, and what was more, do it easily and as needed. He gave Ramón the piece of obsidian to keep; this grounding stone would aid him in grounding until he could do such quite automatically. An additional gift of a carnelian would help protect him in times of psychic stress and furthermore would provide links to his own inner power.

Then he taught Ramón how to tap the power of the ley lines, the power that would enable him to Heal.

Prudence had awaited their return to the mission house eagerly. She wanted to see more of the children made well. There had been such a change in the three that had been Healed: they were out of bed this morning; laughing and eating well, no longer laying languidly on their cots.

She had gone out into the surrounding wood that morning and spent time in grateful prayer for the coming of this wonderful doctor. Surely he was heaven sent!

It made her angry though, that Reverend Brewer and Brother Ezekiel still seemed to think that Doctor Stillfield was some kind of demon. Sister Rebecca seemed more inclined now to be thinking her way, that the doctor was good, not evil. Sister Rebecca had confided to her Handmaiden that the Wicked One or one of his minions would not know the powers of the Healing Herbs, and could not even touch them without burning from Holy Fire.

Prudence was not certain what the doctor was doing with the Indian from the mines, but when the two young men returned she could at once see a difference in the Indian. Not only was he clean and clad in better clothing but he had somewhat of the same air that Doctor Stillfield had, a type of glow, a feeling of goodness, that Prudence, sensitive to such things, could feel and almost see.

Reverend Brewer and Brother Ezekiel, watching form the sidelines, glowering, but Sister Rebecca stood almost beside Prudence, wanting to see as much as was possible.

Prudence hoped that three more children, at least, would be helped today. Indeed, when Julian arrived back with Ramón he chose three of the children: Pia, Vasco and Léon. These three were not as ill as had been Angelita, Guillermo and Benito, but they were sick enough with asthma, bronchitis and dust allergies.

Prudence had insisted that Julian tell her the children's names and she was happy to be able to call them by name and hear them call her *Señorita* Prudencia, even if she could not understand much else of what they said. She was happy in the thought that tomorrow Lola, Chimo and Tomas would also be made well. She did not realize that Tomas was beyond the aid of even a Wizard Healer.

Julian drew, with his wand, the Healing Circle about the bed of the first child. He encircled Ramón as well as the child, himself and Siofra, again cautioning Prudence not to cross the Circle.

The candle at the head of the narrow cot was lit and Julian turned to Ramón. "When I tell you to do so," he instructed, "touch the power of the earth. I will bespell you so that you will be able to see as I do and see the child being Healed."

Ramón nodded in assent, his heart beating fast.

The first child was Lola. She was ten, thin and small for her age. She had a hacking cough that seemed to be stealing her strength from day to day, so that she only could lay listlessly in the bed.

Siofra lay under her hand, purring. Lola smiled to see Ramón, whom like most of the children in the tribe, she thought of as a big brother. Since the *Señor el Médico* had made the others well, she had lain awake the night before, hoping that she would be helped as well. It would be so good not to cough as it interfered with speaking, walking and eating, making her utterly tired.

"*Hola*, Lola," said Julian, sitting down on the edge of the cot and smiling at the little girl, with his wand in one hand. He put his other hand on her forehead and said "I am going to make you feel better. I will not lie to you–this may hurt a little. I have to chase away the illness."

She nodded. "*Sí, Señor*, Benito told us last night that it hurt a little but afterwards he felt so good. I am ready. I want to be well."

Julian nodded at Ramón and said. leveling his wand at Ramón said "*Particeps*."

This was a spell of sharing, used very often in teaching, that enabled the pupil to see what the teacher did, particularly in spells such as Healing, in which a great deal of the magic was hidden from view.

Ramon felt a jolt as if the earth had shifted beneath his feet and then he watched in amazement as the green light ran off his teacher's hands and entered the child's body. He could follow that light with his eyes and see it enter the chest and lungs, now as visible to him as if aid bare.

Ramón was conscious of power, green-gold. sweet and good, and extremely strong, pouring into Julian and then into the child. She gasped a little and looked frightened for a moment but Siofra turned up the volume of her purr and Lola began to relax, closing her eyes and slipping into a sort of trance.

The disease could be seen as a darkness in the lungs, an evil growth, advancing and choking the health from them as an invasive weed choked out a garden. The green-gold light attacked the darkness, beating it back, making it turn in upon itself, seeking it out where it tried to hide. When it had all been thoroughly routed, then the light soothed and Healed what injuries were left behind, leaving health and easy breathing in its wake.

The power, Ramón saw, surged back through Julian, taking the darkness with it and went back down into the earth. Ramón was able to see it be taken in to the earth and there its destruction was completed, and it was harmlessly dissolved in the goodness of the earth.

Julian remained seated for a moment until Lola opened her eyes. "Take a deep breath," he said to the little girl.

She did so and gave him a look of wonder when there was no pain and she did not cough. *"Gracias, gracias, Señor!"* she said, with tears in her voice.

As Ramón observed, the next two children were helped as well. He watched almost breathlessly, closely looking at what happened. He felt the power and saw what it could do. He was also certain that he could do it in time. He felt the power surging in his own self and it filled him up, seeking an outlet.

But there was a price to pay for this gift, he saw when Julian finished with the last child. His mentor staggered when he rose from Vasco's cot and he looked tired and drawn.

Ramón could understand this. Had he not himself felt the strength of that pull in and going out?

Wearily, Julian commanded *"Claudere,"* and Ramon felt the connection cease. Julian took down the Healing Circle and snuffed the candle. He looked so tired that Ramón gave him the support of his arm.

Sister Rebecca bustled forward and said briskly, "I've made tea and there is fresh bread. Come, Doctor, there is enough for both you and your friend."

"Thank you, said Julian gratefully, as much for the tea as for her acceptance of Ramón and took a seat at the table with his pupil as the fragrance of St. John's Wort wafted up from the tea pot. Prudence, her great pansy brown eyes full of stars, served them with fresh baked sweet bread, made with honey. Gian-nah-tah came forward to sit at Ramón's feet, while Siofra, with a restorative purr, climbed into Julian's lap. Ramón could feel the fox's approval of the proceedings, although the animal said nothing.

But again Julian could feel the malignant glare of the Reverend Brewer. The minister had remained quiet this time but he did not look as if he had come to accept the Healing. Brother Ezekiel's face, lost in that magnificent beard, was not as easy to read. He seemed to be reserving judgement. His wife, however, by her offer of a herbal tea that was meant to allay exhaustion, seemed to have accepted the Healing as a force for good.

Julian and Ramón, however, no more than did the rest of the occupants of the mission, could not know that this act of compassion had now put the childrens' existence in mortal danger, not only of their very lives, but of their souls as well.

Chapter Twenty

Reactions

The dragonets could not stay in the cave: that was readily apparent. It was too far from food and water and from their bond-mates.

They could not fly, of course and it was too great a distance for such young ones to walk. Nicholas and Sabrina ended in rigging a sling from the mesh carry-alls on the breast harness of the two adult dragons and transporting the dragonets two at a time back to camp in a sort of hammock strung between Erianne and Varian.

Nothing could convince Amyas that Erianne was not his mother. Whether it was because she was the only adult female or perhaps now that his scales had turned the colour of a summer maple tree, making them roughly the same colour, as hers, no one could tell.

He did not wish to be separated from her for even the short space of time that it took to make two flights back and forth.

Only Sinclair was about when the dragonets were brought to the camp. He had been sitting under the canvas canopy, reading one of the dime novels Nicholas had brought along, when the two adult dragons landed simultaneously and the dragonets tumbled out of the mesh. The first flight had brought Amyas and Seneca, along with Nicholas and Atalanta.

"Baby dragons?" Sinclair said in surprise, letting his book drop and coming to his feet. Mr. Lutterworth was not going to like this! Sinclair's employer was at present in his tent, writing an angry letter to Washington. He had already delivered a long tirade about how little work had been done on the treasure project while the railroad line sat idle, waiting for them to find and remove the treasure. What delays would baby dragons cause? Sinclair hung back from going up and approaching the dragonets. He did not know if they would spout flame or be aggressive. His knowledge of dragon-kind was almost non-existent.

Amyas let out a low moan of protest when Erianne and Varian took off again almost immediately. He did not want to be separated from "Mama".

"She'll be right back," Atalanta, who with Nicholas had stayed behind to see to the dragonets' needs, tried to soothe him.

Seneca, rather jealously, came to stand between Atalanta and the Maple dragon. Atalanta was *his* property, his glare seemed to say and Amyas backed away from him, looking shyer than ever.

"That's enough of that, Seneca," said Nicholas sharply. "You will need to learn to share Atalanta's time and affections." Dragons, if not taught otherwise when very young, could become exceedingly possessive of their bond-mates, which could then make any other relationship with a familiar or a spouse, other family members, or even a lover, difficult indeed. This was a lesson usually taught in the Incubatory by the matron, an older female dragon, or by the dragonet's parents. Nicholas supposed that Erianne was going to have to act in this capacity. The dragonets would recognize her authority. It was bred into them to obey an adult dragon, just as it was instinct to never harm a human being.

Talking softly and low, Nicholas approached Amyas and began to stroke the little dragon's eye ridges. This caress was more than acceptable to any dragon, young or old, and the little Maple relaxed under this attention. Varian, Nicholas knew, would not mind if he gave some attention to Amyas. Varian was exceptionally self-confident and well-adjusted and knew that his bond-mate studied and interacted with other dragons as a profession.

The rest of the party was back shortly, the dragonets Pacho and Eda joining the others. They immediately set up a clamor for more food.

Amyas ran to Erianne, looking up at her adoringly. She felt an extreme urge to bring her wing over him and hold him against her side. This was a natural impulse of a mother dragon towards a newly hatched dragonet, but she was surprised at it happening to her with Amyas, as he was not from any egg of hers. She had never quite understood how Nicholas's parents could so love children not born of their union, as if the children were really theirs. But now in a sudden rush of feeling it came to her that parental love was not limited in that manner, given the tenderness she was beginning to have for Amyas.

At the sudden noise made by hungry dragonets Lupe emerged from the cook tent, and gasped at what she saw. "*Madre de Dios!*" she said, slapping her cheeks with both hands as if to contain her astonishment. She was even further shocked when she saw *Doña* Marisela caressing one of the creatures.

"Look, Lupe!" the *Señorita* called out. "This is Pacho! Is he not handsome? And he is mine!"

"And I am hungry!" said Pacho plaintively.

"Is there anything left for them to eat?" Nicholas asked Sabrina, worriedly. Eda was indicating that she too, wanted more food, by rubbing her head along Sabrina's arm and widening her eyes in an appealing manner. They would eat at least three more times before sleeping tonight and then would want food as soon as they were awake.

"We have some ham, some preserved fowl and tins of meat for Torin," she answered. "But we shall definitely need more meat, quite a lot of it. I'll go and ready what we have." Eda followed her closely.

Fascinated in spite of her fear, Lupe came closer to Marisela and her new dragon companion. "*Doña* Marisela," she said slowly, "what will your parents and *Don* Rafael say to this animal? They will not be pleased! You cannot mean to take it back to the *Hacienda!*"

Marisela looked taken aback. In her joy she had not even thought of the consequences of obtaining a dragon. Suddenly she realized how her parents would view a dragon. He would frighten the horses and the cattle and probably even most of the *péons*. But one objection did not matter in the least. "*Don* Rafael has nothing to say about it!" she said.

"But, *Señorita*, if he is to be your husband–"Lupe protested.

"Your husband?" said Nicholas sharply, turning to stare at Marisela. He felt as if he had been jolted by a sudden strike of lightning which left behind a most unpleasant feeling.

"My parents wish me to marry him but I will not do so. He is an *idiota*," said Marisela dismissively. "He knows nothing about dragons. He cannot even ride a horse. He would faint if he were to try and fly."

"You can't marry anyone like that," said Pacho. "I wouldn't' like it. But now I am so hungry!" He looked up at her, his eyes huge and pleading.

"We shall have to renegotiate the contract with your father, *Señorita*," said Cillian. "We are going to need a lot more meat."

In the midst of the second feeding both Lutterworth and Dr. Beck emerged from the tents. Lutterworth had been writing a very nasty letter to 'his' Senator, Robert Marden of New York. Why was he making generous campaign contributions to Marden if the Senator did not protect the interests of A. J. Lutterworth? How had that snake, Rankin, been able to sneak into Taos, Albuquerque and Phoenix territory? The telegrams he had sent in Albuquerque should take care of the problem, but it was a problem which should not have come up. And to make it even worse, the whole affair had interrupted the treasure hunt. Even now he could have been reveling in his discovery.

He was still fuming when he came out of the tent, letter in hand, to be given over to Sinclair for mailing. Delays and more delays in what should have been a simple operation! He supposed that none of these people had stayed behind to search for the cave. As usual, he would have to make them toe the mark.

"What the hell!" he exclaimed when he saw the dragonets, who were frisking about as they waited for their food to be warmed.

Most people found dragonets as irresistible as kittens or puppies. All Lutterworth saw was something else he had not planned on, yet another spanner cast into the works. "Delamar!" he roared. "What the hell is this–an archaeological dig or a home for orphaned dragons? What are these damned things doing here?"

"At the moment, waiting to be fed," said Ellery calmly, although his feeling more and more was really that he wished to place a nice flush hit on Lutterworth's angry face.

"Get rid of them!" Lutterworth ordered. "I won't pay to feed them or have someone who ought to be worrying about my interests wasting time on taking care of them!" His pugnacious jaw stuck out in a most antagonistic manner.

"We have not asked you to pay for the dragons' food," said Ellery coldly, "nor will we do so."

"And as for getting rid of them," said Nicholas, looking up from the meat he was feeding Amyas, "you much mistake the matter if you think we shall do any such thing! They will die without care. They are orphaned–"

"How is this my concern?" Lutterworth snarled. Once again his face was very red.

"It isn't," said Nicholas, trying to be as calm as Ellery always seemed to be around this impossible man. Nicholas wanted to tell him a thing or two in no uncertain terms. "I, however, am a Dracophilologist and dragons must always be my first concern."

When Atalanta heard Lutterworth declare that he would not pay to feed them she had a sudden sinking feeling. She had been so stupid! How was she to pay for the food for a full-grown dragon, never mind that of a constantly hungry dragonet? She had no money of her own, only a small allowance, given her grudgingly by her father. And there would be other expenses as well: the saddle and harness for one. What would her father say when he found out that one of these dragonets was hers? All she had thought of was the happiness of having a dragon, a bond-mate. She looked down at Seneca who had his short snout in a pot of meat she had just been given, magically warmed for him. As if he felt her eyes upon him, he looked up at her. His amber glance was full of love and trust.

She felt her heart turn over. Somehow, she would find a way to provide for him. She could not give him up. She would talk to Sabrina. Perhaps the Irishwoman would know what she could do. There seemed to be a lot of dragons in her family.

While everyone's else's attention was on Lutterworth Dr. Beck had stared hard at his daughter. What did she think she was doing, feeding a small dragon? That young Stillfield, who seemed to be obsessed with dragons, had no doubt cajoled her into it. That was not part of her duties and she ought to be seeing to her father's evening meal, as the time was drawing near for its preparation. Surely she did not expect him to eat the food that the Native woman cooked! It was inedible, with all of those chili peppers or whatever they were. He was not certain exactly what the spicy taste was but he was sure of one thing: he didn't like it. He thought he had made that clear to Atalanta this morning after breakfast. His eyes narrowed as he looked at his daughter. There was also something different about her as well, something odd.

Then as she moved, putting down the now empty bowl, he saw what it was and was outraged, "Atalanta, what is that immodest garment you are wearing?" he said severely, his voice indignant.

Surprised at the angry voice Seneca turned around to look at Dr. Beck. Was this man speaking to his bond-mate?

"It's a split skirt, Papa, for riding. I've been wearing it all day," she said patiently. It was typical of him that he only now noticed. Unless it had a direct bearing upon his own self, he very often failed to see what was right in front of him. "Miss Delamar loaned it to me so I could ride dragon-back."

"Go and change at once!" her father demanded. "It shows your limbs in a shocking fashion! It's disgraceful! And stop playing with that creature!" he added, looking with distaste at Seneca. "It is time you were beginning to think about my evening meal. I cannot eat what that woman cooks! She gave us another unpalatable mess for luncheon while you were off gallivanting who knows where. You have been neglecting your duties shamefully since we have been on this expedition!"

"Don't you talk to her like that!" said Seneca, his eyes blazing with draconic fury. Subconsciously copying the stance of an adult dragon in a confrontation, he stood braced, with his neck thrust out and his head down. His eyes were narrowed to slits and if he had been able to produce any, steam would have been trickling from his nostrils. His sharp teeth, although still small, showed menacingly in his maw. He placed himself in front of Atalanta as if protecting her. "She's my bond-mate and I have to defend her from people like you!" the dragonet declared. Through the bond, as new as it was, he had felt her reaction to her parent's harsh words. She had been made most dreadfully unhappy and embarrassed.

Seneca's belligerent tones attracted the attention of the other dragonets and they looked towards the scene of conflict.

"Bond-mate?" said Dr. Beck incredulously. "What does this animal mean by that?" he demanded of Atalanta, shocked. He did not like the look on the dragonet's face. Although it was small it was still a dragon.

"It's true, Papa, we bonded when he hatched this afternoon," said Atalanta. She could tell that this was going to send her father into one of his snits, if not a full-blown fit of temper.

Dr. Beck was not un-ignorant of dragons as several colleagues kept the creatures. He even knew about the bond between dragon and rider as it was normal with American dragons. Of course, his colleagues who kept the beasts were far better paid than he was, teaching as they did at larger colleges and universities and many had private means. He knew, as well that keeping a dragon could be an expensive proposition.

"How dare you let this happen!" he said wrathfully to Atalanta. "Do you suppose that I will pay for this creature to eat us out of house and home? Where do you suppose that it will live? We have no facilities to house it, even did it not get any larger! How could you have been so irresponsible?"

In the background, Lutterworth had been ranting and raving and Ellery had paid less and less attention to him. Mr. Sinclair had come up and, in attempting to expostulate with his employer, was managing to turn Lutterworth's fury upon himself. Mr. Sinclair could see that both Dr. Delamar and Dr. Stillfield were rapidly losing their tempers, although neither of them grew red-faced or loud-voiced as did Lutterworth. Unused to Wizards, Sinclair was not certain whether or not one of them, goaded into it by anger, might turn his employer into Something Nasty. Sinclair, however, was not certain as to whether or not he really minded if Lutterworth became Something Nasty. It might be preferable, particularly if the Something Nasty had no voice.

Ellery noticed the increasingly heated scene between the New York Gold and his bond-mate's parent. Atalanta looked wretched and Ellery felt again, which had been happening quite often, a spurt of ill temper at Dr. Beck. The man treated his daughter abominably.

Ellery walked up beside Seneca and laid a hand on the little dragon's head. "*Quietus*," he said softly. This was a soothing spell used at Incubatories when dragonets became over-excited.

It worked instantly. Seneca, who had been trying to rear up on his back legs as if he were about to spring at Dr. Beck, subsided.

"I wouldn't worry about the cost of feeding Miss Beck's new companion," Ellery said in as pleasant a tone as he could muster to Dr. Beck. "There are subsidies available to people who have bonded with dragons that will help feed and house them. The government here appreciates dragons and their riders. Miss Beck and her dragon might even obtain a position with the government. And as for housing, a dragon can be perfectly happy with a sand wallow and a canvas cover. Nicholas has informed me that even Montgomery Ward features a very nice dragon shelter in its catalogue at a reasonable price. I would be very happy to come and create a ley line warmed wallow for Miss Beck, *gratis*."

Dr. Beck looked taken aback. "But it's dangerous!" he said "Did you not see how it looked at me?"

"You were making Atalanta unhappy!" said Seneca. "And I am not an it! I am a male and my name is Seneca!"

"Seneca?" Dr. Beck repeated blankly.

"After our college, Papa," Atalanta said. She was most grateful to Dr. Delamar. Her father seemed to have run out of steam in mid-tirade under the influence of his calm and reasonable demeanor. However, knowing her father as well as she did, this would not be the last of it. He would disapprove of Seneca merely because the dragon would take her attention from his needs.

"Is everything all right?" Nicholas came up to them. looking concerned. He had seen the agitated dragonet.

"I was just about to tell Miss Beck about the government's dragon program," said Ellery.

Nicholas smiled. "It's a great program," he said enthusiastically. "It enables people who ordinarily could not support a dragon to do so and benefits the government as well. We've now something much the same in the Six Nations. I can put you in touch with the right agency, Miss Beck, when the expedition is over. In fact, I shall post a letter tonight. The current head of the Federal Agency for Draconic Development is a close friend of my grandfather's and I know him quite well."

"Thank you," said Atalanta gratefully. It seemed her problem was about to be solved and she would not have to face perhaps giving Seneca up for his own good.

"Varian and I are taking *Doña* Marisela back to the *Hacienda*," Nicholas then told Ellery. "We need to get some more meat and she has to break the news about Pacho to her parents. She needs my support. Pacho will have to remain with us for a while at least. It's probably better that way. Erianne and Varian can teach them what they need to know and dragonets do better with dragon companions around them at any rate."

"Aren't you forgetting your promise to Julian, Nick?" Ellery queried.

Nicholas looked horrified. "It went out of my head completely!" he exclaimed. "All I could think about has been the dragonets! He'll have my head on a tray!"

Ellery nodded towards the sky. "And I see Torin coming down. I foresee more fireworks!"

Julian was a fair-mined man, Nicholas thought. Surely when he saw the dragonets he would understand why every other consideration had fled from his brother's mind. Nicholas only hoped that his brother had not actually begun the passing ceremony. He would then be feeling the effects of an aborted ritual and in no mood to be logical and just.

Chapter Twenty One
More Treasure?

"I'm so sorry, Julian," Nicholas began as his brother dismounted from his hippogriffe and took Siofra from her travel basket. "I completely forgot–"

"I can see why," murmured Julian, looking at the dragonets, who having finished eating were immensely curious about this new creature who had landed amongst them. "No matter, Nick," he continued "the boy died naturally this afternoon. It was sudden, but not unexpected."

Something in his voice made Sabrina look at him sharply. "You look exhausted!" she said to her nephew. "How many of those children did you Heal this afternoon?"

"Three of them it was!" Siofra answered for her Wizard. "And he was after guiding the boy to the angels as well, even though 'twas bein' the boy's time to go."

"I should have come," began Nicholas in distress. seeing how heavily fatigue sat on his brother. Guiding, even when the person being helped was at the point of death, was exhausting for the Healer and the support of another magus was always welcome.

"No, I had Ramón," said Julian. "He is really the most extraordinary–" he stopped suddenly, too tired to go on and raised no protest when Sabrina took him by the arm and led him towards the tent he shared with Ellery and Nicholas. They were followed by an interested Eda.

Lutterworth had watched this byplay with a deep frown. "Aren't any of you people going to do what I hired you for?" he demanded. "First thing in the morning we're going back to the site and find that cave!"

"We're more than willing to do that," said Nicholas, turning away from Torin and towards Lutterworth. "I saw a whole network of caves below the surface there, just waiting to be explored. "He did not add that he was looking for more dragon eggs. For him, they were the real treasure.

"Are we going back to the cave, Mama?" inquired Amyas a little fearfully. "I like to be here with you!"

"No, dearling, you'll be staying here with me. All of you will stay here with me," she said, looking down tenderly at him and then fixing a stern glance on the other two dragonets still left, who seemed to think that going back to the cave would mean a jolly play-time.

"Thank you, Erianne," said Nicholas gratefully. He could only imagine what mischief dragonets could get into, roaming through a honeycomb of caves.

"I can see that we missed quite a lot today!" said Torin. The other familiars began to bring him and Siofra up to date as Lupe called out that it was nearly time for *la cena*. Nicholas them left with Marisela to take her home before it grew too late.

Sabrina had long ago learned how to tactfully deal with hired foreign cooks and Lupe had cheerfully agreed to make the food less spicy for the *Señors*.

Even Dr. Beck, inclined to fuss at first, ended in enjoying the *Flautas*: corn *tortillas* stuffed with shredded lettuce, mildly seasoned chicken and barely spiced *salsa*, and then sautéed. She had made a cucumber soup, mild rice and a chopped avocado salad with it. Everyone, even the familiars enjoyed the custardy flan with a golden syrup sauce, that was for dessert. Lutterworth, too, made a good meal, although he kept interrupting everyone's enjoyment of the food by making detailed plans for the next day's work.

Everyone retired early. Julian had eaten some soup and fallen into bed. The events of the day had been rather overwhelming for all and it was shown in the sudden outbreak of yawns and sleepiness.

The dragonets had to be dissuaded from sleeping with their bond-mates. "Dragons sleep out of doors or in a proper dragon pen," said Erianne firmly. Amyas was already curled up under one of her wings and she spread and lifted the other for the rest of them.

Pacho was already mourning the loss of Marisela. He could not understand why she had to leave him. Erianne agreed with Nicholas that Pacho staying with the other dragonets was the best idea. She had heard enough about the people at the *Hacienda* from Varian to know that the dragonet would not be welcome there. And there were no older dragons there to teach him how to go on in proper dragon behavior.

Atalanta woke very abruptly, not knowing what had awoken her.

It was very dark and still. Sabrina was sleeping quietly. Whatever had awoken Atalanta had not disturbed her tent mate.

Unbidden, lines from Sappho came into Atalanta's head:

"The silver moon is spent:
The Pleiades are gone;
Half the long night is spent, and yet
alone I lie."

What had made her think of such a thing? As was any classical scholar she was familiar with the poetry of Sappho, and many others. But it had never jolted her from sleep before.

She had never felt less like going back to sleep. She sat up, and drew up her knees, clasping her arms about them and laying her head down on her knees.

Being an intellectual, methodical person, she decided to analyze why she suddenly was filled with a restless longing and awoken with an ancient poem echoing in her mind. So much had happened today....

Finally she tracked it down. When they were swimming, Sabrina had told her that she was actually a widow, that her husband had died before they had even been married for a year.

And now Atalanta remembered the feeling of envy that had come over her. At least Sabrina had known love. She had truly mattered to someone.

A birthday was coming up soon for Atalanta. She would be thirty-five. An old maid, as her mother often sighed. That was another reason Atalanta preferred working for her father at his excavations. Her mother's reproaches about why she had not married and given them grandchildren were even harder to bear than her father's demands.

But other than ribald jests at some of the digs no man had ever paid any attention to her. She had never been kissed or courted. And truthfully, for she was always very honest with herself, she had loathed the social situations that her mother reveled in. In spite of her many illnesses her mother still managed to attend teas and parties and gatherings of many kinds, even when she was exhausted by such events. When Atalanta was at home, during the winter when Dr. Beck was teaching, her mother insisted on her company and tried to introduce her to 'suitable' young men. None of them had been interested in her and she had found none of them to her liking. Too many men disapproved of her intelligence and she refused to act stupid, as her mother urged, just to catch a husband.

But she was a normal young woman and more and more lately, she had been thinking of what she had missed.

Suddenly she wanted exercise and air. The camp was safer than the digs she had been on in Greece and the Levant, for Sabrina had explained that it was warded. No one could enter or leave without difficulty. And dragons were the best watchdogs there were. With six of them now in camp it would be a daring thief or robber indeed who would disturb them.

Atalanta threw aside her bedclothes and found her slippers and robe. The slippers were always placed neatly by the side of the bed and the robe draped over the foot.

Sabrina, with Flann curled beside her, slept still deeply. As Atalanta pulled on the robe one of the cat's eyes opened briefly, looked at her, and closed again.

Atalanta tied the sash of her robe about her waist and pulled the long braid of her hair out from beneath it. She slid her feet into the waiting slippers and left the tent.

It was a beautiful star spangled night or what was left of it, for in the east it was lightening. The time was near dawn.

The air was cool and she shivered a little. But at the same time the chill was rather bracing, like an autumn day at home. Later, of course, it would be much warmer.

"Good morning," came a voice. "Couldn't sleep?"

A little startled, she looked towards the ley line fire and saw Dr. Delamar, who she surmised, had been sitting there in the shadows. "I've made some tea," he said. "Would you care for a cup?"

"Thank you," she said gratefully and joined him at the fireside. "I woke up and felt in need of air." She sat down on one of the handy rocks and took the cup he handed her. "Did you awaken early as well?"

"I am always up with the dawn. I like watching the sun come up. It's not as dramatic here as it is in Egypt but it's beautiful nonetheless. One can see at dawn why the legend of golden cities arose," Ellery answered. "If you like, I shall show you how this rock turns into a castle of gold."

"I would like that," she said a little shyly and sipped at her tea. It was strong and sweet, without milk, and warmed her from onside out. Tea made by the English was somehow different than American made tea.

To Ellery she seemed altered this morning. Softer perhaps was the best description. Her hair was down and her eyes seemed larger without the heavy spectacles. She looked younger and far more vulnerable.

Seeing this vulnerability made him say abruptly, "Miss Beck, if you should ever need a situation, particularly now that you have a dragon that Dr. Beck does not seem to welcome, I would like to offer you a position on my staff. Seneca would always be welcome as well."

"But I am not an Egyptologist," she said, staring at him, surprised.

"But you are a scholar, trained in archeological techniques," he said. "You can learn Egyptology." He hesitated from mentioning the main reason he made the offer. Watching the way her father treated her set his teeth on edge. Having bonded with Seneca was only bound to make her life worse.

"You would actually accept a female on your staff?" she queried.

"Your father—" he began.

"My father, Dr. Delamar, does not count me as *staff*," she said, her mouth twisting wryly. "I am not paid, or even acknowledged most of the time. Anything I have learned is held to be an anomaly of nature, a freak, since of course, females cannot be classical scholars. But since funding is always a consideration of any of our expeditions, my father accepts my help because many times there is no one else to be had."

He swore, causing Atalanta to raise her eyebrows.

"If you ever wish to come to me, I can guarantee that you will be valued. Ask my sister if I do not think of her and treat her s a colleague," he said sincerely.

"Thank you," she said, touched and honored. "I do thank you so very much."

"Now, come with me," he said. "The sun will be up in a few minutes and I want you to see it."

She put down her tea cup and rose. She took the arm he offered, as the ground was rough and she wore but thin slippers.

Ellery lead her to the place he had discovered the very first morning, where the rising sun gilded the cliffs. They stood and waited together. It seemed natural to Atalanta to keep her hand on his arm.

The sky began to lighten and the first rays of the sun began to touch the area.

"Thy rising is beautiful in the horizon of Heaven,O Aten, ordainer of life. Thou dost shoot up in the horizon of the east, thou fillest every land with thy beneficence. Thou art beautiful and great and sparkling and exalted above every land. Thy arrows envelope everywhere all the lands which thou hast made."

Ellery quoted as the sun grew stronger and the walls of *El Morro* shone like gold in the new light.

"That is the hymn to Aten, the sun, is it not, written by the Pharaoh they call the Heretic?" Atalanta said.

"And you are not an Egyptologist, Miss Beck?" He quirked an eyebrow at her.

"I've read all your books, and others besides," she admitted. Turning the subject she said, "I can see why the Spanish thought that there might be a city of gold here," She looked with appreciation at the cliffs before them. "It's beautiful. Thank you for showing it to me. But I'd better go and get ready. My father as well as Seneca, will be wanting breakfast soon."

He stood looking after her as she hurried away. It was a shame and a crime the way she was treated.

Once again Lutterworth was incensed. Julian was returning to the children again today and when Lutterworth found that Erianne was to remain behind to nursemaid the dragonets as well his rage knew no bounds. He had counted on the green dragon for digging.

Both Ellery and Nicholas ignored him, each seeming intent on his own thoughts. Sabrina was busy making certain that the dragonets would have enough food. They would be eating up the last of the tinned food for their breakfast. More freshly butchered cows were to be delivered this morning, and Marisela was to come with them. Sabrina had decided to stay behind. Feeding hungry dragonets was more to her taste than spending much more time in Lutterworth's company and she would have Marisela's help and companionship as well.

Nicholas, of course, wanted to go to the caves to search for more dragon eggs and he was the logical person to do that. Sinclair was to remain behind as well. Lutterworth was expecting some return telegrams. Someone was to ride over from Albuquerque if there were answers today and some one had to be here to receive them. Sabrina thought that Sinclair looked relieved.

Dr. Beck did not seem happy to go cave exploring but he was obedient to Lutterworth's demands. Lutterworth, after all, was paying the bills.

Since Varian had a six person saddle it was not necessary to make more than one trip out to the caves. The dragon was able to carry the necessary digging and lighting equipment and his passengers with no trouble.

The mage lights that Nicholas had created yesterday still hung in the air illuminating the big open cave. In the shadows, at the edges, could be seen many openings that Varian claimed led to other caves. Dragons had a feel for caves. When they were feral, caves had been their homes and most dragons still enjoyed caves and liked to explore them.

These limestone caves were particularly large. They were both high and wide, complete with stalactites, stalagmites, and columns, and all other sorts of weird creations made by water dripping for millennia against the stone. Many of the formations were grotesque and could almost be imagined to be strange and dangerous creatures by persons blessed with an active imagination.

Lutterworth had no imagination. All he could see was the potential for treasure. "There are five openings on this side alone," he said. pointing to the back of the cavern. "We'll each take one, explore and then come back and tackle the rest. Even Miss Beck can find a cave by herself."

Ellery vetoed this at once. "The potential for getting lost is too great. We should split into two parties. I shall take one and Nick the other. We can magically mark our path in so that we may easily find a way out. Who knows how many branches there might be to this cave? Only Varian can explore by himself. He won't get lost no matter how convoluted the trail."

"May I have a lantern, Ellery?" asked the dragon. "You can hang it on one of my horns."

The lanterns that had been brought along were special lanterns, made to hold a mage light. This was a strong pure white light and would burn until the spell was ended. Ellery lit one and hung it on one of Varian's horns. Dragons saw better than humans did in the dark but centuries of dwelling out in the light and away from the darkness found in caves had made them more light dependent.

Varian took of at once to the middle passage, a high and wide route.

The rest of them divided into two parties, Nicholas heroically offering to take Lutterworth, while the Becks stayed with Ellery. Cillian was on Nicholas's shoulder while Bairre rode on Ellery's.

To the left of the pile of dragon eggs was a narrow opening and down this way Nicholas led Lutterworth. The railroad baron was armed with a mage lantern and when his coat swung open Ellery saw that he wore a gun strapped to his waist in cowboy fashion.

Nicholas led the way, the tip of his wand lit and held aloft at its brightest. "Two hours, Nick," Ellery called after him "and we'll rendezvous back here."

"Two hours!" Nicholas called back, his voice echoing eerily back from the opening.

Ellery then led the Becks to the right of the eggs where another opening gaped darkly. Like Nicholas had begun to do, Ellery left a luminous trail behind them as they went in.

Dr. Beck was inclined to grumble beneath his breath but he followed Ellery's lead and obeyed the order to stay close together.

At first it was very dark, illuminated only by the light from Ellery's wand and the mage lanterns carried by Atalanta and her father. The light showed the usual twisted, drip style formations seen in the main cave, but in a tighter, meandering passage.

"It's awfully dark," said Bairre in Ellery's ear. He was holding rather tightly onto the collar of Ellery's jacket.

"You've been in darker places," Ellery returned. "Just think of the pyramids."

"True," said Bairre, "and this cave smells better. But all the same I don't really like this. There could be anything hiding in here, some sort of wild animal! Those shadows look a lot like dangerous creatures such as a basilisk!"

"Or a Minotaur, like the one in the labyrinth in Crete, that Theseus slew," Atalanta suggested.

"Myths and legends!" scoffed Dr. Beck. "That is why the female mind is totally unsuited to science–romanticism always creeps in!"

A strange, all too familiar feeling was beginning to creep over Ellery and he suddenly stopped. Both Atalanta and Dr. Beck bumped into him.

"What are you about, Delamar?" demanded Dr. Beck petulantly. "Give me some warning–"

Ignoring her father Atalanta came forward and took Ellery's arm. "What is it?" she said anxiously. "Do you feel something?"

"Blood," he muttered. "Blood. Death..." The wand, which he had held aloft came down suddenly and ahead of them, something flashed green fire.

"Look!" Bairre cried and leaped from Ellery's shoulder to run ahead.

They could see him digging eagerly at something on the floor in the combined light of the wand and the mage lanterns. Dr. Beck moved closer, holding up the lantern to

213

light Bairre's progress, his eyes gleaming with curiosity and excitement.

Atalanta was more concerned about Ellery. He leaned back against the wall of the cave as if it were difficult to remain on his feet. His eyes were closed and his head was sunk on his chest. The still lit wand hung from a limp hand.

"I've got it!" Bairre called out excitedly. Using his nose and his paws he pushed his find to Dr. Beck's feet.

Dr. Beck bent and picked it up, giving an exclamation of surprise and awe.

It was a large, crudely cut emerald.

Chapter Twenty Two
The Light and the Darkness

Prudence had thought that she would never be able to stop crying. As was expected, she helped sister Rebecca lay out the small body of Tomaso for burial, while the Reverend Brewer intoned prayers over the departed. But all the while tears trickled down the Handmaiden's face. Even a sharp rebuke from the Reverend, that this child of sin had gone to a better place and that she should be rejoicing, not drowned in sorrow, had done nothing to stop the flow of tears.

She had been so distressed when the doctor had not been able to cure Tomaso as he had the others. She could not accept that the boy was beyond any aid. Though Tomaso himself was sinking fast, and prepared, even longing for death, she could not be resigned the fact of his dying.

Even the ritual which had followed, and feeling the presence of what she knew had to be a heavenly being, had not reconciled her to the boy's passing.

There had been no chance to talk to the doctor, to protest his letting the boy die. He had left rather abruptly on his strange feathered mount. Caught up in her own sorrow, Prudence had not seen what the afternoon's work had cost Julian.

She also did not see what effect the Ritual had upon the Reverend Brewer.

Like the others, the Reverend had felt the presence and even thought he heard the rustle of great wings. He had fallen to his knees and covered his face in awe when the pure light had begun to grow around the boy as he had breathed his last in the doctor's arms.

Peering between his fingers, the Reverend had seen the moment when the boy's soul had passed into the care of the angels and he had been filled, not with a sense of peace and love, but with a jealous rage.

He was the man of God, properly ordained! *He* should be the one to call up angels, to bask in the Holy Light. And what made it even worse was that the so-called physician had been assisted by a native, by one of an inferior race, who was not even a proper Christian! The native had been allowed within that   glowing Circle. It was obvious that a minister should have been there instead, offering up prayer and then able to commune with that celestial Light!

Such hatred filled his being that it physically affected him. His hands shook and his heart beat loud in his ears and it grew difficult to breathe.

All his life he had been certain that since he had been called to the ministry that one day he would be able to work miracles and be at one with God. It was just a matter of waiting and being as pious as he could be.

But now this interloper, a man who he still suspected of being in league with the Prince of Darkness, had usurped all of his position. Even his helpers at the mission now looked at this stranger as they had used to look at him, their spiritual guide and leader. For even Brother Ezekiel had been won over when he had felt the attendance of the divine being.

And the women! Reverend Brewer had always known females to be the weaker vessels but these two had shown them selves to be weaker than most. They were enthusiastic supporters, with their instant obedience to any of the doctor's commands. He had thought at least Sister Rebecca had better sense.

To think that he had considered honoring Prudence Cromwell with his hand in marriage! She had seemed so suitable–her parents were high in the Covenanter hierarchy: her father a deacon of the church, her mother a deaconess, her grandfathers on both sides men of the cloth. She was even distantly connected to the founder of the Covenanters, Oliver Cromwell, who had brought them from England three hundred years earlier in search of religious freedom and safety from the pernicious influence of magic and magicians in the British Isles. Prudence was young and even attractive, and could be trained out of any flightiness by hard work and prayer. She was the right age to be molded into a proper wife for a man of God.

But after seeing the wanton way she had followed that limb of Stan about, hanging on his lips, with her eyes as bright as stars, Reverend Brewer wanted nothing to do with her. She was unworthy of the distinction of being his bride.

And today, as it had been every day, that charlatan was to come and Heal the remaining children and he would have to somehow stand seeing his followers fawn on the man. It was past all bearing.

Something would have to be done about the situation.

It was very early for either Brother Daemon or Brother Satyr to be at the ice cave, but they had plans to discuss and no place else was as private.

Both had journeyed to the cave by round-about routes, careful not to be seen. This was another good reason to make this meeting as early as possible. Few people would be about this time of the morning.

They both wore their robes and rings, even though there was to be no Work done today. There was not even a woman present. Brother Daemon in particular, was disappointed by this. The last whore had been so satisfying.

In spite of the early hour, Brother Satyr poured them a large measure of a very fine brandy. Brother Satyr liked his comforts and the brandy was poured into balloon glasses of fine crystal.

The brandy sent warming fire through the veins. The cave was cold without any pleasurable activities to warm one's bones. The ride here, in the chill of just after dawn, had been cold as well.

The two men lingered over their brandy until Brother Satyr said at last "All precedes apace. Our plans will soon come to fruition. I have had communication from the Brotherhood as well. They are with us, if we can deliver the promised goods."

Brother Daemon said doubtfully, "But how? It will take money as well as guns and men. You have a fortune of your own but I–"

"Do you think that I will spend my own money on this scheme? I am willing to take the risks with everything but my fortune. Should this enterprise fail I will still be able to live the life I enjoy, even though it might have to be somewhere else, " said Brother Satyr complacently. "If we win out, which we cannot fail to do, given the support of the Evil One himself, we both will be rich, heaped with honors and glory." He paused and swirled the brandy around in the glass, watching the patterns it made on the sides of the crystal. "No, I have two plans for an alternate source of monies for financing our design. Are you aware that there are treasure hunters at *El Morro*? They are searching for Coronado's gold."

"Coronado's gold?" said Brother Daemon in disbelief. "Every child knows that it does not exist!"

"Were you aware that they found a very fine piece of jewelry there?" said Brother Satyr softly. "Old legends are often correct, my brother. Where there is one piece, there are probably more. If they do find something I intend it to be ours, not go to some *Norteaméricano!*"

"How do you know this?" Brother Daemon wanted to know.

He could not see the slow smile that spread itself over Brother Satyr's features, for the drawn up hood hid his face well. "Oh, I have my sources," said Brother Satyr in a voice that sent a chill down the smaller man's spine.

"And there is a second wellspring of funds just waiting to be tapped. All that is required is a little ingenuity on my part to obtain it," Brother Satyr continued. "I anticipate no problems in that, however. More brandy?"

Brother Daemon pushed his glass forward. "And the rest of it? When does it come off?"

"Sister Diabla tells me that the time will be right in the next few days for her little ceremony," Brother Satyr said as he poured a good measure in each glass. "And then I think that the next few weeks will see the rest take place. By the beginning of the summer things should be well in train. If everything goes as we planned, by autumn all should be complete."

Brother Daemon shivered in delight. Not only did the end of all they had been planning excite him but Sister Diabla's ritual was so erotic! Although the Sister herself was physically unprepossessing she brought an eagerness and an expertise to the Rituals that was irresistible. She truly enjoyed every minute of them.

"Drink up, Brother, until we meet again. I will send you word when we shall join with Sister Diabla," said Brother Satyr.

Brother Daemon envied his superior. From what he had let drop, he had access to Sister Diabla at all times. Sometimes that visions in his brain about what they might be doing together caused Brother Daemon to wake up at night in a hot sweat of desire.

They drained the glasses and departed separately, again carefully, so that no one could see, fetching their horses from the shallow overhang they had been hidden beneath and from there to ride off in opposite directions.

Once again Ramón was eagerly awaiting Julian's coming. Not even seeing the strength that was drawn from his new teacher for the Healing power had dissuaded Ramón from wanting to learn more, to be able to do that kind of Healing.

Prudence too, was waiting. Her eyes were less swollen as Sister Rebecca had made her lie down with a cloth dipped in lavender on her forehead and a packet of cool soothing herbs on her eyelids.

She had fed Ramón and even offered a plate to his vulpine companion, who turned it down.

Julian had explained to Ramón that one ought to eat a good meal before attempting Healing as it sapped the strength so utterly. Ramón had expressed a worry to Tadeo, yesterday evening, that good food might not always be available.

But Gian-nah-tah had calmly stated that Ramón was not to concern himself with minor matters like that.

Tadeo had stared at the fox in consternation. "You are *loco*, fox!" he said, tapping himself on the forehead in the age-old gesture denoting lunacy. "Who is going to give us good food? Today we are having tortillas again, with little inside them, unless Nan-kah-yen returns with a buffalo!" The blue dragon had not yet come back from his hunting trip to the Great Plains.

"What you need will be provided," said the fox.

Tadeo threw up his hands and gave up. Perhaps

Ramón was right; perhaps the fox was a spirit and knew things that they could not know. He just wished that the fox would not make statements that seemed to have no way of becoming truth.

"My teacher has promised to come with me to our camp here and Heal those who are sick," said Ramon happily. "Soon I will know how to Heal, Tadeo, and I can take care of us."

Privately, Tadeo thought that their tribe needed a great deal more than Healing of minor illnesses. They needed work and food and knowledge. But he felt for Ramón as if the other were his brother and he was not about to tread on his dreams.

"It's a regular delegation you have waiting for you, Julian," said Torin cheerfully as he began the descent. They were so close to the mission that he had flown slowly and low and so was able to converse with his rider.

Indeed it was. Ramón awaited them, a look of eager expectancy on his face. Prudence Cromwell waited as well, her face painted with anxiety. Sister Rebecca and Brother Ezekiel stood on the steps of the mission, looking happy to see him. The only one not in evidence was the Reverend Brewer.

Today would see the Healing of the final two children. Julian had given his word to Ramón that they would then go and see his tribe and see what might be done for them. It sounded from Ramón's descriptions that they suffered from only minor illnesses. An afternoon's work that would be and then he would be free to concentrate on Ramón's training. In a week or less the Healed children could go home and leave the mission, unless the Reverend Brewer dug in his heels and refused to let possible converts go back where they belong. Julian would have something to say about that if it proved true.

Prudence hurried up to Torin, barely allowing the hippogriffe to land before she was saying "I have to talk to you!" in an urgent voice to Julian.

"Mistress Cromwell!" Sister Rebecca called sharply.

"Let the doctor be. He has work to do!"

"It's quite all right, ma'am," said Julian. The girl was distressed. On the periphery of his consciousness yesterday he had acknowledged her pain at the boy's death but he had been simply too exhausted after three teaching Healings and a death-bed to do anything for her. There were calming spells a Healer could use for distressed family members and others who shared a death watch (used with the person's permission of course) but he had not anticipated such a depth of grief from any of the missionaries. Ramón, who had known the boy from the moment of his birth, was far more stoical about Tomaso's passing. In the mines, one saw death far too often and many times it was a mercy.

Julian dismounted and took Siofra from her travel basket, placing the little cat on his shoulder. "I'll be right there," he said to Ramón. "Would you please unsaddle Torin so that he can roll and sleep comfortably?"

Torin had wasted no time in getting on terms with Gian-na-tah, who then made the hippogriffe known to Ramón. Ramón was inclined to be frightened of the strange creature at first, but Gian-nah-tah accepted him so placidly and Torin was so friendly that soon Ramón found himself talking with Torin quite naturally. Now the native American was quite glad to be able to do something for his *maestro*, his master/teacher, as he had begun to call Julian, which embarrassed that gentleman no end.

Julian led Prudence away, out of sight of the mission house, almost to the pool where Ramón had bathed.

"What is it?" he asked when he thought that they were private enough.

"Why did you let Tomaso die?" she cried. "You Healed all the others, why did you not help him? Didn't he deserve to live as well?" New tears sparkled on her lashes and her cheeks were flushed with her passion.

"My dear girl," Julian began.

Prudence stamped her foot, "Don't talk down to me!" she spat. "Tell me why you let him die!"

"Even magic has its limits, Miss Cromwell," he said quietly. "Tomaso was far sicker than any of the others. I will not perform an autopsy on him but I would be willing to wager that he had an underlying weakness of the lungs even before he was sickened by the dust and bad air in the mine."

"He was after having no health in his lungs at all," put in Siofra, who had helped her Wizard write up his notes on the case. "There was bein' no healthy tissue for the Healin' to work on."

But you didn't even try to Heal him!" Prudence protested. "Surely if you had tried–!"

"I am not God, Miss Cromwell," said Julian gently. She really was upset. It was not the first time that a non-magical person failed to understand that even magic could only do so much. "I cannot work miracles, however it might seem. I am fortunate enough to have been born with Healing powers, given to me by the Light, but that does not mean that everyone I try to help will be helped. Sometimes, when a patient is as ill as Tomaso, all I can do is help guide them into the care of the angels and to make that passing as easy as possible. Tomaso knew he was going to die. He was ready."

"He was even lookin' forward to bein' with his Ma again," said Siofra.

Prudence burst into tears. Somehow she ended up in Julian's arms, with her head on his shoulder. "I never saw anyone die before," she sobbed. "And it is so unfair! A little boy like that who had no chance to live, to be a child instead of a slave!"

Siofra said a little sarcastically. "And who has been after tellin' ye that life is fair?" But she reached a velvet paw forward and wiped a trail of tears from the part of Prudence's face that was not buried against Julian. "Let her cry it out," she added kindly. "I'll be chaperone, for 'tis doubtful that Sister Rebecca will be approvin' of this!"

Don Casimiro was again hiding in his library. There had been a great stir and bustle in the house since early morning. After coming in late last night with no reasonable explanation of where she had been, Marisela had been locked in her room by her mother.

Today was the day that Marisela was to be measured

for her *ajuar,* her bride clothes. The dressmaker from Albuquerque had arrived at nearly dawn, complete with a wagon full of bolts of fine fabrics, trims, laces, a sewing machine and an assistant.

Don Casimiro was anticipating another shouting match as the stubborn girl refused to admit that she was going to marry *Don* Rafael and there was an end to it. He was certain that once she was wed, and saw the advantages to being the wife of a wealthy *caballero,* and once there were children, she would thank her parents for making her honor their choice.

But when *Doña* Milagros had gone above stairs to let Marisela out of her confinement, the girl was nowhere to be found.

Then the shouting had truly begun, as *Doña* Milagros accused everyone from Marisela's maid to the cook of letting the girl out when the orders had been that she was to remain in her room.

Her horse was discovered to be missing from the stable but *Don* Casimiro had refused to take any of the *vaqueros* from their work to look for his daughter. Last night Marisela had told him that the beef order to the camp at *El Morro* was to be substantially increased and old Curro and his man were needed to go to the high plain and bring down more of the vast herds of the *hacienda* that were ready to be butchered. The gold that would be received when the cattle were delivered was far more important that another of Marisela's wild starts. The girl would return when she was over her fit of the sulks. The seamstress could wait. It was not as if she was going to be paid. *Don* Casimiro hoped to foist off the bills for Marisela's finery onto her new husband.

Don Casimiro was reading a favorite prose volume of Lope de Vega, *El peregrino en su patria,* when the old butler knocked on the door and announced in his quavering voice, "Don Rafael begs a moment of your time, *Señor.*"

Casimiro was surprised. It was not yet ten. Surely this was an early hour for *Don* Rafael to be abroad?

Nonetheless he made his future son-in-law welcome, offering him a seat and a glass of wine.

Rafael seemed delighted at something and could scarcely contain himself, waiting for the polite routine that the two men went through as wine was offered, accepted and poured.

"I have received the most incredible news," Rafael began at last. "And who better to share it with than those who are to become family? An elderly relation has died in Spain, a relation of whose existence I hardly knew. I am his heir!"

"*More money in his pocket,* thought Casimiro rather sourly. *Why could he, Casimiro, not have a rich old relative that would die and leave him everything?*

"Not only is there a substantial fortune left to me, but there is a title as well!" Rafael continued happily. "You see before you the new *Marqués* de Venegas!"

Casimiro congratulated him insincerely, trying not to sound too envious.

"Of course, this changes everything," continued Rafael. "We had spoken of an autumn bridal, but I must go to Spain almost immediately and lay claim to the title. There are many papers to be signed and legal matters to be attended to. And naturally I would wish to take my bride with me. She will no doubt be presented at Court, in Madrid. Could we be wed within the month?"

"Within the month?" Casimiro sputtered in surprise. "The women would never agree! There are too many preparations....No, it is impossible!"

"I am prepared to expedite all matters with a suitable application of gold. What woman would not like to see her daughter a *Marquesa* and an ornament of the Court? I have no idea when I shall be returning to *Nueva España*. It might be years before I come back and by then your daughter may not be marriageable." He smiled silkily at *Don* Casimiro.

Faced with the possibility of an old maid daughter, Casimiro managed to overcome all his objections and found that *Don* Rafael was even willing to pay for the bride clothes.

There was only the mater of Marisela's *dote*, or dowry. This was a discussion that had been a source of dread. Her *dote* was small and shrinking in value.

To Casimiro's joy *Don* Rafael was willing to give up all claim to the *dote* in exchange for a deed, the deed to the old silver mine that had not been worked in over two years.

Suddenly it seemed too simple. "That mine is probably played out," Casimiro said. "You will not come back years from now, claiming that you have been cheated?"

Rafael laughed. "My dear Casimiro, I am become one of the wealthiest men in Spain! Her *dote* is but a token. It is Marisela herself I want, her beauty and wild heart. She will cause a sensation in Madrid, properly dressed, of course. I will be quite content with the deed to the silver mine."

Without further protest *Don* Casimiro shook hands and agreed to meet the next day in Albuquerque at the office of Rafael's *abogado,* to sign the final papers. Marisela would be married and off his hands in less than a month. And at a very low price to him.

Chapter Twenty Three
In the Caves

Nicholas paid little attention to Lutterworth's mutterings and curses behind him as they ventured deeper into the cave passage. It was rather rough going: it was a narrow passage and the various dripstones, the stalactites and stalagmites and other forms, were thick. There were pillars and columns and even the gravity defying helictites with their twig-like projections that looked almost like trees, intent on escaping from the walls, but frozen for all eternity. These were quite delicate. Lutterworth shattered some with his outstretched hand as he tripped and swore, sending the shards to the cave floor.

At any other time Nicholas might have been fascinated with the weirdly beautiful formations in the cave. It was like lacework or intricate carving wherever one looked. Chandelier like formations hung from the ceiling and the columns might have been sculpted by a Baroque artist. There were waterfalls of stone and even patterns that reminded Nicholas of frost. On the floor were sheets of flowstone, looking like an ocean tide, stilled permanently at the very moment of lapping up on the shore.

But Nicholas could not stop thinking about Marisela.

When he had left her last evening she had insisted on being put down some distance from the *Hacienda*. He had planned on seeing her parents with her when she told them of her acquisition of a dragon. He could explain the many advantages of having a dragon, acquaint them with the government programs that would help pay for Pacho's keep, and help reconcile them to the notion.

But she had not wanted him to come in with her and was evasive as to why she did not want his support.

All he could think about was Lupe's mention of *Don Rafael*. Lupe seemed to think that Marisela was to marry this man. In spite of Marisela's dismissal of this Nicholas was still uneasy.

When they had talked so easily to one another, she had informed him that she was only twenty, not yet of age. Could her father compel her to marry the man of his choice?

Even back home Nicholas had heard of arranged marriages, particularly amongst the nobility. And Marisela's family was of the *Hildago* class. Presumably they married other members of the nobility, not for love but to increase their holdings in land, in wealth, in short, making a suitable alliance, something that those in his family cared little about. They had all married for love, giving little thought to social status or fortune.

It made Nicholas feel sick to think of Marisela given to some man she had described as an idiot. She deserved better than that. She deserved some one who would love and understand her.

Behind him Lutterworth stumbled and cursed yet again.

"Hold your lantern a little higher and it will cast more light in front of you," said Cillian. He rode on a quilted pad on Nicholas's shoulder.

"I don't need advice from a talking pincushion!" Lutterworth growled.

Cillian chuckled. He was not insulted. He found this attitude amusing. Non-magical people often wondered how any one could keep a hedgehog as a familiar. They seemed to think that a hedgehog's quills were the same as a porcupine's. They were not. They were not barbed (or even poisonous) and could not easily be removed from the hedgehog. A hedgehog could defend himself by rolling onto a ball and presenting the spines to an enemy. However, most hedgehogs ran from danger, for they could run quite fast and climb as well. And naturally Cillian would never hurt Nicholas with his quills. They knew how to interact with one another.

"I don't think there's anything here," said Lutterworth in disgust. He finally raised the lantern higher. "Look at this!" he went on. "It's getting to be a stone jungle in here! These damn rocks are so close together! I don't think anyone's ever been through here, even two hundred years ago!"

Nicholas had to agree. The further they had gone into this cave, the lower it had become and the more confined. The lace of the dripstones had grown more profuse. Up ahead it was obvious that only a small adult or a child could wind his way through.

He leveled his wand and said *"Explorare"* and the

image that came back to him was that of stone and stone alone, ending in a blank wall.

"The cave ends just up ahead," he told Lutterworth.

"You can tell that with your damned wand?" Lutterworth sputtered. "Then why the hell don't you just stand in the central cavern and do that?"

"Because there is no spell that will tell me if there is a treasure in any cave. We don't know what form this treasure takes—"

"It's more than likely gold," Lutterworth interrupted him impatiently.

"But is it buried, in a chest, or even in a lead lined box? Any of those will give a false reading, what we call an anomaly," Nicholas explained. "The wand can tell me if there is something besides stone, but not exactly what it is. For that you need to actually see it. If it is buried in the ground I would not even get an anomaly until we were almost on top of it."

"And exploring caves is fun!" added Cillian. Hedgehogs, who slept in dens in the wild, were quite comfortable underground.

Lutterworth shot him a glance of purest aversion. He did not know which of the animals he disliked the most: this walking cactus, the know-it-all ferret, those mouthy cats, or those damned dragons. They all had too much to say and got too much encouragement from what Lutterworth thought of as their owners. Animals, like children and women, ought to be seen and not heard.

"Why can't you use that thing like a dowser does?" Lutterworth demanded, pointing at the wand. "I saw a water dowser once. It was the damndest thing I ever saw. He had a bent twig that led him straight to water. Why can't you Wizards do something like that with treasure?"

"Magic is not all powerful, Mr. Lutterworth," Nicholas began. "It has its limitations—"

"Excuse me, Nicholas, but some one is shouting for help," Cillian said urgently. He had very keen hearing and a sharp sense of smell, unlike his poor eyesight that necessitated his wearing spectacles.

"They found it!" said Lutterworth excitedly. "They need help moving it!" He turned and took off at a stumbling run.

"He'll kill himself trying to hurry like that through these rocks," said Cillian placidly.

"I hope he does!" Nicholas muttered. He kept to a fast walk as he followed the luminous trail back to the main cavern. There were all sorts of side passages. He hoped Lutterworth had the sense to follow the trail provided. Nicholas had no desire to spend time searching for a lost Lutterworth.

When they arrived back at the main cavern where the eggs had been found Nicholas found his uncle slumped on a rock, with Bairre at his feet and supported by Atalanta. Ellery's eyes were closed and he looked none too well. Dr. Beck looked miffed and Lutterworth, with a look of greed on his face was holding an good sized stone as green as a leprechaun's eyes. Varian, too, had heard the cry for help and had hurried from his cave.

Nicholas knelt beside Ellery. "What happened to him?" he asked Atalanta, and moved to take some of his uncle's limp weight from her.

"It was so sudden," she explained. "one moment we were walking along, talking about labyrinths and the next minute he fell back against the wall and began muttering about blood and death and then Bairre found that stone," she said with a nod at the emerald.

"Properly cut, it might be as much as twenty carats!" exulted Lutterworth.

Nicholas wondered that Lutterworth did not pull a jeweler's loupe from his pocket and check the stone for flaws.

"Why did you people stop searching for the rest of it?" Lutterworth demanded, finally taking his greedy gaze from the emerald. "There had to be more! This probably was dropped."

"I was far more concerned with Dr. Delamar!" said Atalanta stiffly.

Lutterworth made a gesture of impatience. "You could have kept looking!" He turned on Dr. Beck.

"Search a dark, strange cave by myself?" the classical scholar said in outrage." I think not, sir! What if I were to be lost and wander for days beneath the earth? When you presented me with this proposition nothing was said about caves! Archaeologists *dig*, they do not rummage about in caves!" This was not precisely true, for many exciting archaeological discoveries had been made in caves, but Dr. Beck had been feeling increasingly uncomfortable in the caverns. What if another part of it collapsed on top of them? He did not find the rock shapes interesting, but thought them grotesque. He could see no beauty in them. It was hard to breathe down here as well.

"Nick, I think we ought to get Ellery back to camp so that he can lay down and perhaps have Julian see to him," said Varian anxiously. "I know that Erianne would want me to take care of him."

"Isn't someone going to look for the rest of this loot?" Lutterworth yelled. "What the hell am I paying you for?"

Nicholas looked at him in dislike. "I'll stay," he said shortly. "Varian, you take the others back to camp. Ellery does need to lie down and I think Dr. Beck has been down here as much as he can bear."

"Thank you, young man," said Dr. Beck warmly. "I am glad to se that *some* of the members of this expedition have some sense!"

This was agreed to and Varian indicated that he would return to help Nicholas search.

Lutterworth did not want to wait for Varian's return, so Nicholas told his dragon companion that he would leave a trail for him to follow.

The cavern was large enough that Nicholas was able, with Atalanta's help, to secure Ellery, who seemed to be sliding into sleep, to Varian's saddle. Atalanta sat behind him to hold onto him, with Dr. Beck behind her. Varian walked off, carefully instructing his riders to duck their heads as the opening for the ramp Nicholas had created was a trifle low.

Before the dragon was even out of sight Lutterworth was ready to go back into the cavern where the emerald had been found. He thrust the stone into the pocket of his coat and Nicholas could see that he repeatedly put his hand in the pocket, as if caressing the stone and reassuring himself that it was still there.

Lutterworth was content to follow Nicholas, for the light from the tip of his wand, maximized, was far stronger than the mage lantern and illuminated almost every corner of the caverns they traversed.

Marisela often felt thankful that her late brother had treated her as a playmate and companion. She had learned so much from Rodrigo and his loss was a still constant emotional ache.

From him she had learned to shoot, to swim, to ride like a *vaquero,* to use a *lasso* and to handle the cattle. But for one thing he had taught her she was especially grateful, particularly when her mother locked her in her room.

The *Hacienda del Sol* was honeycombed with secret passages. And Rodrigo had found the hidden means to entering them. He had taught their concealed ways to his sister.

Even *Don* Casimiro did not seem to know about them. Rodrigo and Marisela saw no need of informing him. It was too delightful and useful a secret.

When Rodri found the first passage, leading from his bedroom, it was obvious that no one had used it in a very long time. Festooned with cobwebs and dust and sagging walls in some places, it was a place for ghosts and the shivers. But Rodri soon saw the possibilities in it. He had many a nightly adventure after his parents thought him safely in bed.

Now it was Marisela's escape from both boredom and what she saw as unjust imprisonment.

She had been unable to tell her parents about Pacho, for the minute she had arrived home her mother had pounced upon her, full of tearful reproaches that had quickly escalated to a show of temper. Marisela was locked in without her supper, and told to meditate upon the behavior of a proper young lady, one who did not ride about the *hacienda* astride, coming in dirty and windblown and refusing to marry the *caballero* her parents had so wisely chosen for her.

Marisela wasted no time. Scarcely had she heard the key click in the lock and her mother's footsteps go down the hall and then down the stairs when she went to the panel behind the wardrobe and slipped through. The big wardrobe was attached to the wall panel and closed so firmly that no one could see where it opened and the latch was ingeniously hidden in the carving that surmounted the wardrobe.

Lack of supper was no problem. She went to Curro's house and begged a meal of tortillas and beans from his wife. She slept there as well, rolled up in a blanket in front of the fire as she had done many times before.

The first thing in the morning, before almost any one was up, she saddled Vittoria herself (the intelligent animal had come home on his own) and rode back out to *El Morro*. She knew that her mother would not be out of bed much before noon and that the *vaqueros* would be busy going out to bring in more cattle. Her father would not bestir himself to come after her. She would have a good block of time before she was missed.

If she was disappointed that Nicholas had gone off treasure hunting, it was not obvious. Pacho was thrilled to see her and she was just as happy to see him again. She was in time to feed him and listened eagerly to all Sabrina could tell her about the care and feeding of dragons. As far as Sabrina knew there were no books on dragon care available in Spanish and there would be no such thing as a translation table anywhere here. Marisela had to confess that she could not read English very well at all.

In one way Sabrina was glad that the three dragons had bonded to women. It was about time that this had happened in her opinion. But she could see a lot of difficulties ahead for the two other women.

It was not a problem for her. She had the resources to care for a dragon and when she was at home, there was plenty of room for Eda, as there were many dragons, both bonded and employed by the various members of her family.

But Atalanta was already facing the fact that Seneca was going to be a considerable cost to her. Her means were very slender. Sabrina, unlike Nicholas, was not certain that the government would welcome a dragon and his *female* partner. And in Marisela's culture, just a few short years ago, dragons had been proscribed, hunted down and killed or enslaved. Very shrewdly, Sabrina thought that Marisela had found it impossible to tell her parents about her new

233

companion. The girl's evasive answers as to queries about how her parents had reacted to the news confirmed this.

They had scarcely finished the second feeding of the morning and were busy measuring the dragonets for growth when Varian arrived back with Ellery, Atalanta and Dr. Beck.

After seeing Ellery safely bestowed and hastily explaining what had happned Varian took off again.

Mr. Sinclair, who had been talked into dragonet feeding duty, helped get Ellery into bed. He was sleeping naturally now. Sabrina thought it the best thing to just let him sleep.

After her brother was taken care of she went to talk to Atalanta, who had lost no time in first getting her complaining father a cup of tea and then going to Seneca's side. The dragonet was overjoyed that she had returned.

"I cannot understand where these jewels are coming from!" Sabrina said to her friend worriedly. "Is it possible that there is actually a treasure? All the literature and even common sense would seem to be against it!"

"Dr. Delamar spoke of blood and death before the gem was found," Atalanta told her as she petted and made much of Seneca.

"Not more pirates!" Sabrina said, rolling her eyes. The notion of pirates in this area seemed ridiculously far-fetched. "I suppose we won't know until he wakes up. I wish this pyschometry business did not hit him so hard. It seems to be getting worse as well. I shall have to ask Julian if there is anything he can do about it."

She sighed. "I hope that Nicholas does not end in killing Lutterworth. Any court worth its salt would declare it justifiable homicide but why take the chance? Lutterworth is not worth a hangman's noose"

Nicholas was indeed nursing most uncharitable thoughts towards Lutterworth. The man's impatience manifested itself in snarling and sarcasm. When Varian joined them again Lutterworth asked him jeeringly if he had flown the party to China as he had certainly taken long enough to get back.

Varian looked hurt at this, and kept away from Lutterworth. "Don't mind him," said Cillian in Gaelic to the dragon. "He's an ignorant blowhard. I doubt anybody else could have got them there and come back as fast as you did."

"He doesn't know anything about dragons," said Varian in the same language. Nicholas gave him a glance of sympathy.

On and on they went deeper and deeper into the cave. It was getting larger, with a wider corridor and a higher ceiling. At Lutterworth's urging Nicholas had several times used his wand to tell them what was ahead.

There had been several anomalies, which excited Lutterworth no end. But one proved to be the bones of some animals, long dead, and another was a cache of pottery. It was not clear why it was there. It was in very poor shape, for in this part of the cave they could hear dripping water. In places a thin film of it ran over the floor of the cave.

The cave had now become large enough, Nicholas thought, to qualify as a Baroque cathedral. The stonework was certainly elaborate enough. One could almost see the apse and the nave and the angel roof. Lost in this fancy, Nicholas did not see Lutterworth stop until he almost walked into him. Only Cillian's cry of "Look out!" saved them from a collision.

"God damn it all to hell!" Lutterworth swore. "Look at that!"

"That" was a huge rock fall. It must have been twenty feet high and almost as far across. It completely blocked the way ahead.

"Well, you're the Wizard!" Lutterworth said contemptuously to Nicholas. "Do something about this! Wave that damned wand! We're going to go on looking if it means removing every one of these fucking rocks!"

Chapter Twenty Four

Cursed?

Once again Ellery found himself awakening with a face hanging over him. This time it was Sabrina's.

"Good!" she said when she saw his eyes open. "You're back in the same day."

Holding his head, which ached, Ellery sat up. "What was it this time?" he asked crossly. Bairre, who had been sitting on his pillow, scampered across to the bedside table and fetched Ellery's spectacles.

With the donning of these the world came into focus and Ellery saw Atalanta sitting on Julian's cot on the other side of the tent, gravely regarding him.

"It was a large emerald, Ellery!" Bairre answered first. "The light from your wand made it flash and I dug it out of the ground."

"Where is it now?" his Wizard wanted to know.

"I am afraid that Mr. Lutterworth could not be persuaded to part from it," said Atalanta in her dry way.

Sabrina snorted in a most unladylike fashion. "He insisted that the exploration of the caves keep up. Nick, bless his heart, volunteered to keep that jackass busy. Varian returned as well, once he had you and Atalanta and Dr. Beck back here. They are still there, even though it is getting late." She frowned, glancing out at the open flap of the tent, where shadows could be seen to be lengthening.

"Was it a piece of jewelry or a loose stone?" Ellery inquired.

"A large, rough-cut emerald," Atalanta answered. "I am no judge of such things, but it appeared to be rather crude, and about the size of a large thimble. Of course, that is just a guess. I was not allowed to touch it."

Bairre nodded in agreement. "About this big." He made a circle with his paws. Dr. Beck had snatched it away from him as well, and then reluctantly given it up to Lutterworth.

"What did you see, Ellery?" Sabrina wanted to know.

He frowned. "Three men were fighting, quite violently, with swords. They were shouting in Spanish and they looked almost crazed. I got the impression that two of them died and the third perhaps was mortally injured. I'll know more when I can see the gem again."

"I'd rather you did not see it again!" said his sister emphatically. "This pyschometry is getting worse, Ellery! I've never seen it quite as bad as it has been here. It usually never sends you into a swoon! The headaches and dizziness were bad enough!"

"At any rate I doubt Mr. Lutterworth will let any of us anywhere near it," remarked Atalanta.

"Sabrina, I want to know where it came from and even more importantly, how did it get here!" Ellery protested. "The fact is, that such a thing should not be here, any more than that piratical treasure necklace should have been here. Indeed, I can think of far more scenarios to account for the necklace's presence than I can for finding a very large emerald in a limestone cave in this part of the world. If I can advance our knowledge by studying it with my pyschometry I shall not let minor considerations–"

"Minor considerations?" Sabrina interrupted hotly. "Making yourself ill? I intend to ask Julian if there is not some way that this so-called gift of yours cannot be blocked before you do yourself irreparable harm!"

Ellery sat up and put his feet on the ground. "You will do no such thing," he stated, his features set and his eyes determined. "Even were you our mother I would not allow it. I and I alone am responsible for my health. I am not a child. Now," he added firmly, "if you ladies will excuse I have to change," he gestured at his rumpled garments " and perhaps a bath might be in order as well."

Sabrina exchanged a look with Bairre, but she stalked out of the tent, followed by Atalanta, who gave Ellery a look that told him that she agreed with him. Scholarship came first, scholarship and the answer to a mystery that was becoming more intriguing than they had ever suspected.

There was a sensible woman, Ellery thought. There was more than a little to admire in Miss Beck.

"Ellery," began the ferret. "Perhaps Sabrina is right."

"How else are to find out what we need to know?" Ellery said to his familiar. The ferret's black-masked face was concerned. "A little faintness is worth what we well be able to find out."

"If Lutterworth lets you even see the emerald," said Bairre. "The look on his face when he saw it–it was so greedy! Why are some people not content with what they have? He is a wealthy man and yet he always wants more. I don't understand it."

It was difficult for an animal to comprehend the motivations of people, particularly the type of monetary greed that Lutterworth suffered from. Such avarice was not confined to those like Lutterworth who had pulled themselves up by their bootstraps as the saying went. Even people born to wealth could be inflicted by a need for more and more.

"I think perhaps everyone wants something badly, whether it be money or love, or adding to a prized collection," Ellery said thoughtfully.

"I know what you want the most," said Bairre, looking up at his Wizard. "You want knowledge and you are willing to do anything to obtain it."

His familiar was right. He had to *know*. And right now he had to know about the truth of this treasure.

"Well, Stillfield?" said Lutterworth impatiently. "Are you going to move those Goddamned rocks or not?"

"Don't be ridiculous!" said Varian, shocked at his stupidity. "Even with magic Nick cannot move something like that all by himself! Why, there must be twenty ton of rocks there!"

Nicholas had been making minute explorations with his wand and a few muttered spells. Now he said, "You're just about right, Varian. I daresay there is about twenty ton of rock there. It's a deep fall. It looks, from what my wand tells me, that a part of the ceiling crashed in. There is an anomaly in there too–"

"The treasure! I knew it!" Lutterworth declared, his eyes lighting with triumph. "Now move the rocks, damn it!"

"I can't," said Nicholas simply. "It will need all of us, no doubt to move that much stone. Even if I were a geomancer, I doubt I would be able to do it, but the magic of the earth is not my speciality."

"Didn't you learn anything when Nicholas and Sabrina had to rescue Varian?" asked Cillian, peering at Lutterworth through his spectacles. "To move that much rock will take stabilization spells as well as lifting and moving."

"And we shall have to wait for tomorrow for Ellery to recover. We'll probably need Julian as well," Nicholas added.

"I can help by doing some digging from the top," added Varian.

"Not until it is stabilized," said Nicholas firmly, looking sternly at both the dragon and at Lutterworth.

"I want to get in there tonight!" Lutterworth shouted. His face was turning red and he glared angrily at Nicholas.

"It's quite impossible," Nicholas said in as reasonable a voice as he could muster.

"You people have been more than eager to take my money," Lutterworth declared "but what am I getting for it? Delays and more delays! What if I refuse to give the money I promised to your uncle's school? When the Dean or whatever he is gets wind of that being screwed up your uncle will be out of there on his bony British ass!"

Varian snorted, a trail of steam escaping from his nostrils. "Ellery can just make it up to them," he said.

Lutterworth gave a short sharp laugh with no mirth in it. "Where is Delamar going to come up with fifty thousand dollars?" he sneered.

Varian stared at him. "I'm certain that he would be able to do it easily. The current rate of exchange is the pound sterling is 4.86, 6 1/2 to a dollar, which would make it, rounded up for ease, two hundred and fifty thousand pounds on the gold standard. I can give you the exact amount if you like. Ellery has easy access to far more than that."

Nicholas almost laughed aloud at the look on Lutterworth's face at being told rates of exchange by a creature he thought of as just a step above a dumb brute. There were few bankers or businessmen that knew as much about finance, money, rates of exchange, precious metals and stones as a dragon. It was a holdover from the days when each dragon had a hoard of gold, silver and jewels. Now, instead of sleeping on their wealth in a cave, they invested it.

"When we each came of age, Lutterworth, my great great grandfather, who is Ellery's great grandfather, gifted each of us with one hundred thousand pounds, or five hundred thousand dollars in your terms. With the help of his man of business we have each invested it," Nicholas said. "We are all quite well to pass now. Perhaps you've even heard of my great great grandfather, the Duke of Chenevix? Some call him the richest man in the world. So don't threaten us with what you will or will not do with your damned money. That blackmail will not wash. This rock will be excavated tomorrow, safely," he said, giving Lutterworth an even, steady look. "Now," he added pulling his watch out of his jacket pocket and flipping it open, "It's getting late. We'll discuss this over our evening meal."

"I'm starving!" said Varian. "I hope the dragonets have left enough for us!"

Lutterworth was forced to follow them out of the cave as Nicholas quite calmly doused the mage lantern, which left them dependent on the light at the tip of his wand. No more than anyone did Lutterworth relish being deep in the bowels of the earth without a light.

"All right," he said curtly. "You've got me over a barrel, damn it. But I want to set a guard on this cave. We'll stop on the way back and get that Yates here tonight."

Varian rolled his eyes. Whoever was going to steal an apocryphal treasure from beneath twenty tons of rock?

Nicholas, although he quite agreed with Varian's unvoiced opinion, decided that he would leave Yates with not only a good many mage lights but a ley line fire as well.

Marisela had spent as much time with Pacho as she dared. As evening began to draw in she realized that she would have to return to the *Hacienda*.

She had thoroughly enjoyed her day with the little dragonet and learning about dragons from Sabrina. She had fed Pacho about four times and rubbed him with a soft cloth as well to buff his scales to a shine. He now more like he had been dipped in starlight than ever. His scales were too young to need oil as yet but the both enjoyed the grooming.

She also basked in the adoring looks he gave he. With no one except Rodri had she ever experienced this unconditional love. Her mother and *duenna* were always trying to change her and correct her while her father wanted her to stop causing him grief. He would never listen to her or take her side, retreating to his library every time there was an argument.

"Do you *have* to leave me?" Pacho asked wistfully as she reluctantly made plans to go, and saddling her horse. Pacho had followed her to where Vittorio had been tethered all day so that he could graze. The horse had been frightened of Pacho at first but Flann had spoken to him in Animal Speech, and now Vittorio had actually touched noses with the dragonet, rapidly coming to accept him.

"I have to go, Pachito," she said sadly. "I live with my parents and they expect me home at night."

"But why can't I come with you?" he said, his eyes large and sad. It wrung her heart to see that look.

"They don't know about dragons," she said evasively. "They would be afraid of you."

"Afraid of a dragon?" he said, puzzled. "But no one here is afraid of us! *You're* not afraid, Marisela."

"Things are different in *Nueva España,*" she said. "Until very recently, Pacho, I was afraid of dragons too."

This he found hard to believe. "But you are my bond-mate now and we should be together always!" the dragonet protested.

"Right now, that cannot be. I have to arrange things properly," she said and turned back to brushing Vittorio so that she could put on his blanket and saddle. "Besides, it is better for you to stay here with your other dragon friends, no? Where you can get plenty of good food and learn from them?" She kept turned away from him so that he could not see the tears in her eyes. How could she love him so much when yesterday she had not even known he existed? She did not realize that since Rodri's death she had been starved for love and acceptance.

"I suppose so," said Pacho slowly. He did like being with the others and he liked being near the older dragons.

242

"But I will miss you," he added "Will you come back the first thing in the morning?"

"I will try," she said. She could not promise. Suppose her mother locked her in a room in which there was no entrance to the secret passages? The servants were too afraid for their jobs to set her free.

Marisela suddenly wished with all of her heart that she belonged to Nicholas's family where dragons were a part of daily life. She deeply envied Sabrina, who lived her own life and had an interesting profession as well. Even Atalanta Beck, as troublesome as her father was, did not have someone insisting that she marry an *idiota* whose looks and touch made her skin crawl. Once again, she was plunged into a mixture of sorrow and anger that Rodri had died. *He* would have stood up for her; he would have seen that *Don* Rafael was no fit husband for any one, much less for his little sister. Rodri would have even helped her run away....

Run away! Not for the first time this idea beckoned to her. To leave all of this pressure behind, to get as far from *Don* Rafael as possible!

The idea was in the back of her mind as she bade Pacho a tender farewell. As she put Vittorio to a ground-eating lope in the gathering dusk she thought of little else. Nicholas had spoken of how the United States government helped support a dragon and sometimes even had positions for dragons and riders. She could be self-supporting that way and not worry about feeding Pacho.

She could see no possibility of having him with her now. Her parents would never stand for it. And if she married, even to someone other than *Don* Rafael, would that *caballero* allow his wife to have a dragon? Hatred and fear of dragons ran deep in her country.

Nicholas would help her, she was certain. He knew all about dragons and he might loan her some money as well. She could pay it back when she and Pacho had a position. She had little money of her own. Her father saw no reason to give her much of it as he provided her food and clothing and there were few places to spend it, other than at the small market in Diablo and in the collection plate at church.

As she neared the *Hacienda* in the almost dark she wondered what new recriminations and demands she would face that night. It was too bad, a small voice whispered in her mind, that she could not marry someone like Nicholas, who would welcome a dragon into his home.

The emerald sat in the middle of the table, the light from the mage lights overhead making it sparkle.

Lutterworth had reluctantly allowed the others to see it. Sabrina had cleaned and shined it with a quick spell, removing the last of the dirt and bringing all of its deep green brilliance to the fore.

Further cutting and polishing by a jeweler would enhance it, but even rough hewn as it was, it was a beautiful thing.

They were all seated about the table, even the familiars, while the two older dragons leaned close to the canopy over the outdoor table. Erianne had put the little ones to sleep, their stomachs full of their final meal of the day. At this stage, dragonets, like kittens, preferred to sleep in a tumbled heap together. Amyas wanted to stay near Erianne, but Pacho, feeling very lonely without Marisela's comforting presence nearby, offered to sleep close to him, and with Erianne's assurance that she would come later and take them all under her wings, the shy little Maple dragon was persuaded to go off to bed. Erianne was as curious as any of the others about the emerald. Through her bond with Ellery she had felt an echo of what he had that afternoon and had very nearly flown off to the cave that afternoon, feeling that he needed her.

Even Julian, looking tired, had joined the group. Siofra, from a perch in his arms where she was being stroked, looked with interest at the emerald.

"That is after bein' a Healer's stone, that is!" she said admiringly. "Wouldn't that be lookin' fine on th' end of yer wand, Julian!" she said to her Wizard.

"And waste it like that?" said Lutterworth, revolted by such an idea. "Stick to the glass you are using for these wands of yours...."

"Glass?" Nicholas said while the familiars snickered. "What use would glass be? All of us use real jewels to tip out wands. Gemstones are important in magic as conduits and focus stones. Jewels are used in spell casting as well. My wand is tipped with a real fire opal. Ellery's got a diamond, while Sabrina has a pink topaz. And Julian has an emerald."

"Most Healers have emeralds, or some other green stone" Julian put in. He took his wand from his belt loop and put it on the table. A good sized emerald shone on the gold tip of the wand. It was less half the size of the stone they had found that day.

For one moment it seemed as if Lutterworth would snatch at it, for his face wore such an expression of covetousness that Julian quickly withdrew the wand and put it back on his belt.

"I had thought that Dr. Delamar was to give us one of his dramatic readings about this stone. That is the purpose of this gathering, is it not? " Dr. Beck said sharply. "I am longing for a cup of tea and my bed, in that order. I for one, would wish the performance to be over and done with." His voice was querulous.

"Yes, let's get on with it," said Sabrina. She was glad that Julian was there in case Ellery became weakened by this evening's work. She was very much against him proceeding further. He was aware of this but there was little else she could do to prevent whatever he might want to do with his pyschometry.

Ellery reached out and picked up the emerald. A protest died on Lutterworth's lips as Ellery gave him a level look. If Lutterworth had his way, the emerald would still be in his pocket. He had not even allowed poor Sinclair to see it until this moment.

At once, images began to flit through Ellery's consciousness as contact with the stone clarified his impressions.

Oddly enough, actually touching it steadied him and allowed him to convey what he saw to his audience.

"It was mined in South America," he said, concentrating. "it has a long history, passed hand to hand, once in a game of chance, most often by force." He closed his eyes to focus better upon the images in his mind.

"Blood and violence cling to it like a smell. I can see the three men. They are all shabbily dressed, almost in rags, as if they had undergone a long and difficult trip. They are fighting with swords in a desperate fashion, each claiming the gem as his own. One is in a dying condition. The others –" he broke off suddenly, his expression changing and began to shout in Spanish. The emerald suddenly grew brighter.

It was as if another face, a face full of greed and anger were superimposed over his. He was shouting "It is mine, you devil! You shall never have it! I will kill you!" all in Spanish and began to rise to his feet, his arm lifting as if he bore a sword, causing Bairre to tumble to the table top.

"Take it from him, Nick!" Julian shouted. "Throw it on the table!" Nicholas was nearest his uncle and he reached out and grabbed the stone, tossing it to the middle of the table. The stone was glowing as if lit from within.

"*Silentium!*" Julian commanded, leveling his wand at the emerald. A burst of violet light surrounded it and the pulsating light left it. Julian then ordered "*Actum!*" and it became just a dull green stone.

"What the hell are you doing?" Lutterworth yelled. "If you've compromised the value I'll have your ass!"

Ellery was slumped against Nicholas's shoulder. "I think he's unconscious," said Nicholas in concern. Sabina had started up and come around behind them to lay a hand on her brother's forehead. What had Ellery not listened to her?

Bairre, much distressed, put a soft paw to his Wizard's cheek. "Is he ill? Julian, is he ill?"

"I think we took it from him it in time," said Julian. He looked at all of them, a very serious expression on his face. "There may be a very good possibility that this stone is cursed. I silenced it and shielded it so it cannot touch any of us. I shall give Ellery a counter-curse potion and conduct tests on the stone—"

"Cursed!" cried Erianne, steam pouring from her nostrils and her tail lashing. "And Ellery with reading powers? It must be destroyed before it can hurt him any more! And the best way to do that is with dragon fire!"

Chapter Twenty Five
Wait For What Will Come

Ramón was so wrought-up that he could not sleep. Instead, with Gian-nah-tah at his side, he had restlessly walked the perimeters of the camp on the mountainside.

It was a beautiful night. Later in the year there would be many thunderstorms and clouds, but now, in late spring, the desert air made the brilliant stars seem very close. The air was cool but Ramón barely noticed. Almost, he could be walking on air. He felt very close to all of nature tonight, all his senses heightened.

"Did I not tell you that you would be trained?" said the fox softly. "Did I not tell you that you should trust me?"

Ramón looked down at him. "I was wrong to doubt you," he admitted. "It is something I thought could never happen."

The afternoon had been full of learning. He had had the satisfaction of seeing all the members of his tribe cured of all of their ills, from a badly scraped side to broken wrist bones set badly.

And his teacher had let him, Ramón, Heal the very minor cuts and bruises! He had done it easily, as if he had been Healing all of his life. Julian had been very pleased and had praised him, words that had filled Ramón with happiness.

There was much more to learn: the more difficult Healings of serious injuries and diseases of the body, the ways of the Healing herbs. But Ramón was now filled with confidence where there had once been doubt. He could do this. His teacher was certain that Ramón could become a great Healer. And after this afternoon's events, Ramón himself felt that it was possible.

He had another cause for happiness. The blue dragon, Nah-kah-yen, had returned this afternoon as well. With him he brought two buffalo.

The tribe had not really known how to deal with skinning and taking the meat from the dead beasts, but Nah-kah-yen had used his talons to good effect and they managed to get at the good red meat.

As he always did, Nah-kah-yen lit a fire for them and soon the air was filled with the mouth-watering smell of roasting meat.

Julian had been present when the blue dragon had arrived with his spoils and had instructed the two who served most often as cooks how to make a strengthening broth from the meat. Packets of herbs from his medical bag added flavor. He cautioned them against eating too heartily as they had been on short rations for a long time. Lastly, he put a spell on the meat that would preserve it and keep insects and predators from it.

It had been more than pleasant to have done a satisfactory day's work and then to enjoy a delicious, filling meal. The corn tortillas that made up their usual fare were stuffed with shredded meat and wiped in the drippings from the meat. There had been more than enough for everyone. This was very rare, to be able to go to bed with one's stomach satisfied.

Sated, everyone else had gone to sleep early on. But Ramón was far too keyed up and only in walking about did he finally began to calm himself.

"You will learn more and more," Gian-nah-tah added as they continued to walk about the camp quietly. "The time is coming when you will be called upon to do a great task, to save lives. It is well that your teacher has come when you needed him, but he and the others with him have set in motion a chain of events that will bring a very great evil to this place."

Startled by hearing this, Ramón looked at the fox and said "What do you mean? Should my teacher not have come here?"

Gian-nah-tah stopped walking and sat down on his haunches. He was barely a gray shadow in the night. "I do not mean that," he said evenly "but it is a fact of life that for every good thing that comes, there is usually a price to be paid. I can not see far enough ahead to tell what the evil might be, or when it might come, but the feeling of it makes my fur stand on end. I tell you this, Nantan Lupan, not to frighten you, but to tell you to be on your guard. All you may do now is wait for what will come and trust your heart to tell you what to do when it does."

In spite of the fox's calming words, Ramón felt a thrill of fear. What peril, what *evil*, could Gian-nah-tah be speaking of? Ramón had no doubt that his spirit guide knew what he was talking about. He had been correct in every particular up to this point. Wait for what will come–to take this advice was going to be difficult.

"Is there such a thing, in these modern times, as a true curse?" Atalanta queried.

Ellery, doused with a potion, had been put to bed with Bairre in attendance. Dr. Beck and Lutterworth had retired as well, Lutterworth incensed because Julian adamantly refused to let him have possession of the emerald again until it had been thoroughly examined for black magic.

But Atalanta and Mr. Sinclair had joined the three remaining mages and their familiars at the table over the universal British panacea of a nice cup of tea.

Erianne, still upset, had at last been convinced to go to the dragonets and take them under her wings. Varian had sensibly pointed out that the little ones would sense her agitation and might wake and cause problems. She went to them but was still convinced that if there was even the smallest doubt of the emerald's being cursed, it ought to be destroyed as a threat to everyone, but most particularly to Ellery.

"Oh, yes. A certain amount have to be removed every year. Ellery and I have run into a few ancient curses in Egypt," said Sabrina. "But those were reasonably easy to deal with. I don't like the fact that this stone seemed to take possession of Ellery."

"He looked like someone else there, for a few moments," Sinclair put in, giving a little shudder. That had been frightening to see.

"What could cause that?" Atalanta said. "Would a black magician have to be involved?"

She was looking at Sabrina as she spoke, but the Witch shook her head. "This is not my field. Of the three of us, it is really more Julian's bailiwick."

"Wizard Healers learn more about curses and their removal than most other Wizards or Witches," Julian said briefly. "That is because most curses involve illness and death. For a personality to become trapped in this stone would not necessarily take black magic, only the strong desire for it from a dying person with an equally strong personality, not to be parted from this stone or to prevent others from getting it. I am just afraid that in Ellery's reading of the emerald he might have awakened that something trapped in the stone."

"The curse?" said Sabrina sharply.

"That, or a presence," Julian said.

"Ye are meanin' a spirit?" Flann inquired. "I was feelin' no spirit, Julian," she said. "Did you, Siofra?" Cats were especially attuned to spirits. In fact, cats were one of the few creatures on earth that actually enjoyed being in a haunted house.

"Nay, then," Siofra replied, "But neither one of us was after bein' in the cave when Ellery was first sensin' the thing, were we now? The spirit might have been fleein' then."

"Then what was that face?" Sinclair said in confusion. "If that wasn't a ghost, what was it?" He absently sipped at his tea, forgetting that he really didn't like it and preferred coffee.

"A revenant," said Julian. "A remnant of a spirit. It would not feel like a true spirit to you familiars since it is mostly an impression."

"Does that mean that if Ellery were to hold the emerald again we might not see that face?" asked Nicholas with interest. Cillian, who was laying on his back on the table so that Nicholas could rub his stomach, opened one eye behind his spectacles.

"Ellery is not going to touch that thing again!" Sabrina exclaimed. "And I don't want any of you encouraging him to do so!"

"When I am done with it, the stone will be perfectly safe," said Julian. "I am reasonably certain that I can remove any curse—"

"Reasonably certain is not *positive*," Sabrina retorted. "I am more than a little tired of seeing my brother laid low by pyschometry. What if the next time he does not recover? He is

250

too stubborn and pig-headed to realize the damage he is doing to himself!"

One has to take certain risks in the pursuit of knowledge, Atalanta thought. From what she had seen of Dr. Delamar she did not think that his sister's protests and a fainting fit would stop him. Like her, he wanted to *know*.

"When are you going to work on it, Julian?" Nicholas queried. "I'll be glad to lend a hand, if you need another magus."

"Thank you, Nick, it will be easier with two of us," said Julian gratefully. "I intend to get right at it–"

Siofra twisted in his arms to look up into his face." And that ye will not be doin'!" she exclaimed, disapproval in every small inch of her. "And were ye not after Healin' two more children this morning' and then Healin' all of those little matters this afternoon as well? 'Tis laid down upon yer bed ye should be and 'tis me that'll be seein' ye go there right now!"

"Siofra–" Julian began, but as she continued to stare at him belligerently he realized that she was right. "Very well," he at last agreed. "I'll go to bed. I am rather tired."

"It's been a long day," said Sabrina. She stood and began to gather up the tea things. "But I want it understood by everyone," she added, looking at each of them in turn. "Ellery is not to go near that damn stone until it has been made safe!" Her look was so fierce that they all agreed to this prohibition. No one wanted to see Ellery in a swooning condition.

"Mr. Lutterworth will very likely want to go out to the mine immediately after breakfast, if he will even wait that long," Sinclair warned.

Varian, who had remained silent and just listened now said," Well, he will have to wait until the rest of us are ready, which is when I will be flying out there. He's welcome to walk, but I am afraid it would take him a very long time. And it's not as if he could move those rocks by himself, although perhaps he is stupid enough to try." He yawned when he finished speaking, revealing very large, white teeth that Sinclair regarded in fascinated horror. Even his volatile employer could not argue with something that possessed teeth that large.

Nicholas and Julian rose early and began examining the stone before anyone else in the camp other than Lupe was stirring. Accompanied by their familiars they set up a small laboratory a little ways from the tents.

Like most Wizards, they each carried the portable laboratory in a bag, developed by their three times great grandfather, Lord Lyonshall. Everything that might be needed in the field was found in this handy tool, from beakers to neatly labeled vials of mermaid's tears (helpful for divination) to a sliver of unicorn horn, which could purify even the worst of black magics or pollution. They all had a personal bit of unicorn horn as well, to purify the local water.

Cillian took notes, with his paw in the stylus that enabled him to write. He wrote in runes, which most Wizards did as a matter of habit. Non-magicals did not very often understand runes and in the wrong hands a Wizard's notes could be dangerous. Curious adolescents, even non-magical, had been known in he past to try to duplicate magical spells, which could lead to disastrous results.

The first few tests revealed that it was no longer inhabited by even a revenant. Something had been there without doubt, but it had fled. It was unclear whether the revenant had accomplished its purpose by appearing to them or if a spirit had indeed been released.

Julian stood in front of the stone, frowning down at it. "We'd best be prepared for a spirit manifestation," he said at last. "that stone has a minute residue remaining. I do not like the feel of it. There is nothing definite, but–"

He did not have to explain further to either Nicholas or the familiars. They knew that intuition counted for a great deal in magic.

"'Tis being most likely that a spirit will come at night," said Siofra. "But many are bein' bound to but one place and cannot be travelin' about. 'Tis more than likely that since this stone was bein' found in that cave, that is where the spirit will be after bein' contained."

They all listened closely to her. Cats had an inborn

knowledge of spirits and their peculiarities that other animals and humans lacked.

"In my experience ghosts prefer nighttime to the light of day," said Nicholas. He had actually quite a bit of practical knowledge of ghosts and hauntings from a time some years ago.

"Is there a curse on it?" Cillian inquired.

Instead of answering Julian leveled his wand at the stone and commanded, *"Bacchato maledictio!"*

The stone gave a small leap in the tripod that supported it, but did not flare to life.

"That would be a negative," said Cillian, making a note of the result.

"Is that a new spell?" Nicholas inquired with interest. "It's much shorter than the old curse-revealing spell."

"Brand-new," said Julian absently. "It was in *The Wizard's Lancet* last month."

"I should start reading that," said Nicholas. "*The Gentleman Wizard* doesn't get medically based spells until at least two months later." He turned and looked at the emerald closely. "Well, this stone should be safe enough for Ellery, even in Sabrina's estimation. We've done about every test and containment we know."

Julian agreed. "But I am worried about what we shall find out at the mine. Something was here, but it has gone. Where it has gone is my main concern. Perhaps we shall find out at the mine"

"You're coming with us?" Nicholas inquired.

"Oh, yes. According to what you told us of that rock fall, it will be safest if all of us do a four point stabilization first and then remove the rock in increments, as geomancers do in a railway tunnel. I have already sent word to Ramón that I will be late today," Julian answered.

"That fox was after comin' here early this mornin'" Siofra said. "'Twas if he was knowin' I'd be havin' a message for him. Aye, he's after bein' a knowin' one."

Cillian said "I hear the others stirring. Perhaps we'd better clean up and then join them for breakfast." He raised his head and sniffed in appreciation. "Something smells good!"

Removing the rocks was all Lutterworth could talk about over breakfast. He had wanted to leave without this meal, but as he was the only one who felt this way, he ended in having to wait as everyone ate.

The dragonets had to be fed as well. Erianne would stay with them, as would Torin.

Varian would be making two trips out to the mine as there were eight persons to be conveyed. Lutterworth even let Sinclair come along as he could help dig. Nicholas loaned Sinclair some clothing, as the city clothing Lutterworth's assistant was wearing was neither appropriate nor comfortable for digging in a mine. They were nearly of a size and Nicholas had an extra pith helmet as well, which was a necessity for working in an area where rocks falling were a constant threat.

Atalanta and Dr. Beck very kindly volunteered to remain behind for the second trip. Lutterworth, of course, had to be among the first to go. He practically danced with impatience and cursed aloud at each delay.

In his breast harness Varian carried shovels and picks and several buckets, as well as a chest of other tools such as hammers and chisels, even the small tools and brushes used in archaeology. Ellery was determined that anything of archeological value was not going to be destroyed.

Sabrina had been glad to see that her brother was much restored this morning and looked as if he had been well rested. Julian had more than likely put some sleeping herbs in the anti-curse potion and it had done Ellery good to get a restful sleep. She had been much relieved when her nephews had informed her that the emerald was of no more danger to anyone. And Lutterworth had been more than pleased to be able to restore the stone to his pocket.

The air looked hazy as they landed in front of the mine site. It was going to be hot today, as the blazing sun rising in a brilliant, cloudless blue sky foretold. But below ground they would not notice the heat.

Lutterworth waited impatiently as the others unstrapped and slid off Varian's back. He was in the fourth seat and only Varian's statement that he would not stand for Lutterworth's sitting right up on his neck had prevented Lutterworth from claiming the first seat on the saddle.

"Where's that damned Yates?" Lutterworth demanded as he clumsily dismounted. "I left him here last night on guard! I told him to sit right at the entrance here and guard it against intruders!"

There was no sign of Yates. The ley line fire Nicholas had provided him, at the top of the ramp leading down into the caves, still burned and the mage lights still hung in the air, lighting up the way down into the cave.

A crumpled blanket and a bed roll lay on the ground near the fire. A coffee pot and a tin mug stood to one side of the fire, close by a plate of half-eaten beans.

Nicholas touched the coffee pot briefly. "Cold," he said.

"Where the hell is he?" fumed Lutterworth. "I'm paying that man a damned fortune to guard my interests!"

"Perhaps he is laying somewhere, hurt," said Julian, taking his wand from his belt loop." Perhaps he had to answer a call of nature and tripped and fell, or was bitten by a rattlesnake or a scorpion. I'll do a sweeping search."

"Yates! Yates! Where are you, damn it?" Lutterworth yelled, cupping his hands about his mouth. He chose not to wait for Julian's wand to find the missing cowboy.

A scrambling noise was heard and a few moments later Yates' head appeared over a ridge a little way from the hole in the ground that led down to the cave. When he saw who waited for him he climbed over the top and slid down the rock face.

"Where the hell have you been, Yates?" Lutterworth began angrily as the cowboy drew nearer. "What the hell am I paying you for, anyway?"

Sabrina, far more observant than Lutterworth, said quickly, "What is it Mr. Yates? Are you not well?"

Yates looked terrible. His eyes were blood-shot and his complexion pasty. His eyes appeared huge in his pale face. Sweat beaded his forehead. He hugged his rifle to his chest and appeared to have to pry his hand from its stock before he removed his hat and addressed Sabrina. "No, ma'am, I ain't well a-tall. If I'd a-had what wages was owing to me I'd a-lit out an' not stopped 'til I done reached San Francisco. But I ain't got me a dime yet in my jeans, so's I had to stay. But I don't care if he 'twas to pay me ten dollars a day!" he jerked his chin towards Lutterworth. "There's things a man can't bear an' I draws the line at haunts! Yes, ma'am, that's right, *haunts*!" he said when Sabrina looked surprised. "A- moanin' and a-groanin' an' like to turn my hair white overnight! Haunts as ever was!"

Chapter Twenty Six
Digging

"What do you mean, *haunts*?" asked Lutterworth irritably. He was frowning and impatient.

"I think he means ghosts," said Sabrina." Its that not right, Mr. Yates?"

"Yes, ma'am!" said Yates, at once. "Spooks, or haunts, or whatever you wants to call 'em. This place is full of 'em! An' I ain't staying nowhere near haunts, no sir!"

"What did you see or hear?" Nicholas inquired. "Can you tell us exactly what happened?"

Julian made Yates sit down on a handy rock and began to examine him critically. Yates was adverse to this until Julian told him that he was a doctor.

"Just after dark, I reckon it was," Yates said as Julian took his pulse. I heard this noise like a pack of coyotes a-howling. Didn't pay it no never mind. But then it got worse. There was this laughin' and hollerin' an' I knowed that weren't no coyote! The darker it got, the louder it got. Sounded like a brawl in a saloon after a while. Then there was all of this sound like pots banging and screamin'. When I saw lights a-shining I thought they was comin' for me an' that's when I lit out. It went on till near sun-up. Am I goin' to be all right, Doc?" he asked as Julian removed the stethoscope from his chest where had been listening to the cowboy's heart. "Heard of folks afore now bein' skeered to death."

"Your heart rate, pulse and breathing are accelerated and I have no doubt that your blood pressure is high," said Julian. "Since this affects you so adversely I would recommend that you keep away from this environment."

"Does that mean I ain't got to stay here at night no more?" Yates asked hopefully.

"Yes," stated Julian. Yates looked extremely displeased.

"Now, see here, Doctor!" Lutterworth interrupted. "This man is in my employ and I insist that this area must and will be guarded at night. Night is when most thefts are committed!"

"People *can* be scared to death, Mr. Lutterworth, and

in my medical opinion Mr. Yates is a prime candidate for such a happening," said Julian evenly, putting his stethoscope back in his medical bag. "I'm going to brew him a calming potion and then recommend bed rest for a while until his heart rate decreases. The potion will prevent you from dreaming about this," he added, turning to Yates.

"Well, that's fine by me!" the cowboy declared.

While this had been going on Sabrina had heated up the coffee, adding some water when she found it so strong that it could eat away the lining of one's stomach. She now gave a fresh cup of black coffee to Yates, who said "Thank you kindly, ma'am. That's just what I been needin'." His hands were still shaking as he reached out for the tin cup.

"If all you are worried about is theft, Lutterworth," said Ellery a little sarcastically "we can magically ward this site far better than any guard."

"That's what he said last night," Lutterworth gestured at Nicholas. "But I told you, Delamar, I haven't much use for magic or Wizards and it seems to me that this expedition proves I was right. For all of the magic you people are supposed to possess Stillfield here couldn't remove those fucking rocks and we've been delayed time and again by your damned playacting over these jewels we've found! I want to get in to that cave and I want to get into it *now*, God damn it! Time is running out and I want that treasure!" He stopped, breathing heavily, his square face red with temper and glaring at each of them in turn.

"First of all we'll have the cats check the area for spirits," said Nicholas, trying to speak in even tones. Lutterworth made him so angry and he could see that the rest of his family members were just as annoyed by Lutterworth's attitude. "We could be in danger—"

"So you people believe in *ghosts* now?" Lutterworth laughed mockingly. "It's just another excuse to put off doing what I am paying you for!"

Ellery ignored him. "Varian," he asked the dragon, "Will you please go back and fetch Dr. Beck and Miss Beck? After the cats have checked for spirits we shall go down into the mine and remove the rocks that Mr. Lutterworth is so impatient about. Siofra, Flann," he turned to where the cats had been sitting with Cillian and Bairre, listening to the humans talk as the dragon took off.

But there were no cats there, only the ferret and the hedgehog.

"They've already gone on down to the caves, Ellery," said Bairre. "Siofra said it was best if they checked the area on their own, without humans."

There were no mage lights deep in the cave but the two felines could see well in the dark.

Neither of them had been this way before but they had asked the way of Cillian and Bairre who had both been in this particular cavern. Flann has refused Bairre's offer to accompany them, for she and Siofra were best equipped to deal with spirits by themselves. Any ghosts would be more likely to talk to cats than to other animals. Cats had no fear at all of ghosts. Flann had seen that both Bairre and Cillian did not really wish to go into a cave that might be haunted.

Flann, like most cats, had no fear of spirits at all. Other animals were very afraid, as afraid as humans. Flann had seen both horses and dogs react very badly, with overwhelming terror, to the presence of just one small spirit. How a dragon might react to spirits she was not certain; the only thing dragons seemed to be afraid of was lightning strikes.

To cats, spirits were just another part of the natural world. And interceding with them on the part of their Wizards and Witches, or a medium who wished to contact the Other Side, was a part of their feline function.

Most spirits felt welcome when they felt the presence of a cat. That was one way that a knowing person could tell if a medium was a fraud. If she or he did not keep a cat and have that cat in the room where the *séances* were conducted, that medium was almost assuredly a fake.

Flann and Siofra had walked deep into the cave, whiskers quivering, feeling for ghosts.

"There's been hauntings here all right," Flann said in a low voice to the smaller cat as they drew near the spot where Ellery had found the emerald.

"Aye, they've been after goin' to roost," agreed Siofra. "'Tis naught left but a feelin' of them. They'll be not comin' back till 'tis dark, I'm thinkin'."

"Ye are thinkin' there's bein' more than one?" Flann asked. Siofra was even more attuned to ghosts than most cats. In her family, it was a long tradition for the females to deliver their litters in the shadow of the *Lia Fáil*, the Stone of Destiny, out at Tara at home in Ireland. This gave the kittens born there a paw in both the world of man and of Faerie. The Stone was a very powerful magical object.

"Two, mayhap three, I'm after thinkin'," said Siofra. "But we'll be seein' none of them till the sun is goin' down."

Both cats were well aware that ghost preferred the darkness as they fed off the fear (actually the energy that fear produced) that a lack of light produced in many humans.

From the beginning of time humanity had been scared of the dark, a time when fear of the unknown and the unseen had some basis in self preservation. Humans, cats thought, had to rely too much on eyesight. Other human senses, those of smell and hearing, were paltry compared to an animal's and most cats felt that even human eyesight was lacking. It was easy to be afraid of things one could not sense clearly.

"Let's go back and tell them that it's safe for now," said Flann.

With a last look around the two cats trotted briskly back towards the surface. Whatever spirits there were in the cave were at rest for the moment. Both of them, though, in unspoken agreement, would return to this cave when twilight was done and darkness set in.

"That is a great deal of rock," said Sabrina, gazing up at the rock fall before them. "How far back does it go, Nick? Did your wand tell you?"

They were all standing in front of the cave-in, the party now augmented by Dr. Beck and Atalanta. Varian stood behind the humans and the four familiars

"It's not that deep, perhaps ten feet," Nicholas answered. "It is far higher than it is deep. What I don't like about it is that the ceiling is unstable. I would hazard a guess that that's what caused the original fall."

"How far back is this anomaly you spoke of?" Ellery inquired, looking the rock fall up and down.

"Well behind the fall," said Nicholas.

Lutterworth was seething with ill temper. Why the hell were they just standing there looking and talking? Why didn't' they do something? First there had been the hold up outside while they waited for the damned cats to come back and report. Then the doctor had to brew up a potion for that damned Yates and see him sent back to their camp to rest. Then they had to wait for Dr. Beck and his daughter. There was an interminable trip down here. And now they were just standing around talking. If all the British operated like this Lutterworth found it amazing that they had built an Empire.

He wished he had his dynamite.

After discussion, the four mages decided to do as Julian had suggested earlier to Nicholas: a four point stabilization. This would be the safest thing as no one wished to cause a further rock fall.

First of all Varian would stand up on his hind legs and remove some of the rocks from the top. The layer there was the thinnest and they hoped to insert the magical supports in a gap, which would cause less damage and less chance of more ceiling collapse.

"Everyone stand well back," cautioned Varian as he came forward and reared up on his powerful back legs. He had been unsaddled to make it easier for him to work and his wings were partially unfurled for balance.

To Atalanta, watching, he seemed far larger in this posture. Would Seneca get this big? She had been surprised that morning when she fed him, for he already looked bigger in just a few days. Nicholas, when applied to, had told her that it was common for a dragonet to double in size the first two weeks of his life.

Removing stones was easy work for dragon talons. A dragon had great strength as well; two of the reasons that the Inquisition had been so eager to enslave them in the mines.

Between them, Nicholas and Julian used their wands

and a spell of *Demiterre* to safely lower the rocks Varian was shifting.

"How big a space do you need?" Varian asked. "I think that I will be able to make a gap as there seem to be fewer stones at the top."

"An inch or so will do," Ellery advised him.

To everyone but Lutterworth things seemed to proceed quickly after that. Varian was soon done. The four mages then stood in a square and from corner to corner they sent violet energy, forming a huge X. Almost as soon as it was made the cross became to spread until it looked as it it were a violet blanket hanging in the air between them.

On a signal from Ellery they raised their wands simultaneously and the violet blanket rose above their heads. With a spell of *Inserre* they sent the light towards the gap created by Varian.

The non-magical people heard an audible thump as the blanket pushed itself against the ceiling above the cave-in.

The next quadruple spell was *Stabilitius*, the very spell that Nicholas and Julian's father had helped develop for the safe building of the many railway tunnels in the Six Nations. A team of geomancers, working for a railway company, used this spell, performed just as this one, to stabilize the roof and sides of a tunnel.

The violet light would spread from the ceiling down into the walls and even the floor, making it safe to work inside the area, ten to fifteen feet at a time.

The rocks were removed from the top, a few at a time, with another conjuration, this one the standard spell of removal, *Amovere*.

Dr. Beck, watching this operation, was filled with envy. How easy to dig this way! No back breaking labor of dozens of men, all of whom had to be paid! He noted the careful way the stones were moved, floating to one side of the cavern, out of everyone's way. Little dust was raised and there were few chips of rock.

Atalanta wished that she had magic. It must be a wonderful thing to be able to do so much. She realized that all of them must have studied very hard to learn all of this but she fancied that it would be worth it, to be able to perform such seeming miracles.

Sinclair watched open-mouthed. He had never seen much magic in action. He had come, very reluctantly, prepared to dig, but now could lounge at his ease on a convenient rock while all the work was taken out of his hands.

But all that Lutterworth could think about was how slow it was. Dynamite was much faster. He never gave a thought to how much safer the magic was.

At noontime, when the stone was remove about half way down, Julian, as the group's medical adviser, called a halt for luncheon. Magic required good meals and they had been all Working magic all morning.

Lutterworth was completely enraged by this and followed the party back to the surface yelling "Come back here, you're not anywhere near finished yet!"

The others ignored him. Even Sinclair, Dr. Beck and Atalanta were ready for a midday repast and a cooling drink. Varian and the familiars too, were ready for a rest. Varian had occupied himself in rolling the removed stones out of the way. He had conceived the idea of using the stones to build a cairn of burial above the dead dragon eggs.

They sat in the mouth of the cave that had been created by Varian and ate from full hampers Sabrina and Lupe had packed that morning. There were chicken and ham sandwiches, still chilled under a preservation spell, with a terrine of vegetables, flaky fruit-filed pastries and cold fruit juice, as well as pieces of fruit. There was minced chicken and mushrooms for the familiars and Varian ate a large *mélange* of various fruits.

Lutterworth ate nothing but instead paced up and down, muttering to himself.

"An apoplexy waiting to happen," murmured Julian to his brother as they finished up the meal.

"I wish it would happen sooner than later," Nicholas returned.

"How much longer are you people going to sit here eating?" Lutterworth burst out, interrupting a conversation between Ellery and Sabrina and the Becks comparing digs in Egypt to those in Greece.

"When will all those rocks be moved so we can get in

there?" Lutterworth continued angrily. "I never meant to be out here all day! I want to be able to take the treasure into Albuquerque, before dark, to my office, where I have a safe!"

Ellery looked at him with the dislike he was finding more difficult each day to conceal. "We're not even certain that there is treasure under all of that rock," he said.

"Stillfield said there was an anomaly," Lutterworth stated. "That says treasure to me."

"Not necessarily," Ellery began only to be barged in on by Lutterworth saying "I don't give a good God damn what else you think it can be! How much longer before we get to the treasure?'

"Another two or three hours," said Ellery coldly, after exchanging looks with the other mages.

"Two or three hours!" Lutterworth echoed in disbelief. He looked out overhead to where the sun was already beginning its decline, for it was now after noon. He pulled a large ornate watch that hung on a heavy gold chain from the watch pocket in his vest. "It's after one already! Don't you people know the meaning of the saying "Time is money?"

"Mr. Lutterworth has a sign of that saying up on the wall of all of his offices," Sinclair said in a low voice to Sabrina, whom he was sitting beside.

"Back to work," said Nicholas and stood up.

"At least one of you has some sense and ambition!" growled Lutterworth.

"It's better than sitting here listening to you," said Nicholas sweetly and picked up his familiar. Cillian's laughing face looked back over his Wizard's shoulder as Nicholas walked away.

Lutterworth sputtered in rage.

Three hours later, almost to the minute, they took the last of the stone out of the now stable but narrow tunnel. They would only be able to walk two abreast and there would not be enough room for Varian.

The dragon was much more cheerful and accepting of

this than Lutterworth would have been. Cillian offered to keep him company; the hedgehog had little curiosity about treasure and would rather remain behind, comfortably curled up on Nicholas's discarded jacket.

Lutterworth danced with impatience as the mages lit their wands and the mage lanterns. He had to be the first in, of course. He was followed by Ellery and then Atalanta, with Dr. Beck, Sabrina, Julian and Nicholas following. At the last minute Lutterworth ordered Sinclair to stay behind.

Dr. Beck would have preferred to remain behind as well. He hated the thought of going into a small dark tunnel, but his scholarly curiosity overcame him and he joined the party.

"How will you find this anomaly?" Lutterworth queried as they entered the tunnel.

"With our wands," Ellery answered. Each of them held the wands out before them, the focus stones blazing with light.

Ellery had expected the air to be dank but there was an odd smell in the air, one that he could not identify at first. And the air was better in a way than he had thought it would be. In fact, the further they advanced the more convinced he could feel moving air on his face. If only it smelled better.

"Phew!" said Bairre from his perch on Ellery's shoulder. "Something stinks! Is there something dead up ahead?"

The cats too, complained of the smell and Sabrina began coughing.

"It smells like a burial chamber!" said Atalanta, remembering some of the tombs they had opened in Greece. Sometimes the tombs they disturbed had looted in antiquity and the bodies disturbed and left out in the air. Sometimes those that had been magiced were in the first stages of putrefaction as the ancient spells wore off.

They suddenly rounded a corner and came into a much bigger room, one full of a hideous jumble of things gleaming white and grinning, with what smelled so distressingly sitting on top.

It was an immense pile of human bones, with rotting bodies of recently dead atop it. Above it, up high, a natural window stood open to the sky.

Chapter Twenty Seven
Bones

Marisela was unable to leave the house the next day.

At a very early hour her mother came to her room and insisted she get up and get ready for the dressmakers. *Doña* Milagros was not about to let her daughter slip through her fingers again.

To add to the horror of hours spent standing on a stool while the two dressmakers measured her and poked her with pins, *Doña* Paloma arrived mid-morning to help oversee the selection of Marisela's bride-clothes.

In vain did Marisela protest that she was *not* going to marry *Don* Rafael. All this measuring and sewing was for nothing!

The three older women, Milagros, Paloma and even her *duenna* Trinidad, smiled indulgently at her, as if she were a child having a temper tantrum. The sewing woman, *Señora* Lopez and her assistant, *Señorita* Puente, nodded knowingly. It was but bridal nerves. Such a fortunate young lady, to be marrying a wealthy and now titled husband! And to be going to Spain to be presented at Court! It was every young girl's dream come true!

It was more like a nightmare for Marisela. She wanted to be gone from here and away from all their eyes and hands, staring and prodding. She wanted to be with Pacho. She wanted to be free! This was intolerable. She was never going to marry that fool! She did not want to go to Spain at all. If the rest of these stupid women thought going to Spain was so wonderful, let them go in her place! She did not want to be presented to King Alfonso XII and Queen Maria Christina; they were nothing to her.

"You will thank me for this one day," said her mother complacently as the seamstress draped a length of deep blue satin around her unwilling victim. "When you are a great lady in Spain and a lady-in-waiting to the Queen you will wonder why you did not wish to obey us."

"The blue brings out the highlights in her hair," said Paloma. "Do you have the latest fashion journals, *Señora?*" she asked of *Señora* Lopez.

"*Sí, Doña* Paloma, not from Madrid, but from Paris!" The seamstress, a tall woman who looked like one of her own sewing needles, nodded. "The bodice will be fitted and the skirt draped in the latest mode. Do not worry, *Señora*, whatever I make for the *Señorita* will be fit for the Court. I have experience and skill and I even have a sewing machine!" she added, thinking fondly of her treadle Singer Improved Family Model 15 that could sew anything from silk to canvas. It was now ensconced in the rooms where they would work here on Marisela's bride-clothes, the machine having traveled from Albuquerque on the wagon with the two women and the rolls and rolls of fabrics. "But the *Señorita* will have to be corseted for my creations to fit properly!" she added.

A bare half hour later Marisela, overpowered by the five other women, found herself laced so tightly into a corset that came up under her breasts and down over the hips to a point in front, that taking a deep breath was impossible.

The fittings went on and on. Marisela could not comprehend the number of gowns the women thought necessary. Day gowns, tea gowns. walking dresses, gowns for evenings at home, ball gowns, riding habits, even a tennis dress, although Marisela did not play tennis. She was not even certain what tennis was.

"My son will take her to Worth, in Paris, for the majority of her evening dresses," said *Doña* Paloma smugly. "You need only make enough for shipboard."

As if this were not bad enough, when all the fittings were done they began to deal with her hair. *Doña* Paloma wanted her soon to be daughter- in-law to wear a fashionable hair style beneath the antique *mantilla* she would wear on her wedding day.

The current *à la mode* hair was dressed elaborately, with a 'fringe' on the forehead, made by cutting some of the front hair and frizzing it with a hot iron. The rest of the hair was drawn back and up to show the ears with complicated ringlets and sweeps at side and back.

Marisela had to endure this hairstyle made over and over, as *Doña* Paloma's maid, who had accompanied her mistress, made Conchita practice again and again on her own mistress, until it met with the approval of all of the ladies. In between incarnations her hair was ruthlessly brushed.

Marisela thought she might escape after luncheon. She thought of Pacho waiting for her, wondering where she might be. Was he getting fed properly? Was he lonely?

After luncheon, however, she had to be fitted with the hastily basted muslin patterns sewn by *Señorita* Puente. And while they were eating luncheon, two more persons arrived to torture her: a milliner and a shoemaker. The milliner also made gloves. Marisela had to endure being measured for gloves and shoes and to try on hat after hat over her new hair style, which she hated. The hats made her head ache.

The shoemaker had brought a number of ready-made shoes with him and all were very modish: a boot type buttoned or laced, with high tops, heels and pointed toes. She could scarcely walk in them and felt herself wobble on the high heels. He also brought with him a selection of silk stockings, which were held up by something Marisela had never seen before: elastic suspenders that attached to the stockings. These hung from the bottom of the corset and were quite the most uncomfortable things that Marisela could imagine.

How do women bear these clothes? she thought in despair as she was pushed into a ready-made jacketed gown, with her new *coiffure* crowned by a tiny ribbon draped hat set at an angle on her piled-up hair. *Doña* Milagros had the long pier glass brought down from her room so that Marisela could see herself.

The others in the room were loud in their praise but Marisela did not like what she saw: a very pretty, fashionable young woman who was not the Marisela she thought herself to be. One moreover, who looked frightened, for the possibility of being married over her protests to *Don* Rafael suddenly seemed very real.

Running away looked more attractive by the minute. She could not, would not be turned into the stranger she saw in the mirror. It would kill her and separate her from Pacho, just after she found him.

No one noticed *Doña* Paloma's maid, Teresa, carefully gathering all of the hair from Marisela's brush and comb and pocketing it. No one would have cared if they had seen, as it was quite usual to save the hair caught in the brush and comb to make hairpieces that would perfectly match a lady's hair. This was very useful in the case of a lady whose hair was not thick or full enough to make all of the ringlets and poufs demanded by fashion.

But Teresa was not Marisela's maid and at any rate, Marisela did not need such additions, for her own hair was luxuriant.

Teresa licked her lips in anticipation as she thought of the use to which the hair would be put.

Sabrina prided herself on being able to face almost anything they found in the tombs they had excavated in Egypt. A moldering mummy did not faze her, nor ordinarily, a pile of bones. But there was something about this accumulation of bones and bodies that profoundly disturbed her.

"I have often smelled putrefaction in Greece, where a spell cast by an ancient magician has begun to wear off, but never anything quite like this," said Atalanta calmly. She had taken out an immaculate white handkerchief and was holding it to her nose.

"That," said Julian grimly, "is because the magic used by the ancients to preserve bodies was of the Light. This is not."

"Black magic?" Ellery asked. Nearly all of them, even the familiars, were holding paw or hand or handkerchief up to their noses as the smell was extraordinarily bad.

"Will one of you so-called Wizards do something about this stink?" Lutterworth demanded. "We can't find the treasure with this Goddamned stench in the air!"

Julian turned to face the group and pronounced *"Halitus clarus!"* while making a wide sweep with his wand to encompass everyone in the party. "A useful forensic spell I learned from Grandfather," he said at the looks of inquiry from the other mages. "Forensic Wizards often have to examine corpses in extreme stages of decay and this is a breathe clear spell. Your nose will now filter out the smell."

"What is the meaning of this?" Dr. Beck demanded

querulously. "It appears to be some sort of charnel house!"

"It looks as if the bodies were tossed down that hole," said Nicholas peering upwards.

"I'm not after likin' this at all," said Siofra." 'Tis not being how the dead are to be treated, with no grave, nor shroud, nor even any blessing to take them to the angels. Discarded as so much rubbish they are."

Ellery had taken out his wand and was using it as a dowser. "Hastily applied, badly done, but black magic nonetheless," he said.

"Never mind that!" said Lutterworth forcefully. "They're all dead and gone! Where's the treasure?"

"These bones are more than likely the anomaly my wand felt," Nicholas began, only to have Lutterworth yell "What? Are you trying to tell me we spent all this time clearing out this fucking cave to find a pile of goddamned bones?"

Atalanta, who had gone to stand by Sabrina, murmured "And now we are to be treated to another show of temper. How I wish his mother had taught him better manners!"

Neither Ellery nor Dr. Beck paid him any heed. They were watching Julian as green light from his wand streamed towards the bones, and wound itself through and around the bones to travel up the mound. At the top, the clean, pure green for a few moments turned a sickly, revolting colour. It flashed quickly, burning brightly and then returned to its former colour.

"What was *that*?" Dr. Beck asked.

"That rid us of the last remnants of the black magic," said Ellery in approval. "The Healing magic cleared it out."

"I used another forensic spell to halt the decay," Julian informed them, "in addition to the removal of the necromancy. I want to come back her and conduct a thorough investigation." there would be no need for the others to be present and have to see the bones and bodies.

"But what is the purpose of this burial, if indeed it can be called such?" Dr. Beck queried. "I have never seen anything like this!"

"I think I know what it is," Julian said, looking distressed. "Ramón told me that when someone died in the mines, their bodies were tossed down a mine shaft or taken away and disposed of. In many cases they were taken away when suffering from illness or a broken limb. They were never seen again. From what little I was able to read many of these people, particularly the more recent deaths, might have still been alive when tossed down here. The bones are mostly those of women and children."

"How horrible!" said Atalanta who had turned away form the spectacle of Lutterworth almost frothing at the mouth. "How can anyone be so cruel to other people? Was it the Inquisition?"

"More than likely," agreed Julian. "I should like to ceremonially burn these bones and give any spirits lingering a final rest." He still looked troubled.

Ellery asked "What else is wrong?"

"I don't like this at all, Ellery," his nephew admitted. "That these people were regarded as expendable and dumped like this is bad enough. The examination was quick and somewhat superficial, but several bodies on the very top showed the unmistakable signs of having been sacrificed in a black ceremony and one of them was ritually killed just within the last few days. There is no mistaking or missing something that Dark."

When Lutterworth finally ceased screaming at Nicholas and accepted the fact that the anomaly felt by the wand was the stack of bones and bodies, they left the cave.

All of them save Lutterworth were somewhat subdued. Julian planned to come back as soon as possible with the supplies he needed, as well as Ramón, to perform a ceremony of *os cinis*, which translated from Wizard's Latin, meant literally 'bone ash'. This was nearly always done in cases such as this, when only bone remained and there was some doubt as to whether sprits might still linger, especially if the death had been violent or as a result of black magic. The fire of the Light would turn the bones to ashes, allowing them to return to the earth and give the lingering spirits no reason to remain behind.

It was later than they thought when at last they emerged from the cave. Shadows were growing long and it was time to return to the camp.

"Do you think that the ghosts that Mr. Yates heard were those of the people who died in that mound?" Sabrina asked her brother as they waited for Varian to return after taking the others on ahead. In spite of the heat of the day Sabrina felt chilled.

Ellery shrugged. "I don't know–I thought what little black magic we had to clean up was leftover from the Inquisition. But now..." he allowed his voice to trail off, a frown knitting his brow.

Flann was on Sabrina's shoulder and said "me an' Siofra are intendin' to be comin' out tonight, by ourselves, and seein' if the ghosts will be talkin' to us."

Ellery knew better than to try and change her mind, although with the threat of black magic hanging over them he was uneasy about their doing any such thing. But one could not tell a cat what to do. They were very independent creatures, even more so than most familiars. "Have Varian bring you out and wait for you," he suggested. "If you have to get away quickly, nothing is faster than a dragon." Flann agreed to this at once.

Bairre, like Flann, on his mage's shoulder, shivered and moved nearer until he was pressed up against Ellery's collar. "I don't want to see any ghosts, or black magic!" he said feelingly.

"If the ghosts will be talkin' to us," said Flann, "they might be able to tell us who and where the black mage is bein'."

"But perhaps the ghosts have been released from the emerald and have nothing to do with the bodies," Bairre suggested.

"That's what we'll have to be findin' out tonight," said Flann evenly.

When Nicholas and the others were left at the campsite by Varian it was to find Erianne worried about Pacho. "He's barely eaten all day," she explained to Nicholas. "The others, even Amyas, are eating well, but something is bothering Pacho. I wish you would look at him, Nick. I hope he is not sickening for something!"

Although not a draconic veterinarian, Nicholas, as the holder of a Doctorate in Dracophilology, knew a great deal about dragon diseases.

Pacho was lying apart from the others who were having a game with, surprisingly, Yancy Yates. The cowboy had made a ball-like creation of long grasses and river mud and was tossing this around with the dragonets. "Ain't they the cutest danged little critters I ever seen!" he marveled. This ball had a tendency to fall apart frequently, which only added to the fun.

Pacho lay in a huddle, wings folded and tail drawn up. His head lay between his outstretched forelegs and he looked thoroughly unhappy.

Nicholas squatted down in front of him and reached out to rub that little dragonet's eye ridges. "What is it, Pacho?" he asked in Spanish. "Don't you feel well? Do you have a pain anywhere?" At this age he could gauge the dragonet's temperature by touch as his scales had not as yet hardened. Later on, the scales would dull when he had a fever, but a thermometer would be needed to tell the exact degree. Pacho did not seem to have a fever.

Pacho barely raised his head. His eyes were listless and his voice depressed as he said in low tones. "She never came. I waited all day but she never came."

"She cannot always get away," said Nicholas, trying to be soothing. "I am certain that she would rather be with you, but–"

Pacho raised his head a little more. "Everyone else has their bond-mate with them; Erianne and Seneca and Eda, even Varian has you! Why can't Marisela be with me?" He sounded both bitter and resentful. "And don't tell me Amyas hasn't anyone. One day he'll find his bond-mate and he won't be abandoned like I am!"

Something was going to have to be done about this, Nicholas thought as his heart sank. These early days of the dragonet and his bond-mate getting to know one another were very important. Marisela *had* to spend more time with Pacho. She would have to tell her parents about the dragonet and make arrangements to accommodate him. Pacho could become ill in earnest if he refused to eat and brooded. He could even eventually die of loneliness.

Nevertheless, he spoke sternly to Pacho. "Not eating is not going to bring her here any faster," he admonished the dragonet. "How do you think she will feel when she comes and finds you sick from not eating? It will make her unhappy."

"What if she does not come tomorrow, either?" Pacho asked, sounding hopeless.

"If you promise to eat your supper," said Nicholas, "I will go and get her myself tomorrow."

Pacho raised his head fully from the ground and looked at Nicholas, surprised and suddenly hopeful. "Really? You will bring her to me?"

"I promise," said Nicholas. The dragonet's entire aspect had changed.

"Oh, thank you, Nicholas!" sighed the dragonet and rubbed his face along Nicholas's arm in trust and happiness.

By the time the sewing women, the milliner and the shoemaker packed up for the day, dark was closing in. They would stay at the *Hacienda* while they worked, although they would eat and sleep with the servants. *Doña* Paloma and her maid left as well, wishing to return to their *Hacienda* before it became full dark.

Marisela was left with a splitting headache and a wish to be far, far away from here. She was immensely worried about Pacho. How had he fared by himself all day?

Her mother had insisted on her remaining in the new gown with the new hairstyle so that her father could see it. Marisela doubted that *Don* Casimiro cared for such things or would even notice. Indeed he gave her but a cursory look when *Doña* Milagros pointed out Marisela's changed looks to him. He only grunted, but from the way his wife beamed, one might have supposed him to have praised his daughter's altered appearance immoderately. *Don* Casimiro's only concern was that he was not paying for any of this. The besotted bridegroom would do that.

Food seemed to stick in Marisela's throat. All she wanted to do was to go get out of these horrible restrictive clothes and brush out her hair. It was now far and away too late to go out and see Pacho. One did not stray too far from home or away from a campfire at full dark of night, when wolves and coyote roamed, unless, of course, one could ride a dragon.

They were more than halfway through the meal when a noise was heard out on the hall and old Pedro was heard protesting to someone.

A few moment later, Curro, the head *vaquero*, entered the room. He looked disheveled and angry, covered in dust.

"*Perdóneme, Señora, Señorita,*" said Curro wide-brimmed *sombrero* in hand. He made a slight bow. "But I felt that the *patrón* should know of what has happened with the herd. The thieving dragon has returned. It carried off two cows late this afternoon."

Don Casimiro cursed audibly and tossed down his napkin. "Did you see it well enough to identify it?" he asked.

"*Sí, patrón*" Curro said. "Big and green, as is the one that is with the *Norteaméricanos* at *El Morro.*"

Chapter Twenty Eight
Nightfall

To Lutterworth's disgust, Sabrina invited Yancy Yates to join them for supper.

The cowboy was glad to accept. His normal diet was endless cans of beans and coffee. He also enjoyed playing with and talking to the dragonets. Like most people, he found them irresistible. Only Lutterworth seemed immune to their charms. Even Melville Sinclair had been helping with their feeding and care, particularly since Amyas hadn't a bond-mate and Marisela had not arrived to see and tend Pacho.

After Nicholas's promise to fetch Marisela the next day, the little New Mexico Twilight ate a good supper and went to sleep under Erianne's wings with the others. The humans sat about the fire, listening to Yates' tales of cattle drives in the Colorado and Wyoming territories, clashes with the *vaqueros* of New Spain over 'rustling' cattle and of hunting buffalo on the Great Plains with the Indian tribes found there.

Only Lutterworth stayed apart. Even Dr. Beck seemed to enjoy the tales. Yates was a natural story-teller and quite modest. Although he seemed to have in his young life had enough adventure for two men twice his age, he told his tales without boasting and a humorous self depreciation that was very attractive.

Atalanta, watching Lutterworth out of the corner of her eye, wondered at the man. He sat away from the others, muttering to himself. He was still angry about there being no treasure in the cave and had already informed the party that they were going back the next day. There were many more caverns and passageways off the main chamber and he would not rest until they were all thoroughly explored. He was as certain as ever that the treasure lay there, his for the taking.

In spite of the necklace and the emerald that they had found Atalanta could still not think that a treasure really existed still. If there had ever been something there she thought it possible that it had been found long since and that the emerald was what had probably been left behind. The necklace had more than likely been lost at *El Morro* by a traveler. Atalanta was reasonably certain that most of the others in the party agreed with her conclusions.

When it was full dark, Siofra and Flann decided to leave for the caves. Varian, as Ellery had suggested, took them there, also returning to a reluctant Yancy Yates to his normal post. He utterly refused to go near the cave system at night again and Julian supported him in that decision. This caused more argument from Lutterworth but as he could find no one, not even Sinclair, to agree with him, the tycoon had to give in, although with ill grace, claiming that Yates was stealing him blind.

After leaving Yates off at his original camp some miles from the cave-in site, Varian took the two familiars back to the cavern.

In spite of the still burning mage lights the entire place seemed far more sinister at night. The shadows in the caverns cast by the pillars of stone were somehow deeper and darker. An un-natural quiet seemed to lay over everything. Outside there was not even a wind, only the wide expanse of starry sky. No nighttime animals could be heard and it seemed to Varian that the three of them were very much alone in this totally alien landscape. The dragon could understand why Yates was so frightened. He himself was big and had flame to protect himself, although if there *were* ghosts, flame was no more use than a rifle, but he still had some little trepidation about going near spirits. However, the cats were his friends and he would not leave them here by themselves.

Varian walked down into the cave with the two cats still in the carrying basket on the back of his saddle. The top had been left unlatched so that they could easily push it open with their paws. He called to them and crouched very low to the ground so that they could descend from his back easily.

All his work that day with the stones had ended in the dead eggs being now covered with a pile of rocks, a cairn entombing the lost dragonets. Varian wondered uneasily if the spirits of these dragonets might not chide him, for it was every adult dragon's duty to care for eggs and help them hatch. Varian had counted eleven dead eggs and he had carefully laid them beneath the stones, saying a prayer to the Dragon Lord, to give the dead dragonets rest and to see their souls into the afterlife until they were born again. It was always a sorrow when an egg did not hatch. Not a great many eggs in a year were ever laid, and Varian knew that many elder dragons worried about the future of their species, that it might die out entirely. There seemed to be fewer dragons about each year. Back home, there were long lists of people who wanted a dragon and had to wait until there were sufficient eggs available.

Flann interrupted these somber thoughts. "Ye'll be stayin' here, no doubt?" she asked.

"No doubt," he agreed. "I really don't want to see any ghosts. But if you need to get away quickly I'll be here."

Flann looked amused. "Sure, an' what can a ghost be after doin' to us?"

"'Tis not as if they can be frightenin' us!" agreed Siofra. "An' I should like to be seein' the ghost that would dare harm a cat! Why, 'tis against nature! Sometimes we are bein' their only connection to the world of th' livin', to be conveyin' messages and such, an' should it get about that one of them was after hurtin' one of us," she looked very formidable for such a small wisp of feline "why, then the spirits would not be likin' what would happen at all."

The two cats then sauntered into the cave where Ellery and the others had found the emerald, tails high, as if they were going on a pleasure jaunt. Varian did not wish at all to join them.

A few mage lights, burning low, had been left in the caves. This was as Flann and Siofra wanted it. Ghosts were not over fond of bright lights, particularly mage lights, as they could not douse these as they could lanterns, candles, oil lamps, gas lights and even the new electric arc lights.

"'Twill most like be nearer midnight when they are bein' out an' about," said Siofra. She lay down on the floor of the cave, with her paws tucked underneath her and tail wrapped about her.

Flann agreed with this. She copied her friend's stance and soon both cats fell into a light doze. But they were still on the alert. The slightest sound or happening would wake them instantly.

A sharp drop in temperature was the first thing that alerted them.

Both cats woke at once, their eyes gleaming in the darkness. Both had pupils open wide, making their large eyes seem bigger than ever.

"We're havin' company, no doubt," said Siofra in satisfaction.

Neither she nor Flann moved, still laying at their ease.

A human being, present at the moment would have been feeling at the very least, a deepening sense of unease, even if he or she was blessed with nerves of steel. Those without such nerves would doubtless feel their flesh crawl and would run, screaming, from the cave.

The entire atmosphere of the cave was changing. In addition to the cold, a strange phosphorescence that had nothing to do with the mage lights began to flicker about the walls. It ranged in colour from pale green to a most lurid, sickly shade of yellowish verdure. The air echoed with mocking, blood-curdling laughter which swiftly escalated into an argument, the voices too quick to follow what they were saying.

As the cats watched, the light began to coalesce into a mass, then broke apart into three distinct shapes; shapes that shortly began to resemble human beings.

Then more noise, much louder, began: screaming, cursing and sobbing breaths, and he clanging of steel as blade met blade.

"Oh, this is after bein' a fine manifestation, this is!" said Siofra happily to her companion.

Flann agreed with her.

The similarity to real people continued to grow. Soon the cats could see three men, desperately fighting with swords. They appeared to be fighting each other, not two on one side against a third as might have been supposed.

As the details were revealed they could be seen to be all men of middle years. One wore a full beard and the helm, padded jerkin and breeches the cats knew to be of the era of the *Conquistadors*. Perhaps he was a soldier. The other two were dressed roughly in loose canvas breeches and full sleeved shirts. One was barefoot. This man had a particularly cruel look about him and wore a patch over one eye. He appeared to be winning the battle for he was both taller and stronger than the others. He also had less compunction about dirty fighting than his opponents for as the two spectators watched he kicked the soldier in a particularly vulnerable location and stabbed him in the neck with a dagger pulled from his belt as, gasping in pain, the soldier bent over.

Eye-patch's cry of triumph was cut short by the third man, who quirkily came up behind him and ran him through with what Siofra recognized as a cutlass. Eye-patch collapsed across the dying soldier, who was groaning in pain.

"Mine!" the third man cried in Spanish and bent to the ground to pick up something that gleamed green fire.

"The emerald!" said Flann.

But eye-patch, even in a dying condition, still had fight left in him. "Not while I live!" he roared, blood dripping from his mouth, and with a thrust upwards from where he had fallen, split open the third man's stomach.

He gasped and dropped the stone, which rolled away to the exact spot that Bairre had found it.

"All this fuss over a wee stone!" said Siofra in disgust in an under-voice to Flann. "Come on," she added and got up to walk towards the ghosts. Flann fell in beside her.

The ghosts were in a dying condition, if persons already dead could be said to be dying. Bleeding from many wounds, one with his entrails spilling from between his hands, the curses and moans were terrible to hear. Little wonder that Yates had been so scared.

Neither Siofra or Flann was the least bit frightened. Siofra only hoped that these ghosts were not the type that were trapped in an endless loop, doomed to repeat their last moments over and over again, unable to do anything but that. She wanted to question them.

Many spirits did not speak, even to cats. Often times they *could* not speak. Since they had heard these spirits speaking the cats had hopes that they could and would be able to talk to them. Now was the time to talk, for the cats could already see the luminosity gathering that might signal the spirits' disappearance. They might appear again and they might not.

In the cat's experience (for Ireland was a country with many ghosts) spirits reappeared in the same place, doing the same thing again and again, sometimes only once in the night. They were more like automations than real people. Sometimes malevolent spirits could wreak havoc in a house, or even harm the occupants. And unfortunately, sometimes it needed a medium to break the cycle of the repetitive action for the ghosts to be able to talk to anyone, needing a vessel to inhabit to be able to speak from the spirit world. Many ghosts were not even conscious of any observers, even cats, locked in their own hell of endlessly repeating a moment in time.

As the luminosity gathered eye-patch groaned and muttered a name. With the incredible hearing of felines, both Siofra and Flann made it out.

The ghosts began to fade, turning to clouds. The temperature in the cavern began to rise.

The haunts were gone.

"Shall we wait to see if they would be after returnin'?" asked Flann.

"Oh, aye," agreed Siofra. "We've the night. Even though we are not perhaps bein' able to be talkin' to them I want to be hearin' what he was sayin' again."

Flann agreed with this and they settled down to wait.

Once the non-magicals in the party had all retired and Atalanta was sleeping, Sabrina drew on her robe and slippers and went to join her brother and nephews in their tent.

Ellery had made tea and poured her a cup once she sat down, joining Nicholas on his cot.

All of the men looked quite grim and Sabrina thought that she more than likely looked the same way. Both Bairre and Cillian were wide awake as well.

"There's no doubt about it," said Julian. "The woman's

body that lay on top of the pile was killed by having her throat slit, but even my preliminary spell showed unmistakable traces of demon-use on her. There were traces of arcane symbols left on her body as well. Someone tried to remove them but such evil leaves a residue that my wand was able to read. She was repeatedly raped by a demon as well as a human man."

Sabrina's tea suddenly did not taste too well.

"We'll have to find them and stop them," said Ellery. "We've a sworn duty to do that." They were all well aware of this.

"We need to find out as well if that place *is* the disposal for people from the mines. I would hate to think that black magic has flourished for over two hundred years here and that all of the people there were sacrifices," said Julian. "That argues a very old and persistent evil, deeply entrenched."

"They must have a den somewhere close then," said Nicholas thoughtfully. "I wish I had more experience with fighting the Dark!" he burst out.

"None of us has have any real experience," said Ellery ruefully. "No one in our families who has ever fought the Dark went into it with any experience. It's not as if it is something one might gain practical experience in. One may only be taught theory."

"At least in Grandfather's day," said Nicholas "one had to vanquish a small demon in order to pass *Magistra*. They dropped that requirement over forty years ago. That could be counted as experience."

"The Dark I felt in the ley lines was not profound," said Sabrina. It was not usual for a Witch to tap ley lines but the family had a long history of females using this power. "Perhaps this mage does not use them with any degree of regularity?"

"Was any of her spirit left, Julian?" Ellery asked. "Enough to ask questions of with a spell of revelation?"

"Not that I could discern, no" he answered. Sometimes the victims of black magic left something of themselves behind that could be tapped for information.

"We don't know *anything* about this black magician," put in Bairre. He shivered slightly and pressed closer to

Ellery.

Ellery sighed and pulled Bairre into his lap. "We now have ghosts, at least one demon, a black mage to find and destroy, and perhaps worst of all, Lutterworth and his treasure hunt. It is not going to be easy."

All of them felt that this might be an understatement.

Chapter Twenty Nine

Accused

The four mages sat and talked for over an hour, trying to decide how to combat the menace of black magic. As Cillian sensibly pointed out they could not decide on a plan of action until they knew more about the Dark magic involved: who was the practitioner, how many of them were there, where were their black rituals being conducted and just how many demons and what kind of demons were they talking about?

It was at last decided that much more investigation would be needed and that they would have to be on the alert at all times. There were non-magical people to protect, as well as the dragonets.

But they all agreed on one thing: they had a duty to find and destroy the necromancer.

After Sabrina left for her bed and the others settled down to sleep, Ellery, accompanied by Bairre, went to the artifact tent where he had set up a table to use as a desk. In spite of the fact that this was completely unlike any dig he had been on, he was still writing up his daily excavation log, which Sabrina would then transcribe on her type-writing machine.

A mage light lit the interior and Ellery took his leather-bound journal from a shelf. He opened it to the day's date and took pen and ink from a drawer.

Bairre watched him and said "I daresay there will be no book coming from *this* expedition."

"Not unless the people who read my books, an admittedly small part of the population, want to read my account of how I managed not to kill Lutterworth," said Ellery, beginning to write rapidly. "And who knows, I still might have to kill him!"

"He is awful, isn't he? And he swears in front of ladies as well!" said Bairre. The ferret had a highly developed sense of propriety. He sighed and said, "Sometimes I wish we had not come, especially now, with this threat of black magic. I'm a little frightened," he admitted.

Ellery put down the pen and looked at his familiar in sympathy. "We all are," he said gently. "We'd be foolish not to be. Don't worry, Bairre, we shall do all that we can to protect you and the other familiars."

Bairre looked up at him gratefully. "I know you will. But I'm worried about your safety as well."

The flap to the tent was pulled aside and the two cats entered. "I was after thinkin' ye would still be awake," said Siofra. "I'm hopin' that Julian has gone to his bed, for it's in my heart that he has not been gettin' enough sleep as of late."

"I'm the only one mad enough to still be up this much after midnight," said Ellery. It was well after one in the morning.

"What did you find out about the ghosts?" Bairre asked eagerly.

"We weren't able to be speakin' to them," said Flann. She jumped up on the table top to be nearer Ellery and Bairre, followed by Siofra. "They're the repeatin' variety of ghosts, an' were bein' no more conscious of us than a baby is bein' conscious of mathematics."

"But there are two things we were after findin' out," said Siofra. She sat down beside the ink bottle. "We were goin' into another cave and it was full of bats. We were bein' able to question some o' them that had come in from huntin' an' they were tellin' us that until yesterday, there were bein' no ghosts in those caverns at all."

"That means my pyschometry more than likely released them from that emerald," said Ellery on a sigh. The ghosts would need to be dealt with too: laid to rest if possible.

"Tell us what they were like and what they did," Bairre urged.

The two cats took turns telling Ellery and Bairre what they had seen. "An' 'tis no doubt in me mind at all that the big fellow wi' th' eye patch was the face that showed up over yours," said Flann.

"An' he was cursin' someone just afore he was after dyin', or dyin' again. We both were after hearin' him. He cursed someone called Maldon." Siofra said. "Blamed him for them dyin' so far from home. 'Twas their greed that was after killin' them!" she said in no little contempt.

"Maldon?" repeated Bairre. "That scarcely sounds Spanish! This just gets stranger and stranger," he added.

"There is a Maldon in England, in Essex, in the

Blackwater estuary," said Ellery. "Remember, Bairre, when we were at University we excavated there one summer."

"Oh, yes!" cried the ferret, remembering. "The Battle of Maldon in 991! Viking invaders defeated the forces of King Edward the Elder. Someone even wrote a poem about it!"

"But what connection could an' Englishman be 'havin' wi' an emerald in a cave in New Spain?" Siofra asked.

It was a question that did not seem to have an answer

When Julian awoke the next morning he at once thought of Ramón. His pupil had no doubt been disappointed that his teacher had not come at all yesterday. But this morning he had to see Ramón. He wanted the Native to go with him to the cave. Perhaps Ramón could identify some of the bodies now under a preservation spell and confirm that these were victims of the heartlessness of the Inquisition, not all of black magic.

As Julian sat up, Siofra, who was curled up beside his pillow, opened one eye and looked at him. He had hoped not to disturb her when he began to stir, but there was real little hope of that with a cat as a bedmate.

She yawned and stretched as he asked "What happened last night?"

"I'll be tellin' everyone th' story over breakfast so I am not repeatin' meself," she answered. "An' Flann will be there to be helpin' me wi' the tale."

The tent flap stirred and a dragonet peered in. "Is Nicholas going to fetch Marisela now?" Pacho asked eagerly.

Julian glanced over to where both Nicholas and Cillian still slumbered. Ellery and Bairre were gone already. "Not until after breakfast, I daresay."

"Oh." Pacho's face fell. Then he said "Can't you wake him up?"

Julian was just about to try and explain to the hopeful dragonet why this would not be possible when there was a lot of noise outside. Men were shouting and there was the bellow of an enraged dragon, as well as the still shrill cries of dragonets. Julian could hear horses as well and then there was a gunshot. Pacho turned and scampered away, perhaps thinking Marisela was arriving.

Julian was out of bed, pulling on his clothing, in a trice. Now was the time to waken Nicholas.

But Nicholas was now awake. He sat up quickly, rubbing at his eyes. Even Cillian woke up, looking startled. "What was that?" he demanded.

Siofra scampered from the tent. Julian followed her, as Nicholas struggled in to his discarded clothes. He was after Julian in less than a minute, carrying Cillian carefully.

They emerged from the tent in to a scene of utter chaos. Men on horseback were confronting Ellery, who stood with his wand out. Violet energy hung in the air: he had obviously worked magic of some sort.

Among the riders, who Nicholas recognized as some of the *vaqueros* from the *Hacienda del Sol,* rode *Don* Casimiro. The *Don* looked stern, his eyes flinty. "That creature," he exclaimed, pointing at Erianne with his riding crop, "stole two head of cattle yesterday and injured one of my *vaqueros*! Are you not getting enough cattle from us already, *Señors*, that you have to resort to thievery?"

"I have no need to steal cattle!" Erianne said proudly. She elongated her neck and looked down at the vaqueros, her eyes glittering. her wings were outstretched; Nichols guessed rightly the dragonets sheltered beneath those wings. Her first thought would be to protect them.

Varian stood in front of her, his wings raised and his head down. It was more than likely him that had bellowed. He was very protective of Erianne, even though she was his elder. He would also wish to shield the dragonets.

"Who fired that shot?" Julian demanded. The others were emerging from their tents as well: Sabrina and Atalanta, Dr. Beck, Sinclair and Lutterworth.

"He did," said Ellery angrily, pointing at a young *vaquero*. "I had just taken down the night wards when they rode in. He shot at Erianne," he added. "Fortunately I was able to deflect it. Do that again, boy, and I shall do worse to you than deflect your shot!" he said threateningly to the young man.

"*Don* Casimiro, what is going on?" Nicholas was the

only one acquainted with the *Don* and he now stepped forward. "Our dragons do not hunt or conduct raids on cattle. I doubt Erianne was even in the air yesterday for she has other things to occupy her time right now."

The *vaquero* who had fired the shot, Enrique, said in tones of furious indignation "The big green lizard mauled my brother Emilio with its claws! I *will* have justice for him! I care little for a *brujo* and his *hechiceria!*" This last word was insulting, for it meant black magic.

The other *vaqueros* nodded their heads and shouted support for Enrique. Some of them shook their fists and their rifles in a menacing manner.

A galloping horse was heard. Marisela, hair blowing wildly, her horse Vittoria covered in foam and streaming with sweat, slid to a stop in front of the *vaqueros.*

"Papa!" she cried as she tumbled from Vittorio's saddle. "This is a mistake! These dragons would not, could not, steal our cattle!"

"I told your mother to keep you at home!" her father snapped. "This does not concern you!"

"These are my friends," she said desperately. "The dragons too!"

From under Erianne's wing Pacho heard her voice. Joyfully, he said "Marisela!" And quickly, before she could stop him, he struggled out from Erianne's wing. He saw Marisela as soon as he emerged and ran towards her, giving shrill cries of pleasure and relief. She had finally come!

"Daughter, look out!" *Don* Casimiro shouted in horror as he saw what he thought was a savage beast with gleaming teeth rushing towrds his only child. The *Don's* horse reared as he quickly drew a long barreled gun from a saddle holster.

Marisela, closest to him, saw his intention and with a loud "NO!" flung herself at Pacho.

Before anyone could react the gun discharged and there was a scream of pain. Both Marisela and Pacho fell.

"This is a good beginning," came a husky voice from

behind a mask. "I am pleased with you, my new acolyte."

Teresa could not help but smirk. The first task given to her by Sister Diabla had been easy. She had done everything else that had been required of her. She had fasted, she had bathed in asses' milk (which had been difficult to obtain) and she had even drunk several noxious potions, most of which had given her horrible dreams. Now she was to be initiated into the Sisterhood.

Teresa Avila came from a long line of women who fancied themselves Witches, although they had no real power. They existed on the fringes of the society of New Spain, having to hide their activities from the Inquisition. They did not know that the Inquisition cared little about their sacrifices of chickens and love charms. The Inquisition was only interested in *real* power, not a pack of deluded women who sold love potions to the credulous.

When she had come here from Cuidad Mexico her mother had whispered to her that if she was to leave a certain sign at a certain place she would be contacted by members of the mysterious Sisterhood. This organization had no name that anyone had ever heard, but it was considered an honour to be asked to join. Not everyone was invited. Teresa felt proud that she had been approached after she had left her message of red and white feathers tied in a certain way. This indicated her interest in the Sisterhood. Written instructions (how fortunate that he mother had insisted she learn to read!) appeared in her room and she obeyed them implicitly. But today, she hoped, was her induction into the Sisterhood.

Teresa had been brought to a most peculiar place. Early in the morning, when it was still dark, she had been met at the crossroads as she had been directed. The instructions for this rendezvous had appeared mysteriously, as had the others in her room in the servants' quarters in the *Hacienda* of Don Rafael where she worked. These had told her that on her one day a week out, she was to come to this place and to do whatever she was told by the one who would meet her.

A hooded figure had met her and informed her in a hoarse voice that she must be blindfolded and strictly obey what she was told to do. If she could not obey, she was not worthy and would be summarily dismissed.

Teresa wanted this very badly. Her mother had belonged to the Sisterhood and her whispered tales of Witchcraft and orgies had excited Teresa. She found piety and good behavior boring. She wanted excitement and power, neither of which she was likely to get as a maid, or even worse, a *péon's* wife, liable to have a pack of children before she was thirty.

She obediently bent her head for the blindfold and extended her hands for her wrists to be tied in front of her. She was put in a cart and after they had jolted over a rough road for a while, the cart stopped. She was then carried through what she thought was a rocky terrain and then, as if she were a package, hauled down a ladder and deposited in this strangely quiet place.

When the blindfold and wrist restraints was removed, she found herself facing a hooded and masked figure who introduced herself as Sister Diabla. Teresa, if she was obedient and accepted everything at her initiation, would be her acolyte, her pupil, and would learn the ways of Witchcraft, the ways of the Black One.

"Do you promise?" she said in that low voice, leaning close to Teresa.

"*Sí*," the girl said as a shiver of excitement ran over her. Sister Diabla smelled of some heady, musky scent.

"Do you have what you were told to gather for us?"

Teresa put her hand into the pocket of her skirt and pulled out the hair she had gathered from Marisela's brush and comb. From her mother's tales she had guessed what use the hair was to be put to.

"*Buena*," approved Sister Diabla and took it from her, putting it into a pocket in her black silk robe.

'And now, you must be bound to the Black One and entered into his service," said Sister Diabla. "Are you a virgin?"

"*Sí*, Sister," Teresa answered. She was intensely curious about what went on between men and women, but she had never met a young man amongst the peasant lads that she considered worthy of her giving herself to him.

"Disrobe. I would see your body and what you will offer the Brotherhood," Sister Diabla ordered.

Teresa was conscious that she had agreed to obey, so

she quickly took her clothes off until she stood in front of Sister Diabla completely naked. The odd floor she stood on, a blue green in colour, was intensely cold and she curled her toes up and away from it. She stole a quick look about the room and realized that she was in a cave.

Sister Diabla seemed to approve what she saw. Teresa had always known that not only her face but her body was beautiful. She could not help but shiver slightly as it was very cold in this icy cavern.

"You will not feel the cold when the ceremony begins." said Sister Diabla. "You will sacrifice your virginity to our brothers and to our Lord and master. They will take their pleasure on your body many times. When it is over, you will be one of us. Come, lie on the altar. They will be here soon and I must ready you for their use."

Still shivering, Teresa allowed herself to be led to the altar. She was suddenly eager and felt no terror as Sister Diabla began to tie her down.

Chapter Thirty
ᴥurgery

Abandoning his horse, who was snorting and terrified of the dragonet so near him, *Don* Casimiro ran forward to drop to his knees by Marisela's side. In many ways the *Don* was a negligent father, but seeing his child drop like a stone nearly at his feet had caused him to suffer such a spasm of horror that his legs nearly refused to carry him. And to think that his bullet, meant for that creature, might have done this to her!

She was still conscious, but gasping in pain. A spreading red stain was covering the front of her white blouse and she looked up at her father as if not seeing him. "Pacho!" she said hoarsely. "Where's Pacho?" She was having trouble breathing.

"Be still, Daughter," he said, not understanding what she wanted. He was barely conscious of someone else kneeling beside him. "Let me see," a voice said in his ear as he continued to clutch at Marisela. "I'm a doctor, *Señor*. Let me help."

As Julian with difficulty pried *Don* Casimiro from his daughter's body, Nicholas rushed forward to the injured dragonet. He knew enough draconic medicine to see that the injury was grave as he flung himself down beside Pacho's inert body.

The bullet had entered his shoulder and the wound was bleeding rapidly. Pressure applied to the surrounding area slowed the rush of dragon ichor to a trickle but the little dragonet was unconscious and breathing heavily. Sabrina knelt beside him too and said "I sent Atalanta for some towels, Nick. Can we stop the bleeding?"

"I don't know," he said, his voice tense. He was conscious of both Erianne, Varian and Torin in the background looking on anxiously and of the dragonets crying in shock and fear. "Thank God he is so young and has no gasses built up. It would have been all over for him," he added.

"Nick," Julian called, his voice as stressed and angry as Nicholas felt. "Can you keep him stable? It will be a while before I can get to him. *Doña* Marisela needs immediate surgery. I can do a quick spell for Pacho but–"

"He's lost a lot of ichor," Nicholas said worriedly. Dragon ichor was a much darker red than a human's blood, almost black, and a great pool of it lay beneath the dragonet.

"Then I'll have to put him in stasis," Julian said. He stood up and beckoned to Sinclair. "I'm going to levitate her. Help me steady her. I need to get her to the table under the awning."

"I'll clean it," said Sabrina and jumped up to run to the awning, almost colliding with Atalanta who was hurrying from the women's tent with a pile of towels.

Ellery, meanwhile, was occupied with holding off the *vaqueros,* who had taken the shooting as an opportunity to try and rush the other dragons. A wall of warding had stopped them in their tracks, but now they were beating against the invisible wall and cursing, even attempting to fire their rifles at it.

He was also fending off demands from Lutterworth and listening to the bleating of Dr. Beck, who was shocked and horrified at the violence he had seen and was exclaiming in a rapidly rising voice that this was not what he was accustomed to, not at all!

Lutterworth wanted to know what the hell was going on and why it was holding up setting out for the caves once more. As the entire altercation had been in Spanish, they had no idea what was happening. Lutterworth seemed oblivious to the fact that a girl and a dragonet had been gravely injured.

Sabrina cleaned the table top to an almost sterile cleanliness with a spell used in hospitals, learned from her father. Siofra and Flann went to the tent and fetched Julian's medical bag, carrying it in their teeth between them.

Looking as he might be sick at any moment Sinclair gingerly helped Julian steady Marisela. He averted his face as the movement exposed the full extent of the bloody damage. She was now unconscious, her head drooping limply.

Don Casimiro came to his feet, never taking his eyes off his child. He had blanched and crossed himself when he saw her rise from the ground with no one touching her. "You, a *brujo*, are a real doctor?" he said worriedly to Julian. "You can save her?"

"Yes, I am a *real* doctor. I have a very good chance of saving her," Julian answered. When *Don* Casimiro moved as if he would follow them to the makeshift surgical table, he said "I think, sir, it would be best if you did not watch. The bullet went through her lungs and this will be a tricky bit of work."

When Marisela had been laid on the table Julian quickly went back to Pacho and used a spell of *"Detinere,"* to put Pacho into temporary stasis. This would not only slow the loss of ichor, but would dull the pain and stop infection. It was a temporary state of almost suspended animation. "Pack the wound with one of those towels," he instructed Nicholas.

"Varian," Julian addressed the dragon who was watching the wounded dragonet, his silver eyes darkened with distress. "I need you to find Ramón and bring him here. He has a dragon; he is more knowledgeable than I when it comes to dragon physiology and I shall have need of him if I am to be able to Heal Pacho." He did not add that he would need to tap Ramon's Healing strength as well, for if Marisela was as gravely injured as the preliminary examination had revealed, he was going to be drained by her Healing.

Varian nodded and at once took off, in the opposite direction of Ellery's warding wall. Several of the *vaqueros* cursed and fired tat him. but their shots fell short of reaching him.

Erianne had the dragonets under her wings and they could be heard wailing. Erianne herself wore an expression of both worry and anger. She was trying to compose herself for the dragonets' sakes but it was proving impossible. A dragoness would usually croon to her offspring in distressing circumstances, which would calm them and send them to sleep, but Erianne found herself unable to do so. She was far too enraged. Stupid, stupid men who brought guns into a volatile situation and let their tempers rule! They were always so surprised when a tragedy took place! She was also deeply insulted at having been accused of stealing cattle and actually injuring a human being. If not for Ellery she might have been the one lying there wounded, or even dead as, to an adult dragon, filled with gasses, being shot at such a close range was nearly always fatal.

Ellery paid little heed to Lutterworth or Dr. Beck,

both growing increasingly loud. His attention was divided between Julian, Nicholas and the *vaqueros*. Not until Lutterworth grabbed him by the shoulder did Ellery react. Instinctively, he pushed Lutterworth away with a burst of magic, sending the tycoon hurtling backwards to land on his buttocks. He looked up, astonished, at Ellery, too surprised to even curse.

"If you will both just be quiet!" Ellery said between gritted teeth. "I'll tell you what is going on. But you have to be quiet! Julian is going to need peace for concentration if he is to save that young woman and the dragonet. All this yelling and complaining isn't helping anything." In a few succinct phrases he explained what had happened that morning. Lutterworth opened his mouth once or twice and then closed it again at a glare from Ellery. Dr. Beck subsided to an occasional bleat.

After ascertaining that Nicholas had matters well in hand, (he had the help of Bairre and Cillian) Atalanta went to the fire and with a cloth wrapped hand, took the kettle off the heated rocks and took it to the improvised surgery.

Sabrina had already laid out the few candles and other impedimenta that Julian would need. Her nephew was stripping the clothing away form Marisela's wound and said "Good!" when he saw the hot water. "I may need both of you," he said. "Does blood bother you, Miss Beck?"

"Not at all," she replied in her serene manner." Many times, on our digs, I was obliged to act as doctor for hurts sustained by our diggers."

Sabrina poured the water in to a bowl and took some soap and towels from Julian's bag. As the three of them washed thoroughly, the cats, who had jumped up on the foot of the table near Marisela's feet began purring. Their purrs would keep her asleep so that she would not feel any pain.

As they scrubbed at their hands and nails Julian explained how Marisela was injured and what he was going to do. "The bullet went through her right lung and out her back, then into Pacho. The lung is not only collapsed, but filling with blood. Since it was a heavy caliber bullet and at close range there is a lot of damage. I've got to drain the lung and tie off the bleeding as well as repair the damage. I've go to work fast as a collapsed lung can lead to cyanosis and death."

He glanced over to where Melville Sinclair held Marisela slightly up so that she was not lying flat on the Abel. The girl's breathing was flat and shallow, her normally dusky skin pale. She would be cool to the touch, her skin damp. There was a horrible sucking sound through the chest wound where air was entering the thorax instead of through the nose or mouth as it should .

To Sinclair's intense relief, Julian had Sabrina take his place. Sinclair felt light-headed at the sight of so much blood and staggered away from the table where he was promptly sick. He could not imagine how anybody could want to be a doctor.

Sabrina used an easing spell so she could support Marisela effortlessly. Both she had Julian had worked in her father Stuart's clinic in the poorer part of Dublin. They had seen a fair share of shootings and stabbings. She was now glad for the experience.

After setting up candles at her feet and head, and drawing a Healing circle in the air with his wand, Julian said a quick spell for the help of the angel of Healing to come to Marisela's aid. He opened himself fully to the ley lines and using a scalpel of obsidian entered her chest cavity. The scalpel was magiced against infection. He asked Atalanta to use the clean towels to sponge away the blood that would inevitably ooze out whenever he nodded.

Atalanta, watching with interest, wondered if all surgeons were as fast. Magic, she could see, gave a physician a great advantage. Working quickly, with green Healing light flowing from his fingers, Julian pulled the blood from her lung and re-inflated it. Healing magic flowed into the damaged tissues and mended them. The bullet had smashed a rib as well and this began to knit itself, the bone cracks and chips flying together to make it whole.

The bubbling breathing steadied. Colour began to come back into Marisela's face. "Now to close these wounds," Julian murmured and held his hands over the open wound on her chest. A surge of power went straight through the girl's body as the badly injured tissues and flesh began to Heal from the inside out.

"Oh, my!" Sabrina heard Atalanta say in admiration. Sabrina agreed with her. She had watched her father at work many times and this was as nice a Healing as she had ever seen.

The chest wound closed, sutures of green light appearing along the length of the scalpel wound. These would fade quickly and there would be little or no scarring. "She can lay down now," Julian directed and Sabrina eased Marisela's head and shoulders to the table top.

Julian went to his bag and pulled out a piece of India rubber that looked like a slightly flattened pyramid. This he tapped with his wand, saying "*Spiritus*," and then fitted it over Marisela's face and nose. "That is a respirator. She'll need some help breathing for a while," he said at Atalanta's inquiring look. "She'll need that for at least twenty-four hours and then I can give her a breathing bottle with she can use if she feels the need. Where's her father? I need to talk to him."

"First you need to sit down," said Sabrina firmly, for her nephew looked gray and exhausted. Intense magic, done at top speed, had that effect. And Healing was the most draining magic that there was.

"I'm hearin' a dragon comin'!" announced Siofra.

"Ramón," murmured Julian, sinking in to one of the canvas chairs. "Sabrina," he began, but his aunt interrupted him with "I know what to do. I'll levitate her into my bed and keep her warm. You must rest until you go to Pacho."

Don Casimiro had fallen to his knees a little ways from the scene of his daughter's surgery. He had covered his face with his hands, praying equally for her recovery and for forgiveness for having shot his own child. He had also been frightened by the magic he had seen. He was not certain whether his daughter was being Healed or condemned to Hell.

When he finally dared to look up he saw the frightening sight of his daughter, flat on her back floating through the air–again.

"*Madre de Dios!*" He looked quickly from Marisela to where the *brujo* doctor was sitting, rather slumped, at the table. It was all over? Was she alive? He scrambled to his feet and approached the doctor.

"*Señor el médico?*" he said a little timidly. "Does she live?"

Julian looked up at him tiredly. "She lives and

barring unforeseen complications, she will keep living."

"Then I will take her home!" said *Don* Casimiro eagerly.

Julian shook his head. "She mustn't be moved for at least twenty-four hours. She should sleep as much as possible and she will need help in breathing. I also want her where I can watch her for the foreseeable future. Everything was Healed, but I don't want to take any chances with a lung wound. It's much better to be overly cautious in cases such as hers."

"But what can I do, *Señor*?" pleaded the hapless *Don*.

"It would be a great help to everyone if you could remove those men of yours. The *Señorita* needs rest and quiet and that noise will not help her recovery," Julian said. He might have added that everyone would suffer until the *vaqueros* were made to desist. Even as he spoke more shots and shouts rang out.

Don Casimiro's jaw tightened and he looked suddenly more his old self. "This I can and will attend to!" he said briskly and strode off.

Not inclined to move just yet, Julian watched as not one but two dragons began to circle down. Nah-kah-yen had brought Ramón, accompanied by Varian.

Julian was glad to see him. He need the strength of his pupil and his assistance. Julian had never Healed a dragon and he would need all of the help that Ramón, Nicholas and perhaps even the other dragons could give him.

Chapter Thirty One
Healing a Dragonet

Ramón had been very disappointed that his teacher had not come the day before. As usual, he was assailed by doubts. Perhaps the *gringo médico* had decided he was not worth teaching? Perhaps he had done something wrong, or somehow offended?

But Gian-nah-tah had laughed at him. "He is pleased with you, Nantan Lupan!" the fox said. If the fox had been human Ramón would have said that he was grinning. "Even I could see that! Have no fear; he will come again. A Medicine Man's time is not always his own. You must grow used to that if you are to be a *diyin*." The fox was so sure that Ramón had to be comforted.

And then this morning had come the summons. The pale green dragon had arrived on the mountainside camp, almost breathless from flying very fast. Ramón's teacher had need of him, he said .Both a young woman and a dragonet had been shot.

As soon as Nah-kah-yen could be saddled they were off. Varian had not as yet been saddled when the altercation had happened and he was grateful that the blue dragon was there. It would have gone against every instinct and every bit of training of Varian's to take up a rider with no saddle or harness. He was shocked to see that in fact there was no safety harness on the Nah-kah-yen's shabby saddle. How could the blue dragon be so careless of his rider's safety?

Nah-kah-yen was more eager than he would admit to go to the camp at *El Morro*. He wanted to see that dragoness. She was not mated to the pale green one or to any other and he had been thinking more and more of mating lately. Compared to a human man, a male dragon came to sexual maturity late, usually twenty or even a little older. Nah-kah-yen was now twenty-five, almost twenty-six. In normal circumstances he might have been mated by now, perhaps even fathered an egg. He had not been able to stop thinking and dreaming about the green dragoness since he first saw her.

They landed at the camp just as *Don* Casimiro was

sending his *vaqueros* back to the *Hacienda*. Atalanta had provided him with a pencil and notepaper to apprise his wife of what had happened. He had little fear that she would come out here. It was too far for her to travel (*Doña* Milagros found a trip to Diablo to the small market there far too fatiguing) and she would respond to Marisela's injury by spending hours at the church with the *padre*, and in lighting candles in front of the statue of the Virgin Mary. Once Marisela could be taken home her mother would spend all her time both spoiling her daughter and scolding her.

Ellery was glad to see the *vaqueros* go. They were an unneeded complication. Lutterworth and Beck were bad enough and now he supposed that they would have *Don* Casimiro here as well. He was the girl's father, and would quite naturally want to stay near her, but accommodations would have to be made for him and someone to serve as translator in his interactions with those who did not speak Spanish. Ellery looked back in longing at the most difficult of his Egyptian digs. They had been easy compared to this.

Nah-kah-yen and Varian were able to land unimpeded, without the threat of being fired upon. Ramón slid down at once and followed Varian to where Nicholas still knelt by the insensible dragonet.

"Nick, this is Ramón," the dragon made quick introductions in Spanish.

"It is a deep wound," said Ramón, joining Nicholas where he knelt by Pacho's side. He touched the dragonet's side and said, looking puzzled. "He is not really living yet not dead! How is this?"

"Julian put him in stasis until he could care for him," Nicholas said. When Ramón still looked as if he did not understand Nicholas explained "Stasis–that means stopping. Julian stopped the blood flow and the pain and made him stay unconscious with magic. He won't get any worse but he won't get any better." He did not try to explain that in human medical terms stasis meant the stoppage of some type of fluid of the body. Stasis was a term Wizard Healers had borrowed for this magical state of what could be literally translated as standing still.

A footstep sounded behind them and Nicholas looked up to see Julian approaching. He was followed by Ellery.

Sabrina, Nicholas thought, was more than likely with Marisela. "How is she?" he asked quickly.

"She's doing well for someone who was lung-shot" Julian said. "I expect a complete Healing with hopefully no complications. She'll have to stay here for a day or so. Even if we could rig up a dragon ambulance I don't think it wise to move her."

"And are you going to be able to Heal Pacho as well today?" said Nicholas in concern, both for his brother and for the dragonet. A human could stay in stasis for nearly five days, a dragon only a day, for their metabolism was quite different. Julian look tired and drawn.

"That's why I wanted Ramón here. If he will allow it, I want to draw on his strength and Healing powers," Julian smiled at his pupil.

"Whatever you want from me, *Maestro*," said Ramón gravely.

"That much you owe to your teacher," said a voice.

Ramón turned quickly to see Gian-nah-tah looking at him, sitting on the ground near Varian.

Where had the fox come from? Ramón had left him on the mountain. He could not have gotten here this fast!

The others were paying no attention. "Let's move him away from the ichor and into a clear, cleaned area," said Julian. "I don't think the table will bear his weight."

Julian took out his wand but Ellery stopped him before he could utter a spell. "Let Nick and me do this. You save your strength for the Healing and the linking you'll have to do," his uncle told him.

"Thank you," said Julian gratefully.

Nicholas asked the two familiars, Cillian and Bairre, to fetch a blanket. They scampered off and when they returned with a clean blanket, working together, Ellery and Nicholas levitated the dragonet and moved him to an area near the fire-pit where the grass had been trampled down. They laid him gently on the blanket.

"He doesn't look too well," said Ellery. Pacho's scales were dulling and his breath was shallow.

"He'd look even worse if Julian hadn't put him in stasis," said Nicholas.

"What I need now is a quick lesson in dragon

physiology, Nick," said Julian. "I can look with my hands but I may not know what I am looking at. What I'd like to do is link myself and Ramón to you so that you can explain to us what we are seeing. Ellery, would you help us link?"

Ellery agreed. Linking could be difficult and the more power available the easier it was. Usually Wizards or Witches linked for a Great Working such as raising a cone of power. It was not necessary to have physical contact in such case but here, Nicholas, Julian and Ramón would actually be touching Pacho so that they could see inside the injured dragonet.

Ramón grounded and shielded himself as Julian directed and then together with his teacher and Nicholas, the three of them placed both hands near the wound.

Ellery took out his wand and commanded *"Vinculum,"* and a violet light ran from him to Nicholas and there from Julian to Ramón. It stayed in the air, a stream of violet ribbon holding them in a circle, bound one to another.

When the link was complete, Julian summoned up his Healing magic and suddenly the three of them 'saw' beneath Pacho's scales to the first layer of his muscles where the bullet had ripped a large area.

"None of these muscles are used for his wings?" Julian asked.

"That's right," Nicholas answered. "This is the shoulder muscle, the pectoris major. The wing is governed by the dorsals, on his back. It's nasty, isn't it?" His heart sank as he looked at the torn muscle.

"Let's go deeper," Julian said. "I am worried about the bone." He increased the intensity of the green magic and penetrated to the skeleton.

"This must be the scapula," he said looking at a large heavy bone at the top of the shoulder.

"Correct," said Nicholas. "See, it leads here into the humerus and behind it are the first ribs. In dragons," he explained, "the rib cage extends from the chest all the way back to nearly the pelvis. The ribs are hinged in several places with cartilage in order for the gas cavities to be able to expand. The ribs are connected at the bottom by a band of cartilage as well. The gas cavities surround the internal organs on each side and the lungs, kidneys, intestines, spleen, liver and stomach are far more stretched out than in humans.

This gas cavity in the front is where his fire will come from. There are chambers from each cavity all along his body that empty into and out of each other. A dragon is constantly adjusting his flight and fire cavities, but it's all instinctive. They don't have to think about it any more than we think about breathing. The back of his throat is right behind this cavity."

"Their throats must be made of asbestos! When we have the time I'd like you to explain to me exactly how they breathe fire," Julian remarked. "It looks as if in addition to the muscular damage, which is extensive tearing, that one of these small ribs in the front of the chest is broken and the bullet is lodged in the first gas cavity. Wouldn't that ordinarily be filled with gas of some type, Nick?"

"Not in a dragonet this young," Nicholas answered. "I don't know anything about this particular breed, but to judge from other dragonets he will have no gas for flight or flaming for about a year. The Welsh Red and the Highland Dhu are the only dragons I know of who can flame a little at birth and then the flame is usually burped out and they are flame-less until they are older. If Pacho had been an adult the bullet might have just damaged his scales, depending on the depth of his scaling. But shot at this close range even a heavily scaled adult dragon might have exploded."

Looking worried, he added, "Julian, if the gas cavity is too heavily damaged he may never be able to spout flame or perhaps even fly. The gas cavities are absolutely necessary for flight." Nicholas looked up and met the worried gazes of Varian and Torin.

"Will he be all right?" Varian queried. "Can you help him, Julian?"

"I'll do the best I can, Varian," Julian promised.

"Erianne said she would keep the dragonets away but they won't stop crying. They could use a '*Quietus*', Nick, when you are no longer busy," said Varian, a little apologetically.

"When I'm done here, Varian," said Nicholas.

"Did you see enough?" Julian asked Ramón.

The native nodded. Julian told Ellery to take down the linkage. Next he would link to Ramón, to borrow his strength and his Healing power.

"First of all I will take him out of stasis. Where are

305

the cats?" Julian asked, looking around.

Flann and Siofra had been sitting with Gian-nah-tah, Cillian and Bairre. They now came over, ready to do whatever was asked.

"Do your soothing purrs work on dragons?" Julian asked.

"Sure, an' doesn't a familiar's purr work on every livin' creature?" said Flann.

"Then purr as loudly as you can, for when I remove the stasis spell he is going to be in a lot of pain," Julian directed.

Stasis had to be removed as it also prevented any Healing from taking hold. There were spells that could put a human patient to sleep; Julian would use one on Pacho as he had on Marisela, but he was not certain by how much to increase it. There were formulas to use, (accounting for weight, age and physical condition) for even with a human being, a Healer in a hurry, or not competent to begin with, could send someone into a permanent sleep. It would be best to use a standard spell for a heavy but healthy male and count on the double purrs to keep the dragonet anaesthetized.

With in a few moments all was ready. The dragon's scales had been washed of ichor and the scalpel, which had gone into a magically prepared sterilization vat after Marisela's Healing, was in Julian's hand.

Nicholas advised him to not attempt to cut through the scale but instead to lift it and go underneath. Part of the scale had been imbedded in the wound amongst the muscles and that would have to be removed as well, as, like the fabric pushed into Marisela's lungs, it could cause infection.

Julian linked to Ramón and at once felt Ramón's strength and Healing powers pouring into him. He was full of gratitude that Ramón so freely gave of himself; without him, Julian doubted if he could have undertaken this difficult Healing. What was really needed here was a proper Draconic veterinarian. But none was available.

The bullet first. Using the scalpel to lift the scale from around the entry point Julian sent a pulse of green light into the cavity. Within a minute, the bullet popped out of the entry hole.

"Caught it!" he heard Nicholas say.

Julian took a quick 'look' at the other gas cavity and then set about repairing the damage, matching the damaged tissue to the healthy tissue he saw in the opposite gas cavity. He could feel Ramón watching him as the native 'saw' exactly what Julian was doing. The damage seemed to fold in on itself, leaving only Healing and health behind.

Then the shattered rib was mended. As he had on Marisela, Julian made certain that every fragment of bone was restored to its proper position, so it would not cause problems later.

Back up through the tissues, knitting them together, restoring the injured blood vessels and the muscles to the finest condition, pulling the scale that had been pushed into the wound from where it had lodged, leaving cleanliness behind so that there would be no infection.

All the anxious watchers saw was Julian, frowning in concentration, green light spilling from his hands as a violet ribbon with green spirals running about it linked him to Ramón. The native, too, wore a look of intense concentration.

Twenty-five minutes later it was finished and Julian sat back on his heels, looking gray-faced and drooping with weariness. He cut the link to Ramón and said "That should do it. It's sutured under the scale and the scale itself is sutured as well. He'll need to be kept quiet for a day or so as they mend."

"I think he should be kept near Marisela," said Nicholas. "They 're bond-mates and each will look for the other when they begin to come around. Most injured dragons want their bond-mate near at all times. It will help Pacho to recover."

"I don't think Sabrina will have any problem sharing a tent with a dragonet, but we shall have to check with Miss Beck," said Ellery. "Julian, are you all right?" he said quickly, as his still kneeling nephew swayed.

"I could sleep for a week," said Julian on a yawn. He turned to Ramón and said fervently. "Thank you. Without your help I could not have done it."

"I was honored to help," said Ramón simply. He, too, looked tired but as a conduit for Healing power it had not taken as much out of him.

"Food for both of you," said Ellery firmly as he helped

Julian and then Ramón to his feet, "and then bed. Ramón should sleep here for a while before he goes home. Nick, I'll get them some food and then I will help you levitate Pacho into the ladies' tent."

"It's all over? He's going to be fine?" came Varian's voice.

"It certainly looks as if he will be as good as new," Nicholas reassured his dragon. "They'll both be fine," He added, thinking of Marisela. He would see how she was doing when he took Pacho to lie beside her. He had felt abject, complete terror when he had seen her fall to the ground.

The animals, familiars, hippogriffe and dragon, gave a short cheer and Siofra said rather smugly "There, an' wasn't I after tellin' ye that me Wizard can be Healin' anything?"

The happiness of the moment was all too soon shattered, as Lutterworth bellowed "Delamar! What the hell is taking so damned long? I want to be back at that cave immediately! There's treasure to find!"

Varian rolled his eyes.

Chapter Thirty Two
Dragon Love

Lutterworth sat at the table under the awning and brooded. Delamar had refused to go back to the cave until after luncheon when everything had settled down, and then it would be just Delamar and the Becks who would accompany Lutterworth. Delamar's sister, and nephews would be otherwise occupied. The doctor, when he awoke, would still be hanging over that girl who got herself shot. Miss Delamar was with her now. Stillfield was with the baby dragon that had been injured.

Lutterworth himself had been saddled with a Spanish nobleman who spoke poor English. When *Don* Casimiro had found out that Lutterworth was the owner of the railroad that was heading this way the *Don* decided to try and sell him some cattle to feed the work crews.

Lutterworth had finally fobbed the *Don* off onto Sinclair, saying untruthfully and rather maliciously that his assistant was the purchasing agent for the railroad.

All a flustered Sinclair had to do, his employer told him, was to keep saying "no". Lutterworth already had a very lucrative (for him) contract to get bargain priced livestock from a Chicago slaughterhouse. Many, if not all of the animals he purchased to feed the workers were old and diseased. Most of his workers were former slaves of New Spain or poor immigrant Chinese. Lutterworth figured that to those type of people anything would seem like manna from heaven and he needn't bother with first quality foodstuffs.

It was all the fault of Delamar bringing those dragons here in the first place, Lutterworth decided. None of this would have happened if those dragons had not been here. He glanced resentfully over to where Erianne was talking to Nah-kah-yen while the dragonets frisked around them, playing with Varian. Now that the danger to Pacho was past and it looked as if he was going to be fine, they were full of high spirits.

Nah-kah-yen had been somewhat taken aback to find the dragoness he was so interested in taking care of three dragonets, almost fresh from the egg. It was nearly impossible to talk to her, as the dragonets, relieved of tension, were very high-spirited and kept interrupting, demanding that Erianne look at what they were doing, wanting her to watch and praise them. They did not like that her attention was only half on them and half on the big male dragon. Amyas clung timidly to Erianne's side but Eda and Seneca, their bond-mates busy with Marisela, were loud and boisterous.

"Erianne! Look at me!" called Seneca as he attempted to sit up on his hind legs. At this age, without a long tail to balance himself this was nearly impossible. And when Eda rushed at him, he fell over, which resulted in shouts of laughter.

"Come on, I'll teach you to swim!" said Varian a little desperately. They were making too much noise. If he took them to the water in the canyon they would be further away from the sick girl and her equally ill dragonet. They might wake Julian or Ramón, both of whom needed their sleep. Perhaps enough swimming and their noon meal would wear then out and make them sleep.

They greeted this suggestion with shouts of joy and eagerly followed Varian away from the camp.

"They need some structured play and some toys," said Erianne thoughtfully. "Do you want to go with them, dearling?" she said fondly to Amyas.

The Maple dragonet shook his head and burrowed further into her side, his head down and pressed into her flank. Nah-kah-yen frightened him. The blue dragon was much bigger than either Erianne or Varian and he wore a scowl on his face.

"They need work and discipline," said Nah-kah-yen severely.

"They are only babies!" said Erianne, shocked at his attitude. At home, dragonets were given two to three years in which to mature. They started flying with their humans at a year old but did not go to live with their humans until two or three, living at the Incubatory where they were closely and lovingly taught their earliest lessons by staff both dragon and human. They started their schooling at the Draconic Collegium at Tara, at five years of age and finished when they were ten perhaps, depending upon the course of study. Some studied only a year or so.

"You should make that one go with the others," Nah-kah-yen said brusquely. He was eager to be alone with her and he could not be so with a dragonet seemingly glued to her side.

"He'll go when he is ready. It is in the nature of Maple l dragons to be shy," Erianne said a little shortly. Who was this interloper to come in here and tell her how to treat Amyas? The glance she gave him was not very friendly and she opened her wing to spread it over Amyas protectively. More and more she was feeling as if the little Maple dragonet was hers.

"How can we achieve a mating flight with him so firmly attached to your side? He is not even from your own egg!" said Nah-kah-yen impatiently.

"A *mating flight*?" said Erianne in amazement. "We've only just met! Why would you ever think that I would want to mate with you?"

"Because I am the biggest male here and the strongest," he said, preening himself a little.

"You also have the biggest ego," she said sarcastically.

He frowned. He was not certain what she meant by that. "Why would you not wish to mate with me?" he demanded petulantly. "All females admire size and strength. Do you wish me to fight for you?"

Erianne was revolted. "Don't be so uncivilized!" she said. "Behavior like that is not tolerated! There is no fighting over a female any more, anywhere in the civilized world. No dragoness nowadays expects or want a male to fight for her."

"Then how does a male dragon win a female?" Nah-kah-yen said, his frown deepening. He was going on what his instincts told him. Having been stolen away from his first bond-mate and his own dragon clan he really had little notion of how to behave. The mines did not teach good manners or proper behavior. Nah-kah-yen was only a few steps from his feral ancestors.

"He courts her," said Erianne.

"Courts?" Nah-kah-yen repeated. He obviously had no idea what she meant.

"He calls on her and they get to know one another" Erianne said. She felt a little sorry for him in spite of his conceit. "They talk and perhaps fly together. At home, a courting couple goes to concerts and lectures, meet each other's families, and eat together." A wistful note was in her voice. She had a sudden poignant memory of going with Cormac, her lost love, to hear a famous dragon-bard.

"How long does this take?" he demanded.

"Oh, at least a year. One of my friends was courted for five years before she consented to a betrothal," Erianne answered.

"A year!" Nah-kah-yen repeated in disbelief. "But I want to mate now!" Without thinking through what he was doing he advanced on her and tried to entwine his neck with hers. In dragons this was the first step to a mating flight. He felt that he had to show her that he was in earnest.

To his surprise she pulled back from him, almost sitting up on her hind legs, and hissed in rage, steam and a trickle of flame coming from her maw. "Leave me alone!" she shrieked. "How dare you! Who do you think you are, coming in here and trying something like that! Go away! I wouldn't mate with you if you were the only male left alive in the world!"

"Erianne?" came Ellery's voice. "Is something wrong?"

She came down on all fours, looking at her bond-mate in relief. "This ill-bred male attempted to wind his neck around mine after I told him I was not interested." Her voice was shaking. She had never heard of a male attempting to do such a thing. All of the male dragons she had met before now were gentleman. They would never think to coerce an unwilling female. This arrogant male should have left her alone when she was unreceptive to his overtures.

Ellery looked sternly at Nah-kah-yen. "I think you had better leave," he said.

"But Ramón–" began the blue dragon.

"Will be flown back by Varian when he awakens." Ellery finished for him.

Nah-kah-yen did not attempt to argue with this human, whom he knew to have magic. An ordinary human he would not fear, nor obey now that he was no longer enslaved. But he had seen what magic could do to a dragon. With a last look at Erianne he walked a little ways away and then thrust up into the air, spiraling up until he leveled off and flew away, disappearing rapidly.

Amyas had begun to cry in short gasps. He had been very frightened when Erianne had pulled away and spoke so angrily. Erianne soothed him and then turned to Ellery, who had remained there watching her. "Oh, Ellery," she said "Thank you! I have never been in situation like that before! I hope he never comes back here again. I just can't believe he behaved like that!"

"I'll ask Julian to speak to Ramón and tell him that his dragon is not welcome here until he learns to control himself." He frowned. "I think he owes you an apology, Erianne."

"I'd just as soon never see him again." She shuddered, her scales rippling.

Ellery moved closer and she lowered her head to him. Raising his hand began to rub her eye-ridges. She began to calm down almost at once. She sighed in pleasure and Amyas crowded close to her again, rubbing his face along her side. "Mama," he said happily.

Who needed an arrogant male like that one, Erianne thought, when she had her bond-mate and this little one to love?

But Nah-kah-yen's mood, as he flew back to the Turquoise Mountain was black indeed. He had done something wrong and he could not understand what it was. He thought all he had to do was show her how strong and fit to be her mate he was. He truly could not understand why she had rejected him. Even now they should have been taking their mating flight and satisfying the desire he felt for her. She was the only female dragon in the area that he knew of and he was the only mature male (the pale green one was but a youth). Threfore it was logical that they mate. Why could she not see this?

He would have to talk to Ramón, perhaps even to Gian-nah-tah. Perhaps they could tell him what to do.

He wanted her more than ever.

Between them, Sabrina and Atalanta had put

Marisela into a clean nightgown belonging to Sabrina. Her blouse was ruined. Julian had cut it away hurriedly, making no effort to save the white blouse. She would have to be given something to wear home, as even magic could not mend the blouse.

Sabrina had pulled the cot out away from the wall of the tent. This allowed Pacho to be placed at one side of it and still leave room for her and Atalanta to get in on the other side to attend Marisela.

A mage light, dimmed, floated in the air above her and water stood by her bedside table. Sabrina had magiced it to stay cool.

"It's unlikely that she'll want any water for the next twenty-four hours," said Sabrina, looking down at their patient. "The respirator is bespelled to not only help her breathe but to keep her mouth and air passage moisturized."

"It's amazing that a piece of India rubber could do all of that," Atalanta said, looking at it. It rose and fell softly over Marisela's face.

"It's the magic that goes into it," Sabrina explained. "And Julian will have bespelled her into a Healing sleep. Flann will purr to her at night."

"I never saw anything so fast as that surgery," Atalanta said. "He's very good, isn't he?"

Sabrina agreed. "My father, who is a top of the trees Wizard Healer himself, said Julian had more natural Healing skills than anyone he had ever seen. Marisela is fortunate that he was here for her."

"And Pacho is too," came Nicholas's voice from the open tent flap. "May I come in, ladies? I've some things here to make Pacho more comfortable." He had folded blankets and several small boxes in his arms. After him came Flann and Cillian, the hedgehog yawning loudly.

The dragonet, like his bond-mate, was deep in a spell induced sleep. He lay on his side on a blanket. Nicholas put down his bundle on the floor and, moving the boxes, unfolded the blankets. He knelt down beside the recumbent dragonet and threw them over Pacho. "He has to be kept warm," he explained. The blankets were also magiced to keep a steady temperature.

"It seems odd," Atalanta remarked, "that a creature

who can produce flame has to be kept warm."

"He's too young to have flame yet," said Nicholas. "So there would not be much body heat. With good Healing spells there should not be much danger of fever or infection, but I'll monitor his temperature just to be sure. He's not going to like it, but for the next few days beef broth would be best for him, and milk." He sat back on his heels and sighed. "I shall have to find a source for milk. If I can't find milk, we'll have to give him calcium tablets in water. A sick dragon needs extra calcium. They have a tendency to lose it from their bodies in fighting off an illness or infection."

"Is that what's in that box, Nick?" Sabrina asked. "Calcium tablets?"

He nodded. "It's a good thing I decided to bring four times the amount I would carry. I thought that with two dragons and being so far from any draconic supply shops it might be a good idea to have more than we needed. It's as well I did, for all of the dragonets ought to be getting calcium supplements as well. The eggshell they ate will only last so long"

Atalanta thought that she had a lot to learn about dragons. She would have to get some books on the subject of dragon-keeping as soon as possible. She would not want Seneca to suffer through any ignorance on her part. "And the other box?" she said, indicating a long thin one.

"Dragon thermometer," He reached for the box and opened it to show her. It was bigger even than the equine thermometers she had seen, made of glass, with a mercury line and two red horizontal line bisecting the glass. "The normal temperature for an adult dragon is one hundred and thirty degrees," Nicholas explained. "But a dragonet's is lower until he has actually able to flame: about one hundred and ten. These lines indicate the normal temperature for an adult and below it, a dragonet," he added, showing her on the instrument. "You'll need certain items to care for Seneca. In about a month he'll need to start taking care of his talons when they are hard enough and you'll have to help him. Don't worry; I'll make you a list and write out instructions. I'll give you a list of good books, since there are some very misinformed volumes out there, and a list of dragon care items as well. There are some good shops in New York City.

Marisela will more than likely have to send to San Francisco for her care kit." He looked towards the sleeping young woman as he spoke and Sabrina felt a little jolt of alarm? apprehension? (she was not certain what it was) as she saw the tender look on her nephew's face.

She liked Marisela, but could see only problems ahead if Nicholas were to become seriously involved with her. Marisela had been raised in the Catholic Church and in a totally different environment than had Nicholas. She was unused to magic and dragons and had been taught to abhor both (although she had come a long way to overcoming those prejudices). Her family was *Hildago*: they would never think Nick was good enough for her. His family, his real family, had been gentry but untitled and although his adopted grandfather was a baronet, as an adopted son he would not inherit the title. The only thing that might make him acceptable to her parents was his handsome fortune. And money was a poor reason for marrying.

Sabrina mentally chided herself. Perhaps nothing would come of it. Nick had been involved with young women before but he seemed to enjoy his freedom too much for a serious relationship to develop. *Perhaps I am making too much of one look,* Sabrina thought wryly. It was just that she had never quite seen a look like that on his face.

It was not until after a luncheon that Ellery saddled up Varian with their equipment to take himself and Bairre, Sinclair, the Becks and Lutterworth out to the mine site. Lutterworth had made himself so obnoxious that Ellery finally agreed to an afternoon's work, searching the many still unexplored caves around the site of the cave-in. Nicholas and Sabrina would stay behind to care for Marisela and the injured dragonet.

Ellery hoped that Julian would sleep until dark at the very least. He had never seen his nephew look so exhausted.

Don Casimiro, who had refused to go home until Marisela could accompany him, was most comfortable with Nicholas.

Accommodations for him would have to be made later.

Varian had already flown Ramón back to his camp on the mountainside. A few hours' sleep had restored him.

Ellery ticked this all off from a mental list as he secured Varian's saddle and loaded the breast harness with shovels and picks. They might have to do a little digging as one mage could not move a mountain of rock.

He still had no great hopes of finding anything. He had discussed this with Miss Beck during one of their morning walks.

She had started rising early, as he did and they had fallen into a pleasant habit of walking about together each morning and watching the sun come up. They discussed everything, including her belief that if there ever had been a treasure it was long gone, taken away in times past.

Ellery really enjoyed their conversations. She did not always agree with him and sometimes they had quite spirited disagreements, but he liked that in her. She had a fine mind and there were many other things to admire as well. He was grateful that she was willing to come along on this ridiculous treasure hunt this afternoon when she would rather be helping Sabrina or being with Seneca. Her presence would make it a little bearable.

"Thank you for taking us, Varian," he said as he closed the flap on the mesh breast bag. "Erianne is too much occupied right now with the dragonets."

"I'm glad to get away from them for a while!" said Varian in a low, confidential tone. "I'm very glad that I am far too young to mate and father an egg! Dragonets are exhausting! I took them to the little lake this morning and tried to teach them to swim, but they were so full of high spirits and only wanted to play and splash water on each other and on me! I don't know how Erianne copes with them. Treasure hunting with Mr. Lutterworth will be a lark after that."

"Are you ready *yet?*" Lutterworth bellowed from the table under the awning.

Ellery winced. He could not remember when he had ever met a person he disliked as much as he disliked Lutterworth. He looked down at his feet and met the sympathetic gaze of his familiar. Bairre's black-masked face expressed the same feeling that he had.

"Perhaps, if we are really lucky, he'll be buried in a landslide," Bairre suggested.

Varian was shocked by this but Ellery felt it to be a grand idea.

Sabrina watched Varian spiral up and disappear into the sky. She was very glad that Ellery had removed Lutterworth. His demands and shouting had not created an atmosphere of peace in the camp.

She had a sudden intense longing for Egypt and their digs there. They had received the firman for Saqqara, the cemetery site for the ancient city of Memphis and would be digging there this year, as they had the year before. It was a rewarding excavation, many exciting, but small discoveries had been made. And in Egypt, she felt completely at home. They hired the same crew and servants each year and they all knew each other's ways. Ellery was completely in charge, although he generously shared his authority with his sister, and each year they had staff, graduate students, most of whom were interesting and intelligent. And they knew exactly what had to be done at an Egyptian dig. Here, they were blundering about in the dark.

Lost in thought, she was unprepared when a clap of wings startled her. She wheeled and looked towards where Erianne had been dozing in the sun, her outstretched wings covering sleeping dragonets, who, with plenty of morning exercise and full stomachs, were now ready to nap.

As startled as Sabrina, Erianne opened her yes and looked into the anguished amber eyes of a strange green dragon, a young male who had landed in front of her.

"Help me!" he said desperately. "Help me! They're trying to kill me!" He was panting and shaking.

"I can see why," said Erianne rather dryly as she looked him over.

From a front talon hung a dead Longhorn.

Chapter Thirty Three

Betrayal

Prudence could not remember the last time she had slept so deeply and dreamlessly. Lately she had been laying awake, thinking about the doctor and how the children had been helped. Only yesterday, Sister Rebecca had remarked how good it was to see them running about like normal healthy children.

Both she had Brother Ezekiel had come down firmly on the side of the Healing as 'good'. For Sister Rebecca it had been the doctor's knowledge of Healing Herbs and for her husband it had been the presence of the angels that had changed their minds.

Reverend Brewer had been acting rather strangely as of late. Yesterday he had not said much to anyone, had seemed in a bad, irritable mood, and had walked into the little town of Diablo, rejecting Brother Ezekiel's offer of company. Several times the Reverend had gone to Diablo to preach against the sins of drunkenness and fornication and to exhort the scarlet women at the house of sin to give up their evil ways. He had been singularly unsuccessful in making any converts or weaning anyone away from drinking or whoring. But he nearly always expected Brother Ezekiel to accompany him as the sinners sometimes could become angry at the Reverend's continued admonitions and often times could become violent. Brother Ezekiel was big and strong and looked as if he could subdue a grizzly bear. Sinners thought twice about throwing rocks at the Reverend, or even calling him names, with Brother Ezekiel in attendance.

When the Reverend had returned from town he had been in a better mood and after evening prayers he had even made the children and his helpers a pot of tea with his own hands and served them all with some sweet cakes he had bought in town. These had been purchased at a small Mexican bakery and were squares of a rich moist cake, chocolate, flavored with cinnamon. Both chocolate and cinnamon were treats that were hardly ever found in New Jerusalem and the children had never had such good things in the mines. The little cakes were sinfully delicious and every last crumb and every last drop of tea had been consumed before they all fell into bed.

The hour was advanced when Prudence finally woke. Usually she woke at dawn, but she had been unable to open her eyes, groggily slipping back into sleep two or three times.

She was horrified when she at last woke up fully and saw how high in the sky the sun was. A Handmaiden's function was to rise first, and fetch water, make the coffee, start the breakfast and have all ready when her Elders awoke. She was surprised that Sister Rebecca had not come and dragged her out of bed.

But Sister Rebecca and Brother Ezekiel were still asleep. The curtain about the alcove where their bed stood was still pulled around. There was no sign of the Reverend Brewer but sometimes he went out early to be by himself and pray.

Still feeling sleepy, Prudence set about her morning tasks. All she wanted to do was to crawl back into bed. Each chore seemed much more difficult than usual.

The children were also missing. But the last few days since they had been Healed they had spent every moment out of doors, playing and exploring. Children bursting with new health rose even earlier than a Covenanter Handmaiden.

However, it was very odd that she did not hear them at play. At first they had been anxious about making noise. Noise had been forbidden in the mines. Prudence had tried to encourage them, by teaching them some games such as Hide and Seek or Blind Man's Buff. Since she had no Spanish and they had no English, her gestures and pantomimes elicited much laughter from the children and they made more and more noise as they relaxed. Even in New Jerusalem, children at play were expected to make noise. Children had their chores, as did everyone in Covenanter society, but they were allowed plenty of time for play. It was considered healthful and right, as children were seen as gifts from God. They were never indulged, but they were not over-disciplined either.

When the coffee was brewing and the potatoes and onions ready to fry, Prudence finished placing sausages into a pan and slicing fresh bread for toast. She went to call the children into breakfast. If they had been outside for some time they would need to wash.

But there were no children out in front of the mission. Nor were they in the wooded area near the pond. Where could they have gone?

She was beginning to feel rather frantic when Reverend Brewer came walking out of the woods. He was a trifle dusty, as if he had walked a long way.

"Oh, Reverend Brewer!" said Prudence. "Did you pass the children? I can't seem to find them. They ought not to have strayed so far."

"They're gone," he said brusquely. His good mood of the previous night seemed to have disappeared.

"Gone?" Prudence faltered. "What do you mean, gone?"

"Left, departed, taken off," he said sarcastically. "You never struck me as stupid before, Mistress Cromwell."

She flinched. His voice was not only jeering but mean-spirited and his eyes were hard. The genial host of the evening before had vanished completely.

There was also an air about him that she did not comprehend at all. In any one else she might have termed it one of triumph.

"Where did they go?" Prudence asked worriedly. "Why would they go?"

"Their people came for them early this morning," he said, turning away from her. "They are back where they belong. That is all you need to know."

"But Doctor Stillfield was going to make provision for them–"Prudence began.

He turned so fast that she stumbled back away from him, alarmed.

"I don't want to hear another word about that – that *doctor*, do you understand me?" he snarled, his face contorted and ugly. "As far as I am concerned, he is a fiend of Satan and I ought never to have allowed him near this mission!"

"But the children would have died–" Prudence protested, wondering at her temerity in arguing with a minister.

"All for the best," he returned. "The little bastards ought not to have been born in the first place. They are the product of illicit fornication. They are of mixed blood and of a pagan religion. They are an abomination in the eyes of God!

Now they are back where they belong."

"But–" Prudence protested hesitantly. She was shocked by his intemperate language and the sentiments he expressed.

"You dare to question my authority, Mistress?" he thundered. For such a small wispy person he could have a surprisingly big voice. "You neglect your duties as well! Why were you not out of your bed beforetime, preparing the morning meal? A Handmaiden should not be a slugabed! I shall have to write to your parents and inform them that your conduct has been far from satisfactory. I might even have to call for a disciplinary board of Deacons if you do not try to mend your ways!"

Prudence blanched. Her parents would be most unhappy with her. It had become apparent that she would not return to New Jerusalem, when her time of service was done, betrothed to Reverend Brewer as Mehetabel and Abijah Cromwell desired and expected. They would be displeased and disappointed. To have their daughter be disciplined by the Deacons would be a further blow to them.

She made a little obeisance to the Reverend and murmured that she would have the food on the table immediately.

"See that you do!" he ordered.

Prudence turned away from him and met the shocked gaze of Sister Rebecca, who had come out and was standing, still in her night cap and robe, on the small porch of the mission building.

Prudence's heart sank. Now she would have to endure a scold from Sister Rebecca as well.

Silently, Prudence served the others when the breakfast was cooked. She poured each one of her Elders a cup of coffee and gave each one a full plate laden with sausage, scrambled eggs, and fried onion and potatoes. A stack of golden toasted bread stood on a plate, along with a selection of preserves, brought from New Jerusalem.

Sister Rebecca had said nothing to Prudence. After washing and dressing she had looked troubled, but remained silent, while Brother Ezekiel, in a still genial mood, had chatted about wood cutting to the Reverend, who merely grunted in response. It could get cold here in the winter and some provision would have to be made for wood or coal. Brother Ezekiel discussed, mainly with himself, plans for a woodshed.

Prudence rose when her Elders finished eating, to gather and scrape the plates, before doing the washing-up.

Sister Rebecca followed her, when she went out of doors to fetch water from the cistern for the big wooden tub in which the dishes were washed.

Prudence dreaded the coming reprimand. This time, unlike the reproach for her hair curling, was well deserved. She *had* overslept; she *had* neglected her duties as a Handmaiden. Every reprimand of Sister Rebecca's would be merited.

But to Prudence's surprise Sister Rebecca said quickly to her "Leave the dishes for now. I want you to come with me. I have told the Reverend that we must gather herbs and simples and buy some vegetables in the town. Brother Ezekiel will keep the Reverend occupied here with the plans for the woodshed. I need to talk to you. I have permission from the Reverend to use the donkey and cart."

Prudence was mystified. Why did Sister Rebecca wear an air of secrecy? She looked troubled as well. Prudence said nothing, but followed her elder to the shed where the donkey lived and helped her curry and harness the little animal to the small cart that they used to fetch supplies from the town.

This donkey was actually one of the gentled wild *burros* of the region and had been purchased locally when the Covenanters had first come to this area. All of them were more used to the mules that were commonly used on the farms back in Ohio. The little *burro*, a diminutive gray animal with a dark fringe of mane and tail, was affectionate and very good natured. For his size, he could bear quite a heavy load and was so patient and equable in temperament that Brother Ezekiel had named him Job.

It was not until they were bouncing along in the cart behind Job that Sister Rebecca spoke.

"Something is terribly wrong with the Reverend," she said. "He drugged us with my sleep mixture last night." She looked straight ahead as if she was concentrating on her driving, but her voice was distressed.

"What?" Prudence exclaimed. "That is why we–"

"Slept so deeply and so late," Sister Rebecca finished for her. "You know my sleep potion, Prudence." For the very first time, Sister Rebecca called the Handmaiden by her Christian name alone. It was a mark of her anxiety. "I have added honey and sweet herbs to it to make it more palatable, so that it can be added to any drink and not leave an aftertaste. When I awoke this morning I felt so muzzy-headed that I wondered at once what might be the matter. When Ezekiel felt the same I went to my cabinet and found half the bottle of the sleep mixture gone. I keep careful track of what has been used and there was a nearly full bottle yesterday morning."

"But why would he do such a thing, Sister Rebecca?" said Prudence in confusion. She had been raised to think that a minister could do no wrong.

Sister Rebecca turned to look at her and Prudence was surprised by the look of pain on the woman's face. "I am afraid that he has done something to the children. I was shocked beyond measure this morning when he called them little–" she broke off, unable to say the word *bastards*. "While you were fixing the breakfast I made up the beds."

Prudence had wondered at this as making up the beds was part of her duties.

"Beneath one of the beds I found all the toys we had made for them, in a jumbled heap, as if they had been pushed there," Sister Rebecca continued. "The children loved those toys. They would not have gone back to their people without them."

Prudence drew in a sharp breath. This was very true. She and Sister Rebecca had made simple rag dolls for the girls while Brother Ezekiel had carved toy animals for the boys. She had never seen children so pleased and happy with toys. They had never had any toys before, even modest, homemade ones such as these had been. They had said *"Gracias! Gracias!"* over and over, which, Doctor Stillfield had informed her, meant 'thank you'. The looks on their faces, of joy and pride in having something of their own was something that Prudence would never forget.

"But what can he have done with them?" Prudence could not even imagine what might have happened. "Why would he do such a thing? How could a man of God harm innocent children?"

"I'm a great deal older than you are and have seen more of human nature," said Sister Rebecca. "Reverend Brewer is exceedingly jealous of Doctor Stillfield. I heard outright hatred in his voice today. Jealousy makes people do terrible things sometimes, things that, when they were not governed by passion, they would never dream of doing. But I am very afraid, Prudence, as to what passion may have caused Reverend Brewer to do to the children. I don't know what it is, but I have a bad feeling about it. And that is why," she said, pulling on the reins to halt the cart. "I want you to go and find Doctor Stillfield. We can use his help. I think he is the only one who *can* help us."

Angelita was the first to awaken. She felt dizzy and disoriented, her head feeling as if it had been stuffed with rags and her limbs weak. She was cold, as well, something she had not been for a while, not since they left the mines, where they had no bedclothes.

It was very dark and beneath her groping fingers, as awareness slowly returned, was only hard dirt and rocks.

This was a nightmare. It had to be. She was dreaming that she was back in the mines. In a few minutes she would wake up to a day of sunshine and a smiling *Señorita* Prudencia making a lovely breakfast for them. The horror of the mines was over.

She moved and heard the clink of chains. About her ankle was a heavy cuff, such as she had never thought to wear again.

No, it couldn't be! They could not be back in the mines! Both Ramón and the *Señor el médico* had promised that they would never have to go back!

Her eyes were becoming used to the darkness now and about her she could see the huddled forms of the other children, all of them who had been at the mission house with her; Léon, the oldest, at fifteen; Alma, twelve, a year younger than herself; Lola, ten; Josefina and Vasco, both nine; Benito, eight; Charro, seven, and little Pia, who was barely five. As far as she could see, they, like her, all wore a cuff and chain about the ankle. And they were beginning to awaken as well, some beginning to cry as they realized where they were.

For there was no doubt as to that. It was a mine, deep beneath of the earth. Timbers held up the ceiling and propped up the walls. a single lantern hung from a nail in a timber, providing a fitful light.

"Angelita!" came Léon's voice. "What has happened to us? How did we get back here?" He sounded both angry and frightened.

"I don't know," she said, with a sob in her voice. "I think someone brought us here when we were asleep. I remember I was so sleepy after that tea and the good cake...."

Léon gave a tug on the chain. It had been fastened securely to a large rock. "Who could have done this to us?" he demanded.

Vasco spoke. "They Healed us to put us back to work," he said, sounding as cynical as an old man.

"No!" said Léon forcefully. "I don't believe that! Ramón would not let anyone do that. The *Señorita*, the doctor, they are good. I know it! You saw the angels, Vasco. No one bad can call angels."

"Someone is coming!" shrilled Josefina. "I see a light !"

"Be quiet, all of you!" Angelita ordered. "Don't let them see that you are afraid!"

The others subsided, crying fading away to sniffs and a few trickling tears as the light came closer. Who would it be? Would they find out who had stolen them away?

Closer and closer came the light, bobbing up and down as whoever held it traversed the rough passageway of a tunnel.

A few moments later a black-robed figure, face obscured by a hood drawn well over it, came into the cavern where they lay. "Excellent!" she said. "They are coming around!" he called back over his shoulder.

Another taller, black-clad figure came from the tunnel. He too, held a lantern. It cast shadows up into his hooded face, giving Angelita the impression that his eyes gleamed scarlet beneath the sheltering hood.

"You are our property now," he said to the children, in a deceptively pleasant voice. "You were bought and paid for in good coin. You will work this silver mine for us, as you have been trained to do. Work hard and you will have food. Shirk your duties and you will not be fed and will be punished with the whip as well. And do not think that you will be rescued. No one can possibly learn where you have gone. You will not leave this mine unless you are dead."

The shorter figure came closer to Angelina and bent down to look at her. Suddenly he reached out and tore her blouse down the front, revealing her still immature breasts. "Look here, Brother," he said excitedly. "This one is almost a woman! She might do for our other purpose!"

"No doubt," said the taller one.

Angelita was frozen in terror. Such a feeling of evil came from the black-robed figures that she could not utter a sound nor pull away from the hand that began to fondle her. On one finger gleamed a deep red ruby ring.

"There will be enough time for that later," said the taller, sounding amused. "Get the sacks. We will put them to work at once."

Reluctantly, the other left Angelita's side. "You are mine," he said in a sibilant whisper to the terrified girl.

This could not be happening, Angelita thought. It was all a nightmare. She would soon wake up. It *had* to be a nightmare!

Chapter Thirty Four
Another Green Dragon

The amber eyes looked defiant as the other green dragon looked at Erianne.

"I had no choice," he said defensively. "Do you think I want to steal? But when you're hungry and you see others going hungry, it makes you desperate! This one cow is going to have to feed five dragons and a number of humans as well."

"I understand that, but what do you expect me to do?" Erianne queried. "Hide you, make up excuses for you? I have already been accused of stealing cows and injuring a human in your stead."

He looked contrite. "I never meant to harm that human! It was an accident. He came too close when I was trying to grab a cow and I raked him with my talons. I know better than to ever hurt a human! And I never thought any one else would be blamed for me taking a cow. I didn't even know you were here."

Sabrina, trailed by Flann, came up to the dragons and said "I take it this is the real cow thief?"

"Yes," said Erianne "But we have not as yet been introduced." She gave the other green dragon a meaningful look.

He looked uncomfortable. "My mother called me Rowan," said the young male. "But in the mines they call me Greenie."

"Rowan is a much better name," said Sabrina. She introduced herself, her familiar and Erianne. "We had better decide what we are going to do. If Rowan is being chased I imagine they will be here soon."

Very abruptly, Torin landed a few feet away, running to a stop as a hippogriffe usually did. He had been sunning up on top of *El Morro*.

"There's a group of rather hostile looking men riding this way," he announced. "Not as many as were here the other day during the shooting, but they do not look happy. They should be here soon. I saw them from above. Sabrina, perhaps you'd best get Nicholas out here. Is Julian still sleeping?"

"*Don* Casimiro is the one we need," said Sabrina,

frowning. "They are his men and this is his cow Rowan has killed. But he seems to have disappeared."

"I'll be findin' him," said Flann and loped off.

Rowan looked as if he did not know whether to take off with his booty or remain behind. A stern look from Erianne caused him to furl his wings. He would wait with the others and face what came.

It was afternoon before Prudence finally arrived at the camp at *El Morro*. They had had to go through an elaborate charade of shopping and searching for herbs, because Reverend Brewer had shown up at the store in Diablo just as Prudence was planning to take the cart and donkey and go in search of the doctor.

Was the Reverend suspicious? It seemed as if he had followed them there and he showed far more interest than normal in the buying of foodstuffs, asking question after question. He looked odd; excited and had a tendency to talk in a high, rapid voice and then suddenly fall silent. If he had not been a minister Prudence would have said that he looked and sounded guilty about something. If he had hurt the children on any way he did indeed have a reason to be guilty.

She ended in walking out to *El Morro*, for the Reverend wanted to ride back with them, but Sister Rebecca ordered the Handmaiden to take the basket and go out and find some tansy. She was just about out, she said, with some winks and facial grimaces behind the Reverend's back, and tansy, used for stomach troubles, gout and female problems, cathartic and blood cleanser, was an absolute necessity. Prudence understood what she was to do.

It was a long hot walk at almost mid-day, out to the archaeological camp. Prudence was not even certain that she was going in the correct direction, for she had no map, only a vague notion of where the camp lay, based on where she had seen the doctor's strange creature fly in from.

But the great rock was unmistakable and it was with relief that she finally saw the tents and the camp near the foot of the rocky promontory.

But she was not the only one arriving. As she watched, a dragon with passengers, landed just as a group of angry looking men rode up.

Lutterworth swore, fluently and violently. "That's it then," he exclaimed, throwing down his lantern in disgust. "Where the hell is it?"

"I should hope that the question is purely rhetorical, Mr. Lutterworth," said Dr. Beck in his precise way "for I assure you that none of us have any knowledge that you do not."

They had spent the entire morning searching the rest of the caves, surrounding what Varian thought of as the dragonet tomb. Some of the caves had petered out after a few feet, and the very few that had gone on for any distance had proved empty. There had been no more jewels, or even any startling discoveries such as another pile of bodies. They were just empty caves. Some, it was true, had beautiful and unique drip-water formations, but Lutterworth had no interest in those at all.

But there was no treasure, nor any sign of a treasure having been there.

The caves had been methodically searched, both by eye and by magic, and marked when the survey had been complete, so that no cave was investigated more than once.

Ellery had seen Lutterworth's growing frustration and rage as the search progressed and nothing was found. More than once he found himself exchanging looks with Atalanta.

She was thinking the same thing he was. Lutterworth would never had made an archaeologist. Sometimes the work of archaeology could be disappointing. All signs would be pointing to a fascinating discovery, only to find that robbers, sometimes in antiquity, had emptied a site of anything of interest or value. One learned to live with this.

But it was obvious that Lutterworth was not going to

accept the failure to find any sort of treasure. He was convinced that someone had come and taken it, sounding, to Ellery's disgust, as if someone had stolen it from him, personally.

Sinclair had been looking more and more worried as cave after cave produced nothing. Ellery could well understand why, for Lutterworth would no doubt end in blaming his hapless assistant for the failure.

But it was no one's fault. Ellery could not explain why they had found the emerald or even the necklace, but it was no doubt an aberration. Part of Ellery's mind still believed that there had never been a treasure and that the map was a hoax.

They all left the main chamber and went above to where Varian waited.

The bright sunlight outside was startling after the dark caverns. It was just past three and Dr. Beck, for one, was thinking longingly of his tea. They had fallen into the habit of taking a British tea at four and Dr. Beck had become quite fond of the custom, particularly of the tea sandwiches Sabrina made.

"I would imagine that we will be returning to New York now?" he said as he watched Ellery and Sinclair load some picks and shovels into Varian's breast harness.

Pugnaciously, his square jaw thrust out, Lutterworth said "Why would you suppose such a damn-fool thing? That treasure is here and we're going to find it! I don't care what it takes: magic, blasting or tearing apart every inch of this Goddamned desert! It's here and I'm going to find it!" he repeated loudly, glaring at all of them in turn.

"What an idiot!" said Bairre in disgust. Fortunately he spoke in Gaelic from his perch on Ellery's shoulder.

Ellery could not help but agree with his familiar. Wherever the other pieces had come from it was obvious to anyone but Lutterworth that there was no longer any trace of it. Ellery himself had felt nothing "calling" to him as had both the necklace and the emerald. His pyschometry had not stirred once in any of these caves. If there had been anything within, it was long gone. But where had the two pieces come from? Ellery wanted to *know* and it was beginning to look more and more if there was only one way to find out.

And Ellery knew what his sister would say if he proposed a *séance*.

Pacho stirred and opened his eyes with an effort. He had never, in his very short life felt so tired. And when he tried to move it *hurt*.

He opened his eyes, whimpering a little. He wanted Marisela. She could make him feel better, soothing him with her voice, and her touch. Just to be near her....

Then he remembered what had happened and sat up abruptly. yelping as he felt the extreme soreness in his shoulder.

Nicholas was there at once, kneeling beside him. "Don't try and move too much," he cautioned the dragonet. "Lay back down and rest. I'll have some food for you in a moment."

Food was not Pacho's primary concern. "Marisela! What happened to her?" he demanded.

"She's right here," Nicholas moved aside slightly so that Pacho could see his bond-mate stretched out on the cot. Siofra was perched out on Marisela's pillow, keeping an eye on her. Should anything go amiss, she would run and fetch Julian.

"What's wrong with her?" Pacho said worriedly." What is that thing over her face?"

Nicholas explained, as soothingly as he could, what the respirator did and why it was necessary. "You'll be able, perhaps, to talk to her tomorrow," he promised.

"Tomorrow!" Pacho echoed in dismay. "Can't she wake up now?"

"No, you must be patient. You want her to be entirely well, don't you?" said Nicholas.

Pacho nodded miserably. She was so still and looked unnatural, laying on her back, slightly propped up with pillows and that thing covering her face.

"That man shot us!" he said next. "Why did he do that?"

"Marisela is his daughter. He thought that you were

going to attack her," Nicholas explained.

Pacho looked astonished. "Attack her? But she is my bond-mate and I love her! As if a dragon would ever hurt a human! How did Marisela come to have such a stupid man for a parent?"

"I'll explain later," Nicholas said. He, too, found it nearly incomprehensible that the people here were so afraid of dragons. "Right now you need to have some beef broth to keep up your strength, after I take your temperature. Once you've eaten we could move you closer to Marisela."

Pacho eagerly assented. Just to be near her, even if she slept, would be heartening.

Julian had slept for nearly the length of the afternoon. It was not nearly enough, but would have to be a beginning. Sabrina had cast a spell of *tranquillitas* around him so that even Lutterworth's bellowing would not awaken him. An additional spell of *tenebrae* had made the tent darker, which was easier for sleeping. Witches and Wizards slept far better than most non-magicals because of this ability to control the environment of their sleeping places. Spells could also warm or cool a bed or cure a sleeping partner's snoring or tossing and turning.

He awoke suddenly, done with sleep. It seemed strange to not have Siofra at his side, but she was watching over Marisela, with her purr at the ready should the young woman become restive.

Julian sat up and took down Sabrina's sleeping spells. They hung as a very thin violet haze in the air. He was grateful to her for casting them. As tired as he had been he doubted that he could have cast them himself. He had been at the point where he was almost too exhausted and wrought-up to sleep. He had been performing as many major Healings as would a physician in a large Metropolitan hospital that saw many cases that needed immediate care. He hoped that there would be no more major Healings for the immediate future.

He had scarcely finished washing, shaving and

dressing when he became aware of angry voices outside. "Not again!" he thought in dismay.

Before he could leave the tent Cillian's head poked through the flap. "Good, you're awake!" the hedgehog said. "We've something of a situation brewing out here and we may need all the Wizards we can get. There is someone here to see you as well."

Mystified, unable to think who would want to see him, for he had told Ramón to wait until he was able to come to him, Julian followed the hedgehog out into the bright sunlight and into a babble of angry voices.

Everyone was there: people, dragons, including a strange young dragon, and Prudence Cromwell, who was looking both anxious and frightened. Both Varian and the other green dragon were shouting and the dragonets were crying. Julian could understand why she was afraid, for dragons had loud voices to begin with and when angered, their verbalizations could cause small avalanches in mountainous terrain. In the noise, all Julian could do was smile at her. She seemed too intimidated to speak.

Once again Ellery was holding off some angry *vaqueros*. There were only five of them this time, including old Curro and the young man, Enrique, whose brother had been injured. *Don* Casimiro was shouting at them and they were shouting back, with the dragons yelling and posturing as if for attack as the *vaqueros* leveled their rifles at Rowan. Nothing coherent could be heard until Nicholas, with the aid of his wand, amplified his voice and commanded *"Placidus!"* and an unnatural quiet fell over the entire group.

"Now, what is this all about, Sabrina?" Ellery asked, as his sister had been here from the beginning and Nicholas and Julian had joined them only after he and his own party had arrived.

Briefly, with admirable clarity, Sabrina described everything that had happened from Rowan's arrival onwards. Enrique, especially, tried to break into speech several times but Nicholas's leveled wand kept the words in his throat. Rowan muttered, but Varian, who knew that a *Placidus* spell could be uncomfortable to say the least if one attempted to talk, prodded the other male with a talon and said *"Hssttt!"*

Feeling as if he was judge and jury, and switching

335

from Spanish to English as needed, Ellery said. "As I see it, Rowan owes *Don* Casimiro monies for the cows he has taken and as for Enrique's brother's injuries–Julian, will you go and see what can be done for him? Enrique, if the doctor can mend your brother's hurts will you accept an apology from Rowan? A dragon would never deliberately harm a human. It had to be an accident." Rowan nodded vigorously, agreeing with this statement.

At *Don* Casimiro's prodding, Enrique, rather sullenly, nodded. Nicholas released them from the spell and Rowan tendered a sincere apology which was rather ungraciously accepted. Then he said worriedly "I want to pay for the cows I took, but I can't. I haven't any money. None of us dragons do and the humans we share with have very little as well. Dragons don't get paid where I work, just fed, badly."

"I'll help you out with the money," said Varian. "But don't you earn a wage at the mine?" he asked, shocked.

"Oh, I don't work at the mines anymore," said Rowan. "Not since the war. I work for the Taos, Albuquerque and Phoenix railroad."

Almost as one, the mages and their animals turned to stare at Lutterworth in outrage.

Chapter Thirty Five
Help Is On the Way

Nah-kah-yen had flown back in the direction of the mountainside in an evil humor. He did not land at once, but spent some time gliding overhead in high spirals. He had changed his mind; he did not wish to speak to anyone at the moment, not until he could understand what had happened between him and the beautiful green dragoness. Instead of flying by himself he should have been enjoying the aftermath of a mating flight right now. He could not comprehend what she meant by 'courting'. It sounded like a waste of time.

Her rejection stung. He was accustomed more to admiration, to have others, humans and dragons, dependent on his strength and judgment. If he had chosen to leave with the other dragons released from the mine he would have been their leader. But none of them, of course, had a bond-mate like Ramón. And the band of humans Ramón lead desperately need a dragon who could hunt and provide them with food. Nah-kah-yen did not regret staying with Ramón; they were deeply committed to one another. Nah-kah-yen knew himself to be very fortunate to have found another bond-mate, for it had been a deep need in him to have a human companion.

At first, he had thought he would die of loneliness, grief and pain at having been forcibly separated from his first bond-mate. Some dragons DID die, he knew. But most of them were old, and when their bond-mates had died of old age, the dragons had lost interest in living and faded away, some of them very quickly.

But Nah-kah-yen had still been very young when he had been stolen from his home and brought here. By the time Ramón had come the memories of his old life and his bond-mate had been fading, for the new life was so difficult, so strange and brutal. There was little time to think and even smaller chance to dream of what had been when one was always both hungry and overworked.

From high in the air, with his keen dragon sight, he could still see the camp he had just left. And when he looked back, to his rage he saw a strange young male dragon, green, like the dragoness he so desired. Was this why she had rejected him? Did she favor this youngster?

His first impulse was to reverse his flight, to go back to the camp and challenge his rival.

But then he had remembered what she had said about fighting, and the scorn in her voice.

Perhaps the wisest course would be to glide up here and watch, to see if she preferred this new dragon, if they achieved a mating flight.

He went higher, where they were less likely to notice him.

Prudence shivered. She had always hated loud, angry voices and there were more than enough of those here. Much of the shouting was in Spanish, between an elderly man and a group of very enraged men on horseback. There were dragons bellowing as well and an acrimonious argument between a large, red-faced man and several other people, something about a railroad.

After a short conversation in Spanish with two persons Prudence did not know, the doctor had headed towards one of the tents and had fetched his medical bag, then going off in the direction of the group of the horsemen. Prudence, uncertain as to what to do, followed him.

One of the *vaqueros* wore a sling, his arm inside it clumsily bandaged. He was gray-faced and looked as if he was in pain. His brother had returned to his side, still glaring with hostility at everyone, particularly the dragons.

"Why did you bring him out here?" Julian said in exasperation to Enrique. "He should be in bed, resting!"

"I wished everyone to see the pain Vicente has suffered due to that beast!" said Enrique angrily. "He will most likely lose his arm and then how will he make his living? Of what use is a one armed *vaquero?*"

"Get down off that horse," Julian directed Vicente. "I am a doctor and I shall take a look at your arm."

Vicente, younger than his brother by several years, looked at Enrique as if for directions. At Enrique's nod he rather clumsily dismounted.

338

"Sit here," Julian directed, indicating a nearby rock.

When Vicente sat down Julian unwrapped the ill applied bandages, which were stained here and there with blood.

A long, deep gash, from just below the shoulder to the mid forearm was revealed. It was quite deep, for a dragon's talons were sharp.

"See?" said Enrique accusingly. "Already it grows infected! The beast's claws were filthy no doubt. It meant to kill!"

"It's probably infected due to mishandling," retorted Julian. "I see no signs that this wound was washed or disinfected. And as for the inept bandaging–the less said about that the better. There's nothing here that cannot be Healed, however. First thing to do is get it clean." He turned towards his medical bag, which he had set on the ground before examining Vicente.

To his surprise, Prudence was there, holding the bag. She had it opened and as he looked at her she offered him one of the prepared bags of disinfectant herbal treated cloths he kept made up for quick use.

"Thank you," he said, a little surprised.

"I have to talk to you, Doctor," she said "But that can wait until after you see to this man." She looked a little desperate and more than a little haggard, but he appreciated her forbearance and patience. Many people seemed to think that during a Healing was the ideal time to ask questions or voice complaints.

Vicente's wound was quickly cleaned with herbs which were astringent: carline thistle root and the root of rhubarb, in an alcohol solution. The young *vaquero* winced a little as the alcohol and herbs began their cleansing action.

Then pads were soaked with the contents of a dark bottle labeled *Elixir salubris* and these applied to the length of the wound. It was a brown liquid, a blend of manna, aloe, rhubarb root, senna leaves, theriac venezian (which itself was a blend of seven medicinal herbs), zedoary root, angelica, carline thistle root, myrrh, camphor and saffron in 80 proof spirits. It left a yellow-brown stain around the edges of the gash. With a tap of Julian's wand the liquid left the pad and went into the wound, leaving behind clean, uninfected skin.

Then a short incantation knit the torn flesh, leaving no trace of the wound.

"*Sancta Maria!*" said Enrique, his eyes wide as he crossed himself.

"Look, Enrique!" said Vicente happily, bending his arm back and forth. "The pain is gone! It is as if the beast never tore me!"

"It is the least they can do for you, my brother, as it was their beast who attacked you," said Enrique, with a stare at Julian that seemed to dare him to contradict this statement. "They should have better control over their animals."

Julian did not even try to argue with him. The green dragon was not one of their party and as sentient beings, dragons were not controlled by anyone. Dragons were humankind's partners and friends. Julian had met this type of ignorance before and it was useless to remonstrate against it. "Ignorance is bliss," he murmured to himself and then said courteously to Prudence "You said you needed to talk to me, Miss Cromwell? Shall we go somewhere where it is quiet?"

"Yes," she said gratefully and followed him to the tent. She was hesitant in entering, for she had been taught that one never went into a room alone with a man unless he was a father, a brother or one's minister, but Doctor Stillfield was a physician and the matter too grave to wait upon the proprieties.

She sat down on the cot he indicated and nervously smoothed the skirt of her dress. She accepted a glass of water that he poured from a jug, and gulped it down thirstily, for it had been a long hot walk. To her surprise, the water was as cool as if it had just come from a spring house.

"Sister Rebecca and I don't know what to do!" she finally burst out. "We think Reverend Brewer may have gone mad! And worse than that, something's happened to the children! They've disappeared."

"What?" He looked at her incredulously. "Ramón was planning to come for them later today or tomorrow originally, but he cannot have done so. Tell me everything!" he urged, sitting down on the cot opposite hers and giving her his undivided attention.

Prudence repeated everything that had happened

that morning, from the absence of the children, the discovery of the hidden toys and Sister Rebecca's suspicions as to their having been drugged.

Julian frowned. "What could he have done with them?" he said, puzzled.

Prudence twisted her hands together. "He said that they were back where they belonged," she said distressfully.

"Back where they belong!" he echoed and then as a terrible thought struck him exclaimed "He could not mean the mines! Even Reverend Brewer could not condemn innocent children—in the name of all that's Holy why would he do such a thing?"

"Sister Rebecca said that it was the angels. He can't bear it that you can call upon the angels and he cannot. He is an ordained man of God and they will not come to him when he commands," Prudence offered.

"Good God!" Julian exclaimed. "But I don't *command* angels, I ask for their help. They are servants of the Light as am I and I *request* their help. No one but God can command them. My brother Cary will be an Anglican Vicar and he does not expect to command angels, nor is he jealous of me for being able to call them to help me in my work."

Prudence asked "Vicar? Is that like a minister?"

"The very same," he said and looked at her, saying earnestly, "Miss Cromwell, Reverend Brewer is indeed descending into madness if he let his jealousy goad him into harming those children. We shall have to find them. I will give you all of the help that I can, as will my brother and my aunt and uncle. They will be horrified to hear of this. We are all magical; there will be great deal that we might do to help locate them."

She felt almost limp with relief. "Thank you," she whispered. Sister Rebecca had been right to insist on her coming here.

Lutterworth had grown tired of defending himself. "What the hell do you people know about running a railroad?" he had yelled at the top of his voice when the recriminations and accusations had become more than he could stomach. "Those damned people would not even have jobs if it weren't for me! When the US government came in here all the mines closed down and they were out of work!"

"So working for a substandard, minimal wage is better than starving?" retorted Ellery.

"Not by much," said Rowan. "The humans have to buy their food at his company store. He pays them mostly in what is called scrip. The other stores around here won't accept it as legal tender. The prices at the company store are very high too, the humans say. And the food we dragons are given is bad."

"You can't believe what this big lizard is telling you!" blustered Lutterworth. "At any rate, the railroad workers are just Chinks, mixed bloods, Dagos and Micks, with a few coloreds. They don't expect any better." In his voice was the unspoken phrase: *And they don't deserve any better.*

"And they are certainly not getting it from you!" said Sabrina angrily. "Neither fair pay nor respect it seems."

"All of us here are 'Micks' as you put it," said Nicholas. "We object to our countrymen and the others you employ being so mistreated. And as a Dracophilologist I feel obliged to report your mistreatment of these dragons to the proper authorities in Washington. It is against American law to expect a dragon to work without wages, and that means money, Lutterworth, not rotten food."

"It's none of your damned business!" asserted Lutterworth.

"We're making it our business," snapped Ellery. He turned to the young green dragon. "Rowan, we've paid *Don* Casimiro for that cow. Take it with you now and tell the other dragons and the humans that tomorrow food, good food, will be delivered to them, and medical help as well for anyone who needs it. I take it you don't have a doctor for your workers?" he turned back to Lutterworth.

"Of course not !" Lutterworth said. astonished. "Why should I pay a damned quack to sit on his ass when he's not needed all the time? And if you think I am going to pay for–"

"This is coming out of *our* pockets, Lutterworth," said Ellery. "You see, we don't expect much of you either." He turned his back on Lutterworth as if the railroad baron was of no account. "Where is Julian? I'm certain that he will wish to a part of this," he queried, looking around and not seeing his other nephew.

"If you want to waste your money," Lutterworth sneered. "As long as it isn't coming out of MY pocket! Damned do-gooders!" he spat.

"Really, Dr. Delamar," Dr. Beck said in protest. He had stood there listening with an exasperated look upon his features. "This is not part of an archaeological expedition! Surely his railroad is Mr. Lutterworth's concern, not yours!"

"Papa," said Atalanta, once again feeling ashamed of her father. "The mistreatment of other humans and animals ought to be the concern of every right-minded person." Personally, she found Ellery's attitude admirable.

Dr. Beck looked thunderstruck. You dare to contradict me, girl? This is what comes of educating women beyond their capabilities!" he declared to no one in particular. "They become opinionated, pert and contentious! My daughter has fallen under evil influences," he added, looking straight at Sabrina. His little beard was quivering indignantly.

At the look on Atalanta's face, compounded of embarrassment and tears, Ellery felt such anger welling up in him that for one of the few times in his life he wanted to hit a fellow human being. How dare that old goat criticize his daughter like that? She bent over backwards catering to him and he treated her worse than a lackey! Her fine intelligence, her skills, her tact: all were overlooked.

Dr. Beck was a complete disillusionment. Ellery could not imagine how such a miserable human being had written those delightful books. He supposed that it was not the first time that an author was totally different in person than the impression one gained of him when reading his works. All the same, it seemed a bitter let-down.

It was at this moment that Julian arrived, trailed by Prudence, who had been raised to think a woman's proper place was two steps behind a man.

Before Ellery or any one else could say anything about the railroad, Julian informed them all of the missing children.

As he had known they would be, they were all appalled at the very thought and offend their help.

"I had thought to send for Ramón and inquire after

343

the locations of all the mines in the area," said Julian. Varian had flown Ramón back to the mountain before they had gone treasure hunting.

"I thought all the mines were closed after the area passed into the possession of the United States," said Sabrina, frowning.

Lutterworth snorted in derision. "If you think these damned Spanish gave up something as profitable as a silver mine you're even more wet behind the ears than I thought!" he scoffed. "I'll bet my bottom dollar that there are still mining operations going on behind the government's back. And I can't see why you give a damn about a pack of bastard kids! Come on, Sinclair, I've got letters to write," he brusquely ordered his unhappy minion, who had taken no part in the argument at all, just looking more and more miserable, as he knew he would bear the brunt of Lutterworth's displeasure later.

With an apologetic glance at the others Sinclair trailed off behind his employer.

"How can he stand working for that man?" Sabrina said in exasperation.

"It's his choice, Sabrina," said Ellery shortly. "Go and get Ramón, Julian. We'll get out our maps; perhaps he can show us where the mines might be located so we can start the search. Miss Cromwell, is it? Could you find something for us that the children might have worn or held frequently?"

Prudence nodded. "Back at the mission, Their toys, their old clothes...."

"The clothes would be best," interrupted Nicholas. "Varian and I will fly her back and fetch what we need, Ellery. You're going to do a pendulum search." This was a statement, not a question.

"The best and fastest way," his uncle agreed.

Prudence was terrified to think that she had to get on a–a dragon. But time was passing by–already it was late afternoon. It had taken a long time to walk here and she had slept late that morning. The children had to be found.

Seeing her fear, Nicholas and Varian were very kind and soothing.

They were scarcely in the air before Ellery had the maps spread out on the table.

Dr. Beck, quivering with indignation, stalked off to his tent and ordered Atalanta to bring him a cup of tea and some sandwiches. None of this had anything to do with the purpose for which he had been hired. He was very afraid that Lutterworth would demand his money back.

Chapter Thirty Six

Seeking

Just after Varian arrived back with Prudence and a bag of the children's old clothes, a map of the area had been spread out on the table and Ramón, fetched by Torin, showed them on the map where most of the mines were.

Ramón knew how to read and use a map. By the time he was nineteen, he had been made the leader of a gang of children whose job it was to seek out new veins of silver. As the leader, it was his task to map these areas, where the biggest veins might be and the progress of each day's mining.

The amount of mines in the area was distressingly large. In addition to silver, there were copper and other mineral mines. Ramón admitted that there might be mines of which he was not aware and some that might have been abandoned for as long ago as a century or more.

Prudence had been terrified to ride a dragon. Even Varian's friendliness and the presence of Nicholas had not reassured her and she rode clutching the saddle strap and with her eyes closed.

Varian landed a little ways from the mission and, after Nicholas helped her off, Prudence, on shaking legs, had run up to the mission building to fetch what was needed. She had met only Sister Rebecca there and was informed that Brother Ezekiel and Reverend Brewer were gone out to search out a source of wood to build a wood shed and for fuel for the winter. Covenanters were taught early in life to always be prepared and it seemed odd to none of them to be making ready for winter in early June. This was for the best as the Reverend would not be here to see Prudence until she came back for good. Sister Rebecca cautioned the Handmaiden to return before dark and with a basket of herbs.

While Sister Rebecca fetched the bag from the storage cupboard, Prudence told her that the old clothes were needed to aid in the search.

Sister Rebecca, who had never heard of or even conceived of pendulum magic, assumed that perhaps the doctor's relatives had a dog who could sniff out the whereabouts of the missing children.

It was one of the hardest things that Prudence had ever done in her life, to climb back on the dragon with the bag of old clothes clutched to her breast. She was completely frightened of Varian. All of her life she had been taught that dragons were minions of Satan; that they existed but to kill mankind with their fiery breath and collect souls for Hell.

So many of the things she had been certain that she knew to be absolute Truth had been challenged recently: that magic was evil, that talking animals were imps of Satan, that dragons were demonic...she felt very confused and sometimes wondered if her elders had been telling her lies all of these years. She then felt guilty for even thinking such heretical thoughts.

Fortunately for Prudence, they spent little time in the air, for the distance between the mission and the camp at *El Morro* was nothing to dragon wings.

It had been decided that Julian would be the one to dowse with the pendulum. He had had actual physical contact with the children, which was sometimes an advantage when trying to find some one with a pendulum.

Every Wizard was taught pendulum dowsing as a matter of course. It was a useful tool to find lost persons or even lost pets. Most police forces employed a pendulum dowser, for it could also be used to find stolen goods, victims of kidnappings and criminals.

The tools were simple. A long chain, nearly always of silver, was attached to a pendulum weight of quartz or stone. Anything actually could be used as a pendulum as long as it swung freely. The requirements were that it was symmetrical in shape and was attached centrally to the cord or chain it swung from.

Like the focus stone on a wand, the quartz or stone pendulum was a personal choice and the Wizard would chose a pendulum stone that called to him and felt 'right'. After years of use a stone became attuned to the particular psychic vibrations of the Wizard who carried it. For this reason, the pendulum and chain were always worn, either as a neck chain or most often as an additional waistcoat chain, along with one's pocket watch.

Julian's pendulum was of lapis lazuli, a rich blue

stone with streaks and spots of gold, in a tear-drop shape, cut and faceted to catch the light. It hung on the end of a braided silver chain attached to his pocket watch.

First of all, when everyone had returned, Julian thoroughly grounded and centered himself. To dowse, one had to cultivate an attitude of emotional detachment, to let go of any urgency the answers to the questions might make. Detached curiosity was the proper frame of mind, for the inner self must be calm to connect with the dowsing medium.

Ramón watched with interest as did Gina-nah-tah. The fox had disappeared for a while but as soon as the dowsing was proposed, he was there again, his bright eyes watching everything avidly. He said little but missed nothing.

When she was asked for it Prudence handed over the bag of rags to Sabrina, who opened it and began to sort through it.

In her left hand she held a pink crystal, cut in facets. This would help her identify the piece of material that vibrated most strongly with psychic energy.

Many Wizards rather scorned Witchcraft, other than for the agricultural blessings it gave to the land. They did not think that crystal power was the equal to the power of the ley lines or even to that of the sun and elemental powers harnessed by the Druids.

But Ellery and the others had seen what Witches could do, and did not hesitate to ask for help of Witchcraft. Crystal scrying was powered by moonlight, gathered and stored and as far a divination went, it could scarcely be equaled. If the pendulum dowsing did not work, Ellery intended to ask Sabrina to use the medium of crystal if she did not suggest it first.

They all kept quiet while Sabrina concentrated. Finally she held up a piece of fabric. "This one," she announced. "The wearer of this must have some psychic ability for the vibration is quite strong."

It was a faded piece of calico with a misaligned pint of small flowers on a yellow background. Cheap and flimsy, it had been purchased for its low price as a 'second' or reject, good enough for the children who worked underground and never saw the light of day.

This worn-out clothing that the children had worn in the

mines had been cut into neat squares for use as rags when Sister Rebecca and Prudence had made the children new clothing. "Willful waste makes woeful want" was a favorite Covenanter aphorism.

Prudence recognized the cloth. "That was Angelita's dress," she said.

Julian gave her a grateful look. "That's useful for me to know," he said. "I can concentrate on her. Where she is, there will probably be the others as well."

He sat down at the table, relaxing as much as possible. The other mages stood nearby. They had an audience of familiars, Atalanta, Prudence and Sinclair, and in the background, the two adult dragons and the three dragonets as well as Torin. Both Lutterworth and Dr. Beck were not in attendance.

Rowan, with his cow, had left some time ago. *Don* Casimiro wanted no part of *brujo* work; he was sitting by Marisela's beside. Only Siofra, of the familiars, was not present. She kept watch over Marisela and Pacho to alert Julian if there should be any problems with either patient.

Julian tied the bit of cloth to the silver chain about five inches above the pendulum. He 'spoke' to the pendulum in his mind, asking it to give a positive or negative response to each question he asked. It could only answer yes or no, or indicate where on a map.

Each mage and pendulum interacted in a unique way, but some matters were standard.

In an easy posture, Julian began to swing the quartz back and forth away from himself, letting it fall into a natural rhythm. When it had swung for perhaps two minutes he asked aloud "Do you know the person whose clothing you wear?"

In reply the pendulum, of its own accord, began to rotate clockwise.

"That means yes," Nicholas translated for those who were watching and did not understand what was being done.

"Might you show me where she is?" Julian then inquired.

Once again, it rotated gently clockwise.

"Please, show me where she is," Julian said.

He concentrated on Angelita as he had last seen her

as the pendulum spun around, gaining speed with every circuit. Soon it was a blur of motion.

"It will stop over exactly where she is," Nicholas informed them.

But it did not. Instead it came to a shuddering halt and stood straight out, attempting to jerk itself from Julian's hold. The pull was so strong that he had to let go, for his arm was wrenched. The pendulum then leaped into the air, fell to the ground and skittered across the soil looking as if it was trying to escape.

Flann streaked after it and pounced upon it as if it was a mouse, stopping it in its headlong flight. "Holy Bastet!" the cat exclaimed. " 'Tis quivering beneath me paw!"

"What the hell was that?" Ellery said. "I've never seen anything like that!" He turned to his nephew, who was nursing his pulled arm. "Did you see or feel anything, Julian?"

"Blackness," he said shortly and then commanded *"Exonrare"* causing green Healing magic to ease the pain in his arm.

"Blackness!" Ellery echoed. "I've never heard of such a thing from a pendulum."

"Let me try," suggested Nicholas.

But his results—and Ellery's—were the same. Flann had to chase after each pendulum and Julian had to Heal hurt arms and shoulders.

"Shall I try crystal scrying?" Sabrina offered.

Ellery knew his sister too well to even suggest that it was too dangerous or inappropriate for her to try. Crystal scrying was the *ne plus ultra* of divination. Crystals were created in the earth and were the symbols of spiritual illumination and purity. In addition, Witches imbued their crystals with the power of the moon which enhanced the properties of order, and stability inherent in each crystal. Crystal was not adversely affected by outside forces. Any good Witch had a store of crystals of different sizes and colours, which she spent time handling each day and took with her to the moon power dances, where they were laid on white cloths embroidered with the owner's names and allowed to absorb the drawing down of the moon. They were kept free from both physical and psychic dirt by frequent baths in purified water.

Now Sabrina reached into a belt pouch she had put on before the pendulum dowsing began, She withdrew a small object wrapped in white silk.

Inside was a white, almost clear crystal the size of a crab apple. "Miss Cromwell," Sabrina said briskly, "as I don't know what this girl looks like, I am going to ask you to hold my right hand and give me a visualization."

Prudence was frightened, What she had seen made her think of the tales of possession she had been warned of, back home in New Jerusalem. Jewelry did not leap about of its own accord and try to run off.

But Julian smiled encouragingly at her and said softly "It's quite all right. All you shall feel is a slight warmth. Nothing bad will happen to you."

When he looked at her like that she would do anything for him, even let the dragon eat her. She went to Sabrina and put her hand in the Witch's right hand.

In her outstretched left hand Sabrina held the crystal, still laying upon its garment of white silk.

"What's that thing in her hand again?" Sinclair whispered to Atalanta.

"That's a crystal. The name comes from the Greek *Krustallos*, meaning 'ice'," said Atalanta absently, her attention on Sabrina. "Crystals were believed to be fragments of a perfect crystal on Mount Olympus, the Crystal of Truth. Any found here on earth have fallen from that one stone. Therefore, they have mystical, some say even God-like, powers."

Atalanta felt Ellery looking at her with approval and was very glad that she did not easily blush.

After telling the Handmaiden to think of Angelita and only Angelita, Sabrina closed her eyes tightly and drew from Prudence an image of the girl. When this likeness was fixed in her mind, Sabrina opened her eyes quickly and projected the image into the crystal. She did this several times, each time putting the picture of Angelita she had obtained deep into the crystal.

Then, eyes half shut, she let the image appear on the crystal's surface. When she opened her eyes wide the image still was there.

But as she watched, the image was overtaken by a

cloud of rolling blackness, filling all of the crystal until no brightness remained and even those watching could see it grow black.

Startled, Sabrina dropped the crystal, with an exclamation of horror.

Deftly, Nicholas lunged forward caught it before it hit the ground where it would have shattered. He grabbed the square of white silk from Sabrina and threw it over the crystal so that it was completely hidden from sight.

"Thank you, Nick," said Ellery. His expression was grim. "Well, this proves it," he said, looking from Sabrina to Nicholas and then to Julian. "Four tries, four images of blackness and their location blocked from view. We are definitely dealing with the Dark here. Those children are in the hands of necromancers."

Chapter Thirty Seven
End-of-Track

Nicholas and Varian returned Prudence to the mission shortly before dark, with a basket full of tansy from Sabrina's and Julian's stores. This herb was fresh, and had been kept so under a preservation spell, which was lifted so that Sister Rebecca could dry it as she usually would without arousing the Reverend Brewer's suspicion.

Before she left, Julian gave Prudence a dragon whistle. "You are to blow this at once," he said "if Reverend Brewer becomes dangerous or violent. Either Erianne or Varian will hear it up to fifty miles away and they shall tell me that you are in trouble. I shall try my best to come and see him tomorrow." Julian had not liked the description of the Reverend's behavior that Prudence had given. He did sound like a man teetering on the edge of madness or at the very least a nervous breakdown.

Prudence at first was reluctant to take it. Jewelry of any sort was a vain adornment. Covenanter women did not wear even wedding rings. Only when the doctor stressed that Reverend Brewer might become unpredictable in his behavior, perhaps even perilous to himself and others, did she consent. It would have to be worn beneath her gown where it would be unseen. She would have to show it to Sister Rebecca and obtain her elder's permission to wear it.

When he returned to the fireside where Ellery and Sabrina sat with the familiars, Sabrina thought that Julian looked different. At first, she could not understand what it was and then it struck her; for the first time since Sarah had so cruelly jilted him, his air of unhappiness had disappeared. He looked restored to his old self, as if all the pain of the recent past had vanished and been forgotten. He was busy, too busy to brood, engaged in his profession and interested in something outside himself once more. She was at once glad that they had brought him along on this trip, as frustrating and now risky as it was. And it had proved a blessing to have him here.

The four mages, their familiars and Ramón sat up late, discussing what could be done for the children.

The fact that they were in the hands of black magicians and could suffer a terrible fate, added urgency to finding and destroying the necromancers. But how to find them? That was the problem.

They spoke in Spanish so that Ramón could follow the conversation. His knowledge of the area would be extremely helpful. He said little, but watched their faces and listened to the others speak. He was much struck by the difference in attitude that these people had towards the children than had the former overseers of the mines. They actually cared what happened to children that most of them had not even met. The Inquisition and those who ran the mines for them had thought of the children as disposable commodities, easily replaced and exploited.

Gian-nah-tah remained at Ramón's side, listening to all that was said. The fox, too, remained quiet but Ramón felt him weighing everything he heard. He would speak only if it were pertinent.

Sabrina brought out a note-pad and a pencil. There was a great deal to be done and it helped to see it on paper.

"Our first task must be to find the children and rid this area of the necromancers," she said, making a note on the pad.

"Not as easy as it sounds," said Ellery. "We are going to have to devote some time to searching every inch of this territory. Even with magic, which does not seem to be working too well, it will be a formidable undertaking."

"Varian, Erianne and I thought we might take turns gliding low over the countryside, looking for signs of recent excavations," put in Torin. The hippogriffe was laying near them, his long legs curled up under him.

Ramón nodded and spoke for the first time. "There must be a slag heap from the digging," he offered. "It would be of earth, fresh from the inside of the mine."

"Even once we find them, it will still be difficult,

perhaps," Ellery said, frowning. "We don't as yet know what form this black magic takes."

"I hope to find out a little bit more about that tomorrow, with Ramón's help," Julian put in. "There are tests I can do on those bodies we found to determine just that, and even what level demon we will be dealing with."

"I wish there were no demons!" said Bairre. The ferret was in his Wizard's lap, where he felt comforted. "Demons are dangerous!"

"We'll take very precaution, Bairre," Ellery promised. "But this has to be done, even if the children were not involved."

"We also promised to help the people and dragons at the railroad site," Sabrina reminded them, scribbling on her notepad. "That includes medical help," she said, looking at her nephew. "You're going to be rather busy, Julian, between forensics, your two patients here, who knows how many in need of care at the railway site--"

"And perhaps even a madman to deal with," he finished. "Speaking of my patients here, I want to look in on them before we retire. If Marisela is progressing well enough I shall take her off the respirator in the morning and perhaps even rouse her. The sooner she can breathe normally and begin eating properly the better. If Nick agrees, I should like to see Pacho eat a little solid food tomorrow as well." He rose to leave and this had the effect of breaking up the meeting. Ramón, it had been decided, would spend the night as well so as to be on hand in the next day to go out to the caves.

Marisela felt as if she was swimming up from the depths of the water tank. It was as if she was running out of breath. Where was Rodri? Why had he let her stay underwater for such a long time? He was usually very strict about that. She murmured his name and then coughed.

To her surprise her mouth did not fill with water. She opened her eyes, surprised that she was not in the water as she had been dreaming and did not at first recognize the man she saw smiling encouragingly at her. And then–"You are *Don* Nicolás's *hermano*, no?" she said hoarsely. "The *médico, Don* Julio?" Why was she so hoarse? She tried to lift her hand to her throat and found it a nearly impossible task. She was so weak!

"Julián," he said, giving his name its Spanish pronunciation. Sympathetically he said "Your throat will be slightly dry. Even with a moisturizing spell, there is a slight dryness. Here, I've prepared a drink for you. This should help you feel better." Carefully, he lifted her head and held a beaked decanter to her lips.

It smelled enticing and she wanted to gulp it all down. It was cool and delicious and even as it went down her throat it seemed to not just soothe the dryness but to spread good feeling out into every part of her. Even the slight tightness in her chest when she had coughed eased.

He made her sip it slowly and when she had finished help her lay back against the pillows. "Now, I'm going to examine you and find out how you are progressing."

"What happened to me?" she queried and then suddenly remembered. "Pacho!" she said urgently and tried to sit up. He stopped her before she could manage it.

"He's right here," Julian reassured her. "Pacho, come over and see Marisela so she can see that you are all right."

The dragonet, who had been anxiously awaiting permission, rose from his blankets and went to her bedside. He put his head on the edge of the cot within easy reach of her hand and said happily "You're awake!"

Marisela reached out to him. The drink seemed to have helped her regain her strength as well. She laid her hand on his head and he sighed in bliss. "Tell me what happened to us," she commanded the dragonet.

She listened to her dragonet as Julian conducted his examination. "You are progressing very well," he said at last in satisfaction. "If you keep this up, we shall make your father happy and let you go home tonight or tomorrow morning."

Marisela wanted to see her father and she was also conscious of extreme gratitude to Nicholas's brother that ought to be expressed. But right now what her body wanted to do was to go to back to sleep, with Pacho near enough to touch. As her eyes closed she heard Julian's voice, as from a long way off, say "That's the ticket. You rest now and when you awake again we'll have a meal ready for you."

The last thing she heard before sliding into sleep was Pacho saying "I'm hungry *now!*"

The next morning Sabrina made the proprietor of the little General Store in Diablo more than happy. Not only did she buy a great many of his canned goods and preserved meats, but she paid in gold and made a large order to go to his supplier in Albuquerque.

It had been decided to go out to the railroad site first. Then Julian and Ramón would conduct an investigation of the bodies while Ellery and Nicholas went back to the treasure hunt. Only this last kept Lutterworth in the least bit mollified. He was still angered that they intended to interfere with his railway workers but the fact that they were paying for it had the tendency to make him less argumentative. At least it was not coming out of his pocket.

Someone had to stay behind and watch the patients and Atalanta volunteered for this task. Her father had no interest in going out to the railroad camp and demanded her presence to wait on him and begin copying out his notes. Like Ellery, he was keeping a careful record.

Atalanta was supplied with a dragon whistle; should anything come up, she was to blow it at once. Since the railroad camp was barely ten miles distant Julian, on Torin, could be back in a matter of minutes.

Ellery was conscious of a feeling of disappointment that she was not to go with them. He had, he confessed to himself, looked forward to seeing more of the surrounding countryside in her company. He had seldom come across a colleague whose opinions he esteemed more.

Lutterworth insisted on going along. This was *his* camp and *his* workers and he was going to monitor the do-gooders and make certain that they did not incite his workers to riot. If they wanted to waste their time and money pandering to them and seeing to their ills that was one thing.

But he was not going to stand for a strike. They were behind schedule as it was, due to the treasure hunt. The railroad should have already reached this area instead of stopping so far away.

In the end, the three mages, Lutterworth and Sinclair climbed onto a heavily laden Varian. Julian rode Torin, in order to bring as many of his medical supplies as possible.

Seen from the air, as Varian and Torin approached, the camp looked busy and prosperous. A number of dragons were bringing loads of railroad ties and steel rails from flat cars behind a small tank locomotive. A crew of men was splitting rough cut logs and hewing them into railroad ties, while others with large brushes were coating them with the creosote that would impede rot.

But on closer examination there were too many men standing about idle. No track was being laid.

"Look at that!" growled Lutterworth as Varian landed. "Graders, track layers, spike-setters, bolt-screwers, tampers, all doing nothing and getting paid for it! I've got nearly one thousand men here all getting paid as much as a dollar a day! And they'll leave here and go to work for Rankin if I stop their wages. All because you people can't find the damned treasure!"

"Sir, I see that the telegraph line has reached us and the office has come out here to end-of-track," offered Sinclair timidly, hoping to mollify what he saw as an explosion of temper in the making.

Both the camp and the construction headquarters moved forward every 100 to 200 miles to what was called end-of-track. The tents used to house the workers moved with this as well.

And something else moved with it: a crowd of dirty, sagging tents from which could now be heard loud, raucous noise, the music from a tinny piano and even gunshots.

This tent city was full of what Reverend Brewer would term haunts of vice: gambling establishments where one might lose one's money at three card Monte, keno, faro and other dishonest games; houses of prostitution where one could develop a case of 'the "French pox"; drinking establishments with overpriced, watered-down whiskey and gin; in short, criminals of every type, all eager for one thing—

360

to relieve the railroad workers of as much of their money as possible.

The dragon and the hippogriffe landing attracted the attention of a three men who had been standing next to a small building, talking in low voices. When he recognized Lutterworth, one of the men ran forward and said "Thank God, Mr. Lutterworth! Are we able to go on now?"

He was a tall and lanky dark-haired young man with an immense mustache. He wore a look of anxiety.

"My civil engineer, Jack Ballard," Lutterworth waved his hand negligently in the man's direction. "Ballard, these are the professors I hired."

Ballard inclined his head distractedly in the barest sketch of a bow not taking his eyes off his employer. Sir," he said jerkily "we've got to get these men to work again! This idleness–they are fighting and gaming and drinking heavily. We've caught up with the graders and they're idle as well. Even the survey has halted at your orders. But it won't do, sir! I'm afraid of what will happen if we don't get them to work again."

"We haven't found it yet," began Lutterworth but was interrupted by the arrival of another man on the run.

He was a contrast to Ballard, who was well-groomed and dressed in well-cut tweeds. This man was shabby, with the flat cap and rough clothes of a laborer. The cap he snatched off as he approached and said "Please sirs, and ma'am" he added, seeing Sabrina. "I was after bein' told there was to be a doctor comin' today? Me wife is havin' a baby and I think it's comin' now!"

Julian took his bag from Torin's saddle and said "I'm the doctor. Show me where she is." He put Siofra on his shoulder as well.

"Saint Pádraig bless ye," said the man in relief.

"Damned Paddys breed like rabbits," muttered Lutterworth as Julian left with the Irish laborer.

Nicholas, Sabrina and Ellery exchanged a look and Varian rolled his eyes. Obviously Lutterworth had forgotten that he was talking to a group of Irish persons.

"If we could just lay the track up to where you are looking for your archeological sites, Mr.Lutterworth." Ballard continued to plead. "There have already been so many fights,

361

even a stabbing and many other injuries. We could even lay the track at a slower rate—we needn't do our standard rate of work. Just something to keep the men busy." Ballard was practically begging.

"There will be a bit of a diversion today, Mr. Ballard," said Sabrina briskly. "We'll need tables and a tent set up here. We'll be cooking and giving out food, and having a medical clinic."

"What?" Ballard, for the first time, really noticed her and the others, including the dragon whose breast harness and panniers were bulging. "Are you people from the Salvation Army?" he asked. She was certainly very pretty to be with the Hallelujah Corps.

"No, we just want to help. One of the dragons told us that he was reduced to stealing cows," Sabrina answered.

"Come to the office, Sinclair," Lutterworth commanded. "Now that we've a telegraphic connection close to hand I need to telegraph New York." He turned to Sabrina. "Play the Lady Bountiful, Miss Delamar. Just don't expect any help or one red cent from me. Stop your whining, Ballard!" he snapped as that young man once again tried to engage his attention. "I'm paying you a damn good wage to design trestles and tunnels, not to wet nurse a bunch of malcontents. Let them kill each other! Better yet, tell them anyone who's injured in a fight gets their pay stopped! That'll cure them!" with this he stalked off towards the office building, trailed by Sinclair who looked apologetically back at Sabrina.

"Let's see if we can't turn thoughts to a good feed and a holiday," Nicholas suggested to Ballard.

Ballard sighed. "That will do for today but what about tomorrow?"

Julian followed his fellow Irishman to the squalid tents where the noise level, if anything had grown louder. He was led around the rear of a tent on which a dirty paper sign hung askew. It read: "Bath, Beer, and Screw $2."

Siofra hissed. "'Tis bein' worse than the slums of

Dublin!" She spoke in Gaelic.

" 'Tis Irish ye are!" The man in front of them whirled around, surprise on his face.

Julian briefly introduced themselves and the man said "I'm from County Cork meself, a little village bein' near Castlemartyr. Me name's Lúcás Cinnéidigh, but they are after callin' me Luke Kennedy here."

Julian frowned. "This is a terrible place to keep your wife, Mr. Cinnéidigh!"

"I was havin' no choice about the matter," he said. "The tents are bein' for men only an' there's no housin' for families near. An' I was not bein' able to afford it any road. The mistress of this establishment is after bein' kind to me Biddy and me two young ones. She is payin' Biddy for the sewin' and mendin' an' is keepin' the customers away from her."

At this moment a long scream rang out and a disheveled woman came running from behind a blanket which had been hung up to make a private corner.

"Luke!" she panting a little "Is this the damned sawbones? She's going to pop at any minute!"

"This is bein' the doctor indeed, Flossie. 'Tis our kind friend, Flossie Jennings, Doctor," Cinnéidigh explained.

"The hell with that!" Flossie exclaimed "Get in there, Doc!" She was a woman of later middle age, getting a little stout, with dyed hair of an improbable red hue and heavily made up. Her low-cut, short in the leg gown was of a brilliant shade of purple and heavily spangled. She looked completely distraught. "I ain't never birthed no baby and I ain't gonna start now!" she declared. Nevertheless she followed the two men into the room.

On entering the little room, Julian found a young woman, very pretty, with soft brown hair that was wet with sweat. She lay on a narrow cot and was obviously near her time.

At the foot of the bed were two children, a boy and a girl, who looked frightened to death.

"Is me Ma goin' to die?" the boy burst out. He was only about seven, the girl younger. She was crying.

"This is no place for them," Julian said in a low voice to Mr. Cinnéidigh.

"Flossie, would ye be after takin' the wee ones outside?" Cinnéidigh said urgently.

She nodded in agreement and said "Come on, kids. I've got some sarsaparilla I'll let you have. Nobody's buying the stuff anyway."

"I'll be goin' wi' them and purrin' them happy," said Siofra in Julian's ear. She hopped down from his shoulder and went towards the children, whom, as she had known they would be, were diverted by the sight of a cat eager to be friends.

The young woman on the bed gave a long moan and said through her teeth "Be damned to ye, Lúcás Cinnéidigh! If it were not bein' for ye wantin' that damned treasure yer daft grandad was always braggin' on, sure we'd be snug at home an' I'd be havin' me Ma to hand!" she broke off as another pain came.

Treasure? Julian shot Lúcás Cinnéidigh a speculative glance. This would have to be investigated. But first, there was a baby to welcome into the world. He laid a soothing hand on Biddy's brow and bent to the task at hand.

Chapter Thirty Eight
Digging for Silver

In spite of her fear of them, Angelita had decided that their captors were very stupid. They seemed to think that there were nuggets of pure silver just laying around in the mine, waiting to be picked up. Then all they had to do would be to melt them down into ingots.

They did not know that the silver had to be extracted from the ore and that silver was usually mixed with copper, argentine or lead. The mine the children had worked in formerly had used the pan or *cuzo* method of extraction by which the crushed and ground ore was mixed with salt and mercury and sometimes what the children knew as bluestone, in a shallow copper pan and then heated. This process took ten to twenty hours to extract the silver.

None of the children knew the proportions in which the chemicals were used. Their jobs had been to either dig the ore with pick or hammer and chisel, or take the crushed ore (crushed by dragons) to the shed where many pans were kept on long lines, constantly heated, and amalgamating silver.

The shorter dark-robed figure had actually only given them sacks to fill with nuggets, not even anything to dig with! Both black robes had been angered when Léon tried to explain to them that silver was rarely, if ever, found laying about in chunks as they seemed to think. They grew even angrier when Léon told them that none of them knew exactly what the chemicals were nor the proportions need for the *cuzo* process. They had never been allowed to do that work. Such was for the older workers. The overseer doled out the chemicals and kept careful watch for waste.

The shorter one, whom they had since found out was called Brother Daemon, had completely lost his temper then and had slapped Léon and began to kick and hit him until the taller one, Brother Satyr, had stopped him. "We shall have to move the ore from this place and have it processed elsewhere," he said. "Hitting the boy does no good. He cannot work if he is injured." He then turned his featureless face, hidden deep in the black cowl towards Léon. "Now, boy, tell us what tools you need to dig this silver from the ground."

Léon, his nose bleeding and sporting a rapidly forming black eye, did so. Until the tools arrived, Brother Satyr said with that silky, menacing voice, they could have a holiday. He returned Léon to the group of children, careful to lock his chain to the huge stone into which all the chains were pounded with a hasp. With this the two black robes left the mine, arguing as to where they could obtain tools secretly.

Angelita tore a strip off the bottom of her dress and dipped it in what little water was left in a clay pot that had contained drinking water. With this she began to wipe the blood off Léon's face.

"*Vacaciones*! In what way is this a holiday?" Léon muttered and then swore as Angelita touched a sore spot on his face.

"Not in front of the *niños*," Angelita scolded.

Léon gave her a look compounded of exasperation and anger. "Don't be stupid, Angelita!" he said. "We are captives again in a mine and you are worried about bad language?" As the two oldest, Léon being fifteen and Angelita two years younger, they were the natural leaders of the group.

"We should explore this cave," Angelita announced, ignoring this comment of Léon's. "There may be a way to escape."

"How are we supposed to do that?" demanded Vasco. His face wore a scowl. Vasco was the one who most often saw only the bad in everything. Angelita could not blame him for that. His mother had rejected him as a child of rape and when he was younger, being small and timid, he had been picked on and abused by the overseers. Although only now nine, he had learned to fight and very few people bothered him further. But his life had left him soured and bitter. He now picked up the chain that circled an iron restraint about an ankle of each of them. He jingled it. "Did you forget about this, Angelita?" he sneered.

"We can push this rock," she said calmly. "It isn't that heavy if we all work at it. We can move it about so that we can each explore the wall closest to each one of us. They will only bring us food once a day, that Brother Daemon said, and we will be alone all of that time until they bring us tools."

"Which will probably be tomorrow!" Vasco jeered.

"No, Angelita is right!" said Léon suddenly. "They

were arguing about where they might get tools secretly. That means they might have to go a long way for them. It might take days. We should really find out as much as we can about this cave."

"And they will expect us to know where the ore is, *sí?*" said Benito "And the best places to dig? Always they have expected us to know."

There was some argument about who was to go first, but eventually they decided that the youngest, Pia, would have the first try.

And that was how they discovered the narrow slit in the wall, a slit big enough only for a very slim, smallish man– or a child.

It had been a difficult birth. The baby was in a breech presentation and had to be turned magically.

Midway through, Mr. Cinnéidigh had fainted dead away, eyes rolling back in his head. Flossie Jennings had peeked in, turned pale and hastily left again. But as if in answer to a wish, Sabrina and Flann had arrived, Flann able to help with her purr and Sabrina another pair of hands to assist.

"Thank you, Sabrina," said Julian gratefully as he washed up and she swathed the baby in clean dry cloths before giving her to her mother.

"It's not the first baby we've delivered together," she said. At her father's clinic, where they had both worked, there always seemed to be a superfluity of babies amongst the poor of Dublin.

Biddy was coming around from the mildly sedative spell that had eased the pain for her but still enabled her to 'push' when needed. "What is it bein', a boy or a girl?" she asked groggily.

"A beautiful little daughter," said Sabrina, and gave the little bundle to her mother.

Seeing the look of love and joy that spread over Biddy's features, Sabrina felt a deep pang. She had thought the pain of losing her child as well as her husband had healed but her emotions, amounting almost to jealousy right now, proved that the grief had not truly gone.

Julian was kneeling beside the prone body of Lúcás, waving a little bottle of vinaigrette under his nose. It had seemed easier just to leave him there when they were busy. But now the new father would want to know that everything was fine with mother and baby.

Cinnéidigh's eyelids fluttered and he let out a groan. "Pádraig and all the saints preserve us!" he said and sat up with Julian's help. "It is bein' over with, *Dochtúir?*" he asked, giving Julian his Gaelic title.

"You have another daughter," Julian told him.

A look of delight lit up Cinnéidigh's face. "And me Biddy, she's bein' all right as well?"

"Come an' be seein' for yerself, ye great gowk!" called his wife. "Faintin' away like a maiden lady, a great strong lump of a man like ye!" With Sabrina's help she had pulled herself up against the thin pillows on her cot and was cuddling the baby against her breast. "Lúcás, 'tis in my heart that we should be namin' this new child after the *Dochtúir* here. He was after savin' me life, I think. It would have gone badly with me were he not here tendin' to me."

So it was that the little girl was named Iúile, which was the Gaelic for Julia.

"You could do something else for me, Mr. Cinnéidigh," said Julian after he had washed and sterilized his forceps and other equipment and replaced them in his bag. "I would like to know what treasure you are searching for. It so happens that my aunt here, and I are with an archaeological expedition that is searching for a treasure in this area."

"An archeological expedition is it?" said Cinnéidigh, looking rather guilty and worried. "I'm knowin' what that is, for wasn't one from the University in Dublin come lookin' for barrow graves near to me home when I was but a lad? Hired some if us they did, to help wi' th' diggin'." He seemed reluctant to reveal his information.

"Mr. Cinnéidigh," said Sabrina. "If you have a claim to the treasure we will make certain that you receive anything and all that you are entitled to. You should know the A. J. Lutterworth, the owner of this railroad, claims it is his and will be quite ruthless in crushing, or even stealing from, anyone who he might think is in his way. My brother has influence and friends in Washington, as well as legal knowledge. We can help you get you share."

"I'm not wishin' anyone to be knowin' of this," said Cinnéidigh in a lowered voice. "Who is knowin' who might be listenin' here?"

"No one will overhear us," said Sabrina calmly. "When I arrived I cast a spell of *silentium* so that the customers in Flossie's would not be disturbed by Biddy's birth pangs. Flossie was concerned that they would leave if they had to listen to her. It is still in effect. Someone could stand right outside that blanket and not hear a word we are saying."

Cinnéidigh still looked reluctant but he had been taught by his parents that Wizards and Witches were good, as trustworthy as a priest, or the police. They were sworn to good, and the presence of the two familiars reassured him as to this. Animals knew when people were good or bad and acted accordingly, particularly familiar animals.

And at the urging of his wife, Cinnéidigh gave in.

"Well," he began," 'tis after bein' a family legend. Me great great – aye, so many greats back I can't be countin' grandfather was a venturesome broth of a boy an' ran away to sea when naught but a lad. This was bein' durin' th' time of the Armada. He was wantin' to fight the Spanish, he did, and he was endin' in the service of Sir Francis Drake. Any road, he saw fightin' here in th' Americas. 'Twas bein' here that he heard of a great treasure, gathered up some years afore and taken north. A great a lot of it, there was, all havin' bein' gathered by a pirate from havin' been robbin' the Spanish treasure ships. Drake was wantin' the treasure for the Queen. There was a legend of a devilish pirate lord who was going to lbe lookin' for the Cities of gold and be settin' himself up as an Emperor."

The rest of his tale was simple. There were still people about who remembered in which direction the pirate Captain and his confederates had headed, even though it was years earlier, before Drake's time.

Cinnéidigh's ancestor, with a party of Drake's most trusted men, had gone in pursuit of the treasure. They had traced them to this area but had failed to find any treasure. Hunger and sickness had forced them to turn back and meet up with Drake in the Caribbean.

But the tale had lived on in Cinnéidigh's family, of treasure in the American southwest and fired the imagination each generation. Because of the Inquisition's stranglehold on this area no one had ever dared to go in search of it; for Irish Catholics, who worshipped in the Irish Catholic church were anathema to the Inquisition, almost as if they were Wizards and Witches. But ever since the ending of the war and the opening of the territories now in possession of the United States, Lúcás Cinnéidigh had dreamed of going to America and finding the treasure for himself and his family. When the railroad had come to Ireland looking for workers and he found out what part of America it was to be built in, he had leaped at the chance to get there.

"Do you have a map?" Julian inquired, when Cinnéidigh had finished recounting his tale.

Lúcás shook his head. "That I do not," he said, "But I've been hearin' all me life of three landmarks: a great castle, two rivers an' a blue mountain."

Julian and Sabrina exchanged glances.

"I think, Mr Cinnéidigh," said Sabrina briskly," That you had better give up railroad work and come to work for us. This is scarcely an proper atmosphere for your wife and children at any rate." Ellery had to hear about this at once, she thought. It might actually confirm that the treasure was real.

All evening, after they returned to the camp at *El Morro*, Lutterworth complained bitterly that the archaeologists had turned his railway camp into a carnival. Food had been served to humans and dragons alike, good solid, satisfying and delicious food. There had been a free clinic and Julian had treated dozens of patients. He had been appalled at the condition of some of them. Nicholas, who had learned the game in his youth from an American friend, organized a baseball game and other contests that successfully gave the railroad workers an outlet for their energy.

It was not until Lutterworth, still complaining, Sinclair and Dr. Beck had retired that Sabrina and Julian brought up the subject of Cinnéidigh's revelations. He and his family were settling into a tent borrowed from the railroad.

Atalanta still sat with the others. She had spent an exhausting day looking after the two patients, feeding dragonets and worst of all, listening to he father complain and making his meals, as he had decided that eating Lupe's food would kill him.

When he saw how tired she looked Ellery felt guilty for leaving her behind to bear this burden. When she rose to leave, he begged her to stay.

Cinnéidigh was brought to meet the others and told his tale again.

"Pirates!" breathed Varian, who was sitting near the awning protected table. "I've read so much about them! I always hoped that there would really be treasure but pirate treasure is doubly exciting!"

"Why?" asked Nicholas. "Why don't' you tell us what you've read about Drake and pirates in the Caribbean, Varian? The rest of us don't know much." Dragons loved reading and had very retentive memories.

Varian gave a delighted wiggle at being asked to tell what he knew.... "Well," he began "I would assume that the period Mr. Cinnéidigh's ancestor was in the Caribbean was in the 1570s. Drake was definitely there then. He had two ships, *Dragon* and *Swan*. Drake led his first expedition as a privateer against the Spanish in 1570, and then twice more in later years. Not a great deal is known about his activities in some of these years but there is little doubt that he was engaging in what the Spanish termed acts of piracy, but which made him a hero in England.

"There was a lot of treasure!" Varian said, his silver eyes lighting. "Every year a fleet, or *Flota*, sailed form Seville to the Spanish Main. Once there it was split into three; one called the *Terra Firme* went to Porto Bello to collect the silver that had been collected from the mines of Peru. This had to be shipped over the Isthmus of Panama, called Darien back then. Some galleons went to Cartagena and collected Uruguayan pearls, gold from Ecuador, and Colombian emeralds. A Vera Cruz fleet went to Mexico to collect the silver from that country. And in Vera Cruz they also collected the goods from the Manilla galleon, shipped across the country from the Pacific. That galleon contained trade goods from the Orient, via the Philippines, of porcelain, spices, silks and brocades. There was even a small Honduran fleet that went to Trujillo to get indigo and spices form central America. So a treasure would be silver pieces of eight, gold doubloons, jewels, pearls, porcelains, silks and spices and dyes. Most people don't know this, but most of the precious metal shipped back to Spain was silver, not gold. Much of it was in the form of vessels for the church, like Christamatories, crosses, chalices and reliquaries, made by craftsmen here."

"All of these fleets met in Havana Cuba and went back to Spain in a convoy. In spite of the size of these treasure convoys they were attacked by pirates and looted. They were heavy cumbersome galleons and the English and the other pirates had sleeker, faster ships. A lot of the treasure ships were sunk in hurricanes or other bad weather or in treacherous waters. A great deal of that era is undocumented, though. Perhaps there was a mad pirate. Perhaps he thought he could find the Seven Cities of Gold and be even richer. Many people still believed in them then."

"Thank you, Varian, for sharing your knowledge with us," said Ellery. "That leaves us with one problem. Dare we tell Lutterworth about this latest development?"

Chapter Thirty Nine

Os Tínís

"What latest development?" came a querulous voice.

They had thought themselves alone and private. Now Ellery looked up to find Dr. Beck standing just outside the rim of light cast by the mage lights. He was looking disgruntled. "Are you attempting to hide something from us, Dr. Delamar?" he sneered. "Something which might pertain to the success of this dig? Perhaps it is nothing to you if Lutterworth demands the return of his money if no treasure is found, but it is to me! I have plans for that money!" He nearly quivered with rage and his temper was not improved by seeing Atalanta sitting at her ease amongst the mages. "And you!" he said. "My own daughter, plotting with these people when you ought to have been seeing to my comfort! I have been shouting myself hoarse for near half an hour. I am having trouble sleeping and need another cup of tea. I ought to have been your first concern!"

"I am sorry, Papa," Atalanta began to rise but Ellery forestalled her. He exchanged a look with Nicholas, who said "I was just about to make tea for all of us, Dr. Beck. Pray take my seat and I shall have a pot made in no time."

Grumbling, Dr. Beck did so, his temper not improved by the fact that Cillian lay on the table at Nicholas's place. Beyond opening one bright eye briefly, he went back to sleep and refused to move in spite of Dr. Beck's saying "Shoo, you creature!" several times.

"Now, what is this new development?" Dr. Beck demanded when it became apparent that Cillian was not about to move himself.

Ellery exchanged looks with Sabrina and Julian. They had no choice but to tell Cinnéidigh's tale. To hold back this information would not be ethical or honorable, as tempting as it was to thwart Lutterworth.

Dr. Beck had paid but little attention to Cinnéidigh and his family upon their arrival. He supposed them to be some sort of servants, for they were poorly dressed and obviously of what he considered a lower social order. He regretted the children's presence for he had little use for the young of any species. The dragonets were bad enough but human children would be intolerable.

However, now that Cinnéidigh proved to have some useful knowledge Dr. Beck was all affability, and watched with the others as Ellery showed Lúcás the map and pointed out to him the two rivers and the turquoise mountain. "When it is light out," he informed Cinnéidigh, "you will be able to see this rock's resemblance to a castle."

"This would be seemin' to be th' place," agreed Cinnéidigh.

"Were there any other family stories pertaining to this treasure?" Sabrina queried as Nicholas arrived with the tea.

Cinnéidigh gratefully accepted a cup and shook his head. "Just what a rich treasure it was bein', far more than that of a Leprechaun," he answered.

"An' that would be sayin' a great deal," said Siofra from her seat in Julian's lap. "I've been hearin' afore of Leprechauns wi' plenty o' brass."

"In the morning I'll have to tell Lutterworth," said Ellery resignedly. "It will mean he'll want to go haring back to the sites and look for more caves."

"And in the morning, after I see to *Doña* Marisela, Ramon and I are going to examine those bodies," said Julian. "I've hopes that I can find out more about just what kind of black magic we will be dealing with."

"That will be very helpful," said Ellery approvingly.

"When will Marisela be going home, Julian?" Nicholas inquired casually.

"Perhaps as early as tomorrow, her father is insistent that she be taken home as soon as possible," his brother answered. "She is doing very well and I think we can rig up a type of dragon ambulance to get her home. A wagon of course, is out of the question. The jolting would do her a great deal of harm." He sighed and frowned. "I must make time to see the Reverend Brewer as well. The man sounds as if he is well on the way to a breakdown."

"I'd like to find out if he is truly responsible for the disappearance of those children," said Sabrina. "How someone could even contemplate doing something such as that!"

The talk turned to where the children might be again and Dr. Beck, who had no interest at all in a pack of brats, sipped his tea and glowered at his daughter. He would have to have a firm talk with that young lady. She was neglecting him shamefully for these new friends of hers. Dr. Delamar's ill-advised praise and treating her as a colleague, not as the mere secretary/servant she was, had inflated her opinion of herself. Well, her father was just the man to deflate her ego and it would be done speedily. After all, Dr. Beck's own comfort and well-being was at stake.

To *Don* Casimiro's joy the *médico brujo* declared that Marisela was fit to go to her home. She was breathing on her own, and although still a little weak, could be transported to the *Hacienda del Sol*. She had Healed very well.

Don Casimiro was not as happy when he found out the method of transport arranged. Julian flatly refused to allow her to be jounced over miles of nearly non-existent roads and instead, with the help of Nicholas, rigged out Varian as an ambulance dragon.

They fastened a cot, secured with rope and magic, to Varian's chest harness. He would fly low and slow, keeping the cot steady. She would be secured inside it, perfectly safe. Julian would go with her, to see her bestowed in her bed and to give directions for her at-home care. He would also give her a herbal dose to make the trip easier on her.

Pacho was made most unhappy by the loss of his bond-mate. Even Nicholas could not promise him that Marisela would return any time soon. Again the dragonet wanted to go with her and again, had to be talked out of it.

Nicholas was afraid that some harm might come to Pacho at *Don* Casimiro's hands. He had not liked the look on the *Don's* face every time his glance lit upon the dragonet. *Don* Casimiro seemed to blame Pacho for the shooting, never mind that it was his own folly that had caused the near tragedy.

Nicholas would not put it past him to have the dragonet destroyed. A dragonet of Pacho's age was still vulnerable. His teeth were not the sharp, long ones of an adult, his hide was still tender and he had no flame, as well as not being able to fly away from danger. Dragonets had been killed before by determined, ignorant men.

No, Pacho was better off here, where not only were there adult dragons to keep him safe, but mages as well.

It was a very depressed dragonet that watched his bond-mate being loaded onto the makeshift ambulance stretcher and flown away. Erianne came up to him and put her wing over him, crooning in sympathy. She knew how badly she would feel if she saw Ellery being borne away, with no chance of being near him for who knew how long.

Pacho, still weak after his wound, gave up the fight to be brave and turned around under her wing so that the others could not see him and burst into sobs.

There was little anyone could say to comfort him, for no one knew how soon Marisela would be well enough to come and see him again. Nicholas had promised that as soon as she sent him a message he would fly to the *Hacienda del Sol* and bring her to the dragonet. But no one knew when that would happen.

Marisela was safely tucked into her bed, still dozing. She had withstood the trip well, with no respiratory distress. Julian left carefully written out instructions for her care, and several herbal bottles: a strengthening tonic, a sleeping aid and a fever remedy. He also supplied her with a 'breathing bottle', a large brown bottle with an inflatable bulb that when squeezed into the mouth and inhaled provided a puff of 'smoke' that helped clear and inflate the lungs.

Julian had scarcely left the *Hacienda*, promising to return on the morrow, when *Don* Casimiro said to his wife, who was hovering anxiously over her daughter. "I shall send word at once to *Don* Rafael. As her affianced husband he will want to know that she is now safe here in her own home."

Doña Milagros agreed. She had been shocked at Marisela's appearance. The girl was pale, all her natural colour dulled and she looked as if she might have even lost weight. This was terrible, for none of the beautiful new bride-clothes in her *ajuar* would fit properly!

Julian felt badly that he had been forced to somewhat neglect Ramón as of late. Other than observing at the surgeries and more importantly being a conduit for energy, he had received no training at all. Even today, he would hopefully be identifying some of the bodies and watching as Julian did forensic spells.

They flew to the cave on Torin. Hippogriffes could carry two adults in a pinch and Julian tucked Siofra in the front of his jacket so that Ramón could ride behind the saddle where her basket was usually attached.

Ramón, of course, was used to flying on the back of Nah-kah-yen but he had never even imagined being on the back of a hippogriffe, for they were nearly unknown in America.

Torin landed just in front of the cave complex where the dragonets had been found. Yancy Yates was there. He had no objections to guarding the caverns during the daylight hours but as sun as the sun began its descent he left. Thanks to Julian, he now had a horse, hired at the livery stable, and could put miles between himself and the 'haunts' every afternoon.

It seemed strange that Lutterworth still wanted the area guarded when an intensive search had yielded no treasure. The railroad baron was certain that somehow they had missed it, or that there were more caves off the main ones. He had wanted to come back this morning but Julian wanted quiet for his forensic exams and Ellery had refused to return until Julian was done. What they could learn about the black magus was far too important to let Lutterworth's greed get in the way.

"Howdy, Doc," said Yates as they dismounted from Torin. He casually carried his rifle in the crook of his arm but he was on the alert at all times. "Want to thank you for the horse. Makes a whole lotta difference bein' able to get outta here before them haunts start in every night. Got me a tent up in the hills where the only thing I've got to worry me about is coyotes. Who's this?" he looked curiously at Ramón.

Julian told him, and said "He speaks no English, Yates."

To his surprise. Yates said to Ramón *"Hola, amigo! ¿Cómo estás?"*

At Julian's look of surprise Yates said "Learned me the lingo when I decided to come down here. Reckoned I'd need it."

It was too bad that the missionaries had not felt the same need.

Yates had a tendency to want to follow them until Julian explained that they were going to examine some bodies. Yates changed his mind at once about tagging along.

Ramón followed Julian, who carried Siofra on his shoulder. Torin brought up the rear; he had heard about the caves from Varian and the familiars and was curious to see them. Smaller than a dragon, he could easily fit into the caves.

Ramón studied the cave with interest. He was used to being underground, but all of the 'caves' that he knew were artificially created and had no features such as stalactites and stalagmites. He thought them oddly beautiful.

"There has been death here," he remarked as they walked through the main chamber where the dragon eggs had been found.

Julian explained about the eggs as they continued on towards the passage that lead to the pile of bones and bodies.

"The Inquisition sent men out all of the time to find dragon eggs and young dragons to make their slaves. We heard that they sometimes went very far away to steal eggs and bring them back here to make them hatch," Ramón offered.

"That's what Nicholas thought, since several of the eggs came from a long way from here," replied Julian.

They were now at the entrance to the narrow tunnel that led to the 'charnel house'.

"It won't be after smellin' bad, will it then?" said Siofra, wrinkling her nose.

Julian assured her that it would not, as he had put the bodies under a preservation spell.

It was difficult for Ramón; Julian could see that. Some of the bodies, those near the top of the pile, were people he had known. Even those which were mostly skeletons sometimes still wore an item of clothing that he remembered.

Having Ramón's help saved Julian a great deal of magical work, for they were quickly able to separate those who had been cast down this hole as sick and ailing from those whom Julian suspected had been used in a black ceremony of some sort.

There proved to be about fifteen of these. Close examination revealed them all to be girls or women. A spell of *Chronos,* a forensic spell learned from his grandfather Stuart, enabled Julian to pinpoint the time of death. This dated the earliest back some five years, not, as he had feared, several hundred. The oldest bodies, he found, had been like those Ramón recognized: deposited there by the Inquisition when too old or sick to work any longer.

Ramón recognized the most recently dead woman as did Siofra. "'Tis bein' th' whore that was after propositionin' ye, Julian, th' first day we were bein' in that devil town!" the little cat exclaimed.

"Yes," agreed Ramón. "She came often to the mines to lay with the overseers. It was said that she came from the *bordello* in Diablo."

"She was definitely ritually murdered," said Julian. "Even without a spell I can feel the Darkness on her."

"And the demon-stink!" said Siofra. "Can ye be findin' out more about the demon?" she asked her Wizard.

"I am going to find out what kind of black magic was used on her first," he answered and leveled his wand at the body, now, like the others, beneath a preservation spell. "*Quarere obacurus magicus,*" he ordered.

What followed was the strangest thing Ramón had ever seen. He seemed to be looking at rapidly shifting pictures of things that were not really there. Two black-robed figures did things he did not understand in a very strange looking cavern with a green floor. He understood well enough what they did to the woman that was tied to the top of some sort of platform but he drew back, revolted and frightened, when he saw the creature that appeared, with the legs of a beast and a long forked tail. There were horns upon his head and an ugly look of lust on his face.

"That's all we need to see," said Julian, feeling that there was no need to see her death. He said *"Terminus."* and the vision winked out abruptly.

"Satanists," said Siofra in disgust.

"And a lower level demon, I think," said Julian thoughtfully. "Let us make certain of that. *Congoscere daemon,*" he commanded, pointing his wand again at the body.

This time they were granted a closer view of the demon.

"I'll mark it well," said Siofra. "Were you after bringing the Book of Demon wi' ye, Julian?"

He nodded, intent on studying the face and form before him. While the book could not give them the demon's name it would identify from which level he came and give them an idea of his powers, for each level of demon had its own particular characteristics.

When the vision faded Ramón said hesitantly *"Maestro,* these people who have died–I sense that they are not at rest. Their spirits hover near and they wish to join their ancestors. But the manner of their death keeps them here. No one mourned them; they were treated like so much rubbish and many of them died in anguish."

Julian was again surprised by the depth of Ramón's untrained empathy. "I intend to release them, Ramón," he said. "It isn't right to leave them here. They need to go Home."

"To the Great Spirit," put in Siofra." To Him ye would be calli' Usen."

Ramón nodded. He watched as Julian waved his wand in a circle to encompass all of the bodies and said *"Os cinis."*

Several things happened at once. All the flesh, and fabric or any trace of clothing on the bodies and skeletons fell away and disappeared. The bones began to burn with a clean, green light.

A light almost too brilliant to look at burst through

the hole where the bodies had been thrown. It was pure and white and gave Ramón a sense of elation. He thought he heard the rustle of wings as he began to see the faintest outlines of people rising into the light. The few faces he could make out were filled with joy.

It was quickly over, leaving behind a pile of bone ash on the floor, that a little wind that came from nowhere spread out over the floor of the cave.

"They are at rest now," said Julian softly. He sounded tired but pleased.

Ramón was filled with wonder at what his teacher could do. Would he ever be able to do things like this, to help people in such a way? He hoped so.

"An' now," said Siofra, turning to Torin who had remained respectfully quiet during the proceedings. "Ye can be takin' us back so that we can be tellin' the others what kind of black mages these are bein'."

Julian shook his head. "Not quite. First, I need to go and see Reverend Brewer."

Chapter Forty

El amor brujo

Marisela could not understand what was wrong. Why was she feeling so strange? Yesterday–was it only yesterday? at the camp she had felt so much better! She had been able to sit up and talk to Pacho, to eat a nice little supper of minced chicken, rice and a bit of *flan*, and talk rationally to people: to Nicholas and the doctor, to her father and the two women who had helped care for her.

Now it was as if she were not quite awake and no matter how she struggled she could not really wake up. Her breathing was better, that did not hurt as much and she was less weak.

Yet she heard herself speaking, answering questions. People seemed very far away. They came and looked at her, looking to her eyes weirdly distorted, fading in and out.

She no longer lay in bed, but sat in a chair, fully dressed. Around her, her parents acted as if she was completely well. And what was worse, the *idiota* and his odious mother were present, *Don* Rafael seated at her side, his hand on hers. As much as she wanted to, she could not throw his hand off. It was as if she had no control over her body.

And still her voice went on, speaking. She could not stop it, nor could she make out what was being said by her or to her. Her ears seemed to be blocked.

Whatever she said, it seemed to please them, for they smiled, her distorted perceptions making their faces grotesque.

Someone was taking her hand, urging her to rise. It was *Doña* Paloma, accompanied by Marisela's mother.

Oddly enough, Marisela found herself walking easily with them, responding to their remarks. But how was this happening? It was as if someone else was directing her body, putting words into her mouth.

Once in her room, her own maid, Conchita, and *Doña* Paloma's maid, Teresa, began to remove her clothing. They dressed her in the wedding dress that had been made by the seamstresses from Albuquerque. It was a beautiful garment, made in the very latest style; very slim and tight, covered in lace, with a draped skirt and a detachable Cathedral train. The separate tight bodice buttoned up the front with innumerable tiny fabric-covered buttons from the waist to the high neck. Long sleeves were edged with lace as well and buttoned up to the elbow. The lace was Brussels; the fabric was faille.

With this *Parisienne* ensemble was worn a *mantilla* over her high dressed curled hair. This *mantilla* had belonged to Marisela's grandmother and had come from Spain with *Doña* Milagros. It had been made by nuns in a convent in Seville and was of the most delicately made lace imaginable, and was draped over a *peineta,* or comb, of mother-of-pearl, set with freshwater pearls and crystal. Neither *Doña* Milagros or *Doña* Paloma believed that pearls were for tears.

Marisela was powerless to stop any of this. She felt like a large doll being dressed by these women. When they turned her to the mirror she could not believe what she saw. Gowned for her bridal, she looked happy: she was actually smiling! How could this be? Inside of her, everything was screaming "NO!" She did not want to marry *Don* Rafael!

But she could not move or speak on her own. She could only react to what she was told to do. Her mother knelt with her and prayed as was traditional. *Doña* Milagros then gave Marisela a tiny cross to wear about her throat. It too was of mother-of-pearl and before fastening it about her daughter's throat she kissed it.

"Now we are ready to go to the church!" Marisela heard someone say as from a long way off.

Doña Milagros sighed as she looked at her daughter. She made a beautiful bride! It was such a shame that there was no one left in the neighborhood to see this triumph, her daughter being married to the richest man in the region, to become a titled lady and to be presented at Court in Madrid... it was only one part of this day that *Doña* Milagros would have changed. She had no one to condescend to, to rub their noses in the fact.

There would be no loud noisy reception with the music of *flamenco* and dancing. No guests would surround this couple in a heart shape as they danced the first dance as man and wife. There were no sponsors, no flower girl nor ring bearer. There would be no attendants, no *madrinos* or *padrinos* with their special functions, such as the *madrino de ramo* who carried flowers for the Virgin Mary. Naturally these important posts could not be offered to *péons,* nor could *Doña* Milagros support the idea of *Norteaméricanos* at her daughter's wedding.

But there was no one left to attend the nuptials. When the *Norteaméricanos* had arrived the others of *hildago* blood had fled, many to *Cuidad* Mexico, others to Spain. Only her own family and that of *Don* Rafael had remained in the area, and that, *Doña* Milagros was aware was because the family holdings were too extensive to abandon, and as well, in the case of her own family, they had little money with which to flee.

The wedding would be a sad affair, compared to her own, so may years ago. But at least Marisela would be wed, and not a *soltera,* a spinster. Milagros could write to the relatives in Spain, telling of the great marriage her daughter had made. Things could have been worse, Milagros supposed. Marisela was getting so old that it might have been difficult to find a man who wanted to marry her.

They were now in the hall outside Marisela's bedchamber, heading towards the stairs. *Doña* Paloma gave an exclamation of distress. "We have forgotten the gloves!" she said. "I shall take care of this," she said. "The three of you go on ahead. Come with me, daughter," she gave a fatuous smile and a titter of laughter. "I think I may call you so, for you will soon be my daughter in truth," she said, leading Marisela back into her room.

Once inside again, she quickly located the gloves .Marisela obediently held out her hands as she was directed and let her future mother-in-law draw them on the gloves over the gaudy betrothal ring that now adorned her ring finger. It was a huge ruby of rose cut, with a domed shaped crown, with brilliant style side facets, set about with tiny square-cut diamonds set in a heavy gold band. This, *Don* Rafael had told Marisela's impressed parents, was the betrothal ring of his family and was well over four hundred years old. It had been put on her finger only today.

Doña Paloma looked her soon-to-be daughter-in-law over critically and picked up the cross that now hung on the lace covered bodice. "We do not need this I think," she said and with a quick jerk, tore it from Marisela's neck, snapping the fragile gold chain. *Doña* Paloma threw the cross to the floor and with contempt, ground it beneath her heel.

Julian had gone to see Reverend Brewer, only to be frustrated that no one seemed to know where he might be. The minister often disappeared, Brother Ezekiel informed him, going out by himself for prayer and contemplation. Any examination of him would have to wait.

Taking Ramón with him, Julian then returned to the camp, where he found most of the party ready to depart to search for treasure yet again.

Ellery, to Lutterworth's disgust and anger, made them wait until he had Julian's report.

"Satanists," Ellery said thoughtfully when Julian had concluded and Ramón and Siofra had given their impressions as well. "And a low level demon." The book of Demon had been consulted and the foul fiend identified as a demon of lust. In the hierarchy of Hell they were common and not particularly dangerous. The book defined them as "cowards; their only passion for copulation with human females".

"At least there only appear to be two of them," said Nicholas.

"We can't be certain of that," returned Ellery. "These may be senior members of the group, doing a sacrifice for their own ends. I would like to find this cave of theirs, though."

"We can find it," Bairre offered. "We familiars that is. We can talk to the animals in the area and ask after a cave with a jade-like floor." Jade-like was the best description that Julian had thought of.

"It had a curios luminescence to it as well," Julian now added. "Almost water or ice-like."

"That should be easy to find," said Bairre. "And we shall be able to feel the Dark magic as well."

"You are NOT to go in this cave without one of us!"

Ellery said, looking severely at all the familiars. "We don't want any of you falling into the hands of Satanists. We have no idea yet of how powerful they are, nor even if they are able to tap the ley lines. There was some Dark magic used here before, some of it very old."

"You two are to remember that!" said Sabrina to Siofra and Flann. The two cats were much more venturesome and had less regard for personal danger than either the ferret or the hedgehog. "Satanists would like nothing better than to get their hands on a familiar to sacrifice!"

Reluctantly, the two cats promised not to go off on their own, but to let the cautious Bairre decide how far they would go in their explorations.

Shortly after this the group broke up; Lutterworth, with Ellery, Dr. Beck, Nicholas and Sinclair to go treasure hunting, Julian and Ramón to go out to the railroad camp where Julian still had patients to treat, and where Ramón might get some more practice in Healing, and the four familiars to go speak to the animals in the area in search of the cave with a green floor. Torin intended to hunt for signs of the children when he had left Julian and Ramón at the railroad camp.

This left Atalanta and Sabrina to tend to the dragonets, along with Erianne.

Save for Pacho, who seemed sunk in a deep depression, the other dragonets were exuberant, even little Amyas seemed to have come out of his diffidence and played more eagerly with the others.

Atalanta found it fascinating to watch how Erianne disciplined them. In many ways it reminded her of a mother cat with kittens, which she had seen both at various digs and at home in New York when a neighbor's cat had kittened. The dragoness was apt to grab them by the back of the neck, gently holding them in her teeth or used a taloned forefoot to cuff them lightly. For serious misbehavior, which included being cheeky with her or one of the humans, she singed them with a long thin thread of flame. Unfortunately, Seneca was the most boisterous of them all. He seemed to suffer from excessively high spirits.

"Will he always be like this?" she asked Sabrina as they finished the first feeding of the day.

"No, they are a lot like kittens. When they get to be about a year old they will be much more sober and conscious of their dignity," Sabrina answered.

Atalanta still looked troubled and Sabrina asked "What is it?"

"I am afraid that my father will not allow me to keep Seneca. He dislikes the entire notion of a dragon in our household. He says the expense will be too great. I am dependent upon him financially," she added apologetically. "And I am very much afraid as well, that your nephew's optimistic outlook as to our future employment may be not just optimistic but improbable. I have never seen nor even heard of a female in any of the positions he was telling me about."

Sabrina privately agreed with this. "It's iniquitous," she said. "Which Is why I am proud to say that I am a Suffragette." She was quiet for a moment and then said "Ellery and I had a long talk about your situation the other night and we would like to offer you a position on our staff."

"As I told Dr. Delamar, I am not an Egyptologist," Atalanta began.

"That does not signify," said Sabrina. "You have intelligence; you can learn. I had no idea of what I was doing when I first went out to Egypt with Ellery. You are at least a trained archaeologist. And you would not have to worry about Seneca for he would be more than welcome. Dragons are a great help on a dig and your salary would more than pay for his keep." She then named a sum that made Atalanta blink.

"And do not be thinking that this is some sort of charity!" Sabrina went on. "We have been thinking for a long time that we need more permanent staff; someone who can learn our ways, and be of use from season to season, unlike graduate students who are usually with us only once."

Atalanta felt her eyes fill with tears, much to her mortification. To work with these people she liked so much, to be valued as a scholar and a colleague! And to be able to keep Seneca with her!

Nevertheless she said "May I think it over?"

"Take all the time that you need," said Sabrina easily. "We shan't be going out to Egypt until November or December."

Another such harangue as they had heard from Dr. Beck last night (for he had not attempted to moderate his voice) and she thought that the scales would tip in their favor.

The nightmare continued for Marisela. She found herself led to a carriage decked out in white flowers and ribbons. Curro, in his very best suit, drove a pair of Andalusians. All about them the *péons* were dressed as for a *fiesta* with someone playing a guitar and singing love songs. Her hearing seemed better for she heard someone tell her to wave and she found herself obeying.

"I am so proud this day," she heard her mother's voice say. Her parents sat opposite her in the carriage. "I knew that she would change her mind. See how happy she looks!"

Happy? When every nerve in her body and mind was screaming that this could not be happening, that she could not be going to the church to marry *Don* Rafael! Why could they not see that she could not help herself, that something was making her behave like this? Did they only see what they wanted to see? Oh, this had to be a dream!

The evil dream went on. They arrived at the church where some of the *péon* children threw flower petals at her. Her disobedient limbs took her into the church, up the aisle and to kneel in front of the priest beside *Don* Rafael.

Marisela wanted to scream, to deny this was happening. All she heard was her voice repeating the vows. Why wasn't Rodri still alive? He would know this was not what she wanted. He would not allow this to go on!

When the *lazo* was thrown over their heads, over the groom's head first as was proper, then looped in a figure eight to encompass her neck as well, Marisela heard a gasp from her mother, for it was not an ordinary rosary, but a chain of rubies set in gold.

The Latin Mass seemed long and strange. Marisela's head was beginning to pound. Why could she not break free of this lethargy, not protest being handed over to the *idiota*? Why could the others not see her distress?

When they left the church the *péons* pelted them with red beads for good luck. Marisela could not feel the beads, even those that accidentally struck her in the face.

An interminable meal followed, of which she could eat very little. The wine, which she lifted to her mouth as ordered, tasted sour. "Bridal nerves!" she heard some one say.

Then she was hustled into a carriage with a smirking *Don* Rafael sitting beside her, bowing to the cheering crowd.

Someone was crying. Marisela supposed it to be her mother. She herself was the one who should be crying! If only she could wake!

She was taken to the home of *Don* Rafael and his mother. *Doña* Paloma took her by the arm and led her into the tiled hall. Nearby, a fountain played.

Their *Hacienda* was rich and opulent, with many touches of red everywhere. The furniture was old and heavy And intricately carved.

"I shall prepare your bride for you, my son," said *Doña* Paloma in a soft, silky voice. "Come, girl, you are in for a rare treat. My son is a magnificent lover!" She pulled Marisela after her up a flight of stairs.

The room into which she was jerked was dark and large, with red velvet draperies blocking all light. The room was dominated by a huge bed, draped in red. It was also hot and stuffy.

"Undress," *Doña* Paloma ordered and sat on the edge of the bed as Marisela obeyed.

"Down to the skin," said her mother-in-law. "I want to see what he will be getting."

Once again Marisela did as she was told and soon stood, shivering and naked in front of the vulture-like woman. She shivered not from cold but from fear. She could not make her hands cover herself in modesty. Yet those same hands did what others bid her do.

"Very nice indeed," purred *Doña* Paloma. "He will be pleased." she looked beyond Marisela. "She is ready for you."

A hand clasped itself over Marisela's mouth and a suffocating material came over her head. A pungent odor with an undertone of sweetness met her nostrils and she fell back unconscious as she inadvertently took deep breaths, struggling to breathe, still unable to scream or make any protest at the way her betraying body and these persons were treating her.

Chapter Forty One

The Reason Why

The day after Marisela's return home both Pacho and Nicholas awaited Julian's coming back from the *Hacienda*. They were both anxious to learn what his follow-up examination would show and how soon she could again make the trip out to the camp.

To their surprise they saw Torin returning almost immediately.

"Is that a good sign?" Pacho asked Nicholas and Varian hopefully. "Does that mean she is well and can come and see me?"

"Something's wrong," said Nicholas frowning. "Julian's too good a Healer to conduct a cursory examination. And considering the amount of time it takes to fly there and back he would have had scarcely five minutes with her."

The three of them went forward as Torin landed and ran a little ways forward before folding his wings and stopping.

"They would not let me see her," Julian said before he had even dismounted. He could see from their concerned faces that they understood the visit had gone amiss.

"Won't let you see her?" Nicholas repeated in disbelief. "But you are her doctor! Why would they deny you access to her? That's insane! How do they expect her to get well if you can't tend her?"

Julian undid the safety harness and slid down from Torin's back. He went to the basket and lifted Siofra out.

"Tis a very strange household," said Siofra. "An' I am not likin' that *Don* Casimiro at all, I am."

"The *Don* claimed that he had their own doctor seeing to her," said Julian. He, too, wore a frown. "But as far as I know there is not a doctor closer than Albuquerque or Phoenix. Without a dragon or a hippogriffe it would have taken him a day or so to get here. And any competent physician would have wished to consult with me, to learn my course of treatment and to hear about the surgery." He looked further troubled. "And there's more. I was told that she would not be coming out here any more, and that we were to keep our 'creatures'—I quote *Don* Casimiro—away from his daughter as she would have no more time to concern herself with them, or us. *Don* Casimiro made it very clear to me that we were all of us *persona non grata* in his home. He was actually quite rude about it."

"There was bein' a nasty atmosphere about that place," put in Siofra. "Made me fur stand on end, it did. And wasn't I after tellin' that old besom we would be sendin' him a bloody great bill for medical services! You should have been seein' his face!" she added in satisfaction.

"She's not coming?" wailed the dragonet. "But I need her! Nicholas, can't you go and get her?" He turned a piteous face to Nicholas.

"I can't, Pacho," he told the dragonet. "As much as I would like to she is still underage and still under her father's control." However, his expression was not resigned and regretful but angry.

"*Don* Casimiro is still quite willing to take our gold for his cows, as that is a business arrangement, he told me, and has nothing to do with any social acquaintance between us. He implied that that sort of acquaintance was one that should never been allowed in the first place," Julian said. He gave an exclamation of disgust and said "She needs more care! I was not altogether pleased when the *Don* insisted on her going home so soon, but one can only interfere so far with patients. We cannot make them take a treatment or medicine. That is still their choice. And since he is her guardian...."

"I'm going out there and give him a piece of my mind!" said Nicholas abruptly. "Perhaps if I inform him we shall find another source for meat and threaten to take away the gold he covets, he will listen to reason. Come on, Varian, let's get you saddled!" He stamped off, followed by Varian and an eager Pacho, who was hoping that Nicholas would bring Marisela back to him, where she belonged.

The last two days had been a fruitless search for more caves and caverns. The egg complex, as they has begun to call it, had been thoroughly searched and re-searched. There were no overlooked caves or caverns, for the search had been both physical and magical, using every means from tapping walls with a hammer to sending spells of revelation into every crack and crevice. They had used a candle to search for draughts and a wand to look for more anomalies.

Ellery was thoroughly disgusted with listening to Lutterworth carry on, ranting and raving how the treasure HAD to be here; how the map could NOT be wrong, how there HAD to be more caves. Lutterworth had blamed everyone from Ellery to Cinnéidigh that the cave could not be found; Ellery for not using his powers of pyschometry and Cinnéidigh for not having more useful information. He had threatened Dr. Beck with demanding the return of the money disbursed to him. He thought Nicholas was paying too much attention to the dragonets and the dragons out at the end-of-track. Julian, in Lutterworth's view, was too busy playing doctor with a bunch of malingering railway workers when he ought to be treasure hunting. The women ought not to even be on the dig as they were worse than useless. And of course, poor Melville Sinclair bore the brunt of this, for unlike the others, he could not walk away from Lutterworth's nasty tongue and fits of rage.

This morning had been another abortive attempt at finding caves, Lutterworth had insisted on setting both Yates and Sinclair to digging in a hillside where he was certain that there was a cave, even though Varian had informed him that there was no 'scent' of limestone.

Lutterworth had angrily said that he knew better than some damn lizard. Varian looked hurt and Nicholas lost his temper. He had blasted away the face of the hillside with his wand, revealing sold rock underneath the covering of soil.

It was only when Lutterworth had conceived of the idea of sending a courier to Washington for official geographical survey maps that the party had come back to the camp. Lutterworth had maps that his own surveyors had prepared but as they pertained to the best places for the railroad they did not have the same amount of information as to mines, mineral deposits and such to be found in the area as the USA government maps would have.

Ellery, without a twinge of guilt, had forbore in

informing Lutterworth that a Wizard could do a geological survey; in fact it was more than likely that the government survey team had included Wizards, those whose speciality was geomancy, or earth magic. The United States Government liked to combine teams of surveyors and geologists that also included Geomancers and both a magical and a physical survey was done and compared to one another for accuracy.

A dragon courier from Albuquerque could be back with the maps within two days, two days in which they might have some peace and quiet as Lutterworth had decided that the only method left to use was scientific, not magical. Magic, as he had been certain it would had failed him. This was a new age, almost a new century, and magic was of the past.

However, Ellery had another concern. Dr. Beck, faced with the possible loss of funding for his next dig, had grown increasingly acrimonious. The last two evenings they had heard his petulant voice raised in his tent and Ellery was aware that Atalanta had been the target of his rancor.

This morning, when they had met for the morning walk and conversation that had become a habit, Atalanta, to Ellery's discerning eye, looked as if she had been crying.

He wanted to urge her to leave her father, to come and work where she would be appreciated, but as Sabrina had pointed out, it had to be her decision. But he had never felt more like physically damaging someone than he did at the moment. It would be so very satisfying to inflict bodily injury on Marcus Beck. Only the fact that he was much older than Ellery himself and it would be a most unequal match, stayed his hand.

And then, later this morning when they had all boarded Varian for the flight out to the caves, Atalanta was not one of the party.

When Ellery inquired why she was not coming Dr. Beck said curtly that she had been very neglectful of her duties since they had come here and that he had received a letter from his publisher only yesterday (as their mail was being forwarded here) demanding the finish of his latest manuscript. This concerned the work of the previous year, done on the Greek island of Ios in the Aegean, where Mycenaean settlements had been discovered. It was her job to copy his manuscript out and make it ready for publication.

Ellery was conscious of a feeling of the day's activities somehow having gone flat and stale. He had grown used to exchanging glances and smiles with her at Lutterworth's extravagances of speech, of listening to her comments, which were always interesting and showed a dry wit that he enjoyed.

When they returned from the latest treasure hunt he at once went to the artifact tent where a long work table had been set up for writing reports, and cleaning and labeling artifacts–if they had been fortunate enough to find any.

Atalanta was not there, but all signs indicated that she had left but momentarily for there was a stack of papers and a small pile of freshly inscribed paper covered in a flowing hand. Perhaps Seneca had claimed her attention.

Dr. Beck's handwriting even looked like him: small and crabbed, angular and harsh. Ellery made a face. He could still not reconcile those delightful books with the man he had come to know. With a pen in his hand Dr. Beck was a different person.

Ellery found himself, without meaning to do so, reading the top page of the completed manuscript. It was not as if it were a private letter but he still felt a trifle in the wrong for doing so. But his curiosity as to the subject of Dr. Beck's next book overcame him.

It was the driest, most pedantic writing he had ever encountered. It could have been used as a remedy for insomnia. Dr. Beck's writing revealed him as a man in love with himself, a firm believer in his own superiority.

Frowning heavily, Ellery read a few more pages and then turned to Atalanta's copy.

Here was the Marcus Beck he had admired; fascinating, anecdotal, humble, immensely readable, but with true scholarship evident in every paragraph.

The truth struck him at once. It was not Dr. Beck who wrote those splendid books, but his daughter. And the bastard took the credit for them!

Such a rage rose up in Ellery that if Dr. Beck had come into the tent at that moment he would have choked the life out of the old man, irregardless as to whether or not it was honorable to attack a man at least thirty years his senior.

A noise at the front of the tent alerted him and he looked up to see Atalanta, with a cup of cool water, entering.

"It's you who write the books, isn't it?" Ellery demanded. "I could not reconcile your father with his books; it seemed as if he were two different people. And this is the reason why."

She sat down, put her water on the table between them and said "When my father wrote his first book the publisher hated it, citing it as boring, dry and dull. My father was enraged and objected to the publisher's suggestion that he work with a professional writer. My father did not want to share his royalties or have to pay someone to make his writing more readable. So he informed me that it was up to me, as his secretary, to do as the publisher wished. And it has been that way ever since."

"But you get no credit for it!" Ellery protested, appalled. "At the very least, he ought to acknowledge your contribution."

She smiled rather sadly. "You are a most unusual man, Dr. Delamar _"

"I thought we agreed that you were to call me Ellery," he interrupted.

"Very well, Ellery. Do you really think that most scholars would read a book penned by a woman? Many of my father's colleagues consider me a freak of nature. I have even been told that classical scholarship is too much for the female brain to comprehend. If my name was on the books they would not be taken seriously," she said.

"Of all the stupid, short-sighted, damned idiotic drivel!" he exclaimed. "I can't bear to see you treated like this!" he added. "It's wrong, it ought not to be allowed and I won't put up with it any longer!"

He bent over the table and scribbled something rapidly on a piece of paper. "This is how the title page should look on any book you write from now on," he said, handing it to her.

A trifle bemused, she took it from him. How did he expect her father to ever acquiesce to putting her name on one of 'his' books?

And then she read it.

She felt a roaring in her ears and all the blood drained

from her head, leaving her a little faint.

He had scrawled across the sheet of paper: *"Coronado's Gold" by Ellery and Atalanta Delamar.*

"But this is –" she began weakly.

"A somewhat unorthodox marriage proposal," he finished.

"But you can't mean it!" she protested. "No man has ever–you can't be in love with me–it isn't possible!"

"Why not?" he said, coming closer to her. "I've admired you from the first day we met. I am not quite sure when liking turned to love, but now if I am not near you I am unhappy and feel as if a part of me is missing." He decided that the best way of convincing her that he was in earnest was to show her and this he did so thoroughly that five minutes later she had melted against him and was dreamily agreeing to an almost immediate wedding.

"Atalanta!" came an outraged voice from the tent opening. "What do you think you are doing! Acting like a harlot while I wait for my luncheon!" His face was a study in shock and anger."How dare you maul her about, sirrah!"

"Papa," she began, mortified, and tried to move away from Ellery but his arms tightened around her.

"Dr. Beck." he said "I have just asked your daughter to marry me and she has accepted. You'll have to get your own damned luncheon from now on. I intend to take her to Albuquerque this afternoon and find a minister."

She gasped.

"And I also intend to spend the rest of my life making certain you are valued and loved and treated as my colleague, partner and dearest of wives, with all the respect and honor you so richly deserve," said Ellery to his betrothed, and oblivious to Dr. Beck's indignant sputtering, kissed her again.

"It's very quiet, Nick," said Varian as h e crouched low so Nicholas could slide off near the *Hacienda del Sol.* "You don't; suppose she is worse, do you, and her new doctor has ordered quiet for her?"

"I hope not," he said shortly. What he planned to say to *Don* Casimiro might become rather heated. This was nearly the twentieth century, not medieval times when a young unmarried woman could be kept under lock and key. There was Pacho to be considered as well. A dragonet needed the company of his bond-mate.

Nicholas did not even exam his own feelings: the sick sensation that had swept over him when he thought he might never be able to see her again; that he would never see her smile or laugh; that they would never ride Varian together again, or see her face light up when she played with Pacho... it did not bear thinking on.

Cillian was still asleep in his basket so Nicholas left him behind. Cillian might urge him to moderate his language or try to suggest a compromise.

But Nicholas was in no mood to listen to the wise counsel of his familiar. There were things that had to be said. He stalked off towards the *Hacienda,* determined to face *Don* Casimiro and have it out with him.

Varian waited patiently. It was a lovely day, with a clear sky and a warm temperature. Idly, the dragon wondered how much longer they would be here. It had been disappointing so far. Only that necklace and the uncut emerald had been found. His hopes of coming home with some treasure of his own were turning to dreams.

Twenty minutes later Nicholas returned, walking slowly.

As he came closer Varian cried aloud and said "What is it Nick? You look terrible!"

Nicholas looked as if he had received a severe shock of some kind. "Varian," he said dully, as if it were hard to recognize the dragon.

"What happned?" Varian demanded. "Did you see *Don* Casimiro? Was he very rude? Did you get to see Marisela?"

"He wasn't there," said Nicholas in that same far away voice. "The only person there was the old butler. He said he was too old and in too much pain from his joints to go to the church."

"The church?" repeated Varian. "She didn't die!" he cried, horrified, thinking that everyone had gone to her funeral.

"They all went to the wedding," Nicholas said. "Varian, she has married *Don* Rafael de Veláquez y Montillo today. By now they are on a halfway to Albuquerque, and will take a train from there heading to New Orleans. Then they will board a ship to Spain."

"Without saying good bye to us?" cried the dragon." And what about Pacho? When will they be coming back?"

"According to the butler, never," said Nicholas flatly.

Chapter Forty Two
In the Ice Cave

Marisela came awake abruptly as something cold was flung in her face. Sputtering, she opened her eyes and tried to open her mouth to protest, only to find that she could not speak. A cloth was in her mouth, effectively gagging her.

She tried to lift her hands and remove the gag, but they would not obey her.

She was tied down, she found out when she struggled, tied to something cold and hard in a frigid atmosphere that was creeping into her bones.

Marisela lifted her head as much as she was able and found out why she was so cold. She was completely naked, tied down and spread-eagled on a block of stone in a dark place where the very air was icy.

Was this a nightmare? If so,it was incredibly real, for she could feel both the tightness of her bonds, the hardness of the stone beneath her and the intense frigidity of the air on her uncovered, shrinking flesh.

Unbidden, the memory of the wedding rushed back to her. That had been a dream, hadn't it? What then was this? Was it delirium? Was she sick again? Her mind seemed sluggish.

"Ah, that woke her," said a voice nearby.

Someone else giggled and was reprimanded.

"Look at me, girl," ordered the first voice.

Slowly Marisela turned her head and saw a terrifying sight.

At first glance it seemed a creature out of Hell itself: a horned visage, with gleaming eyes and an expression of evil incarnate. It bore a striking resemblance to a goat, but a goat whose home was the Nether regions.

But as Marisela's mind and eyes cleared she realized that it was a mask atop a very human male body, as naked as her own. Other than the mask he wore only a ruby ring and some sort of slippers on his feet.

Behind him stood two women, naked and masked also. One was young, with a ripe body. She wore a mask of a snarling spotted cat. Marisela had seen this depicted before; it was a jaguar from Mexico and Central America. This woman also wore slippers but bore no ring.

The second woman wore a vulture mask. She too was naked, but her body made it obvious that she was far from young, for her flesh was tough and stringy, her breasts sagging. She did wear the ruby ring and like the others, leather slippers on her feet.

What sort of place was this? Marisela wondered, trying to quell a rising panic. The floor seemed to be made of some sort of green glass, and the walls were stone.

The man chuckled. It was not a pleasant sound.

"She begins to realize that she is in our power," he said. His voice was somewhat muffled and distorted by the mask.

"When may we play with her as you said ?" said the younger woman. Her voice too, was altered, but the eagerness in it made Marisela cringe.

"She is all enthusiasm, your acolyte," said the man to the older woman. "The fervor with which she greeted her very first coupling and her first offer to the Prince told me that you made a wise choice, Sister Diabla."

"Yes," said the older woman. "She is all impatience when she knows she is to come here. Brother Daemon well likes the rapidity with which she opens her legs for him!"

"To answer your question, my dear," said the masked man to the young woman "We will only tease her until Brother Daemon arrives. His duties make him late. And then, after we torment her for a while with lash, hot irons and whatever your inventive little mind might come up with, my Acolyte–and we will only torment, not couple with her–we shall celebrate our mass and make our sexual offering to the Prince. This one will watch us. I want her to grow very afraid before we finally take her. Her fear, terror and pain will be much enjoyed by his Highness. And then," he turned back to Marisela, "all of us will use your body again and again until you wish for the release of death. But that will not come for a long, long time. You shall even have the honor of being mounted by the Prince of Darkness himself." He laughed again and began to stroke her body.

Marisela tried to fight against her bonds, struggling wildly but ineffectually. She had been tied down so well and in such strong bonds that she could barely move.

"You grow frightened," the masked man leaned closer to her, his voice a sibilant whisper, his hands moving intimately over her. "I can see it in your eyes. You know what lies ahead of you: days and days of torment, of pain, of being the instrument of our pleasure. We shall be careful not to kill you, or to let you die too easily, for each day you live and suffer builds power for us and pleases the Prince of Darkness so that he will grant our humble request. The Prince himself told me of a woman in the last century, in France, who was used for forty days before she finally died. We will see if we cannot best that record."

In a frenzy to get away from his probing hands and the threat in his voice Marisela threw all of her strength against the bonds.

But to no avail. They were too firm.

The masked man laughed again and began pinching her breasts. "Come," he said to the two women. "Let us tease her until Brother Daemon comes."

They came forward eagerly, eyes gleaming behind the masks.

Marisela tried to scream.

Varian was worried about Nicholas. He had never seen Nick act quite like this. He seemed sunk in depression and his mind was elsewhere. Varian even had to remind him to do the harness safety check before they took off for the camp.

The dragon wanted to talk to Cillian about what they could do for Nick. Of course, that could not be accomplished until they had arrived back and Cillian was taken from his traveling basket.

Spiraling down to the campsite Varian's heart sank as he saw little Pacho, awaiting them.

Something else was strange. There was no sign of Erianne. Instead there was a strange dragon with the dragonets. Torin was gone as well, and Varian could not see any sign of Sabrina, Julian, Ellery, their familiars or Atalanta. What had happened while they were gone?

To Varian's surprise Pacho did not look hopeful but instead barely waited until Varian had landed before rushing up to them shrieking "Nicholas! Nicholas!" And right behind him was Dr. Beck saying demandingly "Dr. Stillfield! I must protest!"

Pacho reached them first. Before Nicholas could slide off, Pacho stood up on his hind legs against Varian's sides. "Nicholas!" the dragonet panted. "Marisela is in terrible trouble! She's in a bad place and they are hurting her! I dreamed it! It was a true dream!"

"What!" This had Nicholas's full attention.

Part of the unique bond between dragons and humans was the 'true' dream–a vivid dream of warning that one bond-mate could have of the other. Nicholas had read of it and studied it all his life. Dragons and humans had saved each others' lives before with these dreams of danger. It was some sort of psychic ability, magnified by the strength of the bond.

"She's in a dark place with a green floor and she can't move. There are things with strange heads tormenting her and she's so afraid!" said Pacho urgently. He stood aside so that Nicholas could dismount as Varian lowered himself to the ground.

"She's obviously not on her honeymoon!" said Varian.

"Why did the butler lie to me then?" Nicholas said in confusion. What could have happened to Marisela?

"Dr. Stillfield!" came the shrill voice of Dr. Beck. "I must protest! I will not be used as a messenger boy by some animal! That creature belonging to your uncle demanded that I give you this!" He thrust a note at Nicholas. He was quivering with indignation. "First he steals my daughter and now this!"

"Has Atalanta gone missing as well?" Nicholas inquired.

"That uncle of yours," said Dr. Beck through gritted teeth "has abducted her for purposes of his own!"

The note was from Bairre. It told Nicholas that he, Erianne, Sabrina, Ellery and Atalanta had gone to Albuquerque, where Ellery and Atalanta hoped to be married. The note expressed the desire that Nicholas, Cillian and

Varian would join them there.

Nicholas gave a low whistle. "I don't call marrying your daughter abduction," he said to Dr. Beck.

"He is stealing her from me!" protested Dr. Beck, "Who will see to my needs? What shall I do for field staff?"

"You'll have to find another slave," said Nicholas dryly. Good for Ellery! Atalanta was a splendid match for him.

"Where is my brother Julian?" he asked Dr. Beck, thinking that he could enlist his brother's help in finding Marisela. Ellery's wedding would have to be missed.

"The other Dr. Stillfield was called out to the railroad camp just before the rest of them left. Some Chinese woman is in child-bed. That Indian came here and they went off together," said Dr. Beck, his mouth pursed in distaste. He did not approve of this intimacy with the native-born or even, as he saw it, the dregs of society at the railroad camp.

"You didn't go to your own daughter's wedding?" said Varian in amazement, turning his head to stare at Dr. Beck in astonishment. He had been reading the note over Nicholas's shoulder.

"Naturally not! She had neither my approval or my blessing, nor even my permission," stated Dr. Beck.

Varian rolled his eyes.

By questioning a petulant Dr. Beck, Nicholas soon found out that Lutterworth and Sinclair had gone out to end-of-track as well. The only humans left at the camp here at *El Morro* were the cook Lupe, the Cinnéidigh family and Dr. Beck himself. The strange dragon with the dragonets had been brought from the railway camp to watch them while Dr. Delamar's dragon flew the members of the wedding party to Albuquerque. Dr. beck seemed irritable when questioned. But none of them would be of the least help in finding Marisela.

"You must come with me," said a voice at Nicholas's feet.

He looked down to see the fox, Gian-nah-tah, looking up at him. "I can lead you to what you seek," said the fox gravely. "But we must hurry. She is in mortal danger and you will need every bit of your strength and courage. Take me up before you on the back of your dragon and I will direct you."

He had spoken in Spanish so the dragonet

understood. "I want to go too!" he insisted. "Take me with you! I can help! I will fight for her!" He showed his still small teeth. In spite of his small size he looked very fierce and even dangerous.

"It's not a good idea–" Nicholas began, thinking that Varian would back him up but to his surprise his dragon said "I would have to carry you in my talons as you can't fly yet. It won't be comfortable."

"I don't care!" said Pacho stubbornly.

"Varian, I don't think–" Nicholas began.

"Nick, if it was you missing and in danger I would move heaven and earth to get to you," said Varian simply. "Pacho has a right to help find her; she is his bond-mate. He is young and light enough that I can still carry him."

"Dr. Stillfield, I must   protest again!" shrilled Dr. Beck. He had been seething since Atalanta, paying no attention to him at all, had gone off starry-eyed with the man Dr. Beck saw as her seducer, turning her empty head with his flattery. He wanted desperately to complain to someone. Lúcás Cinnéidigh had taken his measure on the first day they met and had warned his wife and children to speak but the Gaelic when Dr. Beck was about. Even if he could have lowered himself to voice his complaints to people he saw as servants or lower, Dr. Beck could not find that whining to someone who did not speak English much of a relief to his feelings.

"Dr. Beck," said Nicholas as he prepared to get back in Varian's saddle, "I neither know nor care what your problem might be. Any other man would be in alt to gain Ellery as a son-in-law. He's well-born, the great grandson of a Duke, and very well to pass. Atalanta will not only want for nothing but she will also be marrying a fellow archaeologist who will treasure her. Any sane man would be happy for her. Now I have far more important things to do than to listen to your jeremiads."

With this he climbed onto Varian's foreleg and from there to the saddle. Gian-nah-tah sprang lightly from the ground, to Varian's leg and to the saddle in front of Nicholas all in one fast, smooth movement. When Nicholas had lifted the top of the basket and briefly told Cillian what they were to do, and had fastened himself in, Gian-nah-tah settled in his arms and said to Varian "Fly to the San Mateo mountains. What we seek is there."

Once his passengers were settled, Varian reared up on his hind legs and grabbed Pacho between his front talons. Then with a powerful downward sweep of his wings and a thrust from his heavily muscled haunches, they were airborne.

"You really are too clever, Léon," said Angelita in admiration. "How did you convince the black robes that we needed a file to dig out the ore?"

Léon looked up from the hasp he was filing. It was the main bolt that held their fetters to the rock. If he could file through it they would be freed. They would still wear the 'bracelets' about their ankles and drag a length of chain, but they would be at liberty. Léon intended that they would all slip into the cave that they had found. He was convinced that there was a way out, for he had fancied feeling a wind on his face when standing in front of the crevice. It was a soft, gentle occasional breeze, but nonetheless it was fresh air. Léon had spent enough of his life in caves to know what that meant: an opening, a way out. Now he said "Those black robes, they are stupid *hombres*. They know nothing of mining; they believed what I told them, that we need to file the ore out."

"That is why you have had us file the edges of some of the ore?"

"*Sí*," agreed Léon.

Except for little Pia, they had all taken turns filing at the hasp round the clock. It was slow going, but they had kept at it twenty four hours a day in turns. Pia was their look-out.

The black robed men came but once a day, with some bad food and a sack to gather the day's output of ore.

A sharp crack sounded. "We are through!" said Léon in satisfaction. "Now I will free us and we will–"

"Someone comes!" shrilled Pia.

Léon and Angelita exchanged startled looks in the flickering lantern light. It was difficult to tell time underground away from the light of the sun but they had become adept at it since all of their short lives had passed underground. Black robes were not due for several more hours. Quickly, Léon hid the evidence of the filing under a handy rock and pushed at the hasp so that it looked as if it were still whole.

The shorter black robe, the one called Brother Daemon entered. He had a box in his arms.

"Well, children," he said pleasantly. "I am afraid that we must say goodbye to you. It has been a profitable acquaintance but it must end now." He put the box down on the floor as he spoke and began to unload it.

"Those are explosives!" Léon said as he saw the sticks of dynamite.

"Clever boy!" said Brother Daemon. "You have become an inconvenience, even a liability to us. It is unbelievable but there are people searching for you worthless brats. And neither Brother Satyr nor myself can take the chance of having our names besmirched by association with such as you. Therefore, you will be leaving us in a most expeditious fashion. Not to die, no, for we will be capturing the essence of your souls in this," He held up a black, stub-necked bottle that shone with a lurid light. "However, your bodies will certainly not be of any more use to you!" He laughed harshly as he opened the top of the bottle and left it by the edge of the rock to which they were chained.

He made a pile of the dynamite as he finished laughing and attached a long fuse to it. "They tell me this fuse burns very fast. It will be over very quickly; you won't feel a thing!" He laughed again.

He bent to light the fuse and then turned and ran towards the entrance of the cavern.

The fuse flashed and began to burn at an amazing speed.

Léon jerked the hasp free and swiftly pulled all the chains off it. "To the cave!" he cried. "RUN!"

The last child had just gone into the crevice when, with a thunderous roar, the dynamite exploded and rocks rained down where but moments before they had all been chained.

Chapter Forty Three
The Glint of Gold

It had been an exhausting afternoon out at end-of-track. The young Chinese woman had been small and her baby large. She had been in labor for some time before they had sent for Julian and he judged it best to perform a Caesarian section.

This was a procedure not often performed by non-magical physicians as it usually resulted in the death of the mother, although it was well known to them. Non-magical doctors were not so conscious of cleanliness as were Wizard Healers, for the Healers' ability to 'see' inside a body had shown them what harm a lack of cleanliness could do. And only a Wizard Healer could halt and seal the excessive bleeding that sometimes resulted during a Caesarian operation. Spells were needed to anesthetize the mother. All of this had to be done at top speed, almost simultaneously. To do this was not a decision lightly undertaken, but he saw little other choice. She was wearing herself out in unproductive labor.

The baby was scarcely successfully delivered when there was another cry for help. Jack Ballard, the civil engineer, came running in to tell Julian and Ramón that a stack of railroad ties had collapsed and had fallen on several men, two of who were seriously injured. Dragons had removed the ties at once, but no one had dared move the men.

One had a compound fracture of the leg, the other a fractured skull. Five men had been involved. Julian had Ramón Heal the others, who had but minor injuries but Ramón hadn't the experience to Heal multiple breaks in a leg, nor work on a skull fracture that was pressing on the brain.

"Sure, an' we've missed Ellery's wedding," remarked Siofra when Julian had at last finished with the latest patients and she noticed the sun lowering in the sky.

"It can't be helped. Ellery will understand; his father is a Wizard Healer and he knows how these things happen," said Julian, yawning. Jack Ballard had made his office available to them for washing up and had even made some coffee. Julian was grateful for it as his energy was flagging and he could use the lift that the beverage imparted, but wished that it was tea. He was exhausted and could only think of crawling into bed.

To Ramón, the coffee was a rare treat. He was also excited over the Healing he had seen this afternoon and by the fact that he himself had easily Healed a dislocated shoulder, some cuts and deep bruising. He was able to see and understand more and more each time he was given the opportunity.

"Nantan Lupan," came a voice from the open door. "You are needed. You are both needed," Gian-nah-tah added, looking beyond Ramón to where Julian sat at Jack Ballard's messy desk. "I have located the children and they are in danger of losing their lives."

Jack Ballard had been sitting in another chair, leaning back with his feet propped on the desk. As Julian translated this for his benefit the chair came down with a crash and he said "Kids in danger? Where? How can we help?"

"There is no time," said the fox. "We must hurry if we are to save them. I have asked the feathered one to be ready to bear you to the place where they are."

Julian picked up Siofra and tucked her inside his jacket. "Where are we going?' he inquired. He picked up his medical bag as well.

"The mountains that are called the Zuni," replied Gian-nah-tah. "There they are trapped." Again Julian told Ballard what the fox had said.

Jack Ballard followed them outside to where Torin stood waiting. "I'll get together a bunch of the fellows and we'll follow on horseback as soon as we can. We'll bring blankets and food, too," he promised.

Julian tucked his medical bag into Torin's breast bag and mounted the hippogriffe. He extended a hand to Ramón, who put a foot on his and swung up behind the saddle.

In an astonishing leap, the gray fox jumped up into Ramón's arms. "I will tell you where to go," he said.

When all his riders were secure, Torin took a few running steps and launched himself into the air, quickly settling into his best speed with huge thrusts of his great wings, a speed which was faster than many of the locomotives could achieve.

The cavern was filled with the sounds of coughing, gasps of pain and some crying from the younger children.

"Are we all here?" shouted Léon. His voice sounded to Angelita as if he were tense or in pain. It was very dark and she could see nothing of any of the others.

One by one the children spoke up, save for Vasco, who Lola said had been the last in the cavern and had been struck by a rock. He was unconscious from the blow.

They all had injuries to report. Benito had fallen and sprained his ankle as well as being covered in cuts from flying shards of rock and scraped hands and knees. Guillermo was certain that his leg was broken; part of the rocks in this cavern had fallen in when the explosion was set off. Alma and Chimo had been injured in this fashion as well one with a badly damaged arm while the other had been struck a blow on the foot and had multiple cuts and bruises. Josefina had been struck in the head by falling rock and was complaining of ringing in the ears. Léon, they found out had either a broken or a dislocated shoulder. Lola's wrist had been hurt. Nearly all had been wounded by rock fragments. But they were all alive.

Only little Pia was unhurt, for Angelita had thrown herself over the little girl as soon as they had run into the crevice. However, this had caused Angelita's hurts: a large rock had damaged her back and she could only lie curled up on the floor, her arms still about Pia.

"I wish we had a light!" Léon fretted, when everyone had been accounted for and their hurts injuries tallied.

"I have one of the little lights," offered Benito."I had just finished putting more oil in it when the black robes came. I tucked it in the front of my shirt."

"*Bueno!*" said Léon in approval. "I have flint and steel in my pocket."

It took some doing to find one another in the deep darkness of the cavern but with much stumbling and a little cursing, the two boys located each other and Benito gave the little lantern to Léon. It had been difficult for him to walk as his ankle was extremely painful and the floor of the cavern seemed to be littered with rocks and things that slid about when one stepped on them. Benito tried not to think about what these things might be. Having grown up in underground mines he was well aware that there could be many far from pleasant things beneath the earth.

Léon fumbled as he attempted to strike the flint and steel together and make a spark that would light the wick in the lantern. He could not lift his left arm as the pain was too great. In the end he had to sit on the floor and felt a vast quantity of something cold and hard slide away from under him with a clattering, chinking sound. It did not sound like rocks.

Léon was suddenly afraid. What had he led them into?

His hands, already unsteady because of the pain from his shoulder, shook and it took him long breathless minutes to create a spark and then guide it to the oil-soaked lantern wick.

The others were quiet; only little Pia still weakly sobbing.

As the light flared when the wick burst into flame they all gasped.

The little cavern they occupied seemed to be lined with gold.

Atalanta looked down at her left hand. A slender gold band, flanked by an diamond engagement ring shone there. On her right hand she wore an oval opal ring, set in diamond chips. Ellery had insisted on buying it for her when she said that she had always loved opals. They were her birthstone, for her birthday was in October. More opals were in her ears. They were bespelled as, as opals could shatter or crack in arid climates.

She had been surprised to find such a nice jewelry shop in Albuquerque. But the wives and daughters of the departed *Hildagos* had liked pretty things and both jewelry shops and dressmaking establishments had done a good business.

It had been a whirlwind morning. First Sabrina had found out the name of a good dressmaker and the two women had visited her. She had several models of popular styles made up to chose from. As both Sabrina and Atalanta were taller than the average she had to sew pleated flounces on the bottom of the dresses they chose: simple, pretty day dresses, Atalanta's in white lawn, Sabrina's in her favorite green. When Atalanta had protested that green was an unlucky colour for a wedding, Sabrina said that it was not unlucky in Ireland, for it was Saint Pádraig's own colour,and Atalanta was going to be an Irishwoman from now on.

Atalanta did not protest. She had a feeling as if her life and its direction had been take out of her hands and she was rushing along to something perfectly wonderful.

Sabrina also insisted that Atalanta buy a frivolous white hat crowned with net and daisies that they saw in a shop window. Although Ellery had given her a wad of bills and told her to buy what she needed she was far too used to habits of economy. Until Sabrina informed her that daisies were Ellery's favorite flower she could not be persuaded to purchase the hat.

They met up with Ellery again, who had been busy. They were to be married by a Justice of the Peace that afternoon, in two hours. Ellery had purchased a marriage license and had made an appointment with a jeweler.

Atalanta had never expected what followed. He insisted on an engagement ring, even though their engagement must be one of the shortest on record, and bought her the opal set as well when she said wistfully that she had always hoped that her parents would gift her with a birthstone. But they never had.

"I hope you do not think that I was hinting that I wanted—oh, I don't want to seem greedy!" she said in dismay as the jeweler, smiling happily at such a good sale, wrapped up the wedding band. She would wear the others, Ellery insisted.

"You don't ever have to hint or hope that soemone will notice what you need or want," Ellery said. "From now on if you want something, you just say "Ellery, I want an opal tiara." and I will do my best to get it for you."

"But I don't need a tiara!" she said, laughing a little.

"You'll need one when you are presented to the Queen," said Sabrina. At Atalanta's look of shock, Sabrina said "Oh, yes, Atalanta, you will soon be the great granddaughter-in-law of the Duke of Chenevix and as such, a member of the Upper Ten Thousand. Ellery is a great favorite of the Queen's. She likes his stories of Egypt and the little golden animals he gifted her with."

"Don't frighten her, Sabrina!" said Ellery quickly at the look on his bride-to-be's face. "We'll spend the summer sin Ireland, mostly and every other year we'll go to Egypt to excavate. I do not spend a great deal of time in London," he said, reassuringly.

Two hours later they were married. If the Justice of the Peace and his wife, a most romantic-minded lady, thought it odd that they wished to be married out-of-doors so that a dragon, a cat and a ferret could attend, she did not comment on it.

It still hurt Atalanta her father had chosen not to attend the wedding. But she had not been about to let him stop it, in spite of all of his protests. She was of age, of sound mind and was not going to let this chance for happiness pass her by. She had , she realized, been falling deeply in love with Ellery for some time now.

She and Sabrina had changed back into split skirts for the return to the camp. Sabrina offered them the private use of her tent for the wedding night, but Ellery had already thought of this and said that the artifact tent, with the addition of one of the larger cots, would be perfect for them.

"It's too bad Nick and Julian could not be here," said Sabrina as they mounted Erianne for the return trip. She put Flann and Bairre in the traveling basket and secured it.

Ellery frowned slightly as he handed Atalanta up into the seat in front of his, "I understand about Julian, as babies wait for no one, but I wonder what happned to Nick?"

"It doesn't look good, Nicholas," said Cillian softly.

They had landed a little ways away at Gian-nah-tah's direction and had carefully crept up on the location the fox had indicated.

Even if he had been looking for it, Nicholas doubted that he would have ever found the entrance to the cave without the gray fox's directions. The small hole in the ground was well hidden.

Nicholas, with the two dragons behind him and Cillian on the edge, lay on a ledge above the cave entrance. Gian-nah-tah sat a little ways away. "A ladder of rope hangs down into the cave. The floor is of ice–" he said.

"Ice! In the desert?" Nicholas said incredulously. Was that the explanation for the green, luminous floor Julian had seen?

"There are others such here, where the temperature below ground is always chill and the cave floor fills with rain water and snow melt," said Gain-nah-tah. "It is there that the black robed ones conduct their rites and conjure evil spirits."

Cillian had volunteered to creep closer as he was the smallest and see what he could see and hear. He asked Nicholas for his 'augmented' spectacles, as these magiced lenses would let him see further and even in the dark.

It was a nerve-wracking twenty minutes while he was gone, Pacho had to be restrained from blundering down the hillside into the cave several times as he wanted to go after his bond-mate.

"There are four of them," Cillian reported when he got back. "Right now they are having an orgy. There are two men and two women, all of them bare as the day they were born, save for some rather ugly animal masks"

"What's an orgy?" Pacho asked.

"A mating frenzy," said Varian. He was not certain that the dragonet would even understand this but Pacho said "Oh," and let the subject drop.

"And Marisela?" Nicholas asked anxiously.

"There's no doubt in my mind but that she's to be some sort of sacrifice, probably a sexual one, to the demon of lust," replied the hedgehog. "She's naked and tied to the altar, beneath an upside down crucifix and she's been tied with her arms up over her head and her legs wide open. I am sorry to have to tell you this, Nicholas, but I think she's been tortured.

There are bruises all over her body and she looks as if she is in pain."

"Do you think she's been–" Nicholas choked on the word.

"Raped?" Cillian finished. "I think they have not as yet called the demon. They'll offer her to him first and then take their turns with her." Cillian had read extensively about Satanists and their perverted masses. He had wanted to understand how people could turn from the Light. He was still not sure how someone could fall that far from grace.

"Did you sense how much power they had?" Nicholas asked.

"I saw no wands," Cillian answered "or any magical instruments. I will tell you one thing I heard, Nicholas. They think that this demon of lust is the Prince of Darkness himself."

"What!" Nicholas exclaimed, laughing a little "Well, that argues that they are stupid Satanists!"

"Don't be complacent, Nicholas," said Cillian in reproof. "Even stupid people can be dangerous, especially when cornered. Be especially careful of the one in the goat's mask. He and the old woman, I think, are the ones with the real power. The others just wish they had it and think they are obtaining it by all these goings-on. I daresay the young woman is there just for the sexual congress. She seemed to really revel in it."

Nicholas sobered at once. "I'll be careful, Cillian," he promised. He looked up to met the worried gazes of two dragons. "If I call, Varian, can you help me with dragon fire?"

The pale green dragon nodded. "Just be certain you've done the fire-proof spell. I should not like to burn you, Nick." He dropped his snout onto Nicholas's hair briefly.

"You'll save her, Nicholas, won't you?" Pacho begged. "Don't let those people hurt her any more! Then Julian can make her better and we can be together!"

Nicholas took his wand from his belt loop and slowly stood up. He had not counted on battling the Satanists alone. Perhaps he could send the gray fox to find Julian?

But Gian-nah-tah was gone.

"Varian," he said "could you go and find Julian?"

"NO! Leave you here by yourself? Never!" cried

Varian. "We can take care of them, Nick! You and I! I am sure of it!" His silver eyes gleamed with confidence. "I have a lot of flame. I ate a good amount of firestone just this morning!"

Nicholas wished he had half the confidence of his dragon. He was conscious of a sick feeling in the pit of his stomach. But he could not let Marissa be assaulted by a demon. He had read of the things a demon of lust did to a human female, the damage that they caused and that made him sicker than the thought of facing four Satanists and a demon. He could not, would not let that happen to her!

First fire-proofing himself with a quick spell in case he had to call in Varian, he then slid down the hill and headed for the mouth of the cave, wand in hand.

Chapter Forty Four

Amyas To the Rescue

At first look Julian could not see where the children might be. Gian-nah-tah had them land on a ledge on the side of a mountain, quite high up.

Once they had dismounted the fox led them to a cleft in the rock, concealed by some scrubby piñon pines. This cleft proved bigger than it looked at first, for by bowing his head and folding his wings close against his sides, even Torin could follow the others inside.

The cleft led into a small cave, barely high enough for Torin to raise his head. Julian immediately threw up two bright mage lights so that they might easily see.

"A tunnel leads through there at the back of this cave," Gian-nah-tah said. "The children are behind it." As he spoke, there was a rumble and several rocks fell down from the wall and the ceiling.

"There" was a wall of jumbled stones. "Those must be moved," said Ramón, and went to the mass, intending to move them one at a time, if needs be.

"Magic will be faster," said Julian and pulled his wand from his belt loop. "First I want to find out how deep this rock-fall is and what may lay behind it."

He pointed his wand at the rocks and said *"Explorare"*. A violet light shot out from the end of the wand and went through the boulders. "My wand tells me that there are definitely living beings beyond this wall," said Julian as the images flickered back to him. "The wall itself is not thick but the tunnel behind is small and narrow. We will have to crawl through it. The ceiling and the walls are unstable as there seems to be recent damage. I thought I heard an explosion of some sort while we were in the air, but Torin was flying so fast that all I could hear was the wind rushing past." Julian frowned. "There is an anomaly in there as well. I can't make out what it is. Metal of some sort?"

"Perhaps silver?" Torin suggested. He did not like caves. Air was his element but he was not about to let Julian and Siofra go into this dark place by themselves.

"The children are trained in silver mining," said

Ramón. "Those who took them would use them for that. There seems to be silver here."

"Let's remove those rocks, very carefully, and then I can stabilize the walls," said Julian.

Are ye daft?" said Siofra. her fur bristling/" Do magical work like that when ye're tired unto death?"

"I haven't any choice, Siofra," said Julian patiently. "The children need rescuing and if I try to find Nick or wait until Ellery and Sabrina come back, it could be too late. This entire mountainside is unstable. Something disturbed it and it could collapse at any time. They could be buried alive."

He used the *Demiterre* spell that they had used in the other cave to cause the rocks one by one to float from the entrance to the small passage, starting from the top on down.

It took a good half hour and by the time it was done Julian was leaning against the wall, Siofra and Torin regarding him anxiously.

Ramón, too, could see the effort that this took and watched his teacher in concern.

What was revealed when all of the rocks were gone was, as Julian's wand had told him, a small, cramped passageway, only big enough for a grown man to pass through on hands and knees.

"Let me be goin' through there first," said Siofra. "'Tis naught at all for a cat and sure, I'll not be needin' a light at all, for can't I be after seein' in the dark?"

"Not until I stabilize it," said Julian firmly and pointed his wand with a command of "*Stabilius*". The entire cave shuddered but no more rocks fell.

Julian, however, staggered and almost toppled. Torin leaped forward and let his friend lean on him. "Are you all right?" the hippogriffe asked anxiously.

"I'm' fine," said Julian shortly. He *had* to be fine; he would be no help to the children otherwise. If he absolutely had to he would draw some strength from Ramón. But he could only draw that strength if they were linked.

"It's bein' safe then?" queried Siofra, and before any of the others could stop her she sped into the tunnel.

It was very dark and very rough going. The floor was littered with rocks and the shaft was narrow and became narrower still as she went on.

When she was, she judged, nearly at the end, she heard voices and began to see a small light shining.

She emerged from behind a rock to find the children in a room full of gold.

"Holy Bastet!" she exclaimed." 'Tis the treasure!"

The floor of the room was covered in gold and silver coins. At least four large chests spilled out their contents of gold and silver items, crosses, cups, plates and chalices, reliquaries and christening vessels. There were also things Siofra did not recognize, but she assumed tht they must be sacred vessels for use in the Roman Catholic church. There were as well necklaces, rings, bracelets, earrings and coins upon coins. She saw ropes of pearls, and emeralds by the score, both cut and those set in jewelry. There were jade figures made by the Aztecs that Siofra recognized from a book of Ellery's she had been looking at. Gold and silver ingots had once stood in stacks as well, but now had tumbled to the ground.

"Holy Bastet!" she said again in wonder. Lutterworth had been right. But they had been looking for it in the wrong places.

Josefina looked up at the sound of her voice. "It is the cat of the *Señor el médico!*" she shouted, grabbing the attention of the other children, who had been looking at the glittering piles.

"Are ye bein' all right?" Siofra asked in her accented Spanish as she advanced into the cave.

"We are here on holiday, no?" said Léon sarcastically. "We are trapped in here, cat!"

"None of yer sauce, then!" she said sharply. "Are ye all alive and how badly hurt are ye bein' is what I was after wantin' to know. Me Wizard an' yer friend Ramón are bein' on the other side of this wall, figurin' out a way to be gettin' ye out of here."

"The hole you came in is too small for us to go through or for them to come through," Benito pointed out.

"Not if we were after rollin' away that rock," Siofra lifted her front paw and pointed at it. "'Tis in my mind thought that very few o' ye would be able to crawl the distance that is needed. We are needin' some way to drag ye out of here. Can ye not be removin' those chains?" she inquired as Léon moved and the ankle chains he wore clanked.

"Not unless we can find the key," he returned.

"That's bein' bad, that is," she said to herself. "I'll be goin' back now," she announced and continued. "I am needin' to tell them what I've been observin'. Be stayin' away from that big rock." Again she pointed to the stone that blocked the entrance to the tunnel shaft. "It may just be blowin' out like steam from a tea kettle."

With this she turned and went back down the narrow passage.

Julian and Ramón were waiting her coming anxiously. Folding his long legs under him, Torin had laid down on the floor of the little cave and had encouraged Julian to sit and lean against him.

"Is it bad?" Julian asked as Siofra came in sight, her fur was in disarray and dusty.

"'Tis bad enough," she answered. She took a critical look at the two men. "I'm thinkin' that only Ramón is goin' to be able to fit in there, for he's shorter, and skinny. Ye're goin' to have to crawl part o' th' way and pull yerself through the rest of it. An' ye will never manage it, not in the shape ye're bein' in." she said frankly to Julian. "An' there's this also. All of those children are drippin' wi' Cold Iron!"

"Cold Iron? " queried Ramón.

" 'Tis as good as poison to a Wizard," Siofra explained. "He goes near that an' what he looks like now will be as naught to the sickness ye'll be seein' then." She looked about, suddenly missing someone. "Where's that fox?"

"He disappeared shortly after we entered the cave," said Julian tiredly. All he wanted to do was to put his head down on Torin's warm feathered flank and go to sleep for a year. But there was too much to be done, he realized as Siofra began to list off the children's injuries.

Ramon said thoughtfully, "Many of them will not be able to crawl through the shaft. Perhaps I should Heal them before I bring them out?"

Julian shook his head. "My stabilization spell is weak. I cannot guarantee it lasting more than an hour. We've got to get them out as fast as we can."

Torin cleared his throat. "Julian, could you strengthen

the stabilization spell for another half an hour if you borrowed some strength from Ramón?"

"I think so," Julian said slowly. "Have you an idea?"

"I was thinking what we needed was an ambulance dragon," said Torin, "He could carry more than one of the children. Of course a full-sized adult dragon would not fit in this tunnel. But a dragonet would! A dragonet is strong and could carry several of the children and drag a litter of the rest, far easier than either of you. And you are too tired to levitate them out of there," he added sympathetically to Julian. The hippogriffe did not say out loud what they all knew: that it was going to take what power Julian had left to maintain the stabilization. The mountain was too volatile to trust. Even with the spell in place they could hear rocks sliding down the outside of the mountain and ominous rumblings.

"In fifteen minutes I can fly back to camp, get one of the dragonets, some rope and something to make a litter," said Torin eagerly. "The dragonets are still small enough that I can carry one easily."

"What are ye after waitin' for?" said Siofra urgently "Fly!"

Ramón came forward to support Julian as Torin stood up. He was out the cave in a trice and in only a moment they heard the great wings beating as he flew away.

"Now, be seatin' yer selves an' link to be holdin' up this mountain," ordered Siofra. "I am not wantin' to be buried alive."

They obeyed her and sat down. Once again, Julian linked to Ramón and felt the vigor of the Native's natural power connect with his. It was like doubling or even tripling the effect of the ley lines.

"I'll be goin' back to see if the children are bein' fine," said Siofra. "I'll be tellin' them that help is comin'."

She also had an idea and wanted to put it in train.

Julian merely nodded, concentrating, as she disappeared back down the shaft.

Ramón. linked to Julian, was conscious of all of the great weight of the earth above and around them. He could feel how unstable the mountain side was: the slightest noise or action might make the rest of it come tumbling down around them. He also could appreciate the power and the effort it took to steady and keep safe tons of stone and earth.

It seemed an age before Torin returned. They heard him outside the cave, the shrill tones of a dragonet and the voice of another man.

Julian hoped that it was Nick or Ellery; he could certainly use their help.

But it was Melville Sinclair that entered the cave before Torin and the dragonet. He was carrying a stack of blankets and several coils of rope hung over his arm. "Good Lord!" he said blankly, surveying Julian and Ramón. "You both look all in! I'm glad I came to help."

"Go on in," they heard Torin say outside. "There's no time to waste."

They heard someone come in. It was Amyas. The dragonet looked both frightened and apprehensive but said bravely," I'm here to help the children."

"He's the smallest of them," said Torin, coming in behind him. "Mr. Sinclair here tells me he's good with knots and can make a litter."

"I grew up around boats," explained Sinclair, beginning to uncoil the ropes. "I can tie anything you'd ever need. My father was a member of a lifeboat rescue team and I know all about making litters and such."

He was working as he talked and in what seemed very little time had made a rope harness on Amyas with a litter made of blankets behind the dragonet. He showed Ramón how to slip the ropes over the children and how to pull them tight and how to secure them in the litter.

Siofra reappeared as they were finishing this up and pounced upon an unused coil of rope. "Just what I am needin'!" she exclaimed. She pawed at the coil until one end came loose, took it up in her mouth and then trotted off with it back down the tunnel.

"What was that all about?" exclaimed Sinclair.

"Siofra has her own reasons for doing things," said Julian slowly. He was leaning back against the wall of the cave, his eyes closed. He was not looking forward to taking down the link with Ramón, but it would have to be done. Ramón was still the best choice to crawl into the cave and load the children on the improvised dragonet ambulance. He was shorter and slighter than either Julian or Sinclair.

After providing both Ramón and Amyas with a mage light to wear Julian took down the link and felt again the burden of the entire precarious mountain. "Hurry, Ramón," he said under his breath. There was one more thing he himself had to do, as Siofra had explained.

It was an immense effort to lift his wand and say "Expulsio". That would move that rock that blocked the entrance to the interior cavern. His arm dropped abruptly and it was only by will alone did he not slide into unconsciousness.

In the shaft, Ramón was pulled forward by Amyas. The dragonet had suggested that it would be easier and faster if Ramón rode on the litter, and it proved so. Amyas made nothing of the rock-strewn tunnel, or the decreasing height. He tucked his wings in tightly and wiggled when he had to do so.

He made it through in less time than it would have taken Ramón, emerging into the gold-filled room. He blinked in astonishment.

"Ramón!" cried Benito joyfully.They were glad to see the dragonet as well, for they were used to dragons and knew that he had come to help them.

Siofra, standing by a length of rope, said "Be hurryin' now, Ramón and Amyas! Me wizard is nearin' th' end of his tether an' this mountain might be comin' down around our ears when he's done in."

Ramón paid little attention to the treasure. His attention was all on the children and getting them secured. Several of them had filled their pockets with coins.

Amyas was now big enough to carry five of the smallest children. Pia sat on his neck; she was small and weighed next to nothing. As Ramón secured them, Siofra scampered back down the tunnel.

She ran out of it and said panting a little, said to Torin, "Please to be pickin' up that rope end in yer beak an' when I am tellin' ye give it a tug wi' all of yer might!"

Torin was mystified by this but he agreed to do as she asked. There was no time to go into long explanations and Siofra had always good reasons for the things she wanted to do.

It was a far worse trip back through the tunnel with

the cargo of ten children than it had been coming in. Amyas was forced to crouch low and dig in with his talons, at times only dragging himself forwards a foot or two.

As Ramón had cautioned them, the children lay still (only moving when Amyas said "Duck low!") and were quiet, allowing the dragonet to do his work. Ramón hung onto the back of the blanket and was drawn along behind the dragonet. It was not a comfortable way to travel for he was bruised by the rocks on the floor and his clothing was torn and scraped. It was not comfortable for the children either, tied to Amyas or bundled together on the improvised blanket litter.

It seemed to take forever to make any progress. Ramón could feel the weight of the mountain pressing down upon them as they traversed the dark shaft. He could hear Amyas panting with exertion and one of the children sobbing under her breath, trying to be brave, but dreadfully afraid. The two mage lights, one on Amyas's stubs of horn and the other on Ramón's bandana, did little to expel the deep darkness of the tunnel. The earth grumbled threateningly, protesting being held back by a spell. It wanted to conclude what had been started with the explosion.

Crawling, dragging and pushing with his hind legs, Amyas at last emerged from the tunnel.

"Thank God!" Julian whispered when he saw them.

"Get me Wizard up on Torin's back!" Siofra yelled at Sinclair. Be pullin' that rope when I am tellin' ye!" she ordered Torin.

"Don't untie them," Torin said quickly as Ramón began to undo the ropes. "I'm sorry," said the hippogriffe to the children on the blanket, "But we are going to have to roll you up like a jelly roll so that you can be carried. It won't be for long. Amyas," he said to the dragonet, "you are going to have to take the blanket in your talons and hold tight."

The little Maple dragonet looked frightened but Torin explained "I can't fly any distance carrying this weight but I can glide to the ground and get you all safely away from here before it collapses."

Ramon and Sinclair, grasping what he needed, quickly rolled the children into the blanket as safely and as comfortabley as they could and positioned it so that Amyas could easily grab it. "Both of you, up on my back behind Julian," Torin directed the other two men.

Siofra, with a tremendous leap, got onto to Torin's back and inserted herself into the front of Julian's jacket. "Out the door!" she cried inaccurately. "Be pullin' that rope, Torin!"

The hippogriffe obeyed, feeling a heavy weight at the end of it. Whatever was it? He kept pulling at it as he followed Amyas out on to the ledge. There he reared up and took a firm grip with his front talons on the rope that wound round the dragonet's middle, forming part of the harness. He took care not to get too near the children strapped to Amyas's back.

"Ye can be lettin' go now," Siofra said softly to her Wizard, patting his cheek with a velvet paw.

With a sigh, Julian did so, as the overburdened Torin launched himself into the air, dragonet in his talons, and still pulling Siofra's rope. Amyas grabbed the rolled blanket with all four feet and hung on grimly.

Torin had been correct; he could not gain any altitude at all, he could only drop from the ledge and hope that he did not drop to the ground with his burden. Using his immense wings as gliders he headed for the ground as the children screamed and behind them the mountainside started to fall in on itself.

Torin still had the rope in his beak and something heavy burst from the cave and swung free seconds before rocks, dirt and scree began cascading downwards.

"Don't be droppin' that!" Siofra shrilled.

Suddenly the noise and fall of rock stopped abruptly. With difficulty, Julian raised his head and saw two violet streams of light heading towards the mountain, coming from the wands of his aunt and uncle, mounted on Erianne.

"Thank God," he said and fainted.

And from the end of the rope in Torin's beak swung an immense, heavy chest.

Chapter Forty Five
Ice Melt

Wand in hand, at the ready, Nicholas slowly advanced to the hidden entrance of the cave. He still found the fox's description of a floor of ice difficult to believe. The weather was warm and would only get warmer. How could there be ice in this climate?

But Julian's forensic spells had shown him a 'green floor'. Was that the ice? Nicholas had never heard of green ice.

He did not like the idea of having to descend into a cave with perhaps four opponents waiting for him at the bottom of it. He knew enough about black magicians to realize that the young woman whom Cillian had told him of, who did not wear a ring, was more than likely an apprentice and therefore probably negligible magically, but he could not be absolutely certain of that.

The first order of business would be to take care of the black mages and the demon if they had summoned him. Nicholas was not concerned with him as much as with the elder magicians Cillian had warned him about. A demon of lust was at heart a coward and Nicholas had learned the demon destruction spell given in the Book of Demon as they all had.

Now he had to decide how to gain the upper hand over the four in the cave. A stunning spell? A freezing enchantment? He was aware that it was his duty as one sworn to the Light, to eliminate mages of the Dark, but he had never before taken a life and the thought made him uneasy.

But it was his duty to do so. This evil had to be purged and Marisela had to be rescued before the demon could have his way with her.

At the thought of Marisela and what she must be suffering, he quickened his pace, full of resolution.

Teresa lay back on the heavy buffalo robes that shielded their bodies from the cold ice and provided beds for the activities they had been indulging in. For the moment she was sated, but Brother Satyr was about to call up the Prince of Darkness, and Teresa would be very happy when he arrived and turned his attentions to her.

The Prince would take his pleasure on the virgin sacrifice first, Brother Satyr had explained, but then would give his attention to the two other women. The Prince was very lusty and had power and enough to spare for any number of women.

Teresa was also looking forward to tormenting Marisela again. Within herself she had discovered not only a nearly insatiable sexual appetite but a strong liking for inflicting pain. Sister Diabla had whispered to her of the many things they could do to the sacrifice when the Prince had thoroughly used her and Teresa, thinking about it, licked her lips in anticipation. She hoped for many times such as this here, with many more victims and many more bacchanals. Her only regret was that there were not more in their group, particularly young men.

But Brother Satyr had promised that when the Prince was pleased and granted him the power to raise his invincible army and drive the *Norteaméricanos* away from here, restoring the government to Spanish hands, there would be many more members of their group returning from Cuidad Mexico and perhaps even Spain. At the thought of bedding all of those delicious *caballeros* Teresa sighed in ecstasy.

Sister Diabla, lying next to Teresa, smiled a little to herself at he sight of the girl's eagerness. The acolyte had been a good choice. She was enthusiastic, greedy and cruel. She had greeted the embraces of the Prince with avidity, not fear, and his Satanic Majesty well approved of that in one of his worshippers. She hoped that the acolyte was still as eager for a male embrace when she had to serve the legions of demons that Prince had promised to fight at their sides.

Now that the first edge had been taken off their lechery, the two Brothers were conjuring up the Prince. The sacrifice's body had been painted with arcane symbols, in blood and the black candles lit. Incense burned in the brazier, a combination of herbs and plant material that heightened the senses and the libido.

Sister Diabla was very aware that in the world outside this cave she would not be desired by any man. But here, both the brothers panted for her, for both her inventiveness and extreme fondness for their embraces and the Prince had always been most eager to come where there was a woman for him to mount. She was very glad that she had found this outlet for what had been, since her earliest days, overwhelming carnal desires. Of course, she always had Brother Satyr near when she felt the need come over her.

With this virgin sacrifice of noble birth they had now offered to him and killed the requisite number of women he had demanded, to do him honor and convince him to fulfill their requests of him. It had not always been easy to find young women and girls who would not be missed. The officials at the mines had preferred to keep the females for their own use. When the *Norteaméricanos* had come to the village of Diablo and had set up a *bordello*, it had become a little easier. Whores came and went and no one concerned themselves over much with one who took off and was never seen again. Some of the victims had been tossed down a mine shaft, others were buried in out of the way places.

Sister Diabla often thought that she would have liked to have become a whore. All those men, day after day–night after night! It was a lovely thought!

Marisela, tied to the altar, unable to move and forced to watch them at their lewd play, was terrified.

First they had hurt her with their pinching, lashing and poking. Then they had killed a black cock and with its blood, had painted symbols on her body. A rank smell was in the air from a brass brazier where something sullenly burned.

The two men stood in front of her, bowing low to an upside down crucifix that hung on the wall above her head. The light from black candles in tall twin candelabras gleamed on their oiled bodies.

Rodri had taught his sister Latin, so that she might help him with his studies and she recognized what followed as a perversion of the Mass.

Then the taller, and she thought, the more brutal, of the two, stood up straight and lifted his hands. He began to chant.

"I do make invocation, conjure and invoke thee, O Prince of Darkness, to appear and show thyself to us, your humble servants. Show thyself to us that we might adore thee and that thou might partake of this virgin sacrifice of noble blood we have prepared for thee as thou hast commanded. I beg of thee to accept this unwilling sacrifice and with that acceptance grant unto me my desire as thou hast promised, to fulfill my will in all those things I so fervently wish to achieve. Come thou, O great Prince, without delay, to manifest thyself before us!"

There was a flash of red light and a smell as of sulphur burning. A strange figure appeared in a cloud of lurid hues. "Hail, Beelzebub!" the two naked brothers cried, falling to their knees. The women too, prostrated themselves.

It had red eyes, the legs of a goat, horns on its head, and as it looked on Marisela, very evident lust.

Brother Satyr, from his position of abject bowing on he icy floor, said "We have fulfilled all your commands, Majesty. With this virgin of noble birth, this makes the thirty women and thirty sacrifices you have asked for. Will you now grant our desires?"

Azaleel, for such was the demon of lust's name, felt himself in a dilemma. When his Prince had sent him here to see what these mortals might want, the demon of lust had listened to their wants and had told them that he, in the character of his ruler, demanded thirty females for his own use and then the sacrifice of such, ending in a virgin of noble blood. He had also demanded that any females in this group of worshippers be made available to him.

But he had never really imagined that they would come up with thirty sacrifices, much less one of noble blood. He had been so sure of this that he had not kept count of all the women he had enjoyed here. Now they expected him to made good on his promise. Of course, being but a demon of lust, he had no power or indeed authority to do so. However, he could lie to them and leave them hanging, waiting and waiting...that might amuse his Majesty as well. But doing this meant no more delectable human females that would be killed when he had finished with them, nor access to the eager members of this unholy fellowship. For he could not return here ever again. Ah, well, he would enjoy this one last time. Not only was there an unwilling woman to take, but the young worshipper was already looking at him with hot eyes.

All of this went through his mind very quickly and at last he said "But of course, you shall have what you want! Are you not my good and faithful servants?" How the Prince would laugh when Azaleel acted out this little scene for him—the demon of lust had a degree of histrionic talent. "But now I shall enjoy your offering, started " he said aloud.

He turned to Marisela and advanced on her. He reached out one dirty finger and stroked it down her body.

She made a violent move of revulsion and threw herself against the bonds, making inarticulate cries of horror through the gag.

"She's afraid," the demon crooned. He grabbed at one of her breasts. "Do you want her left alive for your use?" he said over his shoulder to Brother Satyr.

"If It pleases your Majesty. We had thought that we might keep her alive for some while, as that woman in France you told us of."

Azaleel's eyes lit up. That had been a lovely, lengthy sacrifice. That had been over one hundred years earlier, far too long ago.

"I am going to hurt you a great deal," he whispered to Marisela as he climbed on top of her, "But I shall truly enjoy myself. And that is what matters!" he snickered.

"Get away from her!" someone shouted. *"Daemon edicti obire!"* And a long violet light shot into the cave and struck the demon in the middle of his back.

He screamed, a high thin wailing, and fell to the ice floor where he rolled around, screeching and sobbing, trying to put out the fire in his spine that seemed to be consuming him from inside out. He clawed at himself, making the injury worse.

Brother Satyr looked up, enraged. Who dared to interrupt them, to attack the Prince? He gathered his power and threw it at the intruder, a red bolt of energy like the flames of Hell itself.

Nicholas started down the rope ladder and threw himself to one side as the red bolt came at him. He threw up a violet shield which the red broke against, scattering in all directions, as he jumped the rest of the way to the floor.

The older woman ran forward to the candles at the side of the altar and knocked them over plunging the cave into darkness. Red bolts from three directions came at Nicholas. He crouched low to the ground and parried, thanking his luck and dragon-ball training in giving him good, quick reflexes. He needed light, however. Presumably the Satanists thought that knowing the cave so well would give them an advantage that he did not have.

"In lumen proferre!" He shouted and the cave was flooded with a brilliant light that seemed to spring from the ceiling, showing up every crack, every crevice and the four nude figures.

The demon lay on the floor, dead. The spell had been a killing one.

The smell of sulphur and brimstone hung in the air as Nicholas pointed his wand at three of the four and said *"Obstupefacere!"* to stun them. They fell over like bowls struck by a ball. But where was the fourth one?

"Nick! Look out!" came Varian's voice from the cave entrance.

Nicholas whirled. The shorter man had ducked behind the altar on which Marisela was tied and now he ran out from behind the stone table gathering power in his hands to hurl at Nicholas.

As fast as Nicholas was, Varian was faster, A long thin flame shot out of his maw, catching the man before he could raise his arm to throw. Covered in oil as he was, he went up like a torch, screaming in an agony of pain.

"Finish him off, Varian!" Nicholas yelled as the other man began to stir. The stunning spell had not held him long. Nicholas had not expected it to. He just prayed that the two women were not as powerful and would remain unconscious while he dealt with the man in the goat's head mask.

Varian, occupied with turning his flame up to white-hot heat and keeping it turned on the man who had threatened Nicholas had no thought to spare for Pacho or Cillian, he could hear the hedgehog's anxious mutterings. Magic was beginning to fly back and forth throughout the cave, both the red of the black magician and the violet from Nicholas's wand. Nicholas also was tossing the pure energy bolts he had learned to craft from the Elves.

The little dragonet had wiggled in beside Varian and now when he saw Marisela he gave an exclamation of distress, and oblivious to everything but his bond-mate, pressed forward and fell down the entrance, one of his rear talons catching the rope ladder. His weight and haste tore it from its brackets to fall in a jumbled heap at the foot of the wall. Pacho picked himself up and ran to Marisela and began to tear at her bonds with his sharp little teeth. Although still his first teeth, and therefore not the dangerous weapons they would be come when he was mature, these baby teeth were nonetheless sharper than many knives and the ropes fell away from her readily.

She sat up with difficulty. She had been tied up for a long time and every muscle in her body felt as if it wanted to go into spasms. She hurt everywhere as well where they had tormented her. She ripped the gag from her mouth and said "On, Pacho! Oh, Pacho!" putting her arms around the dragonet's neck. He nuzzled her, overflowing with love and relief that he had been able to save her and be united with her again.

As careful as Varian had been with his flame, some of the wooden timbers and the hangings on the walls had ignited at one end of the cave. This light from the fire and the brilliant mage light lit up the scene and cast long shadows from the dueling mages.

Marisela watched the bolts of raw power fly back and forth, her arms tight about the dragonet's neck. She had never imagined anything like this. It was terrifying. Power broke and spilled onto the floor where it began eating through the ice.

"You won't ruin this for me, *gringo!*" shouted Brother Satyr. "I have planned too long and fought too hard!" The goat's mask slipped and went down over his eyes, blocking his view. With an oath he ripped it off and cast it on the ground.

Marisela gasped in horror. Brother Satyr was *Don* Rafael!

He no longer wore the look of an empty-minded idiot. He looked both dangerous and feral, his face contorted in a snarl as he attempted to defeat Nicholas.

Her attention riveted on the mages, Marisela did not see or hear when one of the women regained consciousness and staggered to her feet.

Sister Diabla took in the situation at a glance. Something had to be done to stop the duelists. She did not like the way it was going. The *gringo* was young and strong and was throwing both energized bolts from one of his hands and balls of violet power from his wand. She made up her mind and headed towards Marisela. A threat to the girl would halt the white magician in his tracks. Those type of people were too worried about the innocent.

If Sister Diabla had known anything about dragons she would have known better than to act as she did. Marisela did not hear or see her coming, but with preternatural dragon senses, Pacho saw and heard her intent and launched himself with a growl at her before she could reach his beloved Marisela. Sister Diabla gave a great shriek, turning Marisela's attention—and that of the duelists—to her.

Under the not inconsiderable weight of the dragonet Sister Diabla flew backwards and struck the wall, her neck snapping with a very audible crack. Her mask flew off and the twisted features of *Doña* Paloma were revealed. Marisela let out a scream as she saw this and also saw that the woman was dead, her neck broken, as her body fell in an untidy heap at the bottom of the wall.

"Mamacita!" cried *Don* Rafael in anguish, half turning as if to go to her.

Nicholas's bolt caught him across the side of the head and he screamed in pain as it sliced through his skull, killing him instantly.

"Nick!" called Varian urgently. "Nick get out of there! The floor is melting!" Cillian's worried face could be seen on the edge of the cave entrance, the fire reflected in the glass of his spectacles.

Nicholas had been aware for some time that he was standing in water but, intent on fighting, he had given it little attention. Now with a ominous creak and snapping sound the ice beneath his feet gave way and he, Marisela, Pacho and the three bodies, including that of the still unconscious Teresa were plunged into cold, deep water. The fire and the heated magic had done its work well.

Nicholas was a good swimmer and he shot to the surface almost at once. Where were Marisela and Pacho though?

As he looked about rather wildly, Pacho's head broke the surface and there was Marisela, clinging to his neck, looking half drowned and limp. "I can swim!" said the dragonet in surprise.

"I can swim too, no?" said Marisela weakly and began coughing.

"Nick!" Varian called down. "Can you levitate out of there?"

"I don't think so, Varian," Nicholas called back. "Not after all the energy I expended dueling. I don't dare tap the ley lines in this place. They're more than likely polluted. What happened to the rope ladder?"

"I ripped it down," said Pacho in a small voice."I think it burned up."

The fire on the walls was still burning hungrily and as they tread water, canisters of oil, stored in a cupboard, exploded and only ducking under the surface of the water saved them from burns.

When they came up the surface of the water was burning in many places.

Marisela gave a small shriek and tried to climb higher on Pacho's neck. "Something touched my ankle!" she said. "It felt like a hand!"

"Oh, my God!" cried Nicholas, "That other woman! She was unconscious!" He dived beneath the burning water to come up again a few moments later, holding a limp body. "She's dead," he said grimly.

The mask had come off. Marisela recognized *Doña* Paloma's maid Teresa. Nicholas let go her body and it bobbed away from them, bumping against the now rapidly melting remains of the ice.

"Nick!" Varian called down again. "I am going to turn around and stick my tail down this hole. Can you climb up it like a ladder, holding onto my back ridges?"

"We can only try!" Nicholas called back up, his voice breaking on a cough.

"Can you do it?" he said to Marisela, looking at her exhausted and bruised face. She coughed as the smoke from the burning oil caught at her throat. A moment later Pacho coughed as well.

She smiled wryly. "I must do it, no, or drown here in the fire. But what about Pacho?" She lovingly rubbed her cheek against the dragonet's head.

"I can tow him up like a mother dragon does when the dragonets are learning to fly," Varian called down again. "He can grab my tail in his teeth and I'll draw him up."

Nicholas went up first so that he could help Marisela if needs be. It was slippery work, but Varian helped as much as he could, lifting his tail higher as Nicholas climbed further up. Cillian rushed up to him at once, exclaiming "Thank the Great Hedgehog!"

When Nicholas was safe on the ground outside he knelt beside the hole and caught Marisela as soon as her head emerged.

He had his flying jacket waiting and wrapped her in it. Even as tiny as she was it was barely decent.

Then Varian drew the dragonet out of the cave and they all collapsed on the ground well away from the cavern entrance. From inside they could still hear the noise of the fire. Smoke hung in the air.

Marisela was beginning to shiver with reaction and cold, for night was closing in. Nicholas put his arm around her. It seemed natural to do so.

"Thank you, Nicolás, thank you!" she said and burst into sobs, burrowing against him.

Pacho started to cry in sympathy and crowded closer. Cillian was between Nicholas and Marisela in his Wizard's lap and Varian had dropped his muzzle onto Nicholas's head.

"Well, done," came a quiet voice and Nicholas looked up to see Gian-nah-tah regarding them. "I can see that you are deserving of a new name," the fox told Nicholas. "You shall be called Ta-ah-yay-say amongst the People."

"What does that mean?" asked Pacho, sniffing.

"Strong swimmer," said Gian-nah-tah, with a vulpine grin.

Chapter Forty Six
Dragon Conflict

Nah-kah-yen had done little besides brood lately. He could think of nothing but the bright green dragoness and his desire to mate with her. He spent hours high in the air over the camp site at *El Morro*, watching her. He never landed or even came too close, for fear the magician would harm him.

The blue dragon had no idea if she was conscious of him at all. She had seldom flown; she spent too much time with those accursed dragonets. He could not understand why she gave so much of herself to dragonets not even her own. It seemed perverse to him.

Every day his anger and longing grew and every day he tormented himself by flying over the camp at least once, sometimes more often. Occasionally he glided for hours above, watching the activities below, which were very busy.

The young male dragon, the oddly coloured one, ignored him, if he was even aware of the older male so high up above them. He seemed busy flying people here and there.

Nah-kah-yen saw nothing between the male and the female he desired to stir his jealousy. He was still suspicious of the other green dragon he had seen. Perhaps the female favored one of her own colour? Females had had stranger prejudices.

Ordinarily, Nah-kah-yen would have discussed his longing for the lovely dragoness with Ramón, but his bond-mate seemed far more occupied with his lessons in Healing. He seemed not to even need his dragon companion, but instead was riding about on the back of the strange feathered creature that belonged to the *gringo médico*. This preoccupation on the part of his bond-mate made the great blue dragon feel more bereft and rejected than ever.

On the afternoon of the day that Ellery and Atalanta were married in Albuquerque, matters came to a head.

Nah-kah-yen had done his best to stay away from the camp. The rational part of his mind told him that perhaps he ought to range further afield in search of a mate and leave the dragoness, who so inexplicably did not want him, alone.

But like so many before him who had nursed an

unrequited passion, he could not seem to keep away from her. He kept hoping that she would change her mind and come to him, to offer herself to him.

He managed to make himself keep away until later in the day. Then the longing, so acute that it physically hurt, came over him and he launched himself into the sky, swiftly winging towards the great bluff of *El Morro*.

When he arrived, it was to find her no place in sight, but a different green dragon with only two of the dragonets.

It couldn't be! He thought, in disbelief. It was that strange dragon he had seen with her before! His dragoness trusted this strange male enough to leave him with the dragonets? Where had she gone? He scanned the entire area, wheeling and banking back and forth in the sky, searching almost frantically for Erianne.

As he flew, his rage grew. Where was she? What had this stranger done to gain her confidence and trust? Had they mated yet?

At last, with a roar of pure rage, he turned in mid-circle and dove at tremendous speed straight at the interloper. He would have an answer from this male or die trying.

Atalanta was growing used to dragon-flight. She quite enjoyed it and imagined what it would be like when she could fly with Seneca.

And there was an added attraction to dragon-flight today. She sat in the very first seat, leaning backwards against Ellery, his arm unnecessarily around her waist. But it felt good to have his arm there: her husband's arm. It still seemed strange to think of him in that way and she supposed it would for quite a while. After all, she had done without a husband for nearly thirty-five years and they had been married for less than six hours.

After tonight she would never again have to wake in the small hours of the morning thinking of the poetry of Sapphic. She would know the mysteries of the marriage bed and what it meant to be loved.

"Oh, my goodness!" Erianne's voice interrupted Atalanta's thoughts.

They were gliding easily and slowly, Erianne's wings out straight to hold her position aloft.

"What is it, Erianne?" came Ellery's voice from behind Atalanta.

Erianne could turn her head on her long neck and look at him. "There's trouble at the camp!" she said hurriedly and a bit angrily. "That blue dragon that tried to force me to mate, he's attacking the dragonets!"

"What!" came Sabrina's voice."Is he mad?"

"We have to hurry!" said Erianne in anguish. "Does he think that harming them will make me want to mate with him?"

"Fly!" Ellery said, and tightened his hold around his new wife. "Bend forward over the saddle," he said in Atalanta's ear.

Erianne took off with a speed that made tears come to Atalanta's eyes. Even bending over the saddle bow Atalanta was conscious of the wind ripping at her hair and clothing. She wore a jacket, but even so it became colder as the Irish dragon speeded up and began a long descent as they neared the camp.

Erianne had been wrong. Nah-kah-yen was not attacking the dragonets–they were attacking him.

Only Seneca and Eda were left at the camp site. Earlier, Pacho had gone off with Varian and Nicholas and just a little while ago, Amyas had left with Sinclair and Torin.

"Mama" Erianne had left a dragon from the railroad camp, who was called Ancelin, in charge of them while she took Ellery, Atalanta, Bairre, Flann and Sabrina to Albuquerque. Naturally enough, she wanted to go to Ellery's wedding. Since the habit of obedience was very strong in a dragonet, they had given Ancelin very little trouble.

The two dragonets had been napping after a long whispered conversation about how it wasn't fair that Pacho and Amyas got all the fun of being flown here and there.

Upon being told sternly to go to sleep, it was nap time, they had closed their eyes and because it had been a long, exciting morning, they both fell into slumber.

Ancelin's scream of rage woke them.

To their horror they awoke to see their new friend wrestling with a large blue dragon. He was attempting to bite Ancelin's neck and bellowing "What have you done with her?" As they watched, he tried to knock Ancelin to the ground where he could use his talons to cut and damage.

"That's the bad blue dragon Amyas told us about!" exclaimed Eda.

"The one Mama doesn't like?" queried Seneca. Like Amyas had from the beginning, the rest of them had begun calling Erianne "Mama".

Eda nodded, her eyes huge with terror as she watched the two older dragons fight. They growled, roared and spat flame, rolling over and over on the ground, churning up dust and clods of earth. In between lunges and feints of defense Ancelin was yelling "Stop it, you idiot! What do you think you are doing?"

"Mama won't like it if he hurts Ancelin," said Seneca. "Come on, Eda, do what I do!"

Determinedly, he headed towards the battling adults. He waited and then jumped as the tip of Nah-kah-yen's wing came towards him. He leaped, and caught the wing between his teeth.

Wings were very sensitive to pain, and in a dragon battle, once a dragon had his opponent on the ground, he would usually attack the sails of the wings, shredding them with tooth and talon. This not only put his adversary in tremendous pain but prevented him flying away and escaping as the torn sails would prevent flight.

Nah-kah-yen gave a great bellow of pain and outrage. He turned his head to try and snap at Seneca, only to have Eda fasten her sharp little teeth onto the tip of his other wing. He gave a great roar of agony and anger just as Erianne landed near him and Ancelin rolled over and stood up.

"What are you doing?" Erianne shrieked at the blue dragon."Have you gone mad?"

"That's what I'd like to know!" Ancelin exclaimed. "Is

this lout a friend of yours? Attacking me for no reason—someone I don't even know!"

"Get these things off my wings!" Nah-kah-yen said between gritted teeth.

"Eda, Seneca," said Erianne sharply. "Let go and come over here by me."

They scrambled to obey and ran beneath her lifted wings.

"Don't you dare!" Erianne said, glaring at Nah-kah-yen as he opened his maw, looking as if he was going to flame.

"Yes, that's quite enough," said Ellery from Erianne's back. The blue dragon looked up to see that the magician had his wand in hind and was aiming it at him. "I think you know what I can do with this," Ellery said. "There will be no more fighting and I want an explanation of this. Erianne, we'll dismount now."

She sank to the ground, not taking her eyes off Nah-kah-yen.

Ellery, too, did not take his attention from the blue dragon even as he slid down from Erianne's saddle and helped his wife and sister down. Flann clung to Sabrina's shoulder after being taken from the traveling basket and Atalanta held Bairre.

"Now, that explanation if you please," said Ellery, still leveling his wand at the blue dragon.

Nah-kah-yen was suffering from humiliation and a still smoldering anger. He had neither defeated his rival not impressed the dragoness. "I was fighting him for you," he said to Erianne, almost shouting. "I won't stand by and watch him take you without a fight!"

"What!" Ancelin exclaimed and then to Nah-kah-yen's amazement and resentment, began laughing and Erianne joined in. It was not kind laughter.

"Stupid male!" laughed Ancelin. "I never before saw a male who could not instantly tell—I am a dragoness! What an idiot!" she said to Erianne. "I can see why you don't want to mate with him! Who in her right mind would want the father of her eggs to be so stupid!"

Nah-kah-yen felt steam trickling out of his nostrils. Now that she had told him he did not know how he had missed so obvious a fact. Her scent, her elegant long neck, her lighter body: everything about her should have told him. But he had been so blinded by rage that he had refused to notice. "You look just like the other one that was here," he said sullenly. "I know he was a male."

Ancelin had a low husky voice, rather deep for a female. Now she said "That's not amazing since Rowan is my brother. We came from the same clutch."

"Where's Amyas?" Erianne said worriedly. "And Pacho? If you've hurt them—!" she said threateningly to Nah-kah-yen.

Seneca poked his head from out under her wing.""I'll tell you, Mama! They both left messages for you."

Ten minutes later Erianne was in the air again, heading for the Zuni mountains and arrived just in time to prevent the mountain's collapse.

It was not how Atalanta had expected or even dreamed of to spend her wedding night.

When Ellery and Sabrina had taken off on Erianne, Atalanta was left at the camp with only her father and Lutterworth for company. Neither man was in a good mood. Dr. Beck was seething with rage at the loss of his daughter/servant and began cutting up at her as soon as Ellery disappeared. Lutterworth was in a rage over his assistant's having taken off too, "to rescue some damned kids," as he put it. "Let the little bastards rescue their damned selves!" he stated and went off on a long vituperation about "bleeding hearts" and "do-gooders". She also had a pair of hostile dragons on her hands. In a hurry, Ellery had allowed him to stay as Nah-kah-yen said that he would wait for Ramón and Ancelin was doing her best to ignore him. The dragonets, overexcited, had been hard to control as well, in spite of having had a good feeding. They insisted on making faces at the blue dragon and then running away, laughing at him in their high voices.

Atalanta tried to ignore them as she was trying to ignore her father, who had not stopped talking about her ingratitude, the duty she owed him, how he could not spare her, and on and on until she wanted to scream at him to leave her alone.

It was with relief that she saw, as twilight began to deepen, Varian circling over head and descending, with Pacho in his front talons.

With Nicholas was Marisela, a Marisela Atalanta barely recognized. Her hair was a tangled mass, her eyes wide in shock. and wrapped in the inadequacy of Nicholas's flight jacket, she was nearly naked.

When Varian had landed, putting Pacho down first, Nicholas swung down from Varian lightly and, after putting Cillian on the ground, took Marisela off the saddle. She hid her face against his neck, and seemed to be shivering.

Nicholas looked around anxiously, not putting her down, but keeping her in his arms.His face lit up when he saw Atalanta.

"I'm so glad you're back!" he said to his new aunt. "You're just the person we need. She's had an awfully bad time of it today. Could you help her with a bath and get her something to wear?"

"Don't leave me, Nicolás!" Marisela said, her hands grasping at the collar of his shirt.

Ellery had spent part of each early morning walk giving Atalanta lessons in basic Spanish and she understood this well enough.

"He can stay right outside while I help you bathe and dress," she said in her rudimentary Spanish. She was picking it up easily, for she already spoke French and Italian as well as Latin and Greek both ancient and modern.

Marisela had to be content with this and Atalanta listened with interest to Nicholas's reassuring murmurs of "You're safe now"; "They can never hurt you again"; and "They're all dead." He carried Marisela into the tent and put her on Sabrina's cot.

Both Pacho and Cillian had followed them in and the little dragonet looked at his bond-mate worriedly. "Will she be all right?" he inquired.

"She's had a terrible shock, Pacho," Nicholas explained. "She needs rest and help. Is Julian here?" he asked Atalanta. "I didn't see Torin outside."

She told him that his brother was off rescuing the children and Nicholas said "I'm glad that they were found and will be safe now."

Then he switched to English and said to Atalanta, while looking at Marisela, "She was almost raped. They tortured her and she was tied for a long time to an unholy altar. She's got arcane symbols painted on her body that are probably adding to her pain. Here," he reached inside his shirt and pulled a chain out and then up and over his head. "put this in the bath water. It will take all of those ugly symbols off."

Atalanta took the object. It was a tiny sliver of ivory.

"It's a piece of unicorn horn," Nicholas explained."A very powerful purifier and quite the best thing to have when one is traveling in a foreign country and not sure of the water. It will negate any harmful substances, especially those of the Dark. It will even take poison from food."

"I'll stay with the *Señorita,* Nicholas," said Cillian. "I shall be able to show your aunt how to use the horn and I can translate too, if there is any communication problem."

Atalanta felt a slight shock as she realized she *was* now Nicholas's aunt.

"Good idea," said Nicholas in relief. Cillian would also come and tell him if Marisela needed him. "Come with me, Pacho. I want to take a look at your wound site and make certain we did not do any damage today. And I daresay you could do with some food," he said to the dragonet.

"I *am* hungry," the dragonet admitted. He hesitated in following Nicholas out of the tent and, turning backwards to look a her, said to Atalanta "Take good care of her, please! I almost lost her!"

It was like handling a large doll, Atalanta thought as she prepared the bath, using the WORD Sabrina had given her to heat the water. She had to remove the jacket from Marisela's grip and help her into the tub. The younger woman seemed dazed and before the water, purified by the magic of the unicorn horn, surrounded her she was shivering spasmodically.

Atalanta expressed her doubts to Cillian that a bit of horn could remove those ugly things painted on Marisela's body but the hedgehog smiled at her, eyes twinkling behind his spectacles and said "Wait and see!"

And she did. When dipped in the water the horn caused rings of a lovely light blue to ripple outwards and envelope Marisela. In less than a moment the horrible bloody designs had gone and even the bruises and abrasions that covered her had lessened.

Emotionally, Marisela relaxed as well. She closed her eyes and leaned back, actually enjoying the water.

"I do so like magic!" Atalanta said to herself.

Finding something for Marisela to wear was a bit more of problem. Both Atalanta herself and Sabrina were a great deal taller than the Spanish girl and their clothes looked on her as if she was a little girl playing at dress-up in her mother's clothing. Atalanta ended in giving her a nightdress and a dressing gown and turning back the sleeves and pinning up the hems.

Then she called Nicholas to come in, for Marisela had been asking, rather anxiously, for him.

He was scarcely in the door when Marisela jumped up from the cot where she had been sitting and flew to him, putting he arms around him. "But for you I should have been raped by that thing!" she cried and hugged him tighter.

"It's all right," he said, feeling a little overwhelmed by her gratitude, not that it did not feel good to have her arms around him. His arms came up to hold her tight as she again burst into tears. "Shh, shh," he said soothingly. "It's all right, sweetheart, you're safe here with all of us mages to protect you. The black mages are all dead now. No one can harm you again." He sat down on the cot with her in his lap and let her cry.

When her sobs had somewhat abated he said "Do you want us to send a message to your parents or perhaps Varian and I might fly you home?"

She threw her head up from where it had been resting so comfortably against his chest. "I have no home," she said coldly. "I have no parents. They sold me to that pig of a black *brujo* for gold! They could not see what was wrong with me and they should have known. They did not care that I did not want to marry him! And they don't want Pacho!" She turned and looked at him beseechingly. "Please, Nicolás. may I not stay here? I will be a servant or do anything as long as can be with you and Pacho! But I will never go back there! They may send me the few things of mine that I want but I never wish to see them again! Never, never, never!" She exclaimed, her voice rising with each word.

Chapter Forty Seven
Aftereffects

It took some doing for Torin to land safely, carrying a triple load of riders, one of them unconscious, holding a heavy dragonet in his talons, (who in turn was carrying ten children) as well as hauling a heavy chest. Everyone was battered, terrified and very relieved when Torin first deposited Amyas on the ground and then landed heavily himself. Sinclair and Ramón dismounted at once, to go to the children.

As if he had been a trained ambulance dragon, Amyas landed on his back legs, frantically balancing until he let go of the blanket which was tightly wrapped around several of the children. He then threw himself to one side, coming down heavily and jarring the children still tied to his back and sides.

Erianne landed at the same time. Ellery and Sabrina were off her back in a trice. Ellery ran to Torin at once, for even in the oncoming twilight he could see Julian hanging limply over the hippogriffe's neck.

"He's utterly worn out, Ellery," said the hippogriffe when he had dropped the rope Siofra had insisted on him retaining in their flight. "He had a full day of Healing, including a difficult child-bed and a skull fracture and then holding up a mountain on the verge of collapse so we could get the children out safely."

"An' wasn't I tellin' him not to be spreadin' himself so thin?" said Siofra. She had climbed out of the front of Julian's jacket and was actually sitting on Torin's head.

"The mountain is still on the verge of collapse," said Ellery. "Our spells won't hold it much longer. What happened to make it so volatile?" He was making a rudimentary examination of Julian as he spoke.

"Th' children were sayin' that there was bein' an explosion caused by one o' those black mages," said Siofra.

Sabrina came up to them. "How is he?" she queried in concern.

"It's as if he's done a Great Working," said Ellery. "He needs bed rest and beef tea with herbs for strength return in

451

short order."

"I helped Sinclair and Ramón patch up the children as best we could. Ramon has learned a lot in such a short time!" she said in admiration. "But we've got to get them all away from here. Even Erianne can't carry all of us. We've a six person saddle but there are ten children, five adults and a dragonet to transport and some of the children would be better off transported laying down."

"Erianne won't even go up if the children are not secured tightly," said Ellery. "Are you still able to fly, Torin, after a strain like that?" He had seen the immense effort it had been for the hippogriffe to glide and land safely. For one moment he had thought that Torin would not make it.

"I can carry one rider," said the hippogriffe. "That's all I can handle at the moment. Perhaps I can take Julian back and if Nick is there by now, I can send him and Varian back for transport."

"Good idea," approved Ellery. "Atalanta is there and you or Siofra can tell her what to do for Julian."

"Before we are goin' anywhere," put in Siofra, "there is bein the wee matter of the chest full o' treasure we were findin.'"

"What!" said Ellery in amazement. "You found it?"

"Oh, aye," Siofra said rather smugly."We can be givin' it over to Lutterworth an' then bein' rid o' him. Bad cess to him!" she added. "A cat's curse on him for makin' our lives such a misery since we were comin' here! 'Tis over there now." She pointed with one paw to a point just beyond whre Amyas had landed. "An' it is in my mind that ye had best make it disappear, for there are wagons comin' and ye would not want th' men in them to be seein' all that gold an' such or there will be after havin' a riot on our paws"

As she finished speaking Ellery and Sabrina could hear the noise of several wagons coming, which Siofra's keen hearing had caught early on.

Sinclair came up to join them. "Who's that coming?" he inquired.

"'Tis more than likely the men from th' railroad camp. Eager to come an' help th' wee ones, they were," Siofra explained. "O' course, they were not bein' able to be gettin' here as fast as us."

"Siofra's right, Ellery. We'd best hide that chest," said Sabrina. She was taking out her wand as she spoke.

Together, they levitated the chest and inserted it in Erianne's breast harness just as the first wagon came into sight, bearing the engineer Jack Ballard and several other men. Sinclair's eyes widened as he saw the chest, but he took the hint when Sabrina laid a finger against her lips.

Ballard's group had brought two light buckboards pulled by two horses each and a heavy freight wagon of the Conestoga type, drawn by two draught horses. The wagons were full of blankets, easily portable food and other comforts.

That quite efficiently took care of the transportation problem.

"Not quite the wedding night I had envisioned," said Ellery *sotto voce* to his new wife, his arm around her waist, as they stood together watching the wagons arrive at the camp at El Morro.

It was quite late. The wagons, much slower moving than a hippogriffe or a dragon, had taken a good while to arrive.

But it had given them time to set up tents, borrowed from the railway camp, for the children, to get Julian into bed and some strengthening herbs down his throat, to get Marisela to sleep in Atalanta's bed with the aid of a sleeping draught from the emergency medical kit and for Ellery to hide the treasure chest as Siofra called it, in the artifact tent, disguised, with a spell, as an empty crate. He wanted to wait until the morning to deal with both it and Lutterworth.

He had had all of Lutterworth that he could take for the evening. Lutterworth had protested at the bringing of the children here to the camp, at Sinclair's going off to rescue the children, at the railway workers leaving the site; there was scarcely anything that had happened that day that he did not have something to say about, growing louder and louder, and more vehement by the minute, his face turning a bright red.

Dr. Beck had followed Ellery about, bleating at him, acting as if he had seduced and abandoned Atalanta, rather that honorably marrying her. But in truth, all the old goat was worried about was his own comfort and who was going to take care of him. At Ellery's suggestion that someone could be hired Dr. Beck had said in horror: "A *foreigner?* One of these Mexican females? Are you mad? And how am I to pay for it, pray?"

Ellery could see that his father-in-law was going to be hanging on his sleeve for some time to come.

Then there were the stories of what had happened to be shared, told by Nicholas, Pacho and Cillian by Sinclair. Torin, Siofra and Ramón. Ellery and Sabrina were appalled by the fact that Nicholas had faced down four Satanists by himself but did admit that he had little choice if he was to rescue Marisela in time.

It was after one in the morning before Ellery was free to carry his bride over the threshold of the artifact tent where Bairre waited for them on a freshly made-up bed.

The ferret was surrounded by the bright yellow faces of desert marigolds. "I picked them for you," he said a little shyly to Atalanta. "A marriage ought to be celebrated with flowers."

"Why, thank you," said Atalanta in surprise. This little animal had been more thoughtful than had her father, who had offered no congratulations, only criticism and complaint.

"And I'm going to go sleep with Flann and Sabrina," Bairre went on. "This is a night for the two of you to be alone." This was a sacrifice for him for ever since he had chosen Ellery when his Wizard was only eight years old, they had never been apart. But since Atalanta was non-magical she might feel embarrassed and awkward in front of him. A wedding night was difficult enough for a human female under normal circumstances, Flann had explained to him. After a brief good-night, he left, leaving the two of them alone.

Atalanta did indeed feel shy. She had given up expecting a wedding night to ever happen to her, never mind it happening in a tent in a the New Mexico desert, with so much drama going on.

She undressed behind a shelf, putting on the white night dress that Sabrina had insisted on buying for her at the dressmaker's. Although meant for a bride and rather demure, it was still more revealing that the white flannel high-to-the-neck gowns she was used to. It was of silk, and dripped with lace.

Atalanta let down her hair and removed her steel-rimmed spectacles and a little timidly came out from behind the shelf. Ellery was waiting for her, clad in a dressing gown, seated on the bed.

"You look beautiful!" he said in approval. He patted the bed beside him and a little hesitantly, she went to sit down where he had indicated..

"I always thought," she said "that if I ever went on a honeymoon it would be to Niagara Falls."

"Where's that?" said Ellery absently, picking up a strand of her hair. "So soft and pretty," he said.

"It's in New York. It's a gigantic waterfall." she said nervously.

"Don't be afraid," he said. "I will do nothing you don't like. You've only to say "Stop!" and I will."

"I–." she began, but what she was to say was lost forever as they were interrupted.

"Dr. Delamar!" came a petulant voice from outside the tent. "Is my daughter in there? I want her to make me a cup of tea. I have not been able to shut my eyes for one minute!"

"I'll make you a cup of tea," they heard Sabrina say."I think that they are otherwise occupied." Her voice was sarcastic. "It *is* their wedding night."

"You don't mean–!" came Dr. Beck's horrified accents. "My daughter is a lady! She would never–no, I won't believe that she would allow herself to be debauched!"

They heard Sabrina taking him away, Dr. Beck exclaiming that his daughter would never, ever do *that*.

"If he is so horrified by *that*," said Ellery exasperated "how does he think he got you?"

"My father believes that I sprang full-grown from his head, like Minerva from the head of Zeus," said Atalanta, her lips twitching. She began to giggle, changing to a full-blown laugh as Ellery saw the funny side of it and joined in. They laughed so hard that soon that were clinging to one another, barely able to sit up.

With their faces so close together Ellery took the opportunity to kiss her. And from there matters proceeded quite naturally and happily for both parties.

It was late the next morning before they all finally assembled in the artifact tent, called there by Ellery and Atalanta after they had finally risen from bed.

Nicholas and Marisela, who would not leave his side, Julian, looking hollow-eyed, and Ramón, and Sabrina all came to join them. All the familiars were there as well. There was a great deal to talk over, not the least matter being the contents of the treasure chest.

Marisela told them all she had heard of the black brotherhood's plans. "They were convinced that *IL Diablo* would give them the power to make an invincible army to drive out the *Norteaméricanos*. They said that there were more of them in Mexico and Spain." She shivered and tightened her grip on Nicholas's hand. "*Don* Rafael made me sick, always, but I never thought he was so evil as to consort with the Devil and to sleep with his own mother! *Doña* Paloma's maid also–she enjoyed hurting me so much!"

"Do you know who the other man was?" Ellery asked.

Marisela nodded. "*Sí*, it was *Frey* Felipe, the priest. I am certain now because when I was–what was it you said, Nicolás?"

"Bespelled," he supplied. When she had told him of how strangely she had felt and had behaved before and during her wedding he had known at once that she had been under a spell of compulsion.

"*Sí*, bespelled," Marisela agreed. "He said the nuptial Mass backwards, as they said the Mass before that foul altar."

"We'll notify the proper authorities and get a team of Wizard Repressors on the trail of the other Satanists," said

Ellery.

"And now there is bein' the matter of that chest o' treasure," said Siofra. "We can be givin' it to Lutterworth an' then be returnin' home to Ireland."

They had all been speaking in Spanish, Ellery translating for Atalanta when necessary and at this pronouncement Marisela cried "No!" with an anguished look at Nicholas and Ramón looked both worried and dejected at the thought of losing his teacher.

"I would like to give Lúcás Cinnéidigh a claim on some of that treasure," said Ellery "and I don't see that sitting well with Lutterworth."

"'Tis bein' enough in that box to make all of ye as rich as Croesus!" Siofra said, citing the ancient Lydian King well known for his fabulous wealth. "But that's not bein' the half of it. There's a lot more where that was comin' from."

"And Lutterworth will want every penny of it, once he finds that out, Siofra!" said Julian, in whose lap she was sitting. He still looked and sounded exhausted, but sleep and a restorative session with Ramón had helped him a great deal.

"An' why must we be tellin' him?" Siofra queried. "There's bein' more in that chest to satisfy even a greedy spalpeen such as himself. 'Tis in my mind that the rest of it is belongin' to those wee ones out there, an' to anyone else, human or dragon, who was bein' slaves in the mines and on the farms and such hereabouts. They could be usin' it for food, for housin' an' schoolin'. We can be keepin' it private. I've already been at the children to swear to be tellin' no one. The four of ye can be goin' to th' hillside and makin' a secret entrance wi' a Word such as Ramón here can use. An' I am knowin' that the things in there can be sold for a lot o' brass!" she finished.

Atalanta was the first to speak. "What an excellent idea!" she said.

Ellery seconded it. "Ever since we came here I have been trying to think of a way to address the great need these people have. This will be better than just some charitable contributions: a ready source of good, steady income, properly invested and handled by an honest, able administrator. And I fancy I know just the firm."

457

"Mariposa and Sons." said Nicholas with a grin, naming the financial geniuses behind the Stillfield/Delamar fortunes. "With offices in London, Dublin, New York and lately San Francisco."

"And probably opening one in Albuquerque with such a sizable fortune to be supervised," murmured Cillian.

It was agreed between all of them: whatever was left in the cave was to belong to the former slaves of this area for their future.

"Part of it," said Julian, "ought to be used to build and staff a small hospital, where doctors and nurses might be trained as well. There is a definite need for medical personnel in this area. In fact," he said, raising his head from looking at Siofra in his lap as he stroked her, to look a the rest of them, "I am going to remain here when you return home. It won't be forever," he said at the look on his brother's face "but Ramón needs the rest of his training and while the hospital is being set up they might need my experience."

Everything in Ramón relaxed all at once when he heard his teacher was not planning to leave right away. He desperately wanted his training to continue. There was so much he did not know as yet.

"A school for the children ought to be built as well," said Sabrina "and scholarships for the brightest of them to go on to University."

They were all full of ideas and discussed them eagerly for a few minutes. Finally Ellery said "That does leave two other tasks for us. One will be to clean up the last traces of black magic in this area in the ley lines, and to find out for once and for all where this treasure came from. And there is only one way we can do that."

"Oh, no, Ellery!" said Sabrina shaking her head. "I know where this is leading and I won't have it! You are not laying yourself open to that!"

"We shall have to have a séance," Ellery said, ignoring her protests.

"And who is going to be our medium?" his sister asked caustically.

"Why I am, of course," he said matter-of-factly.

Chapter Forty Eight
American Midas

A.J. Lutterworth had spent most of the night drinking and brooding. Nothing had gone the way he had planned. The so-called experts that he hired had spent most of their time doing everything else but hunt for treasure or finding it. He grew angry every time he thought about the dragonets now over-running the camp, the bastard children and the time wasted searching for and caring for them, the ex-slaves they were so concerned about, the trouble the dragons had caused with the locals and the interference in the way he ran his railroad. Lutterworth was used to things going just as he had planned them, through a combination of his forceful personality and utter ruthlessness. Neither seemed to make much of an impression on these people.

It was late when he woke the next morning, alone in his tent. His head ached slightly and his mouth tasted like cotton wool, but since he had a tremendous capacity for liquor, he was not otherwise discommoded.

His watch had stopped last night as he forgot to wind it, but the morning must be quite advanced, he thought as he emerged from the tent The sun was high in the sky. He winced a little against the brightness of the sun in another clear blue sky.

Where the hell was everyone? he thought in irritation as he looked around. The sides of the tents housing the children had been rolled up and he could see the children sitting up or laying down. He did even see the dragons. What the hell was going on? They hadn't gone out treasure hunting without him! "Sinclair!" he bellowed. Surely his assistant hadn't had the nerve to go off without his employer!

He was rewarded after three more bellows by the appearance of a flustered looking Sinclair."I was just about on my way to awaken you, sir," he said. "It really is the most extraordinary thing! You've got to see this for yourself!"

"Did Stillfield discover another dragon breed? Or is there another damned woman whelping or another wedding?" Lutterworth asked sarcastically. But he followed his assistant to the artifact tent where he found most of the party standing about a table on which rested an empty crate.

Dr. Beck was there as well and said to Lutterworth "Finally! They would not tell me what was going on before you came in!" he said petulantly. It seemed as everyone, including his daughter, knew a secret. Even the animals were in on it.

The back of this tent, too, had been rolled up and the space was filled with dragons, both the two older ones and the four dragonets. Torin also watched with his dragon friends. Ancelin, of course, had returned to end-of-track, and Nah-kah-yen, bearing Ramón, had flown back to the mountain camp.

Ellery turned at the sound of Lutterworth's entrance and said. "We have something here that will no doubt please you very much, Lutterworth." He gestured towards the table.

"A dirty old crate?" Lutterworth said, his lip curling.

"No," said Ellery. He tapped the crate with his wand and said *"Celare contrarium!"* Where has stood a dirty crate now stood a very large chest, made with a domed top, brass-bound and considerably battered. It was closed with a simple hook and eye lock.

Lutterworth stared, his eyes goggling. "It isn't–?" he said in a whisper.

"The treasure?" Ellery inquired. "I would say so. But why don't you open it and look?"

Lutterworth went up to the chest and with shaking hands, undid the hook and threw open the lid, which, if he had not put all of his force behind it might have stuck. As it was, it made a terrible squealing noise.

And as to what lay inside..."I knew it, I knew it!" Lutterworth exulted as he shoved his hands deep in the pile of gold, silver and jewels and then raised them again, allowing them to trickle from his fingers. "It's a King's ransom!"

He turned to look at Ellery. "Where did you find it?" he demanded.

"It was the children who found it, high in the San Mateo Mountains," Ellery answered.

"But that's not what the map said," Lutterworth declared, turning back to the shine of gold and silver.

"We can only guess that it must have been moved sometime in the past," said Sabrina. "Perhaps someone felt it was not safe where it was."

"I don't really care," muttered Lutterworth. "I've got it now and it's all mine." His face shone with greed as he picked up and studied one piece after another.

There were, as well as mounds of gold and silver coins, ropes of pearls, and huge emeralds. A number of jade items of Pre-Columbian art work gleamed green amidst the gold while the mage lights in the tent glinted off a number of sacred vessels, all of which appeared to be stuffed with coins or jewels, both cut and uncut. Necklaces, earrings, bracelets and brooches trickled through Lutterworth's fingers as well as Ecclesiastical jewels meant for the hand of a Bishop, or bejeweled crosses for a clerical neck. Amethysts from Brazil, topaz from Mexico, moonstones from Mexico, emeralds from Brazil, turquoise from here in New Mexico, silver pieces of eight and gold doubloons—the list went on and on. At the very bottom of the chest was a layer of gold ingots.

And the archaeologists knew every piece, for while Lutterworth slept, they had counted, described it and Julian had photographed it, with the aid of a little magic to speed matters along.

"Mine," Lutterworth said again. "This is all there was of it?" he turned to glare at them suspiciously.

"Isn't that enough?" said Nicholas in disgust, in a low voice to Marisela, who stood by his side. "Let's get out of here," he added. picking up Cillian from the floor of the tent and took them both out the front entrance.

"That is all that there was bein' in th' cave," stated Siofra. "An' wasn't I seeing to th' packin' of it me own self?" She uttered the lie without a blink of the eye, her voice strong and firm. "I was givin' the children a wee bit of the coins for their trouble. If 'twas not for them, there would be after bein' no treasure, for 'twas them that shoveled it into the chest and tied the rope about it so that Torin was bein' able to haul it out."

"Gave away some on my treasure?" said Lutterworth, incensed. "It's mine, you mangy fur-ball! You had no right!"

"Mr. Lutterworth, I'll thank you to keep a civil tongue in your head while you are talking to Siofra," said Julian quietly, but intently. "She was the one who saved the treasure for you. The coins the children have are minimal. With what

461

that treasure is worth they are but candlelight to the sun."

He bent down to pick up the little cat and put her on his shoulder. "We need to go to the mission house, Siofra," he said "and tell the ladies that the children are safe. Like Nicholas, I don't care for the atmosphere here any more." With the cat looking backwards from her high perch, Julian headed towards Torin. Siofra, looking back at Lutterworth, stuck her tongue out at the tycoon and made a very rude noise.

"I think you have more than enough reason to be satisfied, Lutterworth," said Ellery. "We have already agreed that we will take no finder's fees. There's enough treasure there for twenty men."

"No finders' fee!" said Dr. Beck, beginning to bleat. "But I agreed to no such thing! Even one percent of that would keep my expeditions funded for years!"

"Ellery and I" said Atalanta with her hand wrapped in her husband's, "have pledged ourselves to keeping your digs properly funded, Papa."

With an unspoken agreement they left the tent as well, Bairre scampering after them, followed by Sabrina and Flann.

"How much can I expect?" called Dr. Beck, hurrying after his daughter and son-in-law.

Sinclair, ignored by Lutterworth, too, faded from the tent. He was a little sickened by the spectacle of his employer's naked greed.

Lutterworth did not notice that he was now by himself, as even the highly interested dragons left the open back of the artifact tent and returned to their sand wallow.

Over and over, Lutterworth ran his hands through the treasure, gloating at its value and beauty, neither knowing nor caring that he had been deserted.

"Nicolás, I must talk to you," said Marisela as they walked away from the artifact tent.

He had been thinking that Lutterworth had looked a

great deal like an illustration of King Midas reveling in his golden touch that had been in one of his childhood books of myths and legends. "Sorry," he now said. "I was lost in a brown study. What is it?" he put Cillian down on the ground, where the hedgehog toddled over to a sun-warmed rock, climbed up on it and went to sleep.

"The cat, she said now that the treasure is found you will be going home across the sea, no?" Marisela said in a rush. "Will you take me with you? I will do anything to stay with you. I will cook and clean or even learn to sew. If you will only take Pacho and me with you, Pacho will work too. We will not be a burden. And," she added with a small voice, her eyes falling "I will come to your bed if you wish and be your *puta* to use as you desire."

"Stop talking like that!" he said roughly and took her by the shoulders. The top of her head just came up to his chin. "Marisela, look at me. Look at me!" he said again when she was slow to do so. "I don't want you as my whore, I want you as my wife!"

Her lips parted in astonishment and she looked up at him with wide yes. "Your wife! But I have been dishonored. I have been naked in front of all of those people and they handled me. I am the widow of a foul man who worshipped the devil!" she added bitterly.

"I don't care!" he declared. "When the butler told me that you had been married, the thought that you now were with someone else nearly killed me. And when I saw you tied to that altar I knew I would kill four hundred Satanists if needs be to prevent them harming one hair on your head. The way you have turned to me since then has been the sweetest—" He broke off. "It's too soon to speak of this. We won't be leaving for a while yet. I want to interview those dragons out at the railhead and Ellery wants to do some actual archaeological work in the ruins on the top of *El Morro.* I am afraid that if I press you to marry me right now you will mistake the gratitude you feel—"

"No, no, no!" she cried. "Since first I met you, you have been all I could think about. I often wished that *Don* Rafael was you, come courting me. Even when I was bespelled and standing in front of the altar with him, I wished it was you."

"Are you certain?" he queried, looking intently at her.

"*Sí*," she answered and put her arms up around his neck. "*Querido!*"

"*Mo mhúirnín bán. Ta grá agan duit,*" he said in Gaelic and kissed her. There was no need for translation.

Cillina, looking at them with one eye open, yawned and said to himself "It looks like another trip to Albuquerque."

Prudence had spent part of every day watching the skies for the hippogriffe. He had said he would come.

She had come very close to blowing the dragon whistle more than once. The days seemed so long since he did not cone daily.

Sister Rebecca said that since Reverend Brewer had been so quiet lately, they must be patient and let the doctor and his friends hunt for the children. Doctor Stillfield could not be running out here every ten minutes because Prudence was nervous. This was said kindly, for Prudence now had a much better relationship with Sister Rebecca and Brother Ezekiel. They now treated her as if she were a beloved niece.

They had been both shocked at the Reverend's treatment of the children. Sister Rebecca had cleaned the discarded toys and put them away carefully, for when they would be wanted again and began making several small aprons, suitable for girls of different ages. Brother Ezekiel had begun to carve more toys: wooden horses on wheels and wooden trains with wheels that turned, both pulled by cords.

If Reverend Brewer even noticed this activity he said nothing about it. He spent much time mumbling to himself and taking long walks in the woods. His appetite disappeared and he became more frail than ever, his often wild-eyed looks adding to his air of one not long for the earth. Sometimes for no apparent reason he would laugh like a mad man, hugging himself in glee as if he possessed a great secret.

Such was the situation when near mid-day one morning Prudence, sweeping the floor of the mission, heard the unmistakable clap of great wings folding as outside Torin landed.

"Oh!" she cried in delight, and dropping the broom, ran outside.

Sister Rebecca, sewing at the table, looked up in surprise and put her sewing aside, rising and going out of doors in a more decorous fashion.

Brother Ezekiel was already out of doors, working on the winter wood-pile. He called out a greeting as Torin came to a halt and Julian dismounted.

Siofra still rode in the front of Julian's jacket for her traveling basket had not as been yet restored to its place behind the saddle. She crawled out of this and sought her usual perch on his shoulder. "Will I be tellin' them or will it be you?" she asked her Wizard.

"I'll do it," he said and said in a louder voice. "I've come with wonderful news! The children are found and they are all well."

Brother Ezekiel and Sister Rebecca said almost as one "Praise the Lord!" Prudence burst into tears of relief and ran to Julian, throwing herself into his arms.

Sister Rebecca and Brother Ezekiel tactfully disappeared as Prudence continued to sob, her worst fears now relieved. He was here, with her again and now everything would be all right. He would even take on Reverend Brewer.

Julian took out his handkerchief and mopped her face with it. She was one of those fortunate women whose looks were enhanced by tears; they made her eyes sparkle and put a pretty colour into her face.

At the look she turned up at Julian, Siofra said in the Gaelic "Holy Bastet, Julian, what was I after warnin' ye about? Th' girl;s fair in love wi' ye!"

In the same language he said "Nonsense! That is insane."

"Look at her, man!" Siofra almost howled. "Never would I have been thinkin' I'd have to call ye stupid, but the time seems to have come!"

Julian looked at her shining eyes and her lips, parted as for a kiss, so close to his. One of her hands had crept up and twisted itself about the lapel of his jacket. His heart sank and he pulled away from her so abruptly that she staggered and nearly fell.

"What is wrong?" she faltered, looking like a child that had been deprived of all her Christmas gifts at once.

"Miss Cromwell," he began, feeling ill at ease and awkward. "Siofra tells me that you seem to be entertaining certain feelings for me–"

"Yes," she said happily, not denying it at all. "I feel wonderful when you are near me! I feel barely alive when you are not here."

"It is not uncommon for a patient. Miss Cromwell, to fancy herself in love with her doctor," he began, only to have her laugh at him.

"I am not your patient!" she said. "And please call me Prudence, Julian," she added a little shyly. "God tells us whom and where to love and the object of our affection is worthy of the great love that God sends."

Siofra rolled her eyes and let out a sigh of exasperation. Had the fool girl never heard of unrequited love or known another woman deep in love with a worthless scalawag?

"Prudence," Julian said a little desperately. "I am certain that I am very honored that your feelings should have lit on me, but I am afraid to have to tell you that I do not return your affections. I don't know if I will ever fall in love again," he added, thinking that if he explained about Sarah she might understand. He quickly outlined, without going into details, what had happened in the spring and that it had left his feelings in shreds. "So you see," he finished up "I am simply not ready–"

"I understand," she said, thinking that this Sarah was the greatest fool in nature. To be loved by such a wonderful man and to throw it over for carnal sin with a married man! God would surely punish her.

But Prudence was also convinced that God had been saving Julian for better things, in other words, to be *hers*.

"You do understand?" Julian said in relief. Telling her had given her thoughts a new direction.

Prudence nodded. He would have been appalled to realize that his confession had only fueled her love for him.

Ellery and Atalanta were having a quiet cup of tea with only Bairre in attendance. Everyone had disappeared on their own business. Sabrina, with Flann's help, was typewriting the notes they had made that morning, Julian was still at the mission with Siofra and Torin, and Nicholas, Cillian and Marisela had flown off on Varian. Lutterworth, of course, was still with his treasure, drooling over it, as Bairre said sarcastically. Sinclair, after staying away from the magnate, had headed back towards the tent. The dragonets and Erianne, like the children, were dozing in the heat of the afternoon. It was *siesta* time, a yawning Lupe said.

It was a warm, rather somnolent afternoon and they had finally gotten rid of Dr. Beck when he had decided it was time for a nap.

Ellery spoke idly of doing an archeological survey of the ruins atop *El Morro* before leaving the area and Atalanta, encouraged by her new spouse, had added her ideas to his.

The thought of a nap with his bride, in which there might or might not be any actual sleeping, was beginning to seem most appealing to Ellery. He was just about to suggest it when they heard someone running and Sinclair, looking wild-eyed, burst into view.

"Dr. Delamar!" he cried. "It's Mr. Lutterworth! I think he's had a heart attack!"

Chapter Forty Nine

Stroke

Ellery, closely followed by Atalanta, ran with Sinclair to the artifact tent. Bairre ran along behind them.

On the floor of the tent they found an unconscious Lutterworth surrounded by gold and silver coins. His face was twisted with pain.

"What happened?" Ellery asked, kneeling beside Lutterworth after kicking away a pile of coins.

"He was telling me what he meant to do with the treasure to safeguard it and suddenly he seemed to have trouble speaking. His next attempt to speak didn't make any sense and then he seemed to lose his balance and fell over. He slipped on the coins on the floor," said a miserable Sinclair. "I think he hit his head on the edge of the table when he fell as well."

Ellery felt the back of Lutterworth's head. When he withdrew his hand it was red with blood. "You're right. Atalanta," he directed, "there's a medical kit in Sabrina's tent. There is a jar of willow bark in it. Will you bring that and some water here, please?"

She nodded and left.

"Bairre," Ellery said. "Go tell Erianne what has happened and ask her to go and fetch Julian from the mission house. We need him."

The ferret nodded and ran out of the tent.

"Let's make him more comfortable," Ellery suggested.

Sinclair agreed and knelt beside him near the afflicted Lutterworth.

"When I was a boy," said Ellery as he loosened Lutterworth's collar "our butler had an attack like this during dinner one evening. Fortunately for him, my father, who is a doctor, was at home. He put the man on his side," he began to turn Lutterworth from his back position in which he was laying and Sinclair quickly helped "and he administered willow bark tea as a first treatment." He straightened Lutterworth's limbs as Atalanta entered the tent once more.

"I saw Erianne take off, going to fetch Julian, no doubt," she said in her calm way. "Here is the willow bark and a tea pot of water. You can use the spout to get it down his throat more easily." She also carried a blanket and pillow and some soft cloths. She put down the bottle of willow bark beside her husband. "Should we try to get him into a bed?" she inquired. The bed she and Ellery had shared was now in another tent, one formerly used for the camp kitchen, as this artifact tent was now housing the treasure. Lupe was now cooking beneath an awning.

"I think it best not to move him until Julian says it's safe," said Ellery. "The pillow and the blanket are a good idea though," he added, smiling at her.

Ellery took out his wand and heated the water, quickly brewing a pot of the tea. Then he used the spigot of the tea pot as an invalid feeder to get as much of the tea as he could into Lutterworth. A good amount of it dribbled down his chin, which Atalanta wiped off. Remembering what his father had done so many years ago, Ellery massaged Lutterworth's throat with his hand to help him swallow. Atalanta cleaned the head injury with one of the cloths and held it in position to contain the bleeding.

All the same, Ellery was very relieved when he heard outside, the noise of both Erianne and Torin returning.

The three of them sat over another cup of tea, Ellery and Atalanta discussing in low tones Lúcás Cinnéidigh's joy when they had given him a share of the treasure, still leaving more than enough for Lutterworth's greed. The Irishman had, with Erianne's help, taken his little family in to Albuquerque early that morning, from where they intended to go back to Ireland.

Sunk in misery, his head buried in his hands, Melville Sinclair sat with them, his cup of tea stood untouched in front of him.

"The doctor's been in there such a long time," Sinclair muttered. "When will we know something? I need to send some telegrams," he added. "If Mr. Lutterworth is to be incapacitated any length of time there will have to be provisions made for the running of his businesses."

"I can have Erianne take you to the telegraph line at the railway camp," said Ellery "Or perhaps Nicholas–where *is* Nicholas?" he inquired, as he realized that he had not seen his nephew in quite a while.

"I believe he took Marisela flying," said Atalanta. "They have been gone some time."

Bairre looked a little uneasy and then blurted out. "They haven't just gone flying," the ferret said. "Cillian told me. They've gone to Albuquerque to get married."

"Get married?" Ellery echoed in shock. "But he scarcely knows the girl! He's only known her for–"

"About the same length of time that you have known me," Atalanta finished with a level look at her spouse.

"And then Cillian said that they were going to go to the *Hacienda* to collect her things," Bairre said in a rush, "Cillian didn't think that they would return until this evening."

Marisela had wanted nothing to remind her of the first ceremony she had undergone with *Don* Rafael. She wanted no flowers, no decorated carriage, no white dress. Nicholas bought her new trousers, shirt, vest and boots and she was married in these. She chose a simple gold band for her new wedding ring and made the jeweler stammer in happiness when she gave him the band of rubies placed on her hand by *Don* Rafael. She never wanted to see it again and was uncaring of how much it might be worth.

Nicholas, too, was glad for a simple ceremony. He was afraid that Ellery or Sabrina might try to talk him out of marrying her. Doing so was an impulsive decision, but he was certain that it was one he would never regret. He was also afraid, as she was, that if her parents found out they might cast a spanner into the works. They were both relieved to find out from the Justice of the Peace, that in the new United States Territory of New Mexico, the age of consent was eighteen, not twenty-one, and once she was legally married to Nicholas, no one could do a thing about it.

The ceremony was short and simple and to Marisela, who was used to a long mass in Latin at any of the weddings she had attended, it seemed strange. It was in English too, parts of which Nicholas had to translate. The only witnesses were the Justice's wife, Varian and Cillian. Since dragons familiars were sentient creatures, it was quite legal for either one of them to be a witness.

"I shall have to learn better English, no?" she said when they left the Justice of he Peace's home. They had been married in the garden so that Varian could be with them.

"It might be very useful for you to learn the Gaelic as well," suggested Cillian from the crook of Nicholas's arm. Varian, walking in the street beside the board sidewalk, nodded his head in agreement.

"Two languages?" Marisela said in dismay.

"Don't worry, *mo mhíle stór*," said Nicholas "I have a friend back in Ireland who can teach you a language faster than you could ever imagine." He smiled, thinking of Oberon.

"Was that English, what you called me?" she demanded.

"That was the Gaelic. Translated it means 'my thousand treasures' and is generally used to mean 'darling', " he explained.

"My thousand treasures," she repeated in delight.

"Much more dear than any treasure of gold, silver or jewels," he said softly. "I will show you just how dear tonight when we are alone. But now we have to go and see your parents."

A shadow fell across her face. "Nicolás, I don't want–" she began.

"You need never see them again after this," he said. "But they ought to know what happened to *Don* Rafael and that you are now my wife. They need to be warned about the black magicians in the area. And you want your things, don't you?"

The only thing she really wanted was her little photograph of Rodri and she wanted that very much. It and her memories were all that she had left of him.

Don Casimiro sat in his library feeling put upon. He had just sustained two very trying visits.

The first had been from his banker. His account, even with the gold from the *Norteaméricanos* for the beef, was overdrawn. There were just too many directions for the money to go.

The *Don* had been surprised at this, for *Don* Rafael had promised to place a significant sum in the account of his future father-in-law once Marisela was his. Casimiro had fully expected a draught from Rafael on the afternoon of the wedding as he had promised. What could have happened? Could Rafael just have forgotten? But no, Rafael was a *caballero* and would not do such a thing; it would be dishonorable in the extreme.

The problem was that Casimiro had no idea how to get in touch with his new son-in-law to perhaps jog his memory about the money. He supposed that the bridegroom and his bride were halfway to New Orleans by now, given how fast these new locomotives were. He had read in an Albuquerque newspaper that there were trains which could go as fast as fifty miles an hour. Casimiro was stymied as to what to do. He needed that money he had been promised! The bank refused to honor any more overdrafts.

The second visitor had been *Frey* Felipe's housekeeper. The priest seemed to have disappeared. He had not been seen since the wedding ceremony. And as *Don* Casimiro was the natural leader of the Spanish community here, the housekeeper had come to him.

Unfortunately for the housekeeper *Don* Casimiro had no more idea what to do about the missing priest than he did about his credit problems. He supposed he could send some *vaqueros* out looking for the man. He might have been paying a parish call and fallen somewhere, perhaps been too injured to get on his feet again. He promised the housekeeper that this would be done and sent for Curro, to tell him to direct the men in a search.

When this was put in train he sat for some time in his

library, brooding. The gold of the *Norteaméricanos* might not be his too much longer. That *hechicero brujo* Stillfield had looked none too pleased when he had been told that none of them were welcome here any more. In spite, they might withdraw from the contract. The *Don* was not certain that a United States court would take his side against them, even if they had broken the contract.

But at least the danger of his daughter's involvement with them was past. Marisela was safely married, and on her way to glittering future as the wife of one of Spain's most noble *caballeros*. Soon, hopefully, all of the *Norteaméricanos* and their dragons would be gone as well. The only thing *Don* Casimiro would regret was their gold.

He hoped that he would never have to deal with magical persons and their creatures ever again. He did not like talking animals, creatures that could breathe fire or the fact that one never knew if a *brujo* might take it into this head to turn one into a donkey.

For some time he had been becoming conscious of a great deal of noise outside the thick door of his library. There had been some shouting, even a scream and the sound of running feet. He supposed it to be some kitchen crisis perhaps, or even a bill collector. These Americans did not know their place. In the old days, no one would have dared call upon a *caballero* to demand money of him. It was an honor for them to be owed money by a man like himself.

So suddenly that *Don* Casimiro jumped in fright, the door was thrown open and his wife was there, looking wild-eyed. "Casimiro!" she said in a shrill, hysterical voice "Come at once! It is Marisela! She is back!"

"Our daughter has returned?" he said, frowning. "What has happened? Was *Don* Rafael not pleased with her?" A horrible thought came into his mind. Perhaps all of the freedom they had allowed Marisela had caused her to be unchaste. Perhaps *Don* Rafael had discovered this on the wedding night and he had repudiated her. Perhaps he would demand compensation for being dishonored!

He rose and went with his wife. She had to run to keep up with his long stride and she panted out disjointed phrases that made no sense to him about *brujos* and dragons in the courtyard and Marisela telling stories.

The *Don* found the inner courtyard a scene of turmoil. He had to fight his way through a crowd of servants, all staring at the never even imagined sight of a pale green dragon curled about the fountain.

There was his daughter, shamelessly clad in trousers, an outfit he had never thought to see her wear again. There was no sign of Rafael, only the Stillfield *brujo* and his cactus-like creature.

Don Casimiro was filled with anger. Had he not made it plain to these people that he and his family wanted nothing more to do with them? And to bring a dragon here, into the innermost part of their home! What was Marisela doing with the *brujo*?

"Daughter!" he thundered. "Where is your husband?"

Marisela looked him right in the eye and said "Here," laying her hand on Nicholas's arm.

"He's had a massive stroke with considerable damage," said Julian. "The stroke was caused by a blood vessel in the brain bursting and spilling into the brain. I've sealed up the damage as best I can but with that type of stroke, brain cells are damaged immediately and even those beyond the burst vessels are damaged when they are deprived of blood."

"A stroke–that's the same as a heart attack, isn't it?" said Sinclair.

Julian shook his head. "That's a common misconception. A heart attack causes damage to the muscle of the heart, usually caused by a blockage to the flow of the blood into the heart, in very simplified terms. A stroke is a brain injury in this case, caused by, as I said, a bursting blood vessel. The usual cause of such an attack is uncontrolled high blood pressure."

He had spent over an hour with the stricken Lutterworth, Sabrina helping as much as she could. She and the two cats, purring their most soothing purrs, were sitting with Lutterworth while Julian came out to talk to the others.

"Do you know if Lutterworth has a personal physician, perhaps back in New York?" Julian asked Sinclair. "I would really like to talk to him, either via a telegram or a scry bowl, if possible. I would like to know if Lutterworth has been in treatment for his high blood pressure. Any competent physician would have referred him to a Wizard Healer, who could give him injections of mistletoe-based medication for the blood pressure."

"He saw a doctor called Morton Grant," Sinclair answered, "several times. But Mr. Lutterworth always called him 'that quack' and said he was an old woman. I know that he had a list of recommendations but Mr. Lutterworth paid no attention to them. One of the recommendations was to curtail his drinking."

"Which is why he is in the state he is now," said Julian. "The prognosis is not good. There is paralysis on the left hand side and he is suffering from a mild concussion as well. He struck his head with some force. Before I started the treatment he had another minor stroke. When the pressure is that high, for as long a time as I suspect, it can cause the small arteries in the brain to become brittle and rupture very easily. Even with magic, there is only so much sealing and restoration I can do. And it's delicate surgery. Right now, I've put him into a healing sleep." Again, he looked drawn and tired, scarcely recovered from the previous day's work.

"There's a strange dragon coming!" Erianne called, "With a rider!"

Ellery stood up. Who could this be?

A brilliantly red dragoness spiraled down and landed neatly near Erianne and the dragonets. She wore a black harness that had a large gold saddle cloth. On the sides of the cloth was emblazoned "UNITED STATES GOVERNMENT".

They watched as the dragon crouched down and her rider slid off. The rider pulled off his flying cap to reveal the face of a complete stranger, a young, dark-skinned man with friendly features. "Dr Ellery Delamar?" he called out.

Ellery stepped forward. "Yes?" he said. What was this all about?

The young man came to meet him, with an outstretched hand and an engaging grin. "I'm Benjamin Swift. I'm from Senator Connelly's office. I understand there is some dragon trouble out here? Selena and I are here to fix it," he said, indicating his dragon.

"Good Lord!" said Ellery. He had almost forgotten the telegrams he had sent to Washington. What was going to happen next? he thought wryly.

Chapter Fifty
Another Wedding Night

Both Benjamin Swift and his dragon accepted a cup of tea. While the dragoness went to talk to Erianne and coo over the dragnets, Swift sat down with the humans after removing the rest of his flying suit. After introductions had been performed, Julian excused himself, going back to his patient.

"We've actually been in the area for several days," Benjamin Swift admitted cheerfully as Atalanta poured him a cup of tea. "We like to scout out a situation. One of the things we looked at was the railroad camp. We noticed that there are more than a few dragons employed there."

"We have recently found out that it was the dragons from the railway camp who were stealing the cows from the local landowners," Ellery told him. "They were forced to do so as the owner of the railroad was neither feeding them adequately, nor paying them for their labor."

One of Swift's mobile eyebrows rose. "Oh? That's a serious Federal offense," he said, sipping at his cup of fragrant Darjeeling. "Not paying a dragon for his or her work is tantamount to slave labor and expressly forbidden by law. Why, we'd be no better than the Inquisition! What railroad line is it again?"

"The Taos, Phoenix and Albuquerque," Atalanta supplied.

Swift took out a small notebook and a stub of a pencil from a pocket inside his jacket. "That's owned by Aloysius Jochebed Lutterworth, isn't it?"

"Mr. Lutterworth prefers to use his initials," said Sinclair.

"I can see why," murmured Atalanta, glad to hear of someone with an even worse name–and two of them–than hers. Somehow, her name did not sound half as bad when Ellery used it.

"I shall have to talk to Mr. Lutterworth," said Swift, finishing his notes and then draining his cup. Atalanta poured him another. "Thank you, ma'am," he said, smiling at her. "There's nothing like a cup of British-made tea." Atalanta did not point out to him that she had made it and she was an

American.

"Mr. Lutterworth is actually here at the moment" Ellery informed the young man "but I doubt anyone will be talking to him for a while yet. He had a stroke earlier this evening. My nephew, Dr. Stillfield, whom you net so briefly, is attending him."

Swift frowned. "Then who is in charge?"

"I'm not certain," said Sinclair. "I knew the attorneys back in New York would have insisted on a contingency plan in case of illness, but I need to get to end-of-track and telegraph."

"Selena and I will take you there," Swift offered. "We want to interview the dragons and we'd like to know as soon as possible who will be empowered to answer question for Mr. Lutterworth, particularly if there may be a criminal investigation."

"A criminal investigation?" Sinclair blanched.

"Sometimes these things can be settled out of court with a stiffish fine," said Swift cheerfully. He drank the last of his second cup of tea and stood up. "It's almost dark. It will be a good time to interview the dragons' after they've finished up for the day." He thanked them for their help and hospitality, then called to Selena. She left Erianne and the dragonets with a quick goodbye. Soon Swift and Sinclair were strapped in and the red dragon took to the sky.

"It sounds as if Mr. Lutterworth could be in a lot of trouble," said Bairre. He had his own tea cup. Atalanta was going to have to get used to brewing enough tea for ferrets and dragons. "Poor Mr. Sinclair is very upset."

"And Lupe will be very upset if we do not come to dinner soon," said Atalanta, rising and beginning to collect the tea things. "She has been waving at us from the cook-tent for nearly half an hour. Should I go and wake my father, Ellery?"

"Since I have known your father, he has never been late for a meal." said Ellery wryly. "And here he is," he added, as Dr. Beck emerged from his tent, looking cross. He began at once to complain that he had gotten no sleep with all of the noise of people coming and going; the clap of wings and dragons and who knew what else taking off and landing.

Atalanta opened her mouth to apologize to him but

instead felt Ellery's hand on hers. "It is no longer your concern," her husband said softly. "If he chooses to be hard to please and unhappy ,the choice is his."

It was that simple, Atalanta thought gratefully.

"I wish you had not given my parents money, Nicolás," said Marisela frowning at her bridegroom as they set up a wedding night camp site in the little canyon on the other side of *El Morro*.

Nicholas straightened up from the ley line fire he was constructing with a pile of rocks. "It's customary even in Ireland, amongst moneyed families. We call it a settlement. If we had been married in Ireland we would have met with your family's lawyers and mine and the exact financial details of what exactly you and your family could expect from me. You'd know to the penny what you would get for pin-money–"

"What is pin-money?" she interrupted.

"An allowance, or pocket money," he explained. "Most women also get a dress allowance."

She made a face. "I prefer my trousers, no?"

"There will be times when you have to wear a gown," he began.

"But it will be of my choosing and it will be comfortable, no? And I will never wear a corset, no matter what my *suegra* my mother-in-law) thinks," Marisela stated.

"Nicholas laughed. "My mother will be delighted that you won't wear a corset. She never has. But I felt I ought to offer your poor father some compensation," he said teasingly. "They were so disappointed that you are not to be a rich *Marquesa* and shine in Madrid society."

"But did you see their faces when I told them of *Don* Rafael and his mother consorting with the Devil!" Marisela said, almost gleefully.

"I thought your poor mother would have an apoplexy," said Cillina on a yawn. He had hammered out the details of the settlement with *Don* Casimiro and had not let the *Don* take advantage of Nicholas's offer.

Varian, laying nearby, said nothing. Used to the close ties and genuine love amongst Nicholas's family, he had been more than a little shocked at the callous attitude of Marisela's parents. Her mother was more horrified by the scandal, when at last she could be brought to believe the *Don* Rafael and his mother were as bad as Marisela was telling them. They had shown little compassion for their daughter, only berating her for marrying a *Norteaméricano* not of her faith and not going into mourning for a man who had nearly debauched her. It was remarkable how the scolding had turned to false smiles when Nicholas had offered them money. If Marisela was a little hard towards them, Varian could understand why.

"This is a nice spot for a wedding night," the dragon said into a sudden silence.

"You won't mind sleeping out under the stars?" Nicholas inquired of Marisela. "Varian will keep watch over us–"

"And we will give you your privacy," Varian said, looking at Cillian.

Marisela smiled a trifle sadly. "You have already seen me naked, *amigo.*"

"But it would be very, very rude and ill-bred to watch you and Nick being – er – together," said Varian. If dragons could blush, his face would have been red.

"As to that," Nicholas began. "Marisela, if after today, you want to wait until we become intimate, if you are in the least bit shy or frightened, I understand. We have all of our lives in front of us and we could even wait until we get back to Ireland if you would feel easier about it." This was a great sacrifice on his part, for he was eager to make love to her. But he wanted it to be right for her as well. After what she had gone through today....

She stood up from the rock she had been sitting upon and, coming up to him, wound her arms about his neck. "Never would *Don* Rafael make such an offer," she said. "Nicolás, in one day you have been my *novio,* my *fiancé,* my *esposo,*my husband and now you will be my *amante,* my lover also." She bent and kissed him.

Cillian closed his eyes and Varian turned his back.

It had been a quiet evening. Julian and Sabrina and their cats had remained with Lutterworth. Atalanta and Ellery had taken trays to them and fed the again ravenously dragonets, then tried to enjoy their own meal, which was difficult in the face of Dr. Beck's constant complaining.

He could not reconcile himself to the fact that he was going to lose Atalanta's services as secretary and general dogsbody. While they were eating he proposed that he resign from Seneca College, go to Ireland and live with them. That way Atalanta could still accompany him on his digs when Ellery went to Egypt.

Horrified, Atalanta started to exclaim against this until she heard Ellery say, in a pleasant but firm way "No. My wife will be accompanying me to Egypt. You will have to go to Greece or Rome by yourself. Atalanta's new field will be Egyptology. And as for living with us; I don't approve of starting a marriage off with in-laws under the same roof. It isn't necessary as we won't have the financial constraints most young couples have. We'll either buy or build a home in Dublin and I have a more or less permanent home in Egypt as well. But there will be no room for you in either one."

Dr. Beck looked at him in amazement, his jaw dropping. "Are you going to let him talk to me that way?" he demanded of his daughter.

"Yes," she said and put her hand in Ellery's.

"Let's have a swim in the cache basin before bed," Ellery suggested. Dr. Beck was not included in the invitation.

After a satisfying interlude both in the water and on the bank of the pool, they walked back to the camp site.

It was now full dark. The camp looked deserted, lit by mage lights and the light of the moon and stars. A low light shone from the tent where Lutterworth was being watched.

Erianne had been watching for them and now came forward.

"You missed Varian," she said. "He came by briefly to tell us that Nick and Marisela won't be back until morning. They are camping out in a nearby canyon."

"A wedding night under the stars," said Atalanta "How romantic."

Erianne said shortly "Yes", looking rather distracted and then burst out "I need to talk to you both about Amyas."

"Is something wrong with him?" Atalanta asked quickly. "He seemed fine when we fed them."

"No, it's just that I was talking to Torin earlier and something he said made me realize that we will have to transport four dragonets and two adult dragons home. Eda is bonded to Sabrina and Seneca to you, Atalanta, and Pacho to Marisela. But Amyas belongs to no one. He is extraneous."

"He belongs to you," said Atalanta.

"You don't think he should be left behind, for someone else to take care of?" Erianne said.

Ellery kept quiet. This conversation might establish the relationship between his wife and his bonded dragon and he wanted that to be a good one. Atalanta was already getting on very well with Bairre.

"Four dragonets won't be any more trouble that three and we can't leave him behind. You won't want to be separated from him any more that he would want to leave you," Atalanta said. "As far as we are concerned, it's as if he was from your egg." She hoped she had phrased that properly.

She had. A look of relief spread over Erianne's features and she briefly touched her muzzle to Atalanta's hair, a caress from a dragon to a human he or she felt affection for.

Ellery's satisfaction was complete, when of her own accord, Atalanta made a nest of blankets for Bairre up above their pillows and invited him to share their bed that night as they would be going to sleep, having already enjoyed a most satisfactory encounter near the cache basin.

"Tomorrow," she promised the ferret, "we'll work out a signal to tell you when we want to be alone."

As Ellery fell asleep, with his arms around his wife, his familiar contentedly sleeping above his head where he could touch his Wizard when he wanted to do so and feeling through the bond with Erianne her happiness, he himself was conscious of a deep, overwhelming contentment and slid easily into sleep. All was right with the world.

In the morning when they woke for their sunrise walk, Ellery and Atalanta found Melville Sinclair sitting at the table under the awning drinking coffee. He looked weary, as if he had not gotten much sleep and also, Ellery thought, a trifle bemused, as if something had surprised him.

After greeting them he said "A lot will be happening in the next few days. For one thing, the railroad will be starting up again and will come within a few miles of here. When it does, we'll be moving Mr. Lutterworth to a train and then transporting him back to New York. Dr. Stillfield has already agreed to accompany us. I've put Jack Ballard in temporary charge of the railroad's progress until I can find a good manager."

"Until *you* can find a good manager?" Atalanta said. "It sounds as if you've been put in charge, Mr. Sinclair."

"I have," he said, a strange expression on his face. "I was never more surprised. It's all in his will, just as he said. But I never thought–" He shook his head as if to clear it and said "You probably thinking I'm crazy. But, you see, Mr. Lutterworth is my real father, although he never married my mother. I was adopted by the Sinclairs when I was a baby."

"How did you find out?" Ellery asked.

"When I graduated from college one of his attorneys came to see me and told me the whole story. They had always kept track of me on Mr Lutter– on my father's orders."

"He had a proposition for me. If I came to work for him and proved worthy, he'd leave me his estate." He smiled ruefully. "It was too tempting to resist. I had grown up poor and I had put myself through college. The Sinclairs, whom I will always think of my *real* parents, were getting old and would need financial help. And I hoped to get to know him, and to learn about my real mother from him. I can't tell you how many times I almost walked out. He isn't an easy person–"

An understatement if there ever was one, Ellery thought.

"I was flabbergasted when the attorneys told me that I had been in his will almost from before the time I went to work for him," Sinclair continued. "And as his heir I am his natural successor. Dr. Stillfield thinks a full recovery is extremely unlikely and Mr. Lutter – my father, will be lucky to regain even part of his faculties. So I have to take charge and it will be all made legal as soon as we reach New York."

"But there will be a lot of changes," he said, looking at them both earnestly. "I had a long talk with Mr. Swift and he said if I institute reforms there will be no charges laid. I intend to pay back wages to all the workers, including the dragons. There will be better food and a company doctor. There will also be a claim against part of the treasure by the government, so we won't be able to keep it all. In fact. Mr Swift and a US Marshal will be coming here a little later today to take charge of the treasure."

He also assured them that the monies promised to Trinity and the additional bonuses for finding the treasure would be paid. He then excused himself and went to sit with Lutterworth.

"Well", said Atalanta, looking after him as he walked away. "What a strange turn of events! Somehow I cannot see Mr. Sinclair as a ruthless railroad baron."

"The railroad will be in good hands, though," said Ellery. "A lot of people and dragons will be better off, treated fairly for once."

"So now we are free to do real archaeology again?" Bairre asked eagerly from Ellery's shoulder.

Ellery shook his head. "Only until we can have that séance. I must know how that treasure got here! And don't take sides with Sabrina, please," he said to his spouse. "I have to know."

"I quite agree with you," she said in her brisk, no nonsense fashion. "When would you like to have it?"

"You are a woman in a million!" he said gratefully and gave her a quick kiss on the cheek.

"Knowledge must be served," she said. "And besides, I

want to know as well."

"We'll do it when Julian gets back from New York," he said. "Wizard Healers are trained in these matters."

Chapter Fifty One
Voice of the Dead

It took several days for the railway to be built close enough to the camp at *El Morro* for Lutterworth to be transferred to a train and from there transported to New York.

In that time there was little improvement in his condition. He was still paralyzed and unable to speak, even with Julian's best efforts. Lutterworth had regained consciousness, but his vile temper, even when doused with a herbal relaxant, caused him to have another small stroke which impeded his progress towards recovery. He was still able to glare and even move his right arm enough to throw things at those who were trying to help him. Julian and Sabrina put a stop to this with a magical barrier. Julian told Lutterworth that if he did not quit, he would make certain that his right arm was rendered useless by magic. He would not do such a thing, of course, but Lutterworth did not know it.

It was with relief that the other inhabitants of the *El Morro* camp saw Lutterworth transported to a train and depart for New York, with Julian and Sinclair at his side, along with two nurses hired from Albuquerque.

By the time they left Ellery and his wife and sister had already begun a systematic survey of the ruins atop El Morro. An expert, or as much of an expert as anyone could be on a subject so little explored, was coming from California, to take over the excavation.

While the archaeological business was going forward, Nicholas. with Varian, Cillian and Marisela, was interviewing dragons both at end-of track and those who lived in the hills. These last were brought to Nicholas's notice by Ramón, who waited anxiously for his teacher's return. Nicholas was able to compile a chilling picture of the exploitation and evil treatment of the native dragons by the Inquisition, and discover several hithertofore unknown breeds.

To Ellery, it felt wonderful to get back to real archaeological work, even though it was not in his beloved Egypt. He soon found that Atalanta worked effortlessly with both himself and Sabrina, her mind quick, her training every bit as good as his own.

And to their immense relief Dr. Beck returned to New York with the Lutterworth party. He was totally uninterested in the archaeology of the southwest and wanted to go home to prepare for his next expedition to Greece in the autumn, now that he had funds and the prospect of more.

The only disagreeable note in all of this was Sabrina's complete dislike of conducting any sort of *séance* at all, much less one where Ellery had volunteered himself as the medium. She was unalterably opposed to it. It did not matter where the treasure had come from. She felt that sometimes one just had to accept that it was not possible to know these things.

But Ellery was adamant. The presence of the ghosts in the caves and the spirit revenant clinging to the uncut emerald told him that there was a way to solve the mystery and he was determined to find out the hows and whys. A *séance* seemed the only way to secure this knowledge. When Julian returned, there would be a *séance* in the cave where the cats had seen the ghosts.

Sabrina could convince none of them that this might be dangerous. Nicholas had had more experience with ghosts than any of them and even he could not be brought around to Sabrina's way of thinking. They all insisted that as long as there were other mages present, particularly a Wizard Healer and more particularly the cats, there was little danger to Ellery. Both a trained Healer and a cat could control a ghost or even ghosts. But Sabrina was miffed with Atalanta that she did not want to protect her husband from malign influences.

However, Atalanta agreed with him. It was shoddy scholarship not to use every method of finding out the reason *why*. Both Flann and Siofra had assured her that they could command the spirits and by now she had enough confidence in them to believe this.

All the same, she was quite curious as to what happned at a *séance*. For some years now, spiritualism had been prevalent in American society. Several of Atalanta's mother's friends, who had lost spouses or children, had visited mediums, hoping for messages from 'the other side'. But

490

Atalanta had never attended one of these gatherings, nor, if truth be told, had much interest in the subject. But of course, it was different now, for she was intimately connected to the main participants.

One morning shortly before the time scheduled for Julian's return, Ellery and Atalanta were working, not on top of the cliffs, but on the rock of *El Morro* itself, where they were copying and noting both the petroglyphs and some four hundred years of carved inscriptions. Julian had already taken extensive photographs of these, but Ellery liked to have a scale drawing, a written description a coloured painting as well as a rubbing, if possible. They had already completed a detailed survey of the area. Bairre, keeping them company, was stretched out on a sunny rock, dozing in the sun, which was now growing warmer as the month of June advanced.

Atalanta admired her husband's thoroughness. She did not find his insistence on detail at all tedious, but commendable. It was just how she would have done it herself. No matter what Dr. Beck's objectionable personality traits might be, he was a praiseworthy, careful and meticulous excavator and he had trained his daughter well.

Atalanta had decided to make as many rubbings of the inscriptions as she was able. Armed with a small brush, a rounded ball of black wax and sheets of rice paper she chose a particularly florid carving to rub to obtain an image and industriously cleaned it with water and a small brush, coaxing debris from the carvings and cleaning the work surface.

"Oh dear," she said, when ready to begin rubbing. "I forgot to get some flour from Lupe to make a paste to hold my paper in place."

"No need," Ellery said and took out his wand. Pointing it at her stack of rice paper he said " *Visidus.*" The paper gave a small leap and then subsided. "The paper will stick to any surface you like now," Ellery told her.

Atalanta picked up a piece and found that it nearly tore itself from her hand to adhere to the rock. "Oh, I do like magic!" she said gratefully.

Ellery watched her with pleasure as she worked. She was brisk and competent and he could not have bettered her technique. Beginning at the bottom, with smooth, even strokes, she rubbed a piece of wax over the rice paper, producing a reverse image of the inscription.

"I cannot read Spanish," she commented, "but it seems to me that some of the words in these inscriptions run together."

"They do," Ellery agreed "and there are some every creative abbreviations as well. It will be a challenge to decipher them, almost as if one were breaking a code."

They worked in companionable silence for a moment. Ellery was taking exacting measurements of the inscriptions with a tape.

Finally Atalanta asked "I am afraid I am quite ignorant about *séances*. What exactly happens?"

Ellery put down the measuring tape and turned to look at her. Her gaze behind the spectacles was bright and curious with little trace of the looks of trepidation Sabrina had been wearing lately.

"We'll gather in the cave at midnight, which is the best time to contact the spirits. Julian will put me in a trance to which I hope the sprits respond and they will speak to the rest of you through me. We'll also have a *planchette* for automatic, or spirit writing and several other methods as well. I am hoping for a physical manifestation," he answered.

"What is that?" she asked.

"There are two types of manifestations," he explained "one is mental, in which the medium reveals the presence of the spirit by clairvoyance or clairaudience, or perhaps writing with the planchette, or using a spelling glass. A physical manifestation would be a table rising of its own accord, knocking, lights, rushing winds, levitation and even spirit materialization."

"It sounds a little frightening," she admitted, laying down her wax and looking at him. Now she wore a frown and there was a look of anxiety in her eyes. "Ellery, I've only just found you. I could not bear it if–"

He got up and came to sit beside her on the ground. Putting an arm around her, he said soothingly," I am having Julian put me in a trance rather than trying to enter it on my own for safety's sake. He will be in control and will be able to bring me back immediately should there be any problem at all. And both cats will be there. Spirits like and respect cats.

Cats have special powers over spirits and ghosts. No one can be harmed by a ghost when there is a cat present."

She hoped he was right. She was beginning to understand why Sabrina was so against this.

They went by dragonback out to the caves the very night of Julian's return. Varian and Torin, in a rare spirit of sacrifice, agreed to stay with the dragonets so that Erianne could be near her bond-mate in this undertaking.

The dragonets knew that something was going on and as a result, were boisterous and difficult to control. Pacho especially was in high spirits now that Marisela was available to him all of the time. Upon finding out that he was to stay with the rest of his friends and not remain behind when the others went to Ireland, he was wild with delight. In his opinion, Marisela could not have chosen a better husband than Nicholas, who knew and understood dragons so well.

Marisela was more than little nervous about the *séance*. She had been raised to believe that such things were wrong; that the Inquisition and the Church forbade such unholy black magic.

Sabrina had provided both Marisela and Atalanta a robe to wear to the *séance*, as no Witch or Wizard went anywhere without a selection of appropriate robes. Marisela had listened in some dismay as to the meaning of the soft, violet coloured robe which was beautifully embroidered with sprigs of lavender. "It is one of the colours of air and a séance is an air ritual. Don't worry," Sabrina told her kindly when Marisela looked confused. "You'll get to learn all of the colours and what they signify and what ritual soaps and oils are used at what time. Nick's mother will take you under her wing and be sure that you learn these things. As the non-magical wife of a Wizard you can participate in our rituals by dressing appropriately."

Marisela did enjoy the ritual bath with lavender soap in the purest clearest water she had ever seen. Then Nicholas helped her anoint herself with sandalwood oil. That part she enjoyed very much. Sandalwood oil among other things, opened the world to spirit guides.

She was somewhat startled to learn that she was to wear the robe over her bare skin, closed only with a sash of intertwined blue, violet and yellow cords. It was in an intricate pattern that Nicholas told her was Celtic knot work.

He wore a hooded white robe, with a sash like hers. "I wear white because I am also a Druid," he explained.

Marisela looked perplexed for a minute. She had no idea what this meant. "I have much to learn, no?" she said at last.

"And there are any number of people and books in Ireland to teach you," he said "including me. And for right now I would advise wearing a pair of knickers under your robe before the ceremony begins. You do not want to sit on a dragon saddle without some protection."

It was a bit different for Atalanta. She had read of some of the Ritual clothing and symbolism behind the practice of magic, for her reading was wide and eclectic in nature. She had read of Witchcraft Rituals: how the Witches gathered the goodness of the moon into their uncovered bodies and sent it into the earth through their dances for the benefit of the crops, and of Wizards' Rituals as well as those of the Druids. Magicians made no attempt to hide their secrets; indeed non-magical persons were often invited to come to Rituals and observe and even participate in a limited way. It was rather thrilling that she would now, as the wife of Wizard, take part in all of this.

She did not find the robe as strange as did Marisela, nor was the colour symbolism as confusing. Since far back in history colour had significant meaning in different cultures and she anticipated having no trouble ingesting all the new information she would have to learn.

She was surprised when Ellery, after donning his white robe, turned it to silver with the aid of his wand.

"Silver develops psychic abilities," he explained. "As I

am to be the medium tonight, I need it to help me on the highest level. It usually is not done, to change the colour of one's robe magically, but a silver *séance* robe is not one I usually carry with me."

"Why are you the medium?" she queried.

"Becuse I have the most natural psychic talent of any of us, except for Julian," he said, knotting the corded sash about his waist over the shimmering silver robe. "My pyschometry makes me the best candidate as Julian is needed to put me into trance and then hopefully, release the spirits to a higher plane so that the caves will no longer be haunted."

She looked worried and he gave her a quick kiss. "Don't fret. It will be all right. We've a highly trained Wizard Healer and the cats and after tonight we will know the answer to the riddle of where this treasure came from."

It was a half an hour before midnight when Erianne landed her party outside the cave where Varian had fallen.

Earlier, Nicholas and Julian had come out and made some initial preparations. They had cleansed the site of psychic dirt, set up a table and chairs taken from beneath the awning at the camp and placed the dozens of candles that would illuminate the scene and served the purpose of dispelling stagnant energies. They were white candles, which had been blessed.

As it had not yet become dark yet, Yancy Yates had followed them into the cave, curious as to what they were doing. When he heard they were going to try to deliberately contact the 'haunts', he declared his intention of being nowhere near the caves that night. Sinclair was still employing him to guard the caves as the new railroad tycoon had not decided what to do with him. Sinclair had no desire to put the cowboy out of work. He hoped to find a position with cattle for Yates, perhaps in herding good quality beef on the hoof for the railroad workers.

It was cool out when they landed. Atalanta and Marisela both felt chilly in thin robes over bare bodies but the others seemed impervious to the cold air.

Julian was dressed in Healer's green, in a robe embroidered with representations of feathers, symbolizing the air ritual that a summoning of spirits was.

He lead the way into the caves, lighting all the candles in the corners with a wave of his wand as he passed. The two cats trotted ahead while Bairre rode on Ellery's shoulder and Nicholas carried a sleepy Cillian.

There were literally dozens of these candles, of all heights and widths, and all were white. Julian had brought them back from New York for this night's work.

There were no mage lights. In contrast to the bright steady light that a mage light gave out, the candlelight was wavering, causing long shadows to race over the walls, the flames stirred by the slightest breeze. Dark corners behind the speleothems, or cave deposits, seemed to be full of moving creatures.

Erianne followed them into the main cave where there was enough room for dragons. She lay down, not too close to the table, wings folded, tail curled around her haunches and legs tucked underneath her body. She shared Sabrina's dislike of this Ritual and was determined to keep a stern draconic eye on Ellery and snatch him away from danger if necessary.

Julian had them take their seats, seating clockwise Ellery at the head of the now round, magically altered table, with Atalanta beside him, then Sabrina, Julian at the foot, opposite Ellery, then Nicholas and lastly Marisela. Cillian sat in his Wizard's lap. Atalanta was touched when Bairre asked if he could sit in her lap, for Ellery would be otherwise occupied.

From his Wizard's casket Julian took more candles of blue, yellow and violet and a large white one which he set in the middle of a very rough looking crystal candleholder, which none the less was of a delicate appearance and sky blue in colour. It was translucent and of a vitreous lustre.

"That is celestite," Ellery whispered to Atalanta. "When he lights the candle you will feel at peace. It has that effect on people. Sprits like it as well and it is a direct channel, some feel, to the angels."

With a wave of his wand Julian lit the candles and

then with his wand drew a large Circle of interlaced blue, violet and yellow about them. This Circle was large enough to include Erianne. She knew better than to move or go outside the Circle once it was drawn.

Marisela shivered and wished she could sit a little closer to Nicholas. The appearance of the cave was rather frightening with deep shadows and the odd shapes of the natural formations.

But as the candles caught and began to burn in front of Julian she felt herself relaxing as the magical properties of the celestite rock came into play.

On the table in front of him Julian lay out some feathers and even a dragon scale as a symbol of air. He also placed a box about two feet long, made with two holes in front, at either end, and strung with 16 strings of equal length, raised above the surface of the box with frets. It was obviously a musical instrument of some sort.

"This is an Aeolian harp," he explained. "Since this is a ceremony of air, I am hoping that sylphs will play upon it When they are needed."

"I thought that random gusts of wind made the strings of an Aeolian harp vibrate," said Atalanta. "That is one of the type made to fit in a window, is it not?"

"Many times it is the wind that plays the harp," said Ellery quietly. "But if you hear a passage that sounds much more harmonious, it is usually a sylph. They are air elementals and attracted to anything of air."

Julian pulled out his watch and looked at it. "It wants but five minutes to midnight," he said. "At precisely twelve I shall cast the spell and we shall see what happens. Siofra and Flan have said that we may hear the ghosts further back in the cave as well. Please don't be frightened," he added, looking at Marisela and Atalanta. "This Circle that I have cast will protect us and I shall maintain control of the situation. Wizard Healers are trained to deal with the dead as well as the living."

"And there's bein' us," put in Siofra. She and Flann had climbed upon the table and were sitting by the candles, in much the same posture as Erianne. Cillian too, had gone upon the table top. Nicholas took a notebook and pencil from the pocket of his robe. He fitted a stylus over Cillian's paw, explaining that the hedgehog would make a transcript of all that happened.

Silvery chimes from Julian's watch struck the hour.

Several things happened at once. Braziers set about the cave began to smolder, admitting a fragrance that Atalanta later learned was mimosa. This scent opened channels of communication with both spirits and with one's self.

With a sweeping wand gesture that included everyone at the table Julian pronounced *"Bonum benedicto."*

Both Marissa and Atalanta knew this meant roughly "good blessing" and they both saw and felt what happned next.

Colour like being immersed in a rainbow, swept over each living being at the table, including Julian himself. Starting at their feet the colour was a darkish brown, which blended into the colour of autumn oak leaves, At the top of the legs (this could be seen most clearly on the animals) a rich crimson blossoming into orange, then yellow on the abdomen and green in the heart region. Across the chest and throat was a blue band, with violet across the forehead, all ending in a brilliant white light atop the head. All of these colours had deeply symbolic meanings ranging from strength and stability to psychic awareness.

Julian took a rowan twig from the casket and bound it with a red ribbon, This he handed to Ellery. Rowan was for protection against evil enchantments and for the development of psychic powers, while red was for protective energy.

Ellery made himself as comfortable as possible in the camp chair and leaned back as Julian said, *"Ecstasis"*, pointing his wand at Ellery.

Atalanta had thought that they would have to all hold hands, as she vaguely remembered her mother telling her this, of course, her mother had never attended a *séance* conducted by Wizards.

She saw Ellery stiffen beside her and his eyes closed. His head dropped forward on his chest and his breathing slowed.

Almost immediately the atmosphere in the cave changed. The air grew colder and a little wind sprang up from nowhere, making the candles flicker madly, the candle flame in the celestite rock nearly bending over completely.

"This is bein' excellent," said Siofra in an under-voice.""Tis certain that we will be seein' spirits tonight!" Raising her voice she said "We are after seekin' th' one responsible for th' treasure left here. Will ye be comin' to us and be speakin' your secrets? If ye be tied to the earth an' are wishin' yer rest, we can be offerin' that in exchange."

How *odd,* Atalanta thought, *I really thought that in speaking to the other side one would use more flowery, formal language.*

Marisela gave a little scream and Atalanta's attention, which had been on Siofra, turned back to her husband.

Something was definitely happening. A vaporous, luminous mist was forming about Ellery's head and shoulders and growing in size even as they watched. The temperature dropped again and for a moment another smell which Atalanta could not identify overcame the mimosa in the braziers.

"Ah,'tis bein' the ectoplasm!" said Flann in satisfaction. "A nice manifestation we'll be havin' for sure."

The mist rose until it hung over Ellery but still seemed attached to the top of his head. It churned and rolled and something began to form within it.

But before the formation was complete a voice boomed out "Who seeks to speak to the dead?"

Chapter Fifty Two
The Confession

As they watched, a face began to materialize in the midst of the ectoplasm.

It was very clear. They could see every detail of the face, that of a very old man, with lines etched deeply into his skin, wisps of white hair hanging nearly to his shoulders. He wore a white shirt, such as the Mexican peasants wore, open at the throat. He was visible down to his chest as the materialization coalesced .

"You hath offered me rest," he said in unaccented English that had an old fashioned sound to it. "I now wander between worlds, never at rest, for my sins. Is there rest in Hell?" he added bitterly.

"Heaven or Hell is not for you to judge," said Julian quietly. "That is for a higher authority. I can call angels to guide you above and there you shall be judged."

"Very well," the spirit agreed. "I shall tell you what you wish to know."

A transcript of the spirit's tale, taken down by Cillian Stillfield and rendered into modern English by the same.

My name is Hannibal Maldon. I was born in Essex, in England in the year of our Lord 1510. I grew to early youth in a small village on the Blackwater that leads into the sea, between Mersea and the village of Maldon with which my family shared a name.

My father was a godly, pious man, the Vicar of a small church, and he intended me for the church as well. But I was an idle, brawling boy, who thought more of adventure and silly pranks than I did of books and learning. From my childhood I was more at home on the docks and about the ships in the harbor. My heroes were the sailors who journeyed all over the known world and I never tired of hearing their tales. I longed for that sort of life for myself, a life of freedom, untrammeled by books and petty rules.

As I neared manhood my father's rules began to chafe me further. When he insisted that I give my life to the church,

I ran away to sea at the age of sixteen.

I loved the life. It was everything I had dreamed of for so long. I was free, with good companions and enough adventure to satisfy even my cravings. My first ship plied a trade between Holland and England, and saw some fighting between ships of the Inquisition and ours, as the Inquisition was eager to stop the trade between the heretics of England and heretics of Holland, whose borders were so stoutly protected by Dutch Wizards.

But being an impetuous, venturesome youth I soon grew tired of the unvarying route between England and Holland and longed for more exotic adventures.

There had been many exciting discoveries in the world since before I was born and in all of that time since. In 1492 Columbus had discovered the Indies, followed by the Portuguese da Gama who voyaged to the coast of Africa, India and the Spice Islands. The Dutch had soon followed to the Spice Islands and shortly established the monopoly on those commodities, pushing the Portuguese out with the aid of their magics.

Mozambique, Malabar, Hind, Calicut–those names were magic to my ear and I longed to see these strange lands and peoples for myself, rather than listen to tales of them.

The Dutch had no rules against Englishmen joining the crew of a spice ship, so I set myself to learning as much Dutch as I could and in the spring of 1530, when I was but twenty years of age and by then a seasoned seaman, I joined the crew of a spice trader. I was in a fair way to making my fortune by this venture, for the Dutch were firm believers in profit and allowed each member of the crew not only a share in the spices to sell on his own, but to invest in the ship and her cargo as well, to whatever monies they might afford. I had a little put by from my years at sea, for my wants were few, and I bought a one twentieth share of the ship.

We had a grand voyage and I saw enough of strange ports of call to convince me that I had made a right decision. Strange cities, people, animals and flora were all mine to enjoy and enjoy them I did.

We were all loaded with a bounteous cargo of pepper, nutmeg, cinnamon and other spices for the voyage back to Holland, where the cargo would be sold at auction. We had fair winds as we made the long trip back, even rounding the tip of Africa. It seemed as if fortune smiled upon us.

But our luck ended in a storm in the Bay of Biscay. We began to take on water, to list in the heavy swells. The Captain was considering abandoning ship when, the day after the storm, we saw a sail on the horizon.

Our relief soon turned to dread, for the Spanish galleon bore the pennant of the Inquisition. We knew what happened to both Dutch and English sailors taken by the Inquisition: the fires, if you were magical and imprisonment and slavery even if you hadn't a trace of magic about you.

And so it came to pass, since I had no magic, that I was sentenced to the galleys, to spend the balance of my days chained to an oar for the crime of but being an adherent to my Protestant religion. I hadn't a bit of magic, as the Witch-Sniffers soon found out, but I was a heretic, according to their lights and as such, deserved punishment.

For five long years I was chained to that oar, whipped and starving, in pain—and it did something to me. I became hard and bitter, thinking only of my hatred of my captors and hoping against hope that I could gain my freedom and have my revenge against both the Spanish and the church which had so unfairly condemned me. They had stolen my fortune as well, for our spice ship had been confiscated. Hatred and rage grew in me every day and I vowed to take my vengeance however I could. I have come now to believe that the hatred was what kept me alive when others about were dying.

Then almost five years to the day I had gone to the galleys I won a reprieve. A group of men I later learned were *Conquistadors* came to the galley and chose the fittest among us to go on an expedition to the Americas, as slaves and servants. I was still strong so I was one of the first to be released into their servitude.

I found myself almost immediately on a ship to the New World, to *Nueva España*. The Spanish had been in the New World for over forty years and had exploited the land and its native people, seeking to strip it of all its riches for their own use and the enrichment of both the Spanish court and the church.

The Spanish considered themselves conquerors and

rulers of the new lands. Common labor was beneath them, so there was a great need for slaves.

I had learned a fair amount of Spanish after five years in a Spanish galleon and soon found out that I was part of an expedition headed by gentleman adventurer Francisco de Coronado. Our ultimate destination was Mexico.

For another five years I endured captivity in Mexico, carefully watched, a chain about my ankle during the day, locked in at night, and always within the glance and ready whip of a overseer as I labored in the fields and sometimes in a *hacienda* when extra servants were needed.

Then in 1540, we began to hear more of the rumors of the Cities of Gold that lay to the north. A missionary monk, *Fray* Marcos, had been sent by the Viceroy into those unknown regions and had come back full of tales about tall houses, taller than any in Spain, studded with turquoise, and gold so plentiful that the Indian peoples made everyday implements from it. He had not seen this with his own eyes, but he was a monk, so he was believed.

The Viceroy's heart was filled with greed, thinking that to the north lay another Peru, ripe for exploitation and full of riches. The Viceroy, Mendoza, we heard, provided half the money to equip the expedition and *Doña* Beatriz, Coronado's wealthy wife, provided the rest.

I was chosen to go along to help care for some twenty horses provided by Coronado himself. There were many more than that, of course. Over three hundred soldiers, some one thousand natives and five priests set out from Compostela, capital of the New Galicia province. That was on the twenty-third of February in the year 1540.

Coronado, with one hundred or so men, forged ahead of the main body of the expedition, eager to see Cibola as it was called and the Seven Cities of Gold promised by *Fray* Marcos. I went with him.

But Cibola was always ahead of us, the Indians we encountered told us. We were soon starving and ragged. And when we had come as far as these mountains, we met hostile natives.

It was decided to send *Fray* Marcos back to Mexico as he was no longer safe. The men had come to realize that nothing of what he had told them was true, and feelings were strong against him. He and Coronado both feared for his life and the harm that might be inflicted on anyone who dared to kill a priest. At the very least, the leaders felt, the others in the expedition would be cursed if the monk were molested.

I was with the small group that accompanied the monk. I do not know nor did I care if he was able to safely return to Mexico, for a little more than half way back, I made my escape.

No one bothered searching for me. The members of this little band were ill-equipped and hungry. They more than likely assumed that I had been dragged off by wild animals or by Indians seeking revenge. I doubt they cared over much what had become of a slave.

I made my way, after many trials and much hunger, to the coast, where I was at last able to obtain a place on a ship. The captain asked no questions of me as it was obvious that I knew my way about a ship. He had too much need of competent men to worry about where one had come from.

Hatred still burned in me. Nearly ten years of my life had been wasted in the service of the Spaniards, in which time I had been ill-treated and abused. My back still bore the scars from the many lashings I had received. But how to get my revenge?

The ship I found employment on was a coastal trader, running between ports on the Mexican coast and Panama. It was a small vessel, no proud galleon, but sturdy and well-suited for her labors of hauling mainly foodstuffs. The captain thought such an insignificant ship safe from the pirates who plied the waters, looking for the treasure ships that sailed to Spain after gathering their booty from all over the lands of New Spain.

No one was more shocked than the captain when, on a voyage to Panama, a pirate ship appeared out of nowhere, and fired a raking shot across our bow, demanding that we allow them to board.

Too frightened and weaponless to do otherwise, the Captain ordered us to offer no resistance. The pirates boarded us at their will.

I will never forget my first sight of the pirate captain *Don* José de Hernandez. He was a tall, slender man of middle age, who dressed in gaudy finery, aping the nobles of the

Spanish court. I was to find out that his reputation for both ruthlessness and cruelty was well deserved. He was born of a minor branch of a noble house in Spain, sent out to the Americas to earn his fortune through industry and hard work. He soon proved to have little liking for hard work and thought of an easier way to obtain gold. He would steal it. Even then in those early days, there was a recklessness in his conduct and a glitter in his eyes that seemed disquieting.

The pirates were disappointed with our cargo of mostly food and cloth. But *Don* José had boarded us for another reason. He had need for men and if we would not volunteer, he would take those he needed.

Without a qualm, I threw in my lot with the pirates. They attacked and stole from the Spanish treasure ships. What better revenge than to strike at the Spaniards through their purses? The thought of amassing a fortune of my own was tempting, as well as a chance to kill many of my lords and masters. I did not have to think twice about it.

So began my career as a pirate. *Don* José was extraordinarily successful and his crew and he were growing rich. For years, with the *Don* and his crew I sailed the Spanish Main, plundering, looting and killing too. I eventually rose to a position as the *Don's* second in command, as trusted by him as he was capable of trusting any one. I was known as Pedro the Knife, for Pedro had been the slave name given me by my captors. The deadly knife, thrown or used in hand to hand combat, was my trademark.

Men feared me and I grew rich. Only to a few intimates, men like Cardoza, Enrique the bastard and the Indian Culican did I reveal my true name and home. I trusted these three and the Indian had pledged himself my man forever, for I had saved his life on one occasion.

So matters stood when the *Don* began to talk of retiring from the sea. He spoke of going to the interior of the continent to the north, taking his spoils with him, and there ruling a little kingdom of his own, far from civilization.

I tried to dissuade him, for I had been there and knew it was not the earthly paradise he envisioned. He would not listen nor did Cardoza, a one-eyed hulk, and Enrique the bastard, who had been a foot solider at one time and still affected his armor and helm. There was another companion, a common seaman who served the *Don* as a body servant. he was called Raul.

The *Don* insisted that I accompany them, since they needed me as a guide, as I was the only one of them who had ever seen the northern interior. He promised me such a huge sum of money that I could not pass it up, even though I thought it a foolish venture. I decided that when we reached the interior and I saw them settled I would take my share and somehow return home to England, where I could now live like a king on my share of the treasure. I was nearly forty years of age and the urge for adventure had left me. I wanted a home, a wife, and children at my feet. My desire for revenge had burned low as well.

We set out in the spring of 1558, with a pack train of mules carrying the chests of gold, jewels and other fruits of years of piracy. Such was the fear that the *Don* engendered in every breast that no one attempted to steal from us, or even follow us. Many superstitious sailors thought the *Don* was devil's spawn and made the sign of the evil eye behind his back. The *Don* did everything that he could to encourage this belief. He was a great play-actor and indeed, seemed to have the devil's own luck, never being injured in even the most vicious of fights and always the victor whether with swords or pistols.

At first everything went well. We were well-supplied and full of plans. The weather was with us as well and we saw no hostiles.

And then the *Don* began to go mad. His plans became grandiose; he spoke of setting himself up as Emperor of *Terra Incognita*, where the Indians would worship him as a God.

He began more and more to believe himself a God and became more mad with each day as we drew nearer to this region.

Then one day he had a fit and died. We buried him near here and tried to decide what to do.

Fighting broke out almost at once, for there was the *Don's* huge share of treasure to think of. Should this be divided or shared? Who was to be the mew leader? As the *Don's* second, it would seem that I was to be the new leader, but all I could think of was returning home. I was suddenly heartsick for my own land and had more than enough for the rest of my life.

But the fighting continued, petty quarrels over who got a ring or a brooch or if an uncut emerald was worth more than a gold ingot.

Only I and the Indian stood aloof from this. He had always earned his fair share of our loot, for the *Don* had not cared that Culican was an Indian as he was a good man in a fight and a good sailor. But I had noticed that gold meant little to Culican.

But to Raul, Enrique and Cardoza it was everything. They began to accuse one another of cheating all the others and tempers became frayed.

From the few natives in the area they obtained a potent native drink made from cactus and fermented. They drank constantly, which only served to increase their belligerence.

It was about this time that I began to dream of God and his angels. They were judging me and condemning me for the theft of all this treasure, and for the murder of innocents. Much of the treasure was sacred vessels of the church. I was not a Catholic but a good Anglican, still, I came to think that the best place for the treasure was in the hands of the church. I would even give my share to the church, to expiate my sin. What if I were to die out here, un-shriven, like the *Don*? I would go straight to hell. This preyed upon my mind to a fearsome extent.

When I told the others what I proposed for the treasure they turned on me. I was forced to flee to save my life, with Culican at my side.

But then I knew what to do.

Late one night when they were all laying in a drunken stupor Culican and I stole into their camp and removed the chests with the aid of two stolen mules. The pirates all snored on, oblivious to our actions. We took everything.

I had determined that I would hide it, return to Mexico and tell the church where it lay. Priests could be sent to fetch the treasure and thusly I could settle my conscience and please God. Then I could go back to England. Returning such a prize would guarantee me my freedom from slavery.

The Indian and I did not look back. We left that very

night after hiding the treasure in the mountains, reached with difficulty even by sure footed mules. It was a cave that Culican had found in his many explorations and it seemed an ideal place.

We suffered many hardships on the journey back. At one point my Indian friend died. To this day I do not know where or when, for by then I was myself delirious with brain fever brought on by privation. I have little doubt but that I was near death when at last I stumbled into a town in northern Mexico called Mondrágon.

When I awoke, more dead than alive, it was to see the face of an angel bending over me. She was an earthly angel, my dear Candéla, who became my wife.

For a very long time I had no memory of the treasure at all. My memory came back in bits and pieces, my name first, my real name. I became known as Aníbal Maldonado.

I was already old and crippled by an accident before the memory of a treasure came back to me and of my days as a pirate.

I tried to tell people of the treasure, to tell the *padre*, but they none of them believed me. They thought of me as a fantastic story teller. I drew a map, but the merest mention of the word Cibola caused gales of laughter. Cibola was a myth— everyone knew that and my insistence that I had gone with Coronado merely confirmed that I was *loco*, for everyone knew that Coronado had found nothing, much less treasure.

When I made the map, I did not mark the exact location of the treasure for I was no longer sure of it. If I saw it again, however....

But that was not to be. I was too old, too crippled to make such a trip and my sons and grandsons would not hear of such a fantastic quest.

Even on my death bed, when I tried to tell the young priest of the treasure, he did not believe me. Perhaps now that I have told you my story and the treasure is found, my spirit can be laid to rest at last. It has been too long.

Chapter Fifty Three
Laid To Rest

When the spirit finished talking no one spoke at first, each lost in his or her own thoughts.

Then Siofra said "We were findin' a great emerald not far from here and three spirits fightin' over it..."

"Culican and I did our task in some haste when we moved the treasure from this place," said Maldon. "And I hath not a doubt that the three spirits be Enrique, Raul and Cardoza. Their greed would have driven them to brawl over even the smallest piece they might hath found."

"And there is this," From beneath his robe Julian pulled out the golden cross that had been the first thing discovered. The chain had been repaired magically.

"'Twas Raul's," Maldon answered. "He tore it from the fair neck of a young maid and, being a lazy dog, tied it on with but a bit of string. One day he suffered the loss of it. 'Twas near to the Castle rock, methought, that he had misplaced it."

"Was the maiden killed?" Julian asked.

"Nay," Maldon shook his head. "She was left unharmed, for she was the daughter of a high official of the Spaniards and fetched a goodly ransom." He then looked at Julian."You hath promised me my rest, did I tell my tale."

"And I will keep my promise," said Julian. "I will seek release for all of the spirits that dwell here."

"Hath I your promise that the treasure will be used for good, to go back to the church if possible?" the spirit queried.

"'Twill be goin' to those who were bein' enslaved by the Spaniards, so they can be havin' a better life," Siofra assured him.

Maldon seemed pleased with this. He then waited expectantly for Julian to begin. On his face a look of longing.

From his casket Julian withdrew six candles of violet, and one of gold. He also brought out six beautiful amethysts, a chamois bag closed with a drawstring and a crystal flask with a gold stopper.

This last was lotus oil. Like the others he was

barefoot and now he anointed his head, hands and feet with the aromatic oil.

Taking out his wand, Julian drew on the air around him a six pointed star made of two triangles, equal in size and overlapping. From the chamois bag he poured a stream of sea salt over the invisible star so that suddenly it appeared in the air, hanging in glistening whiteness.

Julian had been careful to seat himself so that he faced east. Now, beginning with the southerly position and moving ever to the right, he hung the six violet candles in the air, at each point of the star.

Beginning again on the south candle, he lit it with his wand and said "Angel Gabriel, lift these spirits with your strength and mercy so that they may come into the Light of judgment". Moving again to the right, he lit the next candle and said "Angel Raphael, Healer's angel, angel of repentance, take these men beneath your wings." The third candle was lit with: "Angel Zamael, angel of death, guide them to celestial judgement and their ultimate eternal home, whether to the Light or to the Dark."

The fourth candle flared into light as Julian said "Angel Cassiel, angel of solitude and tears, take heed of these spirits' tears and lamentations." With number five he invoked "Angel Sachiel, angel of righteousness, help judge them rightly." The final candle was for "Angel Anael, Opener of Gates, angel of the Star of Love, ruler of Divine Love, be merciful."

Julian placed an amethyst next to each candle, where they hung in the air, catching the candlelight which burned pure and steady.

The gold candle he placed in front of himself, it too to hang in the air as if held by invisible hands.

Suddenly, startlingly, the Aeolian harp began to play a haunting ethereal pattern of notes. Atalanta, who had expected it to play at the beginning of the *séance,* heard a definite melody within the notes so lightly plucked by the wind or perhaps an unseen hand.

Julian lit the gold candle and said: "Michael, Prince of Light, angel of mercy, of deliverance and of immortality, take these spirits to their judgement. I do ask this in your names, so if worthy they may be drawn in to the Light. Adonai.

Adonai. Adonai."

All of the candles in the room went out as one.

A breath of some beautiful fragrance filled the room and a soft white light came down from above Julian's head and continued to grow until it lit the entire cave chamber as brightly as daylight.

Maldon gave a cry, but it was not one of fear.

The light was now so bright that the others watching could not really see anything but an impression. There was a warm wind and something seemed to rush by them, or rather, four somethings.

Atalanta thought she heard wings beating and afterwards Marisela said she too heard this.

As suddenly as it had come the Light vanished and all the candles burst into flame once more. They could again see Julian as he moved around the star, putting out the candles, starting with the one lit and ending with the first. As he blew out each candle he murmured "May divine will be done."

Maldon was gone and there was no feeling of any spirits left in the cave, even to the cats. The temperature began to rise again. The ectoplasm about Ellery had disappeared as well.

Ellery opened his eyes and sat up, and said "What happened?"

Cillian looked up at him through his spectacles. "I wrote it all down," he said, taping his stylus on sheets covered with runes. "If Sabrina will be so good as to type-write it, you can read it later. Suffice it to say that we know where the treasure came from, and the ghosts are all of them laid to rest."

There were a few things left to do, to clear up before they could depart for home. There were polluted ley lines to be cleansed. There were four bodies in the ice cave that must be removed and disposed of. The survey of the archaeological site had to be finished to be handed over to Dr. Burke, who was coming from California, all eagerness to delve into archeological sites that had yet to be studied. The children were to be restored to their tribe, who were to have housing, training and a school built. The treasure cave was to be shored up and made accessible to the 'tribe' as well.

With Ramón's agreement, Ellery gave each of the dragons and the dragonets a choice of a piece of the treasure and promised to have a dragon jeweler in Dublin convert the pieces for them to wear. The Native insisted that each of the ladies in the archaeological group was to have a piece of jewelry as well. Even with these generous gifts, and the cut demanded by the government, there was more than enough treasure remaining to provide any number of houses, schools, scholarships and training. The firm of Mariposa and Sons was sending a top-notch investment expert out to work with the freed slaves and dragons and for a while as yet, Julian would remain in New Mexico, training Ramón and helping set up a hospital.

And amongst other distasteful duties Julian had to order the Reverend Brewer confined to a mad house in Texas, for there was none closer.

One morning just after the *séance* the dragon whistle woke everyone up when it caused the dragons to bellow.

Of course they knew at once where the noise of the whistle had come from. Torin, with Julian and Siofra, closely followed by Nicholas on Varian, took off for the mission at once. There they found a strange sight.

On the roof of the mission Brother Ezekiel struggled with Reverend Brewer, who was shouting something in a strange speech and trying to get away from Brother Ezekiel's hold on him.

The two Covenanter women were standing out in the yard looking at the men on the roof. As Torin landed, they both looked up, relieved.

"Oh, Doctor!" Sister Rebecca said worriedly when Julian joined them. Both she had Prudence still wore their night clothes. "He's gone mad! This morning he woke us all, declaring that he was an angel and was going to fly from the roof up to heaven where he would sit at God's right hand!"

"What language is he speaking?" Nicholas queried, joining them immediately after Varian had landed.

"He is speaking in Tongues," said Sister Rebecca.

It sounded more like gibberish to Nicholas.

514

"I had to blow the whistle," Prudence said apologetically to Julian.

"You did the right thing," he said, not looking at her but at the two men on the roof, still struggling. The Reverend seemed to have strength far beyond his frail body. "Nick?" he asked his brother." Will you assist me with a catch and hold?"

Nicholas nodded and took out his wand as his brother did the same.

"Let him go!" Julian called up to Brother Ezekiel.

"But he'll jump and kill himself!" protested the big man. "Suicide is a mortal sin!"

"My brother and I will catch him," Julian called back. "It will be fine, Brother Ezekiel. I shan't let him hurt himself."

Brother Ezekiel had come to like and trust Julian but it was with reluctance that he let go of the Reverend.

With a cry of triumph the little minister ran to the edge of the roof and launched himself into the air.

Sister Rebecca screamed but before he fell even a foot, the Reverend was caught and held by two streams of violet light that wrapped him around and gently put him on the ground. Violet strands wrapped themselves about him and when he tried to run away he could not, held as tightly as if he were pegged to the ground.

"That is bein' a magical strait jacket," said Siofra in satisfaction.

As Nicholas put away his wand he inadvertently looked at Prudence and was surprised to see the look on her face as she gazed at his brother, as if Julian were the end and all of her every desire. Nicholas then glanced at his brother, who seemed oblivious to the girls' adulation. Did Julian realize that she felt that way about him? Nicholas resolved to talk to Siofra as soon as he could manage it. Julian's familiar was certain to know all about it; familiars always did notice even more than their Wizards or Witches.

It took some time to properly dispose of the Reverend and in the meantime he remained at the camp, under Julian's eye, confined to a tent, but well cared for by the members of his little congregation and well fed by Lupe. Julian made a trip to Albuquerque, inquired of a doctor there and then went on to Texas, where he investigated an asylum. He found it to be well-run and kind to patients, headed by an old

515

acquaintance from medical school, an American Wizard Healer, who had become an alienist, specializing in diseases of the mind. It was a suitable place for Reverend Brewer, where he would get the care that he needed in a quiet and humane atmosphere.

Nicholas spoke to Siofra and the little cat spoke to Sabrina, who they felt was the proper person to talk to Julian about Prudence's passion.

It was not until the night before they were to break camp and leave for New York and there to take ship for home that Sabrina found time to have a private word with her nephew.

The last week or so had been very busy. They had cleansed the ley lines in a ritual that involved dragon fire and had removed the bodies from the ice cave, and had seen them cremated, as this was the only safe thing to do with the remains of a Satanist as there was a possibility they could be brought back from the grave by others of their ilk. The ice cave was cleaned of all traces of black magic and allowed to revert to its natural state of a now clean, icy floor. The Satanist impedimenta was burned as well, which cleansed the atmosphere of the entire area.

Dr. William Burke had arrived from California with his staff and was eager to take over the expedition. He was the closest thing to an expert on the ancient Indians of the southwest and he was eager to learn more and greeted Ellery's preliminary work with cries of gladness.

An *abogado*, an attorney from Albuquerque had called upon Marisela. As the widow of *Don* Rafael she stood to inherit his entire estate. At first she wanted nothing to do with it, but wiser heads prevailed and she settled a good part of it on her parents, so that her father would not be expecting more and more money from her husband. She also made provision for the servants on both *Haciendas*. She made over half of *Don* Rafael's lands to her parents as well. Her life would be in Ireland from now on. The balance of the land, the best parts, she decided, would go to the ex-slaves in Ramón's tribe and the *Hacienda* of *Don* Rafael could be used as the basis for the hospital.

Julian was packing up to move to the donated *hacienda* where he planned on starting a clinic. When the rest of his party left for New York the next day he would go there.

Sabrina poked her head into the tent and said "Have you a moment to spare?" Flann followed on her heels.

Julian smiled at his aunt. "For you, always," he said.

Siofra sat on the bed, supervising. With a pencil in her stylus attached to her paw, she had begun making a list of supplies they would need for a clinic. Flann jumped up beside her.

"Julian," Sabrina began "I noticed soemthing the last time Miss Cromwell was here taking care of the Reverend."

"And what is that?" he inquired a little absently, his attention on his medical case that he was checking for depleted supplies.

"She's in love with you," his aunt said bluntly. "Nick has noticed it too."

"An' sure, haven't I also?" said Siofra, putting down her stylus.

Julian put away the bottle of chamomile he had been looking at. "I know," he said."She told me so. I explained to her about Sarah and how I am not inclined to fall in love again. She understood."

"Not by the way she is still looking at you I would say she was only encouraged," said Sabrina dryly. "She is head over heels."

"She'll soon tire–" he began

"But what if she doesn't?" Sabrina interrupted. "She's a nice girl in spite of her Evangelical leanings. I wouldn't want to see her break her heart over you. Nor do I want to see you cut yourself off for a chance for love again."

"Just what I've been after tellin' him!" stated Siofra.

Julian sat down abruptly on the bed beside the familiars. "Sabrina, it's still too soon. I like Prudence; she's a fine young woman. But how can I be certain that I would not be–" he broke off, not knowing quite how to phrase his feelings.

"Gettin' involved with her on th' rebound as they say?"

put in Flann helpfully.

"I suppose so," he agreed. "At any rate, she will be leaving soon. When I took the latest report scryed from Texas to them yesterday I found them packing up to leave. The mission is being closed until such time as there is another minister available. They are going back to Ohio. Prudence says she is going to train as a nurse before they come back here." He did not add what she had said for his ears alone, that becoming a nurse would make her a better wife for a doctor. "I am afraid, too, of feeling obligated to love her because she loves me," he admitted.

"Then some time apart will do you good," she said, privately thinking that if Prudence got out in the world a bit and Julian could get over Sarah and the hurt she had dealt him, there might be a basis for a relationship that might turn into love. Only time would tell. She knew Julian well; he would never trifle with Prudence's feelings.

"Don't say no to another chance for love," Sabrina told him before she got up to leave. "Don't be alone all your life as I am. It's a difficult way to live."

Julian agreed that he would give any relationship a chance, admitting that he did like Prudence and found many admirable qualities in her. With that Sabrina had to be content.

There were many tears at parting the next day. Nicholas urged his brother not to stay away too long. He and Julian were the closest in age and Nicholas would miss his brother quite a bit until he came home to Ireland.

The trip to New York was longer this time; with four dragonets who could not fly they were forced to take the train, which had flat cars for just such a contingency. The two adult dragon flew overhead. And after a short visit to Senator Connelly and his family in Connecticut, they arrived in New York on a night of rain and mist in late June, an evening that almost seemed autumn-like.

Their ship, the *Chivalric* again, was due to sail the next morning.

Sabrina found herself alone on the dockside before boarding, with a mountain of luggage. Ellery and Atalanta had gone to meet Atalanta's parents at Delmonico's, where Ellery was meeting his new mother-in-law and treating his in-laws to a meal at new York's finest restaurant before they boarded ship that evening. Nicholas and Marisela had gone to dinner with a Dracophilologist colleague of his, and the man's wife, from Columbia University. Sabrina's only company was Flann, who was sleeping on top of a suitcase as they waited for the steward and his trolley that was to pick up the bags and take them aboard ship.

Sabrina had been invited to go with either couple. Instead she volunteered to see to the baggage being removed from their hotel and put on the ship in their cabins. She would rather be alone with Flann, for she would be but an extra person in either party.

The fine misty rain exactly suited her mood. She was feeling more than a little depressed. She was happy for her nephew and her brother, having each found a partner, but it made her realize that things would never be the same for her. Ellery's first allegiance would now be to his wife and to any children. Although she would continue to go out to Egypt with him–and his new wife–it would only serve to point out how alone she herself was. "Oh, Hugh," she thought with a sudden pang of intense grief, as raw as it had been seven years earlier, "why did you have to die?"

She stood bareheaded beneath the rainbow halo of a lamp, liking the feel of the dampness on her hair and skin. It reminded her of Ireland. Droplets of moisture sparkled in her copper curls, like Faerie jewels. She was not afraid to be alone, as she had both magic and Flann to protect her.

A slow moving dray was coming and it halted the progress of a horse drawn cab coming at a fast clip towards the dock. *Someone late for their ship,* Sabrina thought idly. A liner was to sail for Southampton tonight before the *Chivalric* departed in the morning. She looked up at the cab as the driver cursed as the horse's iron-shod hooves skidded on the wet wooden planks of the dock.

Due to the moisture coating the glass window of the cab Sabrina could not see the passenger, only an impression of a man looking out at her.

Sabrina could not know it, but she had just had her first glimpse of the man she was to marry.

Epilogue

Egypt, November 1885

A hot sun hung almost overhead in an achingly blue sky. Atalanta, bent over her task, did not notice it, nor the shimmer of gold on the horizon that was the Western desert or the green of the river and a fertile belt that was the edge of the Nile behind her in the distance. She was quite intent on what lay before her–a painted pavement that depicted musicians playing a double reed pipe while girls, clad only in jewelry, danced. The colours revealed were vivid as Atalanta carefully brushed away minute bits of sand that still clung to the painting, even after a clearance spell by Ellery had removed the mountain of sand that had buried the painting.

Her husband knelt on the opposite side of the pavement, engaged in the same task as herself. Bairre was beside him; the ferret held a tiny brush in the paw stylus that normally held a pen or pencil and was as busy as either of the two humans. Flann was busily using her tail for the same task.

Until a few moments ago, Sabrina too, had been with them, but she had answered a call from Ali, their *reis* or foreman.

Now Atalanta looked up as footsteps told her Sabrina was coming back.

"How are Seneca, Amyas and Erianne doing?" Ellery sat up, back on his heels. Atalanta too, sat up, glad for a respite, as her back was aching a bit.

"Erianne thinks they might have found a temple of some sort. She'd like you to come and take a look later, after they've uncovered a bit more," Sabrina answered.

"Is that what Ali wanted?" Atalanta queried.

"No, what he wanted was to tell me that the mail has come and there are quite a few letters." She pulled a thick sheaf of envelopes out of her jacket pocket.

"Applications for the staff positions," she said, putting aside a pile to be dealt with later. "Several from Americans!"

"And letters from home, from Rosamunde, from our parents and a letter from New York for you, Atalanta," she told her sister-in-law.

Atalanta made a face. That would be from her mother, as Dr. Beck was currently excavating in Delphi and would be more likely to send a telegram, usually demanding more funds. Her mother's letter would be the same theme as always: when was she to have the felicity of becoming a grandmother?

"Rosamunde had quite a bit of news," Sabrina said, sitting down in the sand along the edge of the pavement. "Marisela is expecting number two. The Wizard Healer is reasonably certain this one will be a girl."

"Then Roderick will have a little sister," Bairre said. "I wonder if they will both be magical?"

"Also, Rosamunde had a letter from Laura Connelly in Connecticut," Sabrina continued. "Laura included a newspaper clipping from the *New York Times*. Lutterworth passed away in September."

"Finally," said Ellery. The two women looked slightly shocked but Ellery said "What sort of life did he have, paralyzed and almost unable to communicate? It's a merciful release. Even the best Healers could do little for him."

"According to the *Times*, Melville Sinclair inherited everything and took excellent care of Lutterworth until the end," Sabrina said.

"He was bein' a better son that Lutterworth deserved," observed Flann.

"The best news I saved for last," Sabrina continued. "Not only is Julian coming home but he and Prudence are engaged! They'll be married in Ohio so that her parents can be present and then coming home to Dublin. He's going into practice there. Prudence will be working at St Máire's, nursing."

"I'm glad that it worked out for them," said Atalanta sincerely.

Sabrina was too. She did not tell them that a small envelope addressed to her in Julian's hand had come with Rosamunde's letter. In it Julian had scribbled just one phrase: "I am absolutely certain this time."

"Julian also wrote that the new hospital and the school are thriving, that Ramón is fully trained, and has a busy practice of his own. Nah-kah-yen and Ancelin have made a match of it and are expecting an egg."

"Erianne will be glad to hear that," said Bairre "although I will wager that she will wonder how any dragoness could want anything to do with that arrogant male."

Sabrina shared out the letters, giving Rosamunde's to Ellery while she read the one from their parents.

Atalanta quickly read her mother's missive. It was as she thought: a wail as to why she was the only one of her friends who did not have grandchildren to boast of. Atalanta was not about to tell her that finally they had hopes. Time enough to tell her if and when she was safely delivered.

She put down the letter after having only read a few lines. It would be the same thing, reiterated several times until the end of the two pages of thin rice paper.

She looked around her, thinking how happy she was in her new life. Her husband was not only a devoted lover, but treated her as a partner and colleague. The latest Egyptian volume did indeed say on the cover, spine and title page "*By Ellery and Atalanta Delamar.*"

Her father had not been so fortunate. His last two books were still making the rounds of the publishers, for he refused to hire anyone to help him make them fit to be published.

In addition to her new large and loving family, Atalanta still had Seneca, not having to give him up as she had once feared. For the last three years she had been able to fly with him, which had been a joy for them both.

Amyas was still with them as well. He had never found a bond-mate and as a result, was a somewhat withdrawn, quiet, dragon. He still was most comfortable with the few people and dragons he knew best, but had taken eagerly to excavation, his small size a plus when space was at a premium.

And Atalanta herself had discovered a new joy in Egyptology. She had been taken by Ellery to visit a most magical personage whom she still did not quite believe in: Oberon, King of Faerie, who had most obligingly 'given' her the languages modern and ancient, which she would need for life in Egypt. Marisela too, had been given English and the Gaelic by the same royal gentleman.

Who would have thought that Papa's greed, four years earlier, would have led to all this happiness? she thought, gazing fondly at the other four members of her party. A loving husband, a sister-in-law who was more like a real sister every day, even Flann and Bairre, who were both friends and colleagues. And there was Seneca....

When she had first met Lutterworth and gone on the proverbial wild goose chase for treasure, it did not seem possible that the end would have been so wonderful.

Life was good – and in seven months or so, if her wish for a child was granted, it might even be better.

The End